Reviews and End

"A skilled storyteller"

The author, David Thomas Kay, is a skilled storyteller and as such, I highly recommend his latest literary work.

— *Diana Todd-Banks*
3 x International Best-Selling Author Awards

"An atmosphere of mystery and page-turning excitement"

The Ring of Mann is a fascinating and worthy successor to *The Sword of Saint Isidores*. Well-researched, it shows a deep knowledge of the history and geography of the Furness district of Lancashire and so, it has an authority often absent from the historical novel. The well-drawn characters and detailed scene-setting help to create an atmosphere of mystery and page-turning excitement which draws the reader into the complexities of an imaginatively constructed chronicle.

— *Terence Fulton*
B.A.(Leicester) M.A.(Leeds)

"Mann oh Mann! What a great story"

The novel is a meld of historical fiction and Norse mythology and transverses the years 1240AD to1663AD through the occurrence of the mystical runic ring. The suspense is maintained through the evolution of the characters and their interaction of the ring. Death, love, curiosity, horsemanship, and family relations are all well managed in the development of the story. Whilst the characters are numerous, they do not seem superfluous for the convincing events of this novel. The maintenance of the historical accuracy and the culture of the Norse people are interestingly intertwined in this writing. On completing the climax of *The Ring of Mann*, it entices one to read the next volume, *The Inscription*.

— *Graham Pritchard*
Master of Educational Studies (UQ),
Administrator and University Lecturer

"A must read for fans of historical fiction"

The author has crafted a world that allows a reader to immerse themselves in a far-begotten place and time with characters and their surrounds. The novel spans from 13th to the 17th centuries, tracking the many characters over their lifetimes via the main protagonist; the runic ring. Thankfully, *The Ring of Mann* is part of a trilogy, so the story doesn't end on the last page.

—*Jo Edwards*
B.Arch. (Hons) B.Blt. Env. Arch Dip. Screen animation

"Humour"

I totally enjoyed *The Sword of Saint Isidores* and David has continued with his gift for characterisation, and to effectively write humour, is a rare gift in itself.

—*Jane Williams*
NZ Forest Ranger, Dept of Conservation

"Weaving fact and fiction into a thrilling story"

I have read all of David's books and eagerly anticipate every new novel.

The Ring of Mann is a wonderful glimpse into the past, weaving fact and fiction into a thrilling story combining mystery, suspense, and humour.

— *Pete Davies*
Principal EHO, UK

"A psychological thriller"

The Ring of Mann is a psychological thriller; disturbing the serenity of the English Lake District where folk lore, witches and fear of the devil are part of the villager's daily life. The presence of a runic ring and a raven black Arabian horse unleash the restless spirit of a female Viking warrior; and, a young innocent widow is possessed. There are underlying messages of forest preservation and religious persecution. A good mix of fact and captivating fiction. The author's writing is very descriptive, and the story pulls the reader along at such a pace that it is hard to put the novel down.

— *Catherine Joyce Kendal*
Editor, author

THE RING OF MANN

DAVID THOMAS KAY

CIRCLES OF TIME: BOOK TWO

THE RING OF MANN
Book Two: Circles of Time
© David Thomas Kay 2020
First published by David Thomas Kay 2010
Second edition published November 2012

This book is a work of fiction and any resemblance to any person living or dead is purely coincidental.

ISBN: 978-1-922340-35-1 (2020 Paperback)
        978-1-922340-36-8 (2020 eBook)

A catalogue record for this book is available from the National Library of Australia

Cover design © Tracey Leanne Kay (Australia)
Edited by Martin John Kay (Australia)
Printed in Australia by Ocean Reeve Publishing

Published by David Thomas Kay and Ocean Reeve Publishing
www.oceanreevepublishing.com

REEVE
PUBLISHING

THE RING OF MANN

Book Two: Circles of Time
www.davidthomaskay.com

D avid Thomas Kay is a naturalised Australian, married with two children. He arrived in Darwin in 1964, working on Koolan Island in Yampi Sound, before backpacking around the rest of the continent. David then worked in New Zealand, South Africa, and Sydney before settling in Queensland. After retiring he completed a professional writing course at Broadbeach U3A. Genealogical research became the inspiration for his first novel *The Sword of Saint Isidores*. His second novel, *The Ring of Mann*, traces the path of descendants of the Norse immigrants. With a wish to bring the ancient abbey ruins of his childhood neighbourhood to life, the author relates the journey of a group of clandestine Cistercian monks who record the history of the early Norse settlers. A segue moves the story forward to the year 1663 and the reign of King Charles II. North West England and the Lake District are a stronghold of the growing Quaker religion and traits of the Viking migrants remain evident amongst the local inhabitants.

Dedicated to Patricia Lillian Kay

Excerpts from The Sword of Saint Isidores

Author: David Thomas Kay

The Isle of Mann 973 AD

Hrolfr was guarding their retreat and Freydis shouted back to him, pleading, 'I beg of you Hrolfr, I must have his head ... and the ring Hrolfr; the silver ring with the runes.'

The Lake District, England 973 AD

Freydis and Hrolfr stood on the shoreline overlooking the bay of sinking sands. Freydis' hand went to the silver ring retrieved by Hrolfr. Rota had told her that its runes were the symbol of the yew tree, and of Ullr the god of archery. The ring was threaded on a leather string and hung as an amulet between her bosoms. She grasped it lovingly as she thought of her father. 'Thank you for leading us to the new land.'

Whitehaven

Ravenglass

Tarn

The Fells

Coniston

Hawkshead

Ambleside

Windermere

Ferry

Grizedale

Forest

Force Forge

Rusland

Kirkby Hall

Cartmel Priory

Ulverston

Holker Hall

Dalton

Isle of Walney

Furness Abbey

Piel Island

Lancaster

THE LAKE DISTRICT

NORTH WEST ENGLAND

- - - - - Roman Road

-·-·- Monk's Journey

X

Hawkshead

Isle of Mann

Fountains

Furness Abbey

York

Lancaster

North England

fehu	uruz	thurisaz	ansuz	raidho	kenaz	gebo	wunjo
hagalaz	naudhiz	isa	jera	eihwaz	perdhro	eihaz	sowulo
teiwaz	berkana	ehwaz	mannaz	laguz	inguz	dagaz	othala

Runic Alphabet

In a secluded corner of northwest England,
the Britons first hid from Roman invaders.
Then the Vikings came, sailing from a world
in turmoil, determined to make new homes in
a new land. The next wave of invaders was
the Norman French, who became overlords.
French monks followed spreading the word
of God, teaching and converting, building
monasteries and constructing a stable
Christian civilisation.

Character List

Part One: 1240 AD

John de Cancia: Abbott of Fountains.

Brother Joseph: A monk of the Order of the French Knights Templar; dispatched from Savigny to investigate the affairs of Furness Abbey.

Brother Phillip: A close companion and protector of Joseph.

Daniel: A talented novice assigned to Brothers Joseph and Phillip by the abbot of Fountains.

Robert de Wath: Vicar of Dalton.

Abbot Guy of Furness: Under suspicion of murder and of avoiding the king's taxes.

Brothers: Michael the Prior, **Bryan**, the Bursar, and **Henry** (the ghoul), distributor of medicines.

Rolf: A local mason, descendant of the early Vikings and involved in the building of the abbey extensions. Relates his ancestral knowledge to Brother Joseph and wears the runic ring of his ancestors as an amulet.

Helena: Niece of Rolf who is obsessed with regaining her ancestral Ankh amulet from the possession of the abbot.

Gwyneth: Sorceress with links to both Helena and Rolf. She supplies herbs and poisons to the guardians of the abbey's hospice.

Part Two: 1663 AD

Monk Coniston

Robert Johnson: Sheep farmer and widower. No longer a church goer, he attends Quaker meetings for the advancement of his only son, Thomas.

Thomas Johnson: Destined for an apprenticeship in Coniston Forge. He is a compulsive storyteller and thief.

Hannah Inman: Robert's widowed sister and mother of Mary and Damian.

Damian Inman: Thomas' loyal, simple minded cousin. He is a church gravedigger, and keeper of many secrets.

Mary Rigge (nee Inman): Damian's older sister is a throw-back admired for her Spanish beauty. She is the owner of the runic ring and haunted by a woman from the past.

John Rigge: Mary's husband.

James Pritt: A tree feller who disappears after the death of Mary's husband.

Phynius Clayton: Hawkshead School headmaster and Thomas' mentor. He is fascinated and obsessed with the district's history and Mary's elusive runic ring.

Penelope (Penny) Rathbone: Inherits the Manor House from her Uncle Algernon Fleming.

Major Rowan Rathbone: Takes on the duties of Local Magistrate and hounds the Quaker community with a vengeance.

Rufus: The Rathbones' obnoxious son.

Edgar Hollis: The manor's stable manager.

Lizzie Sawrey: House maid.

Mable Fowler: Cook.

Squire Holmes: Cambridge land owner and breeder of racehorses. He vies in a constant battle of one-upmanship with the major, whilst his wife Catherine and daughter Eleanor, manoeuvre Rufus into marriage.

Timothy Atkinson: Statesman Quaker. In enmity with Major Rathbone.

Joshua Benson: Tallow chandler, married to wife **Rachel** and father of **Sarah.**

Part Three: 1665 AD
Whitehaven Harbour

Arthur Grasty: First mate on the Brigantine ship, the *Charlotte.*

Edward Bone: Boatswain.

Julius Laing: Captain.

Edwin Sutton: Highwayman and smuggler.

Coniston Forge

George Ferris: Quaker blacksmith, married to **Rebecca**, father of **William**. He employs apprentices **Oliver** and Thomas Johnson.

Hawkshead Church

Gabriel Braithwaite: Vicar.

Mathew: Streeker (Layer out).

Ruben Goldsworthy: Clerk and part-time bag man for the major.

William Webster: Church warden in charge of the constables.

Francis Watterson: Priest.

Part Four: 1666-1668 AD

Non-fiction characters

Charles II: King of England. The king appreciated his nickname 'Old Rowley' which was taken from one of the stallions in the Royal stud, alluding to his prowess with the ladies.

Catherine of Braganza: King Charles wife and Queen consort of England.

George Monck: Duke of Abermarle. King Charles wearied of the statesmen and Quaker problems in the Hawkshead district and transferred his lordship to the duke for his loyalty and military service.

Samuel Pepys (Peepes): Famous diarist of the 17th century. Secretary of the admiralty, he doubled the size of the Royal Navy during the time of his commission. His eccentricities included carrying his extracted kidney stone around with him in a felt lined box, and like the fictional Major Rathbone proud to show anyone interested.

Colonel Richard Kirkby: District magistrate, and relentless persecutor of the Quakers, related through his wife to:

Sir John Lowther: Earl of Lonsdale and Lord of the Admiralty.

Claude Duval: Norman-born highwayman of Restoration England, popularised as a gallant and courteous rogue.

George Fox: English Dissenter, founder of the Quakers, or Society of Friends who married:

Margaret Fell: Lady of Swarthmoor Hall and founder of the Society of Friends who was imprisoned with George Fox in Lancaster and corresponded with King Chares II.

Contents

PART I

The journey to Furness Abbey: 1240 AD

B rother Joseph was impatient to commence his commission. The journey to Furness Abbey in North West England was proving more difficult than first imagined. He'd been dispatched from France to Canterbury and then on to Fountains Abbey in North Yorkshire. Like most abbeys, the site of Fountains was chosen for its seclusion, and lay in the valley of the River Skell. The Abbot of Fountains, John De Cancia, was a renowned builder, responsible for completing the abbey's recent extensions. Officers of the king had studied the additions and concluded they were comparable in size to those being carried out at Furness Abbey in North West England. It was therefore significant that on completion of the Fountains contract, the same guild of stonemasons transferred their skilled artisans and architects to Furness. The guild's merchants controlled wages and the cost of materials around the country. A visit to Yorkshire had been deemed an ideal opportunity to compare the costs of building and the relevant payment of dues.

On this premise, Brother Joseph sought an audience with the Abbot of Fountains. He delivered a letter from the Archbishop of Savigny requesting access to the building accounts.

Abbot John De Cancia was immediately apprehensive. 'Why should the archbishop require knowledge of our finances?'

'At the present time you are the only means we have of evaluating the cost of building. It is not so much your wealth that interests the archbishop, but the amounts required to fund your building.'

'Then I can tell you that it is the benefactors listed in our records that fund our extensions. These so-called true believers wish to make peace with their maker and help build temples to the glory of God. In their own minds, they are hoping to claim eternal salvation, and so avoid the depths of Hell. But for their funding, we would wither and die. When I grant you access to the accounts you will see that the profits from our many granges serve only to feed the villagers, create employment and promote outside trade. Any surplus tends to dwindle in the bad growing seasons. They would fail to support even the smallest of extensions.'

Brother Joseph studied his superior with interest. There had been no greeting when he entered the room, only a brusque wave and a gesture to sit. *He's a picture of easy living, round face, round body. Not the energetic builder I imagined. He's probably short too, with his chair set high.* Joseph straightened to compensate. 'I must tell you in all confidence that both King Henry and the archbishop are suspicious of taxes being withheld in Furness. The affairs of Furness Abbey, on the surface, are similar to those of Fountains, yet by comparison they have no declared benefactors. The archbishop believes that to extend their abbey in such a manner they must have access to other means of wealth, and that the source has not been declared. We have our suspicions and your costing will go a long way towards calculating the amount of discrepancy.'

The abbot's black beady eyes stared intensely throughout the speech, then dropped to scan the scroll in front of him after the brother had ceased his explanation. *Eyes like a pig* thought Joseph. After making a show of referring to the archbishop's letter of request, the Abbot of Fountains leaned back in his chair appearing satisfied. He spoke slowly with a reedy voice between intervals of scraping a thumbnail over his lower teeth. 'You have ... my permission ... to approach the bursar.' John De Cancia was a cautious man, and thoughtful of any future consequence. *It is likely that the archbishop is investigating more than Furness Abbey.* He pressed down on his elbows, shifted his obese frame around in his chair, then lifted his head and spoke with great deliberation. 'You have a journey ahead of you that could be dangerous.'

'We are both capable men Abbot John.'

'That may be so, but one can never be too cautious. Do you understand the language of the Saxons?'

'Not at all, but Brother Phillip and myself have managed thus far.'

Only then did the true manner and impatience of the abbot become evident. He spoke quickly, and without hesitation. 'Where you are heading for few people outside of the monasteries speak the French language. The dialect is a confusing mixture of Saxon and Norse. You will need an interpreter. I have a young novice in mind, and I will not take no for an answer. The prior will take you to the bursar for a view of the necessary records, so you can leave tomorrow. Now go.' Brother Joseph was rendered speechless and departed without uttering another word. He'd witnessed the business end of the renowned builder and impressed on himself that he must never again judge a person by his appearance.

John De Cancia had an instinct for survival and immediately sent for the master novice. 'I want you to volunteer a young novice for an important service to the abbey. I have such a person in mind.' The abbot flicked a hand across his face, his brow wrinkled in thought, frustration evident. 'We were recently discussing his future. His name eludes me ... er ...' His hand waved in exasperation.

'That would be Daniel. He's almost completed his novitiate. Which service will he be volunteering for Abbot John?'

'He will accompany the two brothers who are presently visiting us from Savigny and travel to Furness Abbey with them. The journey will suit him well. I consider it an adventure he was made for. That young man was never meant to be restrained within the confines of a monastery. There is a restless energy about him. He would be more suited to roving between monastery and church, like a friar.'

'A journey to Furness could unsettle him further Abbot John. He is an excellent student with artistic talents that should be encouraged.'

'Then encourage the young man by setting him a task for his final year. Ensure that it complements the journey and that Furness Abbey is rewarded with a sample of his work. I wish to speak with him before he leaves, for I have further instructions that could be of importance to our wellbeing.' Abbot De Cancia wanted assurance that the brothers of Savigny would be under close observation throughout their investigations.

Brother Joseph was of average height, lithe, energetic and highly intelligent. When confronted with a difficult task, he would become alert to the point of agitation. He suspected that he'd chosen the wrong vocation, but the Archbishop of Savigny thought otherwise, and considered his talents an invaluable asset. Since leaving the Abbey of Fountains he'd become frustrated with what he considered to be unnecessary delays. He'd gathered information at Fountains that could only enhance his investigation into Furness Abbey. His travelling companion, Brother Phillip, was a close and a trusted friend of many years' service with the Templars. They were joined by a novice of the Abbey of Fountains, with the compliments and insistence of Abbot John De Cancia. 'We should have taken a more direct cross-country route Phillip. The priories are safe and comfortable, but we have an urgent task ahead of us. Our time on the road holds no sane relationship to the miles we have travelled and time is short.'

'It is better that we arrive safely than not at all Joseph. We must be less than three nights away and your impatience is unsettling.'

'I still can't understand why we needed a guide. The tides are twelve hours apart and we have to suffer walking our horses for six miles behind a man poking a stick into the sand.'

'They say the high tides are deceptively powerful and lethal for the unwary, returning more quickly than they leave, and the shifting sands have swallowed many a wayward traveller. You saw the church records as well as I did. There are five high tides in the month, and we must respect them, no matter the time taken.'

'Two days in Lancaster Priory waiting for a guide to Cartmel Priory is not my idea of urgency and the closeness of that dismal looking castle depressed me.'

Phillip shrugged his shoulders and shouted ahead to the novice, 'Stop crowding the guide Daniel, and take care with those packhorses.'

The novice was walking alongside the guide, holding the reins and talking with animation. He spoke the local dialect, one of the supposed reasons he was chosen to travel. He learned that the local villager was one of four employed by Prior Simon trained to guide unwary travellers across the sands. They had crossed travellers returning to Lancaster at the halfway mark. The ripples in the sand were firming, pools of water diminishing, and the headland taking shape. 'The guide says we are nearly there, and we can mount our horses. After we leave the sands, we have a short ride across country to Cartmel Priory. We will arrive within an hour's candle after the noon.'

They rode the rest of the way to the shore then walked their horses up an incline from the bay. Half a mile further on the monks came to a fork in the road. 'Whoo lad, hod on, yons reet way if yer gang ter priory.' The guide pointed to the right of the path speaking quietly with Daniel.

'He says we could go left to the coastal villages Brother Joseph and stay the night at one of the inns. We would be closer to the sands crossing there. It would shorten the journey and be quicker than staying over at the priory.'

Joseph respected Phillip's preference and conferred with him before deciding. 'Then we agree, the priory will be safer and more comfortable. If the tide favours us the extra distance will be of little consequence.' Joseph turned back to peruse the bay and was surprised to witness the turn of the tide. Seawater was surging around the shoreline; soft channels were being devoured and reshaped. The distant path they had trodden earlier in the day was already submerged in a glistening sea. He could only feel respect as he watched the sea pouring in, replenishing the hungry bay and quenching its thirst. He grudgingly admitted that the warnings, and necessity of a guide, were warranted.

They rode down into the valley of Cartmel and against Joseph's wishes they lingered at the priory for three days. Their guide had returned to Lancaster early the following morning and Prior Simon explained it would be at least another day before a guide was available to cross the sands to Conishead Priory. 'The tides at this time of the month are extremely dangerous. You must be patient Brother Joseph.'

Joseph gnashed his teeth. He knew it was the horse race causing the delay and he was powerless to intervene. *They make such a fuss over Phillip's horse. I find it hard to fathom.* He was now of the opinion they had taken the wrong option at the fork in the road. 'We should have risked staying over at an inn Phillip. We are wasting time.'

But Phillip showed little concern. He was revelling in the attention. A race with a horse from the brethren's stable had been scheduled for the day after their arrival. They were to gallop twice around a one-mile circular track. A horse such as Phillip's was rare in this part of the country, and news of the race had travelled fast. Daniel joined the brethren and excited villagers at the starting line. He shouted encouragement to Phillip, but Joseph was nowhere to be seen. He was immersed in his own thoughts, buried amongst the tomes of the priory library. Joseph was using the day to study the Furness district. The map he carried showed a large grange to the north at Hawkshead and many similar monastery holdings to the south. Their numbers impressed on him the widespread wealth and power of the Abbey of Furness. The scroll he carried from his superior suggested he should hold a temporary position in the abbey as an assistant to the sub prior. In the saddlebag of one of their packhorses was a copy of *The Anglo-Saxon Chronicle*, telling the events of King Alfred the Great of Wessex. Daniel had transcribed the copy at Fountains. His commission, according to the master novice, was to return from Furness with a transcribed copy of Bede's *Ecclesiastical History of the English People*. He was also to gift the abbey's library a tome recording monastic medicines. Joseph's thoughts on Daniel were interrupted when the young novice burst into the library with news of the race. He was full of enthusiasm at the result. Brother Joseph lifted his head from a tome and turned to him with a glassy-eyed disinterest. 'You say Brother Phillip won the race. Is that important Daniel? Is it important enough to interrupt my studies?'

'I thought you would be interested Brother Joseph.' Daniel's voice and enthusiasm began to wane. 'Phillip's horse was far superior. He won the race by almost a half of the circuit.'

'Then perhaps we should send him on ahead of us Daniel, to inform the abbey that we are on our way.' Daniel found it hard to understand Brother Joseph's lack of interest and thought the sarcasm unnecessary. He left for the dormitory with a drooping head.

They left the priory well behind Joseph's preferred schedule and were guided over the three miles of Cartmel Sands without mishap. Their stay at Conishead Priory was brief, as Brother Joseph insisted they leave at dawn. He was looking forward to the end of their long journey, but it was a ride of another four miles through forest before they were rewarded. They came upon the abbey quite suddenly, catching a glimpse of the isolated monastery at a time when Joseph was beginning to doubt the accuracy of his maps. He was impressed by the abbey's size and its seclusion. He had noted in his studies that Furness was situated on a peninsula, and that the abbey was protected on the north and south by the dangerous quicksands. The abbey was also protected on the west by the Irish Sea and on the east by the wooded fells. He thought it little wonder that the isolation of the monastery was seen as an ideal place to send monks who'd deviated from their path. He had also had time to muse that a deviant's undesirable influence could go a long way towards corrupting the innocents within. The abbey's seclusion had sheltered it from pillaging Scottish invaders in the past, and records showed that the vale had witnessed little of the sounds of war. It also seemed obvious that anyone of importance would prefer to visit the abbey from the sea. Joseph was aware that the king's officers in charge of tariffs preferred the safer passage to and from Piel Island. The trio of horsemen lingered outside the perimeter of the abbey absorbing its size and security, before turning away along another path. With Joseph and Phillip leading the way and Daniel trailing with the packhorses, they took a path that would lead them to the church at Dalton, almost a mile from the monastery. Joseph's instructions were to visit Robert De Wath, the Vicar of Dalton, before presenting himself to the Abbot of Furness. He had thought it strange at first that he should speak to a man who had been set aside from the abbey. But on reflection, he realised that an outside view was essential, no matter how parochial it may seem. Brother Joseph was cautious, hesitant of how he would be received. How would he approach the man on such a delicate matter, and could he trust him on hearsay?

'Bon matin Frère Joseph. Vous êtes invité à rester.' The vicar was overwhelmed by their visit, and after his friendly welcome, Joseph found it hard not to accept his invitation to stay over.

'We have already been delayed on our journey vicar. An overnight stay would be most welcome, but you must not feel insulted if we need to hasten our departure in the morning.'

The vicar was disappointed, his expression scarring a round face marked with the lines of a ready smile. His eyes were bright, his blond hair long and his short body pear shaped. His manner was jovial; Joseph took an immediate liking to the man. *He must be ten years my senior.* The vicar was dressed in cap and scapular, his black under-frock bulging like that of a pregnant woman. *He looks less like a priest than any I have seen, and so hungry for knowledge of the outside world.*

Over a meal and wine, they discussed the affairs of France, the employment of the people, the Abbot of Savigny, and the king's rebuilding of Whitehall. When they spoke of Fountains the vicar became nostalgic. He told Daniel that he'd served his novitiate in the monastery with the present master novice, and that they had remained close friends. When their conversation

11

seemed exhausted Joseph politely led the conversation towards the reason for his visit.

'You say, Brother Joseph, that your quest is to verify whether the abbot is obliging with his subsidy collections, the king's harbour dues and rents of the sheriff's court. I can only tell you that it is common knowledge in these parts that shiploads of wool and iron are being taken regularly to Zealand, Ireland and the Isle of Mann. A great amount of wine is also being imported. The monastery has a warehouse on Piel Island, but you would have an impossible task of proving the amount of cargo being traded.'

'As you are well aware vicar, the freehold laws applying to this district differ from any other in the land, and the Abbey of Furness is exempt of all tithes and taxes. As the exemption only applies within the realm of the monastery's lordship, paying duties for sea trading appears to rankle with succeeding abbots. It is considered that monies due are being avoided as only a paltry sum has been received from their sea trade. The king's officers collect tariffs twice a year and sail by way of Piel Island. They have no means of confirmation other than examining the trading books. I must tell you in all confidence that my intention is to document the quantity and frequency of the abbey's trade.'

'Then you must find means to visit the coastal area, and often. The ships are seasonal and frequently trade between England and Ireland. There could be as many as six ships belonging to the abbey alone. They are of no interest to me, but as you say, if you are to succeed, their quantity and frequency must be confirmed. The Abbey of Furness is a mother monastery with nine houses under her. Filiations of Russen in Mann and Fermoi in Ireland allow the abbot many contacts for trade.'

'It defies belief, Vicar, that an abbot of the Cistercian order could avoid the duties of Rome and the king in such an ungodly manner. If what you say is true, then I cannot think how I could amass enough evidence and convey this message to King Henry and the archbishop.'

'As is the case with the king's officers, your suspicions will mean nothing. If there is anything amiss, hard evidence would never escape the walls of the abbey. The abbots of Furness have always treasured their isolation and that seclusion maintains the abbey as one of the wealthiest and most powerful in all England.'

'I have time on my side, Vicar, and I hope to be working with the sub prior.'

'You are mistaken if you think you have time. The abbot is no fool and the longer you stay the greater your risk. You may find evidence of separate trading records, but I doubt that your task will be so simple, and I must caution you on the dangers of looking into the abbey's affairs. Rumours abound that the death of Abbot William was no accident.'

'I find that hard to believe. But then, it was for outside knowledge and advice that I was directed here.'

'Will you be acting alone, Brother? You have two companions.'

'Brother Phillip is a trustworthy member of the Templar, and we would both unsheathe our swords to protect the church. He looks over me.'

'What of the young novice?'

'Of him, I am not sure. He travels under our protection, and I believe he would defend us. But I have a feeling that there is more to his presence than meets the eye. The Abbot of Fountains insisted we take him for our own good, and to illuminate the final year of his novitiate.'

The vicar smiled his understanding and looked on the energetic monk with compassion. *I wonder if he realises the enormity of his task.* He decided to tell Joseph everything he knew. 'After Abbot William's death the resident smith was called in to open a locked casket in his cellar room. He told his fellow tenants that there were jewels, gold and silver, but Abbot Guy seemed more interested in the Common Seal of the abbey. I can only think that in the past there have been rumours of false leaseholds being forged. The smith was quite taken with a sparkling deep-blue stone. It had a cross with a loop above it, like a halo. He mentioned it to the master stonemason who was convinced it was a missing amulet from the days of the early settlers. One of the older villagers heard of the viewing and said it had been stolen at the time he was a child.'

The more Joseph listened to the busy vicar the more he began to wonder about him. *He has a way of wheedling information from people. It's his ready smile and easy manner. Have I given him too much information about my commission?* 'It's a pity that the smith has such a loose tongue vicar. He could cause unwarranted trouble within and outside of the walls. The amulet was no doubt gifted to the church. But the other matters that you speak of will be in my report. They are of a magnitude that warrants further investigation.' After the discussions with the vicar, the wisdom of his superiors became evident. If Robert De Wrath was to be believed, there would be more to investigate than his commission had inferred.

'Adieu Frère Joseph.' As the Vicar of Dalton bade farewell, Brother Joseph realised more than ever that he would be alone in the gathering of his evidence.

The Abbey of Saint Mary of Furness, in the vale of deadly nightshade: June 1240 AD

They rode the last mile in silence; a monastic peace amidst the monotonous clip-clop of hooves. They came to a halt on a grassy slope where Daniel was assigned to stay behind with the packhorses. He watched his elders canter their charges up the gentle slope and couldn't help but envisage a red cross blazoned across their white robes. Even their mounts stirred his imagination; one a powerful white stallion the other raven black, gracious and elegant. Daniel was already struggling with his calling and to travel in the company of such individuals was even more unsettling. But regardless of his respect for the two brothers, their aura of superiority made him nervous. *Can they sense the real truth of my presence?* He'd been in awe of the brothers since being told of their service with the French Templars. They impressed on him that they had only served in the lower ranks, but the levelling had failed to stifle his dreaming.

He watched in admiration as the two horsemen eased their mounts to the crest of the hill. The white horse whinnied; a hoof caressed the turf, and flared nostrils snorted steam into the crisp, invigorating air. His rider released the reins and the horse's head lowered towards the tempting, lush grass, white capped with glistening dew. Brother Joseph stretched forward lifting slightly in the saddle, his mind alertly scanning the amphitheatre's timbered perimeter. The arena was bustling with activity and the tower bells announcing Prime. The Abbey of Saint Mary of Furness was proclaiming the beginning of a new day. Resplendent in stature, its red stone walls swathed in early morning mist.

Joseph dismounted and gently ran his open palm along the stallion's sweating mane. He patted its neck affectionately and his curved nose wrinkled as he savoured the scent of horseflesh. The white stallion had been his constant companion since leaving France, and they had held many a private conversation on lonely country roads. Despite the innocence of their white habits, the two men were more than capable of their own defence. Both were of a similar stature, of medium height and stocky build, lithe, with their walks upright, brisk and military. Joseph checked that his sword and sheath were strapped securely, a lasting routine from his service with the knights. The Cistercian monk was immaculate in his preparation and it was no coincidence that his habit blended with the coat of his steed. He'd commenced his journey with the aim of being viewed as holier than holy and requested a white horse for his special commission. His intention was to set himself apart from the mundane image of a travelling monk. Workers in the fields had straightened from their tasks to observe them passing in silence. Bother Joseph leading his entourage had been the subject of much speculation. The charade had been more than successful, and Joseph was convinced that it had contributed to a carefree journey on the lawless open roads.

He'd learned from the Fountain's novice master that his young companion was a talented scribe. Daniel had been born in the North Yorkshire Abbey of Fountains. He was the youngest son of secular servants and had attended the monastery school from an early age. He became one of the abbey's most talented students and was invited into the brotherhood. His parents constantly reminded him of the struggles his older siblings encountered outside of the abbey's protection, a world of insecurity and often times of violence. They encouraged their youngest son to welcome with gratitude the offer of a monastic life. On Daniel's acceptance of the novitiate a third of his day became devoted to prayer and meditation, a third to study and a third to manual labour, dining and leisure. Daniel often wondered if he had made the correct decision and his doubts only increased when his thoughts turned to the young secular families. *I should have a family of my own, but how would I feed them?* He had grown comfortable in the ways of the brotherhood, but as the time grew close to the taking of his vows, he was hesitant and becoming restless. *Why did I willingly accept this task with such a feeling of errant excitement?* His orders had been to stay close to his superiors and to assist them if necessary, but not to the detriment of his writing commission. He would obey the orders of the novice master, but the secret instructions of his abbot must be paramount. On the long journey from the Abbey of Fountains he was content to trail behind the packhorses and exchange idle chatter with Phillip. He felt more comfortable that way and if he had any silent moments they were usually in the presence of Joseph. Brother Joseph was informed that Daniel had been volunteered by the Fountain's novice master, assigned for the use of his native tongue, his skills with the pen and for his youth and strength. He was slightly taller than Phillip and Joseph, slim and agile, but more casual in his manner. He was in the last year of his novitiate and if he decided to take his vows, a tonsure would interrupt his curly mop of red hair. Daniel nudged the flank of his old grey mare drawing the idling packhorses together. He watched them contentedly munch away at the lush grass whilst he turned his thoughts to the mounts of his two companions.

Phillip's black horse was smaller than the white stallion. He explained that it was Arabian breed and rare in its colouring. The horse was to be a gift for the Archbishop of York, entrusted to him in France. That the horse was still in Phillip's possession was not a question that Daniel had the courage to ask. Phillip had begun the journey trailing the packhorses, but Daniel had eventually joined him, driven to distraction by the inquisitive probing of Joseph. Before starting out on the journey, the novice had been told that both Joseph and Phillip had been members of a division of the French Knights Templar. For that reason alone, Daniel held them both in awe, and he felt guilty of his envy. They had told him of signing over their wealth and taking vows of poverty, chastity, piety and obedience. And of how they had been allowed to serve for a period of five years after which they were sworn to continue their vows with the Church of Rome. Joseph was a widower who had served beneath the aristocratic knights as a lower-born sergeant. His work involved helping in the administration of the property of the order, a vocation that sat well with his present commission. Like Phillip, he had worn a black tunic with a red cross and a black mantle. Phillip was misguided in thinking that his family were descendants of an aristocratic family and that somehow his ancestors had fallen on misfortune. He had served in the light cavalry, also as a lower-born sergeant and secretly craved the honour of donning the aristocratic white robes. He had gradually become disillusioned with the Templar's monastic order, and finally come to accept that the donning of his white Cistercian habit would have to suffice. The commission of the two monks was unknown to Daniel, but he was sure it would be one to which they were both well suited. He had no doubt in his mind that by their manner they were still acting for the

Knights of the Temple, and that their service was in the defence of the church. If their investigations of Furness Abbey were to the detriment of Fountains, then he would be required to act.

Joseph withdrew his hood and settled it around his broad shoulders. His hands alternately grasped and brushed back his horsetail of long dark hair. He was in a thoughtful mood as he looked down upon the abbey's fishponds and ripening orchards. High wispy clouds swirled unobtrusively across the pale blue sky and the air carried the sweet scent of fruit. The sound of a Gregorian chant drifted in the westerly breeze. Joseph listened enviously to the choir monks' deep tones. Their gentle voices filled the theatre with a lyrical rhythmic song and silenced the chatter of nearby curious birds. He was impressed with the size and splendour of the abbey and pleasantly surprised that despite its enormity, it remained secluded in the deep wooded valley. He imagined an unwary traveller would be astonished by its sudden appearance. Joseph was of the opinion that it was smaller in size to the Abbey of Fountains, but the Domesday papers he'd studied recorded the abbey grounds as totalling sixty-five acres. He observed the porter's lodge and the security of the gated entry, the high walled enclosure and the tall bell tower, all built with local red sandstone. An additional building was under construction and by the height of the scaffolding; Joseph surmised it was nearing the stage of completion. He noted also that there were excavations already underway for further expansion. There was a sudden clamour of activity inside the enclosure and the choir's musical chant was interrupted by the sounds of goods being loaded onto carts and wagons. The wheels of the water mill had commenced their daily grind, driven by the power of the fast-flowing stream. It was recorded that the abbey had over two hundred laymen working in its many outer granges and more than twenty secular servants housed within the monastery.

Joseph took note of an impressive building set aside from the monastery and knew from his own experience with the layout of Fountains that it would be the abbot's residence. *There are many signs of wealth.* A young woman was leaving the building with a brisk stride. She was holding a covered wicker basket in one hand whilst the other brushed vigorously at her apron before lifting to tidy her hair. He returned to the stallion, swung himself into the saddle and drew the hood over his tonsure. He had seen and heard enough for the present. They had witnessed three ships anchored off nearby Piel Island. The seasonal sea trade had commenced in earnest and the haste of their journey now appeared to be warranted. Joseph felt rewarded as he made the first entry in his diary:

Marie Cogge: trading vessel.

The name suggested it belonged to the abbey's fleet, but the quantity of vessels trading, regardless of ownership, would be of the upmost importance. The time had arrived for him to seek an audience with the abbot. With the knowledge acquired from Vicar Robert De Wath, he felt well-armed and confident of success. But the Vicar of Dalton had warned him to be cautious of asking the wrong questions of the wrong people, and Joseph had never been one to disregard what he believed to be well intentioned advice.

The district landholders were queuing in the abbey's service area, collecting their weekly provisions; a payment for their crops and livestock. Women were carrying loaves of bread from the bakehouse and the men loading meat from the kitchens. Others were carrying beer and sacks of oats from the monastery's barns. The sound of the porter's bell alerted a small group of men nearby who stopped loading their wagon to watch the arrival of the three visitors. Joseph made himself known to the porter and as the gates were opened for the monks to enter, the group of men left their work in the loading yard. Joseph had one eye on the three men approaching him and the other on the young woman with the covered basket. *Not the usual woman of the fields.* She slowed to a more leisurely gait and headed towards a wagon. She was lithe and her walk graceful. Without breaking pace, she joined the three men and walked alongside them. Speaking animatedly to the youngest and most handsome of the three, she leaned forward to whisper in his ear leaving him laughing out loud and bright eyed as she walked away. Joseph watched her climb onto the loaded wagon, pleasantly surprised at her beauty. The tunic failed to hide the curves of her full bosom and her long wheat-golden hair had been bunched and pinned. *That's most certainly the young woman described by the Vicar of Dalton.* He remembered the vicar's words. *Take heed that the contents of her basket are not always as they seem. They say the basket is usually empty when she leaves, her purse often full, and she travels often between the witch and the abbey.*

He noticed the wagon preparing to leave as soon as she arrived and then turned his attention to the three men approaching. An elderly bald-headed man was leading the group, his bushy red beard suggesting the hair had slipped from its anchorage. He was of a heavier build, much taller than his two companions and he walked with a swagger and loping stride. Joseph thought the two younger men would almost certainly be his sons and they were lengthening their strides to keep pace. Having little choice, he reined in his stallion and spoke to the three men blocking their path. 'Bonjour mes amis. Que'est-ce que faites-vous?'

Joseph's greeting drew a blank, and the older man turned his attention to the pale-skinned Daniel. 'The brother is asking the nature of your business, sir.'

The bearded landowner welcomed the familiar tongue. He stepped forward and took hold of the white stallion's reins with confidence and an air of authority. Without looking at Joseph he stroked the horse's muzzle with supposedly deep concentration. Joseph was not sure if his manner was one of disrespect or of curiosity. The older man looked up and spoke to Joseph, the phrase rolling quickly from his tongue 'Is t'hoss fer sell?'

Joseph turned and appealed to his novice. 'He's asking if your horse is for sale, Brother Joseph.'

The tall man turned to Daniel and introduced himself. 'My name is Richard of Leece. I'm the holder of farmland close by. This is my eldest son John and my youngest son Adam.'

Joseph didn't wish to offend and considered his answer. 'Tell him that the horses are the property of the church, but we may barter with your horse and one of the packhorses.'

Daniel looked at Joseph in surprise. 'I will need my horse for the return journey.'

'Tell him anyway. I'm sure it's only my white horse he covets.'

Daniel pointed out the two horses. 'Perhaps you would like to purchase those two?'

The landowner shook his head and suggested that either the white or black horse be considered. Joseph showed indifference and turned away, but the tall man Richard was not so easily dismissed. As the farmer guided them towards the stables, he informed them that his family were well known to the abbey and that they attended weekly for their supplies. He insisted that Joseph contact him if he had a change of mind. He then pointed the way to the refectory and explained that most of the landholders would be attending for the main meal. Daniel nodded and turned to question Adam. 'Will the pretty woman be your wife?'

Adam beamed and pushed his chest out. He was about to answer, when his father's huge hand whacked the back of his head. 'Thoo'd best show respect. Your mother carried you months afore you found a way oot, and all you can think of is clamming back in again.'

It was Richard's favourite saying, and he addressed Daniel as if in apology. 'E's young like yourself, but of a different nature.' Daniel blushed and wished he'd never asked the question. They all parted company on good terms, but Richard of Leece lingered and found it hard to disguise his disappointment at the loss of trade.

Joseph's first meeting with Abbot Guy was more convivial than he'd expected and the language more familiar. He had expected someone older, *a little plumper perhaps, with a lack of exercise, and an excess of food?* But Guy was as tall and erect as the landholder he'd recently met in the grounds, lean and athletic with a bony face and setback steel-blue eyes. His tonsure was set amongst wild black hair seeming almost out of place. Joseph knew from his own experience that without his ceremonial robes Abbot Guy could have passed for a soldier in the king's army.

They sat down at the table facing each other. The abbot smoothed down the parchment in front of him then leaned back in his chair, elbows resting, and hands clasped. 'This letter you delivered states that you are here on the behalf of king and archbishop. It also states that your commission is to compare the affairs and finances of the abbey and in relation to that of Fountains. What experience do you hold of such affairs brother?'

'I have studied law and helped in the administration of the property of the French Knights Templar.'

'That may well be, but I'm sure you will have a difficult task. There is little here to compare with Fountains. We serve under opposing laws and are of a lesser size.'

'I believe your administration will prove far superior Abbot Guy.'

The abbot leaned forward, his palms together in the form of prayer, nose resting on fingertips, thumbs supporting the chin. He rocked slowly back and forth, blowing warm air between his palms, and as if deep in thought, he cast a discerning eye over Joseph from beneath drooping eyelids. After a measured silence he rested his hands on the table and leaned back in his chair. 'You must realise that I have been in office for less than a year. I'm in an awkward position, trying to cover up for the deviances and other shortcomings of my predecessor William.'

'I had no idea that William had any deviances abbot.' *Why should he cast doubt over William's character?* 'My presence here is to compare the affairs of Furness Abbey to those of Fountains and to pass on any improvements that may assist other monasteries. Furness Abbey is considered to be one of the most wealthy and successful in the land.'

'If that is a compliment brother, then I thank you for it. You must forget that I mentioned the weakness of our William. His death brought great sadness and came as a shock to us all.' Abbot Guy closed his eyes and crossed himself. 'May the good man rest, in peace.'

Joseph decided not to press the subject. 'As you previously held the position of prior, you will be able to inform me of the running of the abbey in regard to its records of trade and finance.'

'I shall place you with Prior Michael and together with the help of the sub prior and bursar we shall have you out of here in no time at all.'

'Don't be in too much of a hurry Abbot Guy. There are rumours to dispel before I leave.'

'You talk with authority brother, but your manner verges on arrogance. I must warn you of your place, and if you only deal in rumours, then your findings will be worthless.'

He stared at Joseph in deliberate silence, pausing for a reply, but not inviting one. Joseph was feeling uncomfortable, knowing, waiting for the abbot to continue. 'I hear you arrived with a visitor from Fountains, and that he travelled under your protection.'

'The Abbot of Fountains made us very welcome, and when he requested our services we were pleased to assist. The novice has a commission to fulfil before returning. A transcription to be agreed upon I'm told. In the meantime, I'm sure that you could find a suitable task for my travelling companion, Phillip. It would be most preferable if we could all leave together.'

'Phillip has the look of a soldier about him Brother Joseph.'

'You're very observant Abbot Guy.'

'It's a trait I'm familiar with. Your companion shall help with organising the lay brothers in their day-to-day tasks. Prior Michael will see to it.'

From the first day they had entered the walled enclosure and moved amongst them, the brethren knew that Joseph and Phillip were no ordinary monks. Anyone who slept beneath a sword that was hung above his mattress like a Holy Cross had to be questionable. 'When he arrived, I saw him unstrap a dagger from his forearm, and I swear the handle was a bone sculpture of our Saviour.'

The fat monk gasped in horror. 'What do you make of it Brother Andrew. Do you think they still serve the Temple?'

'I'm sure they do brother. We must be careful with our speech and confer often with Prior Michael.'

Joseph had sensed a different atmosphere to that of Fountains. He had immediately set about asking the brothers pertinent questions, and sensed the brethren were secretive. His observations confirmed the belief of the Vicar of Dalton; that there was too much power and wealth in the monastery and that in turn had cultivated greed. But Joseph had more than one problem on his mind and his impatience was evident. He was becoming obsessed with Abbot William's death, even to the point of visiting his place of rest in the monastery cemetery. Joseph thought the gravestone to be suitably impressive and close enough to the grave of Reginald, the King of Mann, to be considered honourable. But he had a lingering suspicion that the abbot had been prematurely deposed from his office. The choir brothers informed him that William's death was from a sudden illness. They said that he was feverish and hallucinating for days before they found him lying in the beck that flowed through the grounds. When he questioned them further, they fell silent and thereafter he found it hard to gain their confidence, and he became suspicious of their meandering explanations. After the information gathered from his meeting with Vicar Robert de Wath whether true or false, Joseph had the mind that no-one should be exempt from suspicion, *not even the vicar.*

Joseph arranged for Phillip and Daniel to accompany him on a visit to Rampside Woods to converse with the local sorceress. Phillip remained on watch outside whilst he used Daniel to question her. 'Have any of the Abbey monks ever asked your advice?'

'What kind of advice brother?'

'They may have asked for information on a poison that would help someone to a slow death.'

'Now why would a learned monk ask a poor ignorant old witch about poisons?'

'You answer a question with a question witch, and that annoys me. You would know the local toxins that are most available, and I search for one that might impart hallucinations.'

'The whole district knows of the deadly nightshade, but you would have to partake in large quantities to bring death to an elder.

Why would the brethren need my advice when they know it grows freely in the dale?'

'You're asking questions again witch. Now, do you deny that you have spoken to any of the brethren?'

'My name is Gwyneth, and the answer is yes, I have spoken to the brethren. The herbalist occasionally calls and asks me for the location of choice native plants.'

'The monastery already has large herbal gardens.'

'He prefers the plants growing wild for his monastic medicines, and he taught me to look for God's signature on the plant to determine which ailment it cures.'

'I have seen the signs witch, and they are true. I often wonder if the Devil marks his poisons in the same way.'

'Not all poisons are bad brother. A small dose can sometimes heal.'

'Was Abbot William given a small dose, witch?'

'My name is Gwyneth, if you please. Are you accusing me or enquiring of my knowledge?'

'Whatever suits your reasoning?' Gwyneth looked Joseph in the eyes with a cold expressionless face. She had no intention of answering. 'You say the herbalist calls on you here ... er ... Gwyneth.'

'Not as frequently. Not since he found work for Helena at the abbey.'

'What kind of work, and who is Helena?'

'She's the granddaughter of a late friend and delivers special herbs to the monastery hospice. She also serves in the abbot's house on occasions, especially when he entertains important people.'

'Would this Helena have hair the colour of golden wheat?'

Gwyneth smirked. 'That would be her.'

'I warn you Gwyneth that I serve the king and archbishop and have authority to investigate any suspicious misdoings.'

'I object to your threatening manner, Brother! And take heed that Helena has a good relationship with the abbot. They say he covets her.' She smirked again as Joseph turned to leave. 'This may not be the last you see of me witch, so be careful.' As they approached Phillip, Joseph caught a glimpse of a blond-haired woman quickly turning away from their path. *She's avoiding me.* Joseph recognised the posture and thought it to be the same attractive woman they had seen on their first day in the abbey grounds. 'Did you see that woman Phillip?'

'Yes. She works for the abbot. The woman is under his protection and sometimes needs to stay overnight.'

'How do you know?'

'I know, because Daniel told me. He has sharp ears and tells me that he's had some sleepless nights in the dormitory. He also finds time to communicate with the secular servants. They dine behind the refectory dividing wall, and they rarely eat in silence.'

Joseph faced Daniel and looked at him in a different light. *He surely keeps himself to himself, and he has a knowing look about him.* 'Well then Phillip, Daniel and I can now tell you that her name is Helena, can't we, Daniel?'

The novice nodded sheepishly. 'Yes, we can Brother Joseph.' *I will have to be more careful in future.*

Helena watched the trio ride out of site before calling on her benefactor. She placed a basket of bread inside the doorway and sat down beside the old lady in front of the boiling cauldron. They both rested with arms on laps, gazing at the simmering liquid in a comfortable silence of familiarity. They listened to the sounds of the forest for a while before Helena gave out a sigh and broke the peace. 'What was his business with you?'

'Whatever it was I didn't like his manner. He was far too inquisitive, and he was interested in both you and the abbot, so be warned my lass. Be warned!'

'How was he interested?'

'He was asking about poisons. Herbal poisons that would cause a slow death. He suggested that I may know something of the late abbot's death, and that you could also be involved in their administration.'

'But I liked Abbot William, he was a kindly man, and they say he died of natural causes. The brothers saw him snatch at his chest and collapse alongside the brook that runs through the grounds.'

'I only believe what I see Helena, not what I hear. The French monk is obviously of the same mind.'

'Uncle Rolf told me they are here to compare the affairs of the abbey to those of Fountains.'

'Then you know more than I do Helena but sometimes the least I know is for the better. I've never asked you this before because it never concerned me. What happens to the herbs after you deliver them?'

'I leave them with the abbot. He says they are for the hospice, but it's none of my business.'

'And you have never seen them taken from his house?'

'Not that I can remember. But that evil-looking Brother Henry is always running to and fro.'

'Am I supposed to know him?'

'He's the small hungry looking one who used to call with Brother Michael before Abbot William's death.'

'Ah yes! He is the knowledgeable one.'

'What do you mean?'

'I mean, he knows about poisons. I'm not a fool, and the more I think of it the more I shudder. He looks like walking death. Perhaps our French visitors know more than they suggest.'

'I would like to think that they are here to bring down the abbot. That would make my task so much easier.'

'What on earth are you talking about lass? They will snuff you out like a candle on as much as the breath of a whisper.'

'I think the abbot already knows the truth about the amulet. He's even taken to giving me the key for the cellar, that I might go and fetch my prize like a dog. And then he shows me off to his important visitors. He teases me, and I hate him for it. But none of that will matter when the time arrives for me to reclaim my inheritance.'

'I don't want to know Helena. I would never have suggested you for the work if I had known of your madness. You have to let go of the past.'

Helena wasn't listening. She was deep in thought, her excitement growing, speaking as if to herself. 'If there is any way I can help them to bring him down, I will. It could be to my advantage to speak in secret with this Brother Joseph.'

Gwyneth shook her head as she listened to the rambling words and felt obliged to interrupt. 'I can smell trouble brewing. Be careful what you say Helena. We know nothing of the visiting brothers, and you could be placing yourself in danger. Brother Joseph is an inquisitor, a man possessed by his devotion to the church. His companion is a silent one who watches over him. The novice is being used but he has knowing eyes and he is intelligent. You should be patient until they have completed their business here.'

'You have learned a great deal of them in such a short visit.'

'I can sense the best and the worst in people, and you would do well to listen.'

But Helena was as obsessed with her task as Joseph was with his. 'The abbot will be sailing at the end of the trading season and when he leaves, the ankh will be in my possession.'

An invitation to partake

A week after Joseph's meeting with Gwyneth, he was invited to partake of bread and wine at the house of Abbot Guy. He was seated at a round oak table in the company of the abbot, Prior Michael, Brother Bryan the bursar and a smaller, ghoulish, hungry looking man that he'd vaguely noticed in the refectory. A mass of candles, equally spaced, in crevices around the room was burning fiercely. Joseph rolled his head and sniffed. His aquiline nose had sensed something other than the odour of burning wax. He'd picked up the scent of rose petals in the room, and the fragrance of a woman.

A shadow flitted across the table and Helena was at his side with a skin of wine and a plate of bread and cheese. Close up she was more beautiful than he'd imagined. 'Peux je vous servir Frère Joseph?' Her voice was soft and calming, and she surprised him with her mode of speech. She leaned over him and whispered in his ear. 'Je pense que je peux vous aider.' She filled his chalice and smiled knowingly as she looked deep into his eyes, then quickly departed from whence she'd come.

What did she mean she thinks she can help me? He remembered his youth, the waywardness and knew that this woman could breach his weakness. He remembered with shame his ordeal with the aristocratic she-devil. In their loneliness she'd taken advantage of his vulnerability, and he'd given in too easily. But what choice did he have? He had prayed every night to cast the Devil aside but eventually took pleasure in the woman's visits. He had betrayed his vows and then been cast aside like a used toy. Joseph crossed himself at the distant thought and heard sniggers from across the table as he looked up from his wine.

The brothers were gloating. They had seen the flattery before. He never realised that he'd been staring so intensely. The abbot was laughing, a deep cynical reverberating laugh. He remembered the words of the witch. *They say the abbot covets her.* The abbot sat back with his hands clasped on his middle and a contented smile on his face. He had witnessed Joseph's pleasure and held a deliberate silence before he spoke. 'Helena is little more than a serving wench Brother Joseph, but I don't want you assume anything ill of her. We've had earls and kings sitting at this very table, bishops and archbishops. They all enjoy her youthful exuberance and charming presence. Choice wine and a good table go hand in hand with pleasure, politics and business.'

Joseph was beginning to feel uncomfortable. *They're belittling me.*

'I have been informed that you recently entered the abode of Gwyneth, a close confidante of an old acquaintance of mine. She is a friendly person and one to whom some people unkindly refer to as a witch. I must tell you that I owe her my gratitude for bringing Helena to me. A beautiful woman who also speaks French is a rarity in these parts. What was your business with Gwyneth, Brother Joseph?'

Joseph had walked into a lion's den and he was flummoxed. He couldn't announce his suspicions to a table of men that he thought could be guilty of a possible murder. And the more he thought of his reasoning, the more ridiculous it seemed. 'I was informed by the locals that she was a great healer and I was interested in her use of herbs.'

'We are skilled in our own medicines within the monastery. I know you are well aware of that fact, and I fail to see why you should deviate from your own interests. What task were you really commissioned for Brother Joseph?'

Joseph sensed a threat in the abbot's choice of words. 'I assure you it was only of a trivial and passing interest Abbot Guy.'

'Then let it stay that way. I won't suffer any more interference with our peaceful existence. I have reason to believe that there is unrest in the dormitory because of your questioning of Gwyneth. I want no more of this trivial probing. You arrived here on high commendation, but I have total authority over my territories, and any actions outside of your commission will be referred to my bailiffs.'

Joseph was wishing himself elsewhere. He was the one who should be asking the questions, but the abbot had made him aware that he'd stepped outside of his commission. *You are an interfering old fool Joseph.* He chastised himself, and condescended. 'I understand Abbot Guy.'

'It is obvious to all, that it is not Abbot William so much as your own mind that has been poisoned. Now, to alleviate any doubt Brother Joseph, and to put your mind at rest, I would like to impress on you the history of recent years.' His eyes locked onto Joseph's, and the pause in his speech held a deliberate protraction that served to emphasise his superiority. His manner was commanding, almost threatening. 'I come from a family of great wealth and social standing, and that is partly the reason for me holding the distinguished position of Abbot of Furness. I came here initially as prior, and I have no qualms in telling you that my position was to have been that of abbot, except for some untimely interference from York via the pope. I must also tell you that Abbot William never left the confines of the abbey during the two years of his service. He was a notoriously bad sea traveller. I personally took on the responsibility of trade with Zealand, Ireland and the Mann, and Brother Michael acted as prior during my absence. So now you may wonder what Abbot William did for amusement.'

'Are you accusing him of circumventing his duties?'

'Not at all Brother Joseph, but you must have heard that the pope had issued a mandate to the Archbishop of York to remove him from his post?'

Joseph had no idea the abbot was being deposed and the shock told on his face. *Why wasn't I told, and for what reason was I denied the truth?*

'Your lack knowledge surprises me brother. I believed it was for that very reason that you were dispatched to investigate our affairs.'

'I must confess that I had no knowledge of the mandate and my commission remains as stated.'

'Then we shall all have to believe you.' The abbot squinted and paused before speaking. 'For the time being, that is.'

'Was Abbot William aware of the mandate?'

'He was, and although it pains me to speak of it, perhaps that was the reason for his death. But Abbot William's life has ended, and we all treat his past with respect, so you will hear no more of it. When I returned from my last sea voyage and heard that he was departed from this earth, and already interred in our cemetery, you can imagine my shock.'

'You were away when he died?'

'Unfortunately, I was away for five weeks and they told me he died less than a week after my departure. He looked so healthy when he bade farewell, and he was only ten years my senior. It was such a tragedy. I was grateful to have had an able sub prior in Brother Michael. He could well be a future Abbot of Furness.' He smiled superciliously as he turned to address the prior. 'But we mustn't delve too much on that subject now, must we Brother Michael?' The prior smiled with closed eyelids and shook his head.

Joseph studied Brother Michael more closely and disliked what he saw. *The man has slyness about him, and he eyes Helena as if with a need.* Then he remembered where he'd seen the other hungry looking brother before. *Of course! He's the brother that sometimes reads from the Bible during the silence at main meal. The one that Daniel thought he recognised.* Joseph had a feeling that it was time to leave, and he'd only just arrived. But he stayed awhile to suffer in silence, nibbling at the bread and sipping the wine whilst he listened to their idle chatter. The main purpose of their meeting had obviously been achieved and for the first time in his life he felt a nonentity.

Joseph was annoyed, and only had himself to blame. But his anger only determined him to take something out of the meeting. His eyes scanned the room for the ventilation mentioned by Rolf. His discussion with the master stonemason had as usual been intense. He had worked on the new abbot's house as an apprentice and explained that there was ventilation for a cellar under the house. The stonemason had also recounted the same tale as the Vicar of Dalton that a tradesman from his village had been called to the cellar after the death of Abbot William and spoken of riches held in a locked casket, and of a blue talisman shaped like the cross. From outside the building Joseph had taken note of two chimneystacks. The warmth of the fire accounted for one. He noticed a cupboard built into a recess between the west windows and believed he had found the other. The mason revealed the location of another vault that lay under the tower, and he said there were rumours of a passageway from a further vault beneath. The iron door to the belfry was only open during the pealing of the bells for the call to prayer. He discovered there was a moveable slab with lifting rings on the first landing of the spiral stairs. Joseph now had two locations that could reveal enough evidence to back up his records, but he doubted that he would ever have the opportunity to gain access.

Helena returned with more wine and Joseph grasped his opportunity to leave. He levered himself from the chair and was about to excuse himself from their company when his eyes closed in on the scintillating blue stone resting delicately against Helena's bosoms. She was running her fingers over its face, a soothing caressing gesture, and staring with glazed eyes as if in deep thought. The deep-blue gemstone's delicate golden specks sparkled from within like stars in the evening sky. Joseph was impressed. *That's a lapis-lazuli stone!*

'You are star gazing again Brother Joseph.'

'I'm sorry Abbot Guy, but Helena's blue talisman caught my eye. The stone is quite beautiful, and I've never seen such an intriguing design.'

'The talisman's origins are Egyptian. It is called an ankh, and to the ancient Egyptians it was the symbol of life and buried with the dead. It is said that the wearing of it will enhance a woman's beauty.'

'I can see the truth before me Abbot Guy.'

The abbot beckoned Helena to him. 'Let us show our brother the stone that you covet so much my dear girl.' As Helena leaned over, Abbot Guy cupped the talisman in his palm and ran his forefinger along the shape of the cross. 'One could be confused into thinking that this is the cross of Christianity, but the loop above tells us otherwise. A talisman such as this was held by ancient kings in their burial chambers long before the birth of our Saviour. In their ignorance they worshipped other gods, and perhaps this symbol of their faith is closer to the Devil than we would wish for. But it is a rarity that was gifted to the church, and if the talisman holds mystical powers, then let us pray that they work to our advantage.'

Joseph looked with deliberation into the abbot's eyes, then into Helena's and back to the abbot, questioning. Abbot Guy interpreted the meaningful glance and was happy to oblige. 'Helena pesters me to wear the talisman whenever she can. Recently the occasions have been more frequent, and on the odd occasion I have had to trust her with the cellar key. But I'm not so naive as to think that she would refrain from stealing the talisman if an opportunity arose.' He looked at Helena as he spoke and smirked as she turned away.

'I can't believe that she would plan to steal from you Abbot Guy.'

'Perhaps she has a death wish, or merely an obsession with rare objects. She once asked me if King John's jewels were hidden under the tower.'

There was an immediate roar of laughter which made Joseph wonder if there really was something of value under the tower. He studied Helena's expression. Her eyes told him that she was aware of being the object of discussion, but she was trying to show disinterest. *How conversant is she with French? She could have been taught a few French compliments in order to charm her guests.* But then Joseph remembered Rolf telling him that she was a relative. *Of course, he speaks fluent French and because of her closeness, she would also be familiar with the layout of the buildings. But why would she risk stealing from the abbot?* Helena gave the abbot a melting smile and turned to her duties. There was steel in her eyes that Joseph hadn't noticed before.

'If anything went missing, Brother Joseph, it would be on her head, as the case would be with anyone else in this room caught stealing.'

His stare lingered on Joseph for a moment, enough to make him feel uncomfortable. *He's trying to intimidate me.*

'When I employ Helena to serve important visitors, it is to my advantage that she adds to her beauty and the blue stone is often a talking point.'

'You flatter me Abbot Guy. To think, that you would allow Helena to serve me as an important visitor.'

'We feel that you *are* important, and we wish for you to inform your superiors of our generous hospitality.'

'And so I will Abbot Guy.' Joseph took his leave but not without being subjected to some parting advice from the abbot.

'Please stay away from the Vicar of Dalton. That man would poison your soul. Bonne nuit Frère Joseph.'

Brother Joseph felt naked. *Is nothing secret in this district?* He was beginning to lose confidence in his own intuition. The witch had told him nothing, but he'd still believed she may have advised or even sampled the brothers a potion. But he was having his first pangs of doubt. *Abbot Guy was at sea when William died, so perhaps the abbot's death was natural after all, or even self-inflicted as suggested. The Vicar of Dalton could have deliberately sowed the seeds of doubt. They are obviously disagreeable to each other.* Joseph felt foolish. He cast Abbot William's death from his thoughts. *If I wasn't so inquisitive, I'm sure my life would be much easier.* He turned to the task at hand, directing his energies towards his true commission. But he was beginning to think the task impossible. *I must learn to be more patient.*

The choir monks settled into their normal days of prayer and Joseph came to spend his spare time in the library above the chapter house. Remembering the vicar's words, he set about befriending Brother Bryan the bursar, asking him the reason for the invasion of horse and wagons every week. He had seen the yeomen delivering wheat to the mill almost daily and at various times they had also delivered cattle. He knew the domestic goods were trading for rent but he asked the question only as a means of conversation. 'I've noticed both yourself and the cellarer organising the loading of barrels of beer and loaves of bread.'

Brother Bryan explained the abbey's means of trade and employment and soon after Joseph was allowed to examine the bursar's records.

'There are no records of the Piel Island trade?'

'They are of a separate matter. We pay tithes on sea trading and the records must be kept apart.'

'Where are the records held?'

'They remain the business of Abbot Guy, and he alone. Why do you ask?'

'I'm simply curious.'

'Forgive me if I'm wrong, but I believe your commission, in your own words, was to compare England's two most prominent abbeys?'

'That's true, and I can only compare them if I take into account all of the trading, Brother Bryan.'

'Fountain's has no sea trade with which to compare Brother Joseph.'

'Exactly brother and that could be the difference between the two.'

'Then, surely as we only pay tithes on the sea trade, the king and archbishop already have the information required.'

The two monks stared at each other in silence. The bursar was now looking aggressive and Joseph was trying to fathom his thoughts. It was Brother Bryan who spoke first, and the words were threatening. 'Unless of course you are insinuating that there is more trade than has been declared.'

'I am not! Your reasoning is quite correct brother. The books would add little to my comparison.'

'If you so desire, you can pursue the matter further with Abbot Guy, but I would strongly advise against any more interference.'

Joseph had initially hoped his investigation into the affairs of Furness Abbey would take no more than the early weeks of summer trading. He soon became aware that there was more to the Abbey of Saint Mary than at first met the eye. His task at Furness was going to be more complicated than his superiors could ever have imagined. Joseph was still finding it hard to believe that an abbey free of tithes and other land taxes could be involved in smuggling to avoid shipping tariffs. But when he looked at the rapid growth of the abbey, he knew that the extensions could only be sustained with ongoing wealth. He now knew that the bursar had separate account books, and that one of them was held by the abbot. There seemed little chance of him acquiring either whilst the abbot was in residence. When the abbot travelled, the books were stored, and after a discussion with the master stonemason he believed he knew the location. He tried to concentrate on other evidence. In the past month his frequent trips to the island had yielded the markings of seven ships trading under the abbot's flag. The distinguishing marks of the ships, the details of their cargos and their frequency of trading would be in his report. Joseph had a change of plan. He had come to the conclusion that because of the situation, it was now convenient for him to sail with the king's officers at the end of the summer season. His records of trade would be handed over to the authorities and compared with those declared by the bursar. Until that time, only Phillip should be aware of the location of his recordings.

The scriptorium

Joseph had been searching for incriminating documents when he was sidetracked by his own curiosity. He had unearthed some unbound parchments relating to the life and beliefs of the early Scandinavian settlers. His curiosity of the local inhabitants was extended when he discovered they still practised the old ways. A conversation with the local master stonemason had revealed a finger ring engraved with four symbols. Joseph could still feel that first surge of excitement. *The ring could be over three hundred years old.* The four symbols matched perfectly with his research. He was studying symbols that resembled a foreign alphabet. The accompanying description of their meanings so fascinated him, that he coerced Daniel into writing a transcription of the original records.

Distant rumbling of stone and sporadic vibration of the timber floor was unsettling Daniel. He had entered the scriptorium shortly after Prime, and he was feeling tired, unable to concentrate. A book lay open on his writing stand and beside it on a piece of parchment, an almost completed sketch of a ship. The young and talented scribe dipped his freshly sharpened goose quill into a phial of coloured ink. He scraped away the excess and with an artistic flourish, put the finishing touches to the curves of the ship's inverted double bow. The novice coloured in the outline of a serpent's head, then set down his quill and stepped back to admire his work. He'd enjoyed sketching the larger perspective of an impressive warrior at the forefront. He thought the original scribe had shown more interest in the Viking warrior than he had on the beached ship in the background. The sea invader was sketched with long wild hair, short beard and eye patch. He wore sheepskin clothing and sea boots and carried a sword, shield and lance. Daniel cocked his head to one side and listened to the muffled sound of hammer against stone. He was bored and his eyes weary from working in dim light. He was being pushed too hard. Brother Joseph had become obsessed with the local history and it was hindering the completion of his commission. *Why is he so intense?* He squeezed his eyelids, rubbed his fingers over them in a circular motion, and blinked. He cracked his knuckled fingers in a handclasp and stretched as he pushed his arms outwards. Transcribing was tedious at the best of times and he'd been made to put aside his task of copying Bede's history to concentrate on Joseph's sketch. *Brother Joseph should be helping me. It is a pity that he's such a terrible scribe, and so impatient.*

Daniel stood up and stretched his body, donned his habit, and doused the candles. He left the scriptorium and went to the library to find Joseph and report his progress. His superior seemed pleased and decided it was time for the novice to meet the stonemason, a man with a direct link to the past. They wound their way down a spiral staircase to the ground floor, moved briskly past the chapter house and entered the courtyard. The upper rooms had been dark and cold. They welcomed the fresh air, the brightness and warmth of God's candle. Choir monks were circulating the cloisters in small groups, chattering with animation, as if making up for lost time.

Joseph often wondered what they found to talk about. *They'll soon be at main meal, eating in silence, talking with their fingers, and listening to the reading.* A small group quietened as Joseph and Daniel approached and like birds-in-a-bush, chattered ten-to-the-dozen after they passed.

A huge wagon tilted, and another load of sandstone thundered onto the turf as a group of carpenters manoeuvred three wooden arches into place. The timber construction would soon support the arched red sandstones until the mortar had set. The monastery lay brothers were helping with the extension behind the cloisters. Phillip's task was organising their labour for the guild's French masons and reporting building progress to Prior Michael. When Joseph and Daniel arrived, he was directing some lay brothers in the adjoining foundation trenches, keeping up a ready supply of the builder's choice stone. He welcomed the appearance of his two travelling companions and told them the whereabouts of the local stonemason.

Rolf was a giant of a man, broad shouldered and sinewy, with alert steel-blue eyes and a gaunt olive-complexioned face. As he leaned forward to chip and scrape over the surface of the red sandstone, his long black hair fell over his forehead and curtained his face. Rolf was a perfectionist. Joseph studied him a moment before approaching, admiring his patience and skill. 'Good afternoon Rolf. You have the patience worthy of a choir monk, but I pray you don't share their silence, for my visits would become less fruitful.'

The stonemason straightened from his work and nodded politely. He spoke in a deep booming voice, and Joseph had a tendency to lean away when they conversed. 'There's little chance of me being silent if you continue with your questioning brother.'

Joseph smiled and took Daniel in with a glance 'At least we have the same interests at heart, sharing knowledge of your ancestors. You must realise by now that there is nothing sinister about us.'

Rolf's eyes darted from the novice to the questioning monk, and his mind was troubled. *I'm not so sure of that.*

'It interests me that you have a complexion similar to my own, not at all like Daniel here, or that of your fellow villagers. With your fluency in our language you could easily have been born of French parents. Were you taught your masonry skills in France?'

'I served the first year of my apprenticeship in the grounds that we now stand upon, Brother Joseph. More than thirty years ago I was apprenticed to stonemasons that had journeyed from France and London. Afterwards I travelled for ten years with the guild, working about the country on castles, cathedrals, and monasteries.' He paused and sniffed through his left nostril. This caused the left eye to wink and his shoulder to hunch simultaneously. It was an affliction that irritated his wife to insanity and one that she'd hopelessly failed to cure.

'Are you of French parentage?'

'My grandmother said I owe the colour of my skin to our immigrant ancestors. They were born of a Spanish slave, a Skraeling, who had married a great Viking chieftain. She voiced many tall stories and swore they were all true. She told me her mother Rota was the only one to be born with my complexion and now my eldest daughter has a son with a similar colouring.'

'Rota is an unusual name.'

'It was an old family name handed down. Our legends tell of a woman named Rota who was a sorceress and could predict one's death. Many of the old names have been lost and replaced with Christian names.'

'I have recently seen the name Rota of Sogn in the history of your ancestors Rolf, and I can well believe you. The name appeared in an old poem that was passed down and transcribed by one of the abbey's first Benedictine brothers.'

'I would like to see these writings Brother Joseph. I was taught in the monastery school and understand a little of the ancient writing. The Rota you speak of could be one of our family ancestors. My mother's mother spoke of one such person in her poetry and there was once a rare blue stone in our family that was said to belong to her.'

'Did you lose the stone?'

Rolf hesitated. *The brother's too inquisitive. He's bleeding me.* 'The wound is deep, and I don't wish to speak of it.' He sniffed again and Joseph stared in amusement as the left shoulder lifted.

'You have a bad habit Rolf. Does something trouble you?'

'My left shoulder often pains me at the end of a long day. Can I see the writings?'

'You may well be able to understand some of the writings, but they are faded somewhat. This is Daniel at my side. He's a novice who has great skills with the quill and at present he's in the process of transcribing a copy of your ancestors' records.'

'Then I wish you God's speed Daniel.'

The stonemason's huge hands swept red dust from his workings exposing two freshly carved symbols. Joseph bent over with interest and then straightened with surprise, completely oblivious of the swirling red dust that settled on his laundered habit. 'Is that a fault in the stone Rolf?'

'It's nothing of the kind brother. All stonemasons leave their mark, and these are my own chosen symbols. They are runic, and once used by our ancient ancestors. They are from the line of runes that you enquired of on my amulet.'

'But you carved those signs yourself. Have you some knowledge of the runes? Are they blasphemous?'

'No Brother Joseph! They refer only to wealth and not to the ancient gods. They are from the same ancient Norse alphabet that you are now transcribing. Our rune master assures me that combined together these two symbols will give the abbey great strength.' Rolf's affliction signalled the end of his speech.

Joseph was pensive for a moment, thinking that he'd been led to this man by the will of God. His task for the past month had been transcribing the meanings of the runes with Daniel and he was of the opinion that he'd become something of an expert. He knew there were twenty-four of them and that each one had a different sound and the ancient ones believed that various combinations altered their magical powers. He had heard villagers referring to them as God runes, magic runes that foretell the future when scattered across the earth like dice. The stonemason leaned forward over his work and a silver ring talisman swung out from his chest, supported by a coloured leather string. He grasped it in his fist and thrust it down into his tunic, smiling sheepishly at Joseph. 'Will you show me the ring again Rolf?' The master stonemason flipped the amulet into the palm of his hand without removing it from around his neck. Joseph's hands looked small as he reached up and dipped into Rolf's huge palm. He scooped up the ring and turned it around with his fingers, trying to guess its age. 'The four symbols are repeated Rolf. The warrior must have thought them to be very important.'

'The ring was to have been passed down to my eldest brother. Perhaps if it had been in his possession during his service to the king, he would still be with us. When father died, I left the guild and returned to marry and take possession of the leasehold. My grandmother gifted the silver ring to me and made me promise to wear it only as an amulet. The ring is a sacred reminder of our ancestors. It would be considered sacrilege and carry ill luck if worn on another man's finger.' He held the ring tightly against his chest as one would swear with hand on heart. 'I would die preserving this ring of our ancestors. It has been in our family since the immigration.'

Joseph was taken aback by Rolf's display of passion. 'Then you know the ring's history?'

'Of course, our ancestors were great storytellers called skalds. My parents taught us all to respect our roots.'

Joseph looked to Daniel and was pleased to see his interest in the conversation. 'Then please tell us about the ring's history Rolf.'

The stonemason leaned back against the wall for comfort and continued. 'This ring I wear as an amulet belonged to my ancestor; a Viking earl named 'Ragnarr the Tall'. He was a bowman warrior of the Norwegian King 'Hakon the Good' and commanded the archers in many of the king's victorious campaigns. My grandmother often recited an ancient poem that told of the ring belonging to Ragnarr, a great chieftain warrior who married his Spanish slave. When their daughter Freydis came of age she was gifted an Arabian horse with a rare black coat as shiny as a raven. Ragnarr was assassinated in his island holiday home, the Arabian horse stolen and Freydis ravished.' Rolf became thoughtful, rolling the silver ring between his thumb and forefinger. 'This ring was torn from Ragnarr's finger as he lay in death and his daughter Freydis became a warrior of revenge. She severed the head of her rapist on the Isle of Mann and retrieved the ring.'

'Are you sure it is the same ring Rolf?'

The mason fixed his eyes on Joseph's, his expression one of disbelief as he blandly recited part of his grandmother's poem.

Ospaki's head was severed
Freydis cast it to the sea,
The assassin Gallin fell to Hauk
And set the settlers free.

Brother Joseph shrugged and waved a hand for Rolf to continue. 'As the poem suggests, her brother Hauk took revenge on their father's killer. The poem tells of a battle in the Bay of Sinking Sands. The same sands you crossed on your way to the abbey.' Joseph looked to Daniel and the novice smiled and nodded his interest as the mason continued. 'The runes that you can see on this ring Brother Joseph, speak of Thor the god of thunder, of a horse messenger of the gods, of an archer and of a sea journey. Who am I to oppose the legends of the ancients?'

'Do you think it was the story of his life?'

'That could be the truth. Or it could be the telling of his future.'

'Explain to me the meaning of the two symbols you have carved on the stone, so that I can compare them with the old parchment.'

'They are the first and last of the rune alphabet. The beginning and end. Fehu has the sound of F and is the beginning of wealth. Othala has the sound of O and is wealth that cannot be sold. I carved them on the foundation stones of this abbey's surrounding walls many times when I was an apprentice.'

'I have seen them before. They are two of twenty-four that are written on the parchment in the library. I will compare them with your knowledge. It will be interesting to see if the meanings have changed over time.'

'I should like to see them if I may, Brother, for they must be as old as my ancestors.'

'I will inform you when Daniel completes his transcription. Are you superstitious Rolf?'

'I am. It is only natural.'

'Your interpretation of the symbols fascinates me, as there can be no doubt that the abbey has already gathered great wealth. What do you think of the meaning of the rune which foretells that the wealth cannot be sold? Do you think that the wealth refers to knowledge, faith or of monetary wealth?'

'The runes have many meanings when they are combined. We may have to wait until the death of the monastery for the answer.' Joseph smiled appreciatively. He enjoyed the banter and listening to the uncluttered thoughts of the locals. 'Now, who is this rune master you speak of?'

The stonemason hesitated. 'He is the last of his kind and lives in the lower Furness district.'

'Then you must bring him to me. You must reassure him that there is no danger. I merely wish to compare his interpretation of the runes with the earlier records.' Joseph knew that there were people in parts of the woods that still worshipped the old gods, but his interest was genuine.

'Will you swear he will be safe Brother Joseph?'

'I swear on the *Bible* and may I bake in Hell if I lie. You have my word.'

'Then I will speak only to you, for I am the son of Rolf of Rusland. My long-departed father was a rune master and taught me the ancient ways. I'm the only holder of the knowledge in these parts since the passing of my brother John.'

The Cistercian monk was stunned, and at the same time excited. *This could be further unrecorded local history.* 'Did your brother die young?'

'He volunteered his service, as is the law relating to the tenants. He joined King Henry in war. He was inspired by our grandfather who often spoke of past family warriors. His brothers had fought alongside Richard in the crusades and returned with honour. My lasting memory of John was as I stood with his family and our proud father, waving him away. He was taller and stronger than I, and he looked magnificent astride his horse. He was dressed in mail garment and doublet armed with spear, sword and bow. We heard that he died bravely but our father never fully recovered from the loss and John's wife was grief-stricken. She wandered from the district with a troubled mind and sought seclusion. She became a recluse and left her only child in the care of our mother.'

'Let us pray that your brother died for a just cause and that he rests peacefully with the good Lord.' There was a moment of contemplation between them before Joseph spoke again. 'I would like you to instruct me in the meanings of the runes as you know them, before Daniel transcribes them. It will be interesting to see if the interpretations have changed with the passage of time. Your ancestor's beliefs must be recorded for posterity in truth, or not at all.'

'I must tell you now, that my father's brother, Roger, was a monk of Furness Abbey. He was taught here and longed for the peaceful living. He gave up his land holdings and all other possessions to join the brotherhood. But on doing so, he left an open wound in the family. There were siblings who believed that certain possessions were never his to own, and they should never have been given away to the church. We have a saying that wealth causes friction between relatives whilst the wolf lurks in the woods. The rare blue stone that I spoke of should have been handed down to my brother's wife, and so on to her daughter, but I wish to say no more.' *I must speak no more of my family.*

'I am certain I have seen the stone that you speak in the abbot's house. There couldn't possibly be two of them Rolf. When we first met you told me you were the uncle of the pretty girl who frequented the abbot's house, and that her name was Helena.'

Rolf feigned surprised and spoke cautiously. 'You know my niece Helena?'

'I can't say that I know her, but I did meet her recently, at the abbot's house.'

Rolf had been told of the meeting. *Helena was right. He could be more of a friend than an enemy.* He decided that he could speak openly. 'Ever since the whereabouts of the ankh talisman became known she has become obsessed with acquiring what she believes is rightfully hers. Her task is even greater than yours Brother Joseph, and I fear for her life.'

'You know of my task?'

'Most things are known within the district, but little is known of the district outside of it.'

'You surprise me Rolf. There seems to be so much secrecy in Furness, and yet there is none.' Joseph paused to gather his thoughts, studying Rolf's facial expression. *How much do they really know?* 'Helena whispered in my ear that she could help me. Was she referring to the task that you mentioned?'

'I don't know her thoughts Brother Joseph. Perhaps you should ask her.'

'I feel that if we were seen alone together her life would be placed in danger. I'm already being closely watched.'

The stonemason thought to change the subject. He smiled, raised his arm, and pointed towards the church. 'My father's brother, Roger, who became a monk, lays buried in the abbey cemetery over there. Rolf pointed to an area north of the chapel. He organised my apprenticeship with the French guild and used to visit me as you do yourself. He told me there were writings in the abbey of our ancestor's beliefs, and a poem of their immigration to the district.'

'Did your uncle discuss the meanings of the runes with you?'

'He only showed a casual interest. He seemed immersed in his inner-self most of the time.'

'Well then, when we compare our knowledge and for my own satisfaction, I shall confirm the markings on the silver amulet that you carry.'

'I would like to determine the history of the woman Rota, Brother Joseph, and the story of the first council.'

'I promise I will read it to you. But in future you should be more open with me. It will save us both our precious time. If you have influence with Helena and I'm sure you have, then you should warn her of temptation. She wears the blue talisman as if it was her own and the monks toy with her emotions.'

'The girl has a strong will. She became homeless again after my mother died and my wife and I raised her like our own. I taught Helena to speak your language in the hope that she might elevate her position in life. I knew that was her mother's wish and my niece showed great determination to master the tongue. Now I'm not so sure that it was a good thing for her. But no matter what she plans, her fate will be in the hands of God.'

'Your words tell me that you have the traits of your ancestors. Do you still believe in a predestined life?'

'That is my way of thinking Brother Joseph. Do you think I should believe otherwise?'

'Having faith in God is all that matters Rolf. I believe he will take me from this earth when my work is done, and I cannot wish for more.'

Brother Joseph left Daniel in Rolf's company and headed for the chapel immersed in deep thought. He believed he was alone in his task and sought consolation in the calm of the church. Joseph sat in the choir stalls whispering a prayer, hearing his voice amplified in the blessed sanctuary. He had visited many cathedrals but found them large and overwhelming. In the confines of the small church he felt a belonging, and at no other time in his life had he been so much at peace. His body had slowed down these past weeks and his mind was less agitated. He faced the east window and studied the partitioned glass paintings of the Crucifixion with the Virgin Mary on the right of the cross and the beloved disciple on the left, and he thought deeply of the sacrifice. Angels were portrayed receiving sacred blood from the five precious wounds, and below the cross, a group of monks in their proper habits with the abbot in a vestment. He wondered if the abbot had been of Furness Abbey and if any of the depicted monks had worked on the transcriptions.

Abbot Guy listened attentively to the accusations of Prior Michael. 'Brother Joseph was suspicious of a murder being committed until we convinced him otherwise. Gwyneth persuaded him that any potion of hers was not enough to kill a baby, let alone a grown man. And I believe we convinced him that it was the vicar that had poisoned his mind about the abbey. But it's now obvious to me that Brother Joseph has more on his mind than the death of our late Abbot.'

'Are you suggesting that our first instincts were correct and that there is a more sinister reason for his visit? Are you convinced that he pursues something other than his stated commission?'

'Yes. We are. For what other reason would he extend his stay? Even the villagers speak of him investigating our affairs for a reason other than comparison. Although the words have passed through many mouths, we must assume there is some truth in the rumours. We must come to a decision of our own.'

'I hear that Joseph has the novice Daniel transcribing more than his commission, a tome relating to the local history. Could that be the reason he lingers?'

'That is an exercise to satisfy his curiosity. We are more interested in his meanderings through the wheat-growing districts of Newbarns and Hawcoat recording the number of carts being loaded within our enclosure. We've sixty-five acres enclosing mills, kilns, orchards stables and fishponds and I've been told he's been seen recording notes at each and every one of them. He's familiar with the Domesday Book and came with knowledge of all our granges in the outer districts. He asked me only the other day if the weekly food being loaded for the freeholders was being transported to the ships anchored off Piel Island. I had to explain to him our method of paying the freeholders for their crops.'

'Brother Bryan has already informed him of our method.'

'Then he asks each of us the same questions and that makes me even more suspicious. His presence has grated on the brethren ever since he rode through the abbey gates on a pure-white horse. Who does he think he is? Jesus Christ? Our French brother hangs around like a bad smell. He walks around with a dagger strapped to his forearm, its carved bone handle depicting our Saviour. Who else would sleep beneath a sword hung above him like the cross of Jesus?'

'I would Prior Michael and I do. Once a soldier always a soldier they say. Remember the Templars fought for the good of the church and their mission is still with the cross.'

'Forgive me Abbot Guy. I had no idea.'

'Know thine enemy Prior Michael, know thine enemy.' *And stop looking at me as though* I'm your *enemy.* 'How much do you think he knows of our shipping trade?'

'He has knowledge of our trading partners in Ireland and Zealand and he must have a fair knowledge of how many ships we own by now. But he can only guess at the quantity of cargo we are moving.'

'Brother Joseph's links to the archbishop and King Henry are dangerous, Brother Michael. Find out what written records he has and destroy them.'

'He examined the bursar records of our general trade Abbot Guy and he became aware that as they attracted a tax, our sea-trading accounts were kept separate from each other.'

Abbot Guy grunted in exasperation as his fist came down hard on the table and one foot stomped the floor. 'Why? Why I ask you, does the king demand taxes when he knows the wealth is needed to create and extend the house of God?' And the abbot proceeded to answer his own question. 'I'll tell you why. He requests wealth that he may waste it on more of his failed army campaigns and on rebuilding Whitehall. That is why!'

'Nevertheless, Abbot Guy, the French agent remains our main concern.'

'That Brother Joseph might set his eyes on both accounts is a matter that we should all take seriously. The book of most importance is safely locked away in my cellar. I will see to it that his eyes see nothing other than the records of our minor trading. If he is still in residence when I depart for Ireland, then you must guard the keys to the tower vault with your life. The records will as usual be transferred there and I will not suffer negligence.'

'We should consider him too dangerous to leave the monastery. He must be taken care of.'

'Then contain him within our walls. He has obviously recorded far too much for his own good. We will have to separate him from Brother Phillip, a bodyguard if ever I saw one. We must hasten Phillip's departure.'

'He will never leave alone. Brother Joseph so much as told me that they would all return as they arrived; two brothers and a novice.'

'He told me he was considering sailing with the king's officers. That would be dangerous for us, and why would he worry about not returning the novice? We will take the matter out of his hands. Arrange for the novice Daniel to leave as a matter of urgency and for Phillip to accompany him. When the time is right you must convince Daniel that he's required back at Fountains, or perhaps that some of our brothers find him unsettling. I will be leaving towards the end of the summer trading, for the Isle of Mann and Ireland. By the time I return I should hope to find our community settled and a peaceful habitat again.'

'Thanks to Brother Henry, our French guest has already acquired a taste for our herbal medicines. Brother Joseph will soon find peace and become easier to handle.'

'You are ahead of me, and that could become a dangerous habit. I must speak with Brother Bryan again. The late Abbot William was excessively greedy, and we are obviously being investigated because of his stupidity. We must make sure the king receives a fair amount of tax this season. They say King Henry's obsessed with rebuilding Whitehall and he must lament over our lawful tenure of Furness. We will have to declare more trade, and the extensions behind the cloisters will be delayed. We shall have good yields followed by bad yields in future, and we shall endeavour to keep the wolves from our door.'

Daniel was overwhelmed by Abbot Guy's interest in his commission. He had never seen the abbot in the scriptorium before and at first, he found it hard to speak with a man of such high standing. 'I must compliment you on the completion of your transcription young man. You are indeed talented, and I wish it was possible for you to extend your visit.'

'I really must leave then, Abbot Guy?'

'Unfortunately, you must. Prior Michael was surprised at the request, but apparently Fountains think highly of you. Brother

Phillip will travel with you of course. Your safety is of the utmost importance.'

'Will Brother Joseph travel with us Abbot Guy? I fear to mention it, but he looks sickly of late.'

'He insists he has further work to complete, and he will travel by ship to London, later in the season. The prior assures me that his sickness is no more than a lack of relaxation, but it is well that you speak of him.'

'We hear that you are also travelling Abbot Guy.'

'That may be true or not. Travel safely young man and ensure that your transcription is fully bound before you depart.'

Daniel would be carrying more than one transcription on his departure and he was fearful of being caught. There had been more than one near miss with Brother Joseph. 'Have you seen anyone riffling through the tomes lately Daniel? They seem to be in complete disarray.'

He had found Brother Joseph's hiding place easily the first time, but after the disarray, his report was continuously moved elsewhere amongst the library tomes.

'The scribes are often looking through them Brother Joseph. What else can we expect?' *He's so immaculate with his placing, always high, almost inaccessible. And he is so suspicious.*

Daniel had no idea that Brother Phillip had been given a copy of Joseph's records until they were stopped leaving the abbey grounds. They were circled by a ring of armed men, and Prior Michael emerged from amongst them with Brother Henry in tow. 'We have reason to believe that you have records in your possession that Abbot Guy considers sacrosanct.'

Brother Phillip went on the defensive, raising his sword. 'I take your accusation as an insult Prior Michael. What could I take from the abbey that would prove offensive to you?'

'That remains to be seen Brother Phillip, and please sheathe your sword, you make me nervous.'

Brother Henry went about searching Brother Phillip's saddlebag. He was disappointed when he found nothing, but before moving on to the packhorses he went to search the saddlebag of Daniel's horse. The young novice was sitting astride the white stallion feeling tall and proud of being allowed to ride back to Fountains on Brother Joseph's mount. Brother Phillip was crestfallen. *Surely, they are not going to search Daniel.* He could only look on helplessly as the ghoul triumphantly lifted Brother Joseph's report from the white stallion's saddlebag and waved it in the air.

Daniel had recognised Brother Henry reading the prayers at his first meal sitting at Furness, only he couldn't recollect where from. It was only now that the memory came to him; at Fountains, many years ago. There had been rumours of the brother being put down on suspicion of administering a poison. *He could be the cause of Brother Joseph's illness? I should have known.*

The prior took the report from Brother Henry and nodded his satisfaction. 'I hope you had nothing to do with this report Daniel.'

The prior waved the report in his face, but the novice had little need to feign surprise. He was genuinely shocked and inwardly shaking. 'I had no idea of the saddlebags contents Prior Michael. I thought to have no possessions other than my transcription.'

The prior was obviously pleased with his success and waved them off with an underhand gesture. 'Then let the innocence remain with your young man. Farewell and travel safely.'

Brother Phillip regained his composure and thought to speak his mind. Their commission had been taken from him, and without a fight. 'Not so quickly Prior Michael. I'm not sure I like you interfering with Brother Joseph's commission. Your life could be in danger if you persist.'

'You are leaving with Brother Joseph's blessing. Whether you return, will be of your own choosing.'

'If any harm befalls my companion whilst I'm away, I will show no mercy. For you can be sure I will return, and neither king nor bishop will stand in my way.'

His stare was threatening and the prior smiled weakly, turned his gaze and walked away without speaking. *So, the silent one has a tongue.*

Daniel's face was white with shock. They rode away with a silence that chilled the air around them. He had so much wanted to ask Brother Phillip if he could accompany him to France. *How can I say to him, I have another copy Brother Phillip? I have been spying on Brother Joseph.* His palm went to his stomach and felt the comfort of the parchment paper under his robes. *Abbot John De Cancia will have to decide on the importance of my transcription and whether he should pass it on to Brother Phillip and the Archbishop of York.*

Rolf was in the Scriptorium admiring Daniel's copy of the Viking ship. 'I've seen a skeleton of a ship very much the same. It's submerged in the sands of the sea below Coniston Water.'

'You're sure it's the same?'

'Not exactly Brother Joseph, but it's similar. All the oak decking has been stripped away and only the shell remains.'

'I must see it one day. Do you like Daniel's drawing of the Viking warrior? He looks to be very tall and he wears animal skins for his outer clothing.'

'We wear similar clothing in winter Brother Joseph. It's most likely a drawing of one of our ancestors, and I'm grateful to you for showing me.'

Joseph placed some more parchments on his stand. 'I read here of an agreement some eighty years ago in the year 1163 regarding disputed boundaries. There was a committee of thirty sworn men representing the Baron of Kendal and the Abbot of Furness Abbey. Amongst them were Scandinavian names like Ravenkell, Ulf and Orm. Your ancestors also held council meetings, such as the Norse people held in the Isle of Mann.'

'My grandparents spoke of the same, Brother Joseph.'

Joseph turned over another piece of parchment. 'Then look closely Rolf and you may imagine that these names relate to your ancestors. They were transcribed and drawn by a Brother Maurice from an original writing by a monk of the Benedict order. But you must also realise that these are only stories written from the spoken words of your ancestors, of poems handed down over generations, and not necessarily factual. You told me that was the nature of your race, their method of communicating your history.

At first the stonemason had difficulty with the swirling handwriting, but as he became familiar, the name of Rota came into prominence, and there was a feeling of belonging. An understanding of the past grew within him. He grasped the silver ring in his huge fist and pressed it hard against his chest. He pondered over the pages, and as Brother Joseph helped him with the translations, he became convinced that the ancestral stories were true. He turned to Joseph as if in a dream. 'Thankyou Brother. You have restored my belief in the voice of my grandparents, and of their ancestors.'

'We are reading an account of one of the first council meetings Rolf, and the names of the principal members. Apart from Rota, there were four more in attendance. There was the chief judge Domari Habrok, Hauk, Hrolfr, and Thorulf. A poem of their immigration was credited to the skald, Drengr Habrok, a warrior and brother of Domari.'

Rolf was concentrating on the parchment, unable to speak, fearing to close his eyes lest it go away. He recognised the first lines of the poem as Joseph recited them to him.

From Halagoland of ice and snow
Hauk guarded Harald's right,
With singing sword and lance and bow
He set the foe to flight.

And further down the page:

Our longboats sailed the Cumberland coast
Across the sea of fields,
We entered the bay of sinking sands
Ships lined with rounded shields.

Joseph stood back and watched the stonemason, trying to comprehend the man's obvious feeling of belonging to an age long past. The learned monk waited patiently in respectful silence, and Rolf eventually lifted his head. 'I think I must go now brother and speak with my wife and children. Can we talk another day?'

'Yes, we can. I would like to transcribe a copy for you, but my time here may be short.' Joseph looked up into the dazed face of the huge man and smiled as the master mason strode through the threshold in a trance. He listened to the sound of the giant's footsteps echoing through the cloisters and paused in his work until they faded away. He dipped his quill in the ink and sighed as his head leaned over the manuscript. Transcribing wasn't his favourite pastime. *It's a shame Daniel had to leave before the volume was completed.* The abbot had been firm and insisted that the novice must be accompanied by Phillip for the young man's safety. His companion would then return from Fountains at his own leisure. Joseph didn't often become attached to people, but he felt isolated and vulnerable without Daniel and Phillip. The past few days he had taken the main meal with Prior Michael and Brother Bryan. He was of the opinion that their attitude had improved immeasurably since Abbot Guy's departure. *Their kindness has helped ease the pain of my loneliness. I am impressed, and I rarely alter my opinion of people.*

Conspiracy

Helena began to panic. The guests had long departed but the ghoul was still hanging around. She felt his hot breath on her neck and spun around, choking on the smell and spluttering a cough. 'What are you doing? Why are you are following me around like a lost dog?' Then she saw the goblet in his hand, and he squeezed a half smile, sniggered and took another sip. Another time she would have laughed. *The chief administer of poisons is having a taste of his own medicine.* 'That's the abbot's drink. He's waiting for it.'

Brother Henry shrugged and continued to empty the goblet, rocking back and forth on his feet. 'Pour him another.'

'You are drunk Brother Henry. I think it's time you left.'

'I will go when Abbot Guy tells me.'

Helena's mind was in turmoil. *He won't be going anywhere shortly. Do I have enough for another concoction?* There had been no allowance for error. Another hour and Adam will have tethered his horse and be scaling the wall. They had to be finished before the bells were rung for Matins. She watched the ghoul sink to the floor. *Now what do I do?* Helena stepped over the sleeping monk, took his goblet, and rushed to doctor another wine. *There may not be enough, but it will have to suffice.* Panic was setting in and time was running short. *I'm losing control.* She took a deep breath and smiled as she walked into the room, the goblet placed delicately in the middle of the tray. 'I'm sorry about the delay Abbot Guy. I was seeing to Brother Henry. I'm afraid he's had too much to drink, and he may have to stay until Matins.'

'Ah! Not to worry. It wouldn't be the first time. He sits around like a lapdog at times. Perhaps I'll leave the drink this time. I'm feeling drowsy.'

Helena's heart pounded. *He's staggering drunk, but will that be enough?* 'You're sailing tomorrow Abbot Guy. You will need a good night's sleep, and this will top you off. Then I'll see you to your bed.'

'That's a very pleasant thought my girl, but I think I have drunk too much already.'

Helena breathed a sigh of relief when he habitually reached out for the goblet and swallowed. She watched him fall onto the bed and prayed for his eyelids to close. 'Bien dormir mon abbot.'

Abbot Guy's mind was wandering, his voice fading, and his words incoherent. He patted and smoothed the space next to him. 'Henry can stay.' And then he was snoring.

The inference shocked Helena into action. She unhooked the keys to both the cellar and casket and went to rescue the ankh. Visions of the abbot and Brother Henry filtered through her thoughts. *He was always running to and fro. Was that only for poisons? And the way the abbot smoothed over the brother's habit, at times affectionately, like stroking a cat. Surely, it's not true. I would never have thought it possible of him.* The cellar vault was empty. Helena stood in a daze, her mind spinning. The casket had already been moved to the tower vault. *I should have known. He's already organised for his departure tomorrow.* Helena checked the two drugged bodies before pulling the abbot's white robe over her tunic. She cautiously closed the heavy door making certain that it was unlocked for her return. She was anxious. The strain of the past few days and the uncertainty of the past few hours were taking their toll. The moon cast shadows from the surrounding trees waving in the gentle breeze. She walked swiftly across the open grounds, almost running, as if the Devil was urging her on. *Adam should be waiting at the tower. It has to work. It's now or never.*

She slowed to a walk approaching the tower, her bare feet stinging on the hardened surface. Helena's eyes nervously scanned the shadows, searching for a glimpse of her accomplice, but the monastery reflections were deceiving. Adam was nowhere to be seen. She stood still, listening to her heavy breathing. The night was clear and the moon cold and silent. Then she saw a movement in the cloisters, a silhouette amongst the columns. 'Est-ce vous Adam? Est-ce vous?' Helena's voice was little more than a whisper. She worried about the echo but cast caution to the wind and lifted her voice. 'It's me Adam. It's Helena.'

Adam came out of hiding and ran to her. 'What have you been doing? I've been waiting here for ages. It's spooky when you're alone out here.'

'I'm sorry Adam. I almost didn't make it. I will tell you why later. We have to move fast.'

'Alright, but I was really scared. Why are you dressed up in those robes? I thought you were a ghost.'

'The robe is my disguise, just in case anyone else is out night walking. I didn't think it would scare you.'

'Well how was I supposed to know? And then you start talking in that stupid language. What did you expect me to do? Jump out and shout, here I am, come and get me!' Adam was holding out a sack, waving it in front of him, jumping up and down.

Helena laughed nervously, almost with relief. 'I've been speaking French all night. I'm sorry.' She dangled the keys in front of him. 'Let us go now, down into the lion's den.'

The keys rattled in the lock and the door's hinges squeaked but Adam lost no more time worrying. He took hold of one of the slab's lifting rings and signaled Helena to take the other. 'Both hands together now.' And he whispered. 'Yan, taen, teddera.' They took night candles from the ledges at the side of the doorway and Adam led the way down the steps.

Helena shouted down to him, 'Can you see anything?'

'There is nothing down here, only a few parchments, tomes, and a lot of wine casks.'

He'd been hoping for a treasure chest and Helena could sense his disappointment. 'One of the tomes will hold the shipping records and they could be enough to bring down the abbot. It must be given to Brother Joseph. Just be careful you don't fall down to the lower level. Uncle Rolf told me about it. We may have to remove another ring slab. I'm coming down to help you.' The slab was directly under the first floor opening and as they slid it aside Helena caught a glimpse of the abbot's casket. She climbed down the ladder and stood with her hands clasped together, staring at the casket in wonder.

'There is nothing valuable down here.' Then Adam spotted a large silver cross hanging on the wall and dropped it into his sack with the tomes. He noticed two round shields propped in a corner, a long bow and a rusted sword blade. 'Why do they bother storing Viking remnants?'

Helena wasn't listening. Her eyes were focused on the casket, her hand shaking as she slowly turned the key and lifted the lid. The ankh talisman was sitting on the top. 'It's exactly where I thought it would be.' She held the blue stone against her breast and stroked it with her palm. 'The talisman is mine.'

'Are there any jewels underneath?'

'If there are you must leave them. To take too much could spoil my plan.'

'That's not *my* plan. I risked my life to steal for you.'

He dipped into the casket and turned over the contents. His palm circled a metal object and his hand tingled as he lifted it into the light. 'It's a gold sword handle.' He opened his palm and saw marked depressions on the grip and pommel.

'The blade has rusted away but I think the hilt was ornamented. Maybe it was studded with rare stones.' He raised his fist and flailed an imaginary sword above his head. 'It must have been a crusader's sword and if there were jewels in the handle, they're probably at the bottom.' He dropped the handle into his bag and went to search the casket.

'If there are jewels you must leave them.' Helena went to him and caressed his cheek. 'Forget the jewels. You have *me* Adam.'

He gulped and his face reddened. 'What do we do now?'

'We continue as planned.' She looped the talisman's leather string over his head, patted the ankh affectionately, and kissed Adam on the cheek. 'I am entrusting my inheritance to you Adam. You must take it with you and deliver it to Gwyneth. She will hold it for me. The shipping records are for Brother Joseph.'

'You should come with me now. He will kill you if he finds out.'

'He won't find out. You know I have to return to the abbot's house before he wakes. If I ran with you now Adam, he would know for sure. This way suspicion will fall on Prior Michael, for after the abbot sails tomorrow he will be the holder of the keys. Nothing will be discovered until the bursar asks for the shipping records. Who else could it be, other than the bell ringer or the prior?'

'You are clever Helena.'

She stretched to kiss him and then pointed to the steps. 'We must hurry. There's only an hour left before Matins.' Helena stopped halfway up the steps and poked her head into the first chamber. 'The slabs will echo when we drop them into place. Check to see if there is anyone about.'

Adam climbed the steps of the upper vault with the candle in one hand and the sack strapped to his waist. His hands still tingled from his grip on the gold handle and he couldn't stop imagining himself a crusader. He was suddenly short of breath and claustrophobic, trying desperately to escape the confined space of the chamber. He was in the midst of a losing battle with his sword arm weakening and the enemy overbearing. He poked his head and shoulders through the entrance and blinked into the dark. Less than a body length away his gaze fell upon a pair of bare feet, toes tapping the floor. His eyes followed the legs up to the torso, and he screamed with terror as he took in the raised arms and the falling sword. The steel blade cut across his chest, bounced across the blue talisman and sliced open his throat.

Helena looked up as she heard Adam's gasp and the gurgle of blood. The talisman was spinning towards her, trailing its leather string. She reached out with one hand whilst the other wiped splashes of blood from her eyes. Helena slipped from the steps under the weight of Adam's falling body and fell backwards to the lower chamber floor. There was a resounding crack like the sound of a whiplash and then a cold eerie silence. Helena lay at rest clutching the blue talisman to her chest, her twisted body motionless amongst the blood of Adam's dripping corpse. The flame of the night candle flickered momentarily, before the tomb was cast into total darkness.

Two days before Abbot Guy sailed for Ireland the tower was locked off by the prior and for two days the bells remained silent.

In the space of one week life at the abbey had changed dramatically. There were rumours of robbery, murder, treachery, people disappearing and the ropes of the abbey bells rotting and in need of repair. Richard of Leece had been called to the abbey. He was shown the rope ladder hanging from the wall and Adam's horse tethered nearby. He was then taken to the tower by the prior and shown the body of his son. 'There are jewels missing from the vault. The thieves obviously fought over the proceeds. His assassin escaped on horseback from the place where your son's mount was tethered.'

Richard of Leece buried his face in his hands. He moaned in anguish and then straightened to address Prior Michael with a stern face. 'My son was no thief. He had no need to steal. Who let him into the tower and where is Helena?'

'Your son, at the least, appears to have accompanied a thief who is now a murderer; a bad influence indeed. We shall search the secular servants' quarters and have a roll call.'

'Where is Helena?'

'She chose to sail with the abbot.'

'I have my doubts that she would do such a thing on an impulse.'

'Perhaps she was saddened by Adam's death and was persuaded that it would be for the best.'

Richard was not convinced. 'Then I would like you to keep me informed of the search for this so-called accomplice. I don't wish our son to be buried a thief whilst his assassin runs free.'

Rolf was worried and deep in thought. He was standing over a freshly dug grave, slowly rolling the rune ring between thumb and forefinger. There were rumours that Helena had left with the abbot and no-one seemed surprised. He hoped they were right, but his instincts told him otherwise. He had known that Helena was planning to retrieve her inheritance, but he was helpless to intervene. He had tried to speak to Brother Joseph, but he seemed to be avoiding him. *Since losing Phillip and Daniel he appears vacant and wanders in a world of his own. He no longer displays the enthusiasm he once had for his commission and he is spending more time with the choir monks.*

Young Adam had made no secret of his fondness for Helena, but Rolf had no idea she'd been planning a robbery with him. Their disappearance on the same day only added to the mystery. It was too much of a coincidence and Rolf gave no credence to the brothers' story of an accomplice escaping with the jewels. He could only pray for Helena's return, but he was already resigned to her death. *What a waste of life. She could have married a nobleman.* He had seen it all before; the bells silent and the brethren, all of them intelligent men, going about their daily chores with blank unseeing eyes. *You couldn't let go of the past, could you? If I should ever possess the ankh, I will place it on your grave that you may rest in peace. God be with you. My wife will recover with time but what of Gwyneth, Helena's true mother? They had only been reunited for three years.*

Brother Joseph finished transcribing the ending of Daniel's manuscript copy, an ending that he considered to be most important.

In this year 1241 AD, a silver finger ring circled with runes was sighted in the monastery grounds. The ring had four repeated symbols: EHWAZ, LAGUZ, THURISAZ, and EIHWAZ and their suggested meanings are recorded in this manuscript. EHWAZ: represents the horse and the forging of an unbreakable bond between horse and rider until their journey's final destination.

LAGUZ: The symbol of water and the power of the tides.
THURISAV: The symbol of the power of resistance against foe, and of Thor, the god of thunder and lightning.
EIHWAZ: The symbol of the yew tree which holds the power of death and regeneration and of Ullr, the god of archery who owned a magic finger ring.

Joseph was unhappy with his eyesight. He struggled in the dim candlelight, troubled by tiredness and sporadic hallucination. He completed the transcription on the afternoon before his meeting. He dated the work, signed with his name and on an impulse, proudly added the words:

Sergeant to the Knights of the Temple

He organised the copy to be bound and placed in the library. He was almost certain that someone had recently been searching the library cupboards and the lingering doubt seemed to justify his earlier instinctive action. He had given Phillip a copy of his records with the proviso that if ever they were separated, he must hasten to the Archbishop of York. He'd misplaced some of his parchments that were hidden between the library tomes. *Why is my body failing me?* He shrugged it off as a condition of the virus he'd recently caught. Every now and then he'd feel tired and have a dizzy spell which went away just as quickly, and for that he was thankful for the brother's herbal tonic.

Joseph received an invitation to converse with the prior and bursar in the abbot's house, and he was curious. They had suggested that now the abbot was away they could divulge some important information, and that they required him to witness some signatures. Joseph was beginning to believe that the Furness monks were contemplating a new abbot. *I've always thought there was something sinister about Abbot Guy. Perhaps they will give me access to the information I require.*

In contrast to the memory of his first appearance, Joseph walked into the abbot's house full of confidence and he was greeted with warmth. There was a completely different atmosphere around the table, and he had a feeling of being accepted, almost wanted. He was seated opposite the prior, sub prior and bursar. It was the same position as when he was humiliated by Abbot Guy, only this time he was cushioned by three most friendly and senior choir monks. He was acquainted with all three, and the obese one in particular had been pointed out to him as a man of jovial nature with an unusual habit. He was renowned for spending many of his leisure hours squatting in the reredorter, reading the scriptures, and totally oblivious to the toiletry habits of his fellow monks. Joseph could only smile at the vision. There was only one other person he could think of besides the abbot that was missing, and he couldn't have been happier.

Prior Michael had a scrolled parchment unfolded in front of him and at the side, a quill, ink, candle and wax. The occasion had the appearance of being more serious than Joseph had imagined, confirmed by the prior's stern look. 'The story has already been told Joseph. We merely need you, as an outsider, and representative of the king and archbishop, to bear witness and deliver our proclamation.'

'Bear witness to what, Prior Michael?'

'We wish Abbot Guy to be deposed and we have both the evidence and the numbers to achieve that end. I must tell you that if everything was written on this scroll it would weigh you down, so listen to me carefully. When Abbot Guy was acting prior, he worked so closely with our departed Abbot William that one used to wonder which one yielded the power. But it was Abbot Guy who brought the complaint denouncing Abbot William. He personally informed the archbishop of William's shortcomings, even though he was as much to blame himself. And we have reason to believe that he organised William's death before he sailed for the Mann.'

'Then my suspicions were justified?'

'We believe that they were Joseph. But one cannot act on suspicion alone and trust him or not, the abbot is the law. We were left to bury poor William and now, in Abbot Guy's absence, we are left to bury his beautiful Helena.'

Joseph's mind was spinning, and he held up his hand to stop the prior continuing. 'Forgive me prior but this is almost too much for me to comprehend.'

Prior Michael at first seemed puzzled, but then his eyes brightened. 'Of course, you would have no idea of the crime. But you must have wondered about Helena and why the tower was out of bounds for two days?'

'We were told by the abbot that there had been a robbery and that the thieves had been taken by their greed. One thief killed the other and then escaped over the wall. I saw Richard of Leece leave with his son's body and it seemed to be common knowledge that Helena had sailed with Abbot Guy. Then we were told of the repairs to the bell ropes. We all found it hard to believe.'

The prior smiled weakly and continued. 'It is little wonder that you found it hard to reason. What I'm going to tell you now is only for the ears of a higher authority.' He stood and made hand motions to the three monks at Joseph's side. They stood up as one and dutifully signed the parchment in silence.

Joseph had paid little attention before but now he began to scrutinise the three monks much more than he would have normally. They had smiled agreeably when he entered the room but failed to speak. He thought to name them the three wise and silent monks. *Brother Michael's 'yes men'.*

Prior Michael waited until they left the room before continuing. 'The bell ropes were certainly in need of repairs Brother Joseph, but the truth is that Helena stayed with our abbot the night before he sailed. That in itself is nothing unusual except that Abbot Guy told us she'd dosed his wine with a sleeping concoction. She planned to rob the vaults whilst he slept, and the farmer's son Adam was her accomplice. If Abbot Guy had remained undisturbed as planned, she would have returned the keys for the treasure casket and those for the bell tower. After he'd sailed that day, no-one would have been the wiser until the records were required. And then who would be under suspicion but the holders of the keys? She was a clever and devious woman. I warned the abbot not to take her lightly.'

'How do you know what she planned?'

'It's merely the supposition of Abbot Guy. She also administered the potion to innocent Brother Henry. He had stayed longer to appease the abbot's needs. The potion should have been stronger for Abbot Guy. The abbot is tall and heavily built, more resistant than Helena anticipated. He said his eyes had flickered and as if in a dream he saw Helena glide past him dressed in his white robes. The tower keys were at her waist. He tried to sit up, but his mind had lost control of his body. After the door closed, he managed to roll his body off the bed and then he struggled to stand on his feet. He managed to find his sword and said he literally staggered out of the house weaving unsteadily from side to side. He followed Helena to the central tower and saw her meet up with an accomplice. They both disappeared into the tower and when Abbot Guy entered, he saw that the floor slab had been removed and he heard them down in the vault. He waited patiently for someone to emerge, and as the young man's body surfaced the abbot was overcome with rage. He raised his sword and slashed down into the accomplice, almost severing his head. The thief fell to the cellar floor and his weight pushed Helena down into the lower vault. Abbot Guy collapsed and he was found by the bell ringer as he arrived for toll Matins. The abbot was covered in blood and in such a state of illness we had to delay the ship for a day. We were told to clean up the mess after he'd sailed and to make sure that neither he nor Helena were implicated in the matter. He still had a soft spot for her and thought it amusing that she would attempt to steal from him. During the past year he had almost wished it on himself. We found Helena's body in the lower vault at the bottom of the steps. She was dressed in the abbot's blood-soaked white habit. Her neck had been broken in the fall, and she was gripping the blue talisman at her chest, as if she would never let it go. The abbot suggested we bury the ankh talisman with her. After all, he said it was considered to be a burial stone by its maker and so he considered it justice.' He paused in his speech and directed his eyes towards Brother Joseph. 'The shipping records were found in the farm boy's sack.'

Brother Joseph was startled by the last comment and felt the brother's eyes on him, awaiting his reaction. He remembered her whispering in his ear at the first meeting, *I think I can help you,* and he felt remorse. *That brave and beautiful woman had sacrificed her life for me.* And then he thought of Rolf. *God help that kindly man.*

'Brother Michael eyes never wavered from Joseph's. 'Helena was such a pretty woman; don't you think so, Brother?'

'She was indeed Brother Michael.' *And you coveted her.* 'It was such a tragedy, that one can but pray for her soul.'

'We discovered a rope ladder on the west wall for her accomplice's entry and no doubt his escape. He had a ready mount tethered close by.'

'We at first thought that you may have been in league with the woman, especially as she held the records you were so much interested in.' Joseph cringed and his eyelids dropped as he absorbed the insinuation. 'But on reflection we all agreed that she stole the records with the naive idea that she might somehow use them for bribery for her own protection, or to bring down the abbot and the prior. We could have saved her the trouble in the case of the abbot, and she would still be with us today.' Joseph breathed a sigh of relief. 'We had no doubt that Helena was obsessed with the stone talisman as you are with acquiring the shipping records. Her accomplice was found with a silver cross in his sack, a gold sword handle and the shipping records. We found it hard to comprehend that the jewels in the chest had been overlooked. That woman was too clever for her own good.'

Joseph was reflecting on Helena's image when a wrinkled hand holding a wine goblet brushed his face and took him by surprise. The sad codfish eyes of the ghoul were a frightening alternative to the softness of Helena. His was the face that Joseph had missed from the table. The monk that Joseph thought looked too small for his habit was now serving him refreshments. Joseph knew him as Brother Henry and privately thought of him as Brother Hungry. The ghoul poured Joseph's drink, his forced smile and puckered lips portraying a sparrow in urgent need of sustenance.

'You look as though you've seen a ghost, Brother Joseph?'

'I wish that I had, Brother Michael. I'm sure that I would feel much easier.' Joseph grinned nervously as he grasped the elusive truth about his hosts. *They don't smile very often.*

It was Brother Bryan's turn to speak. He brought his record book to the table. 'We are aware of your keen interest in the shipping trade, and we now feel that it's appropriate for you to examine the abbot's books. The records in my care are basic and you may take them for comparison. The one you will have the most interest in is no longer held in the abbot's cellar. It is now held in the tower vault. When our business is finished here, we will all pay a visit to the tower and you can copy both records before you depart the abbey. We only ask that you add our proclamation to your report and deliver the truth to the king and archbishop. The committee has detailed everything, and we have all signed the petition. When Abbot Guy returns, he will assume everything has gone smoothly and it will have to appear so. With the treachery and loss of his Helena, he will be in no mood for reasoning.'

Joseph eyes were out of control, but he was feeling exhilarated at the thought of his visit being a success. There would be little bloodshed and he would be leaving behind an organised and lawful abbey. At last he could relax, but as his thoughts drifted towards sleep, a reflex sent a hand to his sleeve searching and ruffling the cloth of his robe. His eyelids closed and his head fell to his chest. *I'm failing in my duty. I've forgotten the dagger.* 'I'm feeling sickly, Brother Michael. Perhaps I should take my leave. There are times when I see double and your bodies waver in ghostly images. My body is telling me it has a need. I have a craving for your tonic.'

'You obviously have that fever again, Brother Joseph, so we will not take too much more of your time. When you witness the signatures, we will go and collect the necessary evidence from the vault. You must realise of course that the records you seek will not be enough to remove the abbot. There is a more serious matter of leasehold forgery and for this the abbot uses the

Common Seal of the Abbey. The forged parchments and seal are kept in a separate vault. When the king's officers arrive, you will show them their location.'

'I had heard rumours of such forgery but thought little of it.' *Vicar De Wath spoke the truth.*

'You do indeed look sickly, Brother Joseph. We must ship you out to London as soon as possible. Brother Henry! Give this poor man another cup of our fever tonic.'

Joseph gulped down the brew and tucked the signed scroll under his arm. He picked up Brother Bryan's records and set off with the three monks towards the tower with the prior and bursar leading the way. His legs were walking of their own accord, but when he faltered, he was steadied by the ghoul and pushed forward by the sub prior. He felt a pain in his stomach and the earth was spinning and he felt sick. The scroll and record book fell to the ground and were quickly scooped up by the ghoul.

Prior Michael unlocked the iron door to the tower and showed Joseph the already opened vault. A slab with holding rings was resting against the wall and Joseph could see steps to the floor below. Brother Bryan lit a candle and eased his way down the staircase. Joseph tried to follow, but he was pulled away from the opening by Brother Henry. 'You have no need to go down, Brother. We will collect your evidence on the way back. I have to show you the location of the Common Seal. You will have a need to show the kings officers when they arrive. Follow me!' The ghoul's voice sounded more distant, squeakier than usual. He led the way holding a candle in each hand.

Brother Michael was calling from the spiral staircase that led to the belfry. 'The location of the seal is far more important for you than the comparison of falsified records.'

Brother Joseph laboured up the winding staircase, his wobbly legs threatening to collapse. He forced himself to remember.

I must have both the records and the Common Seal location. His mind and body were failing but curiosity drove him on. When he eventually spun to the top, his body was wavering, and his vision blurred with ghostly images of Brother Michael and the sub prior. In a state of near collapse, he leaned against the sidewall and rested his elbows on the top slab to support his body. Joseph shook his head to clear his vision and as the two brothers drew close, he sensed danger. His hand searched frantically for the missing dagger. The prior's hands pushed towards him, and then splayed outwards, as if in a gesture of welcome. Joseph was suddenly weightless, floating in a falling dream. He glimpsed the prior's arms waving him away, his eyes wild with anger, his mouth screaming obscenities. Joseph's hands clawed the air, fighting to escape a darkening chasm. His habit swirled about his body and slapped the air. The wind whistled around his ears and turned into a roar like thunder. The world slowed and the heavens widened. Phillip was riding his beautiful black Arabian horse, racing to the archbishop of York. *There's been treachery Brother Phillip! Ride truly my good Brother. Ride safely!* There was a sickening thud like the slamming of a great oaken door, a brilliant exploding light, and then darkness.

PART II

The grammar school,
Hawkshead Village: summer 1663

The thud reverberated around the classroom. Thomas had inadvertently blinked and been sent spiralling into a dark bottomless pit. He was fighting to escape the looming dark chasm when his head crashed down onto the solid oak desk. He straightened as his eyes flooded with light and rubbed the back of his hand across his stinging forehead. He looked around the classroom hoping that nobody had noticed. His face was red with embarrassment. The headmaster paused to glare before continuing with the lecture. 'Remember...!'

Phynius Clayton paused for dramatic effect, waved his forefinger skyward for emphasis and commenced to prowl the classroom like a caged tiger. 'Remember that the Cistercian monks of Furness Abbey lived according to the rule of Benedict. They wore white tunics and a dark scapular, as opposed to the dark grey habits of the earlier Benedictine monk. They elected and swore allegiance to the abbot of their house and elected a prior to run the monastery's day-to-day issues. One hundred and thirty years ago the Abbot of Furness was superior lord over the whole district, controlling Dalton, Colton, and our own parish of Hawkshead.'

The class were beginning to fidget in their seats, hands on knees, fingers tapping out rhythms. The history of the district was their learned teacher's pet subject and fortunately, only a once-a-week sufferance. Thomas was determined to concentrate. He watched his teacher fiddle with his new spectacles balanced precariously on the bridge of his sweaty nose. He only used them for magnifying his reading and was constantly lifting them on and off. Thomas' thoughts went to his cousin Damian and their concealed treasure. He'd felt sorry for Mr. Clayton at the time, having to wait over a month for his new eyes. It would have been fatal to return the spectacles and admit that he'd stolen them. He'd spotted them resting on top of a *Book of Psalms*, and the temptation had proved too much. Like a magpie he hid the spectacles in the treasure pot, secreted away in farmer Smyth's field. The *Book of Psalms* was hidden behind his bed in the cottage. Mr. Clayton's new spectacles were safely secured by a thin cord and looped behind his neck. The small wiry man lifted them from his nose, mopped the sweat from his brow and clumsily stuffed the handkerchief back into his tunic pocket. All the windows were wide open, begging for a cross breeze that might wash the stifling air. 'In the year 1537, Abbot Roger Pele, the Prior, Briand Garnor, and twenty-eight monks surrendered Furness Abbey to King Henry VIII. Ever since that date, and up until only a few years ago, the Liberty and Lordship of Furness remained with the Crown.'

So, what if it has? thought Thomas. It was only the second time he'd been ordered upstairs to mingle with the elite. The first time was for a taste of the birch which remained a lingering painful memory. Today's visit was still a mystery. The headmaster had purposely asked him to attend but never explained the reason why. His attention wavered. *The lower classroom will be cooler.* Thomas sat on a long bench at the front with the important students of the free grammar school; sons of statesmen perhaps destined for Oxford. Others, somewhat less distinguished, sat on benches along the sidewalls. He felt relaxed after downing his bread and cheese lunch and the hot summer's day was making him drowsy. He imagined the huge empty fireplace on the back wall crackling with burning logs and his eyes glazed over. Thomas snapped his head back, forced his eyelids open and inhaled. *There must be a good reason for me being here. It has to be the symbols.*

Phynius Clayton had caught Thomas doodling on a slate board in the lower classroom while relieving his usher and giving the class a taste of real authority. 'I'll see you upstairs in my office Johnson and make sure...' Thomas was already imagining the sting of the birch, when the head teacher's voice trailed away then quickly rose in excitement. 'Do you know what you are spelling Johnson?'

'I'm not spelling anything, Sir. I'm doodling.'

'You are drawing runes. You must have seen them somewhere. Have you visited Urswick or Aldingham?'

'No, Sir. I saw them on my cousin's ring amulet.'

Phynius' brow furrowed. He remained silent for a moment, visibly shocked but unable to conceal his racing excitement. His hands clasped tight, his pulse raced and his feet tapped on the wooden floor. 'I ... I must see this ring, Thomas. It should be in safe hands. You must ... you must bring it to me.'

He was being addressed by his first name and Thomas could sense trouble brewing. He'd already said too much. He needed a way out but found it hard to concoct a convincing lie. 'I can't bring it to you, Sir. Cousin Mary dropped the ring into the lake a long time gaan. It was when we were taking the ferry to Long Holm Island.'

Phynius showed his disappointment, bending forward with eyes closed, bringing his clenched fist down hard on the desk in exasperation. 'Good God, that's a tragedy, Johnson, a tragedy indeed.'

Two days had passed since the doodling incident and here he was, in the upper classroom. Thomas straightened and shook his head awake. The teacher's droning voice was struggling to penetrate his thoughts. 'I can see drooping eyelids, so I will get to the point of this lesson. How many of you have seen Furness Abbey?'

Five students raised their hands. He addressed Thomas. 'How did you find it, Johnson?

'Me fadder took me, Sir.' Thomas felt pleased with the round of laughter and there was a relief of tension in the classroom.

'I was asking you for an opinion Johnson.'

'They are just old ruins, Sir, and there is no roof. Me fadder told me the roof's lead had been melted down for musket balls. Then I saw some farmers with bullocks hauling away some of the huge sandstones.' Thomas had in fact begged his father to take him and Damian to see the abbey. He was fascinated by the stories he'd heard. The monastery was surrounded by mystery. He had heard tales of ghostly monks that rode through the grounds at night, of abbots using the old castle on Piel Island to store and smuggle goods in their ships and the stories of underground passages and runaway kings. There were rumours that King John's jewels and the monastery bells were buried under the rubble of the monastery tower. *Perhaps we could dig there?*

The teacher's voice interrupted. 'I'm sure you were no more disappointed than many others, Johnson.'

'I saw a ghost, Sir!' Thomas couldn't stop himself. He stood with mouth and eyes wide open, waiting for the reaction, wishing that he'd kept his mouth shut. A murmur travelled around the class, followed by an expectant silence.

His teacher's eyes scanned the classroom and noted his student's immediate attention. Phynius loved being in control. 'You saw a ghost, Johnson? Pray tell the class of your unusual experience.'

Thomas looked at the grinning students around him, his head swivelling left and right. He was nervous. His left shoulder and the side of his face twitched and winked in unison, a habit he was often scolded for. He loved telling stories to his family but talking to a whole class of older students was frightening. *They might laugh at me.* 'Do I have to, Sir?'

Phynius leaned his head forward and glared. 'Yes, you have to, Johnson, and I'm assuming that you don't tell lies.'

Thomas perceived the threat in his teacher's voice and hesitated. Taking a deep breath, he nervously cleared his throat then began to speak quietly and ponderously in a deep soft voice. An interruption came from the back of the class followed by rumblings of discontent. 'We can't hear, Sir!'

Phynius held up his hand, demanding silence. 'Speak up, Johnson, or you'll return to the lower classroom.'

Thomas grew angry. Any signs of timidity quickly dispersed as he narrated in his normal deep, penetrating voice. 'Me fadder took me and Cousin Damian to see the castle on Piel Island. On the way home we stopped to explore the abbey grounds. The sky was darkening, and the path home would have been dangerous, so fadder said we should camp in the outside grounds until daylight. He warned us that the abbey is considered sacred at night and restless spirits from the cemetery often roam the grounds seeking peace.'

'Your father told you there were ghosts before you saw one. Are you aware of the power of suggestion?'

'I really saw a ghost, Sir, and so did my cousin. We were camped outside the west gate and I awoke in the middle of the night. I was staring into a full moon and all the stars were clear and sparkling. I never even thought of being scared because it was so peaceful, like being in church. But then a sudden breeze rustled the trees and I felt a chill. I shivered and pulled the rug tight around me, listening. Then the breeze stopped as quickly as it had started, and a shadow fell over me.'

Phynius Clayton was both transfixed and amused. *The lad has hidden talents.* He looked around the class at his students leaning forward with hands between their knees, engrossed. Thomas had risen from his seat and was prowling the classroom, gesticulating in the guise of his teacher. 'Sit down, Johnson!' The class moaned. Their teacher was spoiling the performance.

'Sorry, Sir!' Thomas returned to his seat and weaved quickly into his story again, rocking from side to side, reciting. 'When the shadow fell over me, I shot up to a sitting position and tried to scream, but nothing came out of my mouth. I was terrified. My hands were shaking.'

This time a chorus babbled from the back. 'What did you see, Thomas? What happened?'

Thomas lost concentration but composed himself and gulped as he recalled. 'I saw a monk in white clothing astride a horse, his gaze fixed on something behind me.'

'What was it?'

'Keep quiet at the back!'

'The horse suddenly reared and his hooves came down and thumped straight through my chest, yet I felt nothing. Then the monk wheeled his horse and they galloped through the west gate into a mist. They disappeared like a puff of smoke and the air around us became still and eerie, as silent as the grave.'

The class clapped appreciation as Phynius left his podium to address Thomas. 'You have a vivid imagination and tell a compelling story, Johnson. Your bloodline is strong, and you have obviously inherited the skills of your ancestors. They called the Viking storytellers skalds.'

'I haven't finished yet, Sir.'

Phynius gave Thomas a withering look, and the class slid to the edge of their seats in anticipation. 'Then please forgive my intrusion, won't you?'

Thomas recognised the sarcastic reprimand and apologised. 'Sorry, Sir!' but that's only half the story.'

'Please let him finish, Sir,' the class pleaded.

Phynius prowled the room, eying the pupils. 'You should all be aware that my duty is to teach, not to entertain.' He teetered on a decision then finally relinquished, on the one condition. 'Regardless of the time of day, you will all stay until the lesson is completed.' He stood in front of Thomas, head pushed forward, nose to nose. 'You have my permission to continue, Johnson.'

Thomas grinned and began waving his arms around with a sense of drama. 'I reached across the other side of fadder and shook Damian.'

The same voice came from the back. 'I know him. He's daft, not the full shilling.'

Thomas ignored the laughter and defended his cousin. 'Not as daft as some I know. I told Damian about the ghost and he wouldn't believe me, so I told him to listen and look towards the western gate. Nothing happened for ages then just as we were dropping off to sleep ... the night wind blew a gust of air ... and the tree branches swished around like a witch's broom. There was an eerie silence; a silent silence; and that's when she came.'

The classroom was as still and silent as a corpse and Phynius looked around his students with a smile. *They're so naive, but the lad does have a silver tongue. I could almost be persuaded.*

'The Lady in White had long ghostly hair and was beautiful. She walked around as if searching for something, then turned and followed the way of the monk into the mist of the west gate. She held a cross with a looped top close to her chest. We sat listening for a while, and then decided to wake fadder, but he didn't believe us.'

'I don't believe you either, Johnson. Ghosts don't cast shadows.'

'Have you seen one, Sir?'

'I have not. I don't believe in ghosts,'

'Then how do you know they don't cast shadows, Sir?'

'I know, because it's a scientific fact, Johnson, and for your insolence you can stay behind after school and help the usher. We will have no more of this nonsense.'

He addressed the class again, to impress on them his knowledge of the district. 'Many of you would have heard of ghosts being seen around the abbey and this is an example of how the stories evolve to become exaggerated. Believe what you see and remember, that is not the same as seeing what you believe. There is a legend in the district of a Lady in White and a blue stone talisman. The legend tells of her being murdered for her talisman and that her body is buried in the abbey cemetery. Thus, you have the origin of the story you have just heard. Have any of you seen faces in clouds and watched them disperse?' There was an immediate and positive reaction from the class. 'Then you have the answer. The mists over the abbey streams have a similar effect, swirling amongst the moonbeams, preying on the imaginative minds of visitors.'

'I saw Jesus in the clouds, Sir.'

Phynius cringed. *There's always one in the class.* 'That is another matter, Jennings, and you'd best ask Vicar Braithwaite for an explanation.'

Jennings' question aroused a thought in Thomas' mind. 'Perhaps it was the Virgin Mary I saw in the abbey, Sir?'

Phynius glared down at Thomas. 'Now that's the most ridiculous thing that I have ever heard, Johnson. You will be telling me next that the monk you supposedly saw was her father. It's time you all learned to distinguish between stories of fantasy and those of fact. Ghosts are a figment of the imagination. There is a reason for everything and the sooner you all realise that fact, the better the world will be. Playtime is over! It's back to our studies.'

Phynius unlocked the book cupboard and removed a tome. He set it down on his desk, opened it at a marker and carefully damped down the pages with his palms. The teachers head lifted to scan the class, clearing his throat to signal the continuation of his lecture. 'I treasure this book and consider it very valuable in the recording of the district's history. My own interest in Furness Abbey began when I discovered that the founder of our free grammar school, the late archbishop Edwin Sandys, received his early teachings there. Until the time of the dissolution of the abbeys, your ancestors may have been employed by the Furness monks. Many of them could have been lay brothers working the abbey farms or secular servants living within the walls. Over two hundred lay brothers worked the granges for the abbot. Secular servants were housed in the abbey with a separate dining room and dormitories. They were segregated from thirty or so choir monks by a dividing wall. The Cistercian monks also had great engineering and agricultural skills. They ground their own corn and the statesman's corn in the mill at Butt's Beck, close to the abbey, and then stored it in large granaries. The abbey was the market for all the produce of the fells selling mountain mutton, raw and spun wool, smelted iron and even crates of trout from the lakes. Produce was carried to the abbey and the town of Dalton by barge and packhorse and the local wheat by wagon. Many people argued they were better cared for under abbey rule than under the Crown. However just as many people thought otherwise. Hawkshead benefited greatly from the dissolution and the people grew to accept our freedom of trade.'

'Where did you find the book, Mr Clayton?' Thomas cringed at the whining voice of the tanner's son who was standing eight students away at the far end of the long bench.

'The pages of this tome have been transcribed with the permission of the church. The first copy was transcribed from an original document by a Brother Joseph at Furness Abbey over four hundred years ago. With the Dissolution threatening, Roger Pele rescued tomes from the monastery library and entrusted them to the church at Dalton where he was eventually bestowed the position of rector. Many dispossessed monks continued to act as parish priests in their own churches post-Dissolution. As a past student our own Bishop Sandys had access to the library, and he was kind enough to transfer tomes to our church. Other tomes were transferred to Rome. This particular copy is the work of recent graduates from this school who now attend Oxford. When not in use it remains locked safely away and must be handled with care. Our task this year is to follow the duties of the abbey monks. Select students will transcribe another copy and then translate it back to the original Latin.'

Phynius was warming to his task. 'Brother Joseph was passionate in his interest of the lay brothers. Many citizens descended from Viking immigrants and still practised inherited customs and beliefs hundreds of years old. The district was a mixture of both Norse and Saxon. The first author of the tome, a Benedictine monk, worked closely with them documenting the Norse immigration and their mythology. Decades later in 1241 AD, Cistercian monks transcribed a copy. Brother Joseph signed his name on the final page and below his name inscribed *Sergeant to the Knights of the Temple*. That is most interesting, and I fail to offer an explanation. I can find no record of the ruling abbot in that period as abbots were only recorded after a substantial rule, I suggest that the man had either a short rule or he was deposed.'

'Perhaps the knights killed him, Sir?'

'I doubt that very much, Newman. More likely he was voted down and the decision would need to have been unanimous.' Phynius cleared his throat and turned to a page of symbols. 'Like the Greeks and the Romans before them, the Norse devised written symbols. The symbols were much more than an alphabet. They were called runes, each rune telling a story. The meaning of an individual rune becomes complex in combination with others. There are numerous mystic tales related to them and the Norse believed they stored magical powers. Many monastic scribes were also excellent artists. Observe this drawing of the Viking, a fine example of their work. Our district abounds in Scandinavian place names, but Norse family names that honoured their gods and their goddesses are now disused.'

'What kind of names, Sir?'

'Names like Thor, their god of thunder and lightning, and Freyja, their goddess of fertility, who was said to be a beautiful sorceress attended by hares who rode in a chariot drawn by two cats. Who in this class could believe such a fairy tale?'

'Witches can turn themselves into cats and hares, Sir, but they are all old and ugly.'

'Do you know of such a witch, Newman?'

'There's an old witch called Ada in Tarn Woods, Mr Clayton, and I've heard lots of stories about hares tricking hounds when hunting the fox.'

Phynius shook his head in disbelief. 'They are merely tales to amuse the population. When the Norse converted to Christianity, they were baptised with new names, thereby renouncing the old names identifying them with pagan worship. Earnwulf and Thorulf appear in the Domesday records. Some five hundred years later in the early church registers those heathen names had changed to the likes of Mathison, Stephenson, Nielson or Johnson, a most common name in north Scandinavia and Iceland. And that brings us back to Thomas Johnson of the lower class and his local sighting of Norse runes. Stand up Johnson and tell us your age.'

Thomas was beginning to feel embarrassed. He was the tallest boy in the school and he'd already made an exhibition of himself with his story telling. 'I'm nearly fifteen, Sir.'

Phynius nodded and spouted more of his wisdom. 'Your superior height informs me you are a descendant of the Norse immigrants. Can you recall and draw the runes you saw?'

'Why are they called runes, Sir?'

'In the Norse language rune means secret or hidden. There is a hidden meaning in each and every rune. They were believed to be a source of magic and were relied on for protection and guidance in life.'

Thomas' head was spinning. 'The runes hold secrets like our treasure pot. We've got a rune pot.'

'I would like you to chalk the runes you have seen on your slate, Johnson, and show them to the class. Where you sighted the runes must remain our secret.'

'Can't I tell anyone, Sir?'

'You must tell no-one. Haven't I just explained that rune means secret. If you listen carefully you may see the significance in my following lecture.' *That ring could have been the one recorded by the monk.*

Thomas was feeling special. *I'll have to tell Mary and Damian, and me fadder.* 'There were four symbols, Sir, but I'm only sure of two of them.'

'They will be adequate. I hope your rune markings are more truthful than your ghost stories.'

Thomas chalked the two runes as best he could remember. One resembled a broken arrow and the other a capital M. He passed the slate to his teacher Phynius who held it chest high for the class to see. 'You can all copy the symbols down while one of the Latin students joins me to read out Brother Joseph's description of their Norse meaning. According to the monk's interpretation, each one represents a connection to a Norse god. It is written down that the runes were gifted to mankind by Odin, the god of war, and they foretold a future that the Vikings navigated their life by. The runes were believed to be a source of ancient magic, with each symbol holding a truth and in combination with other runes, holding the secret of the future.'

At last Phynius had the full attention of the class and as the recorded meanings of the runes were narrated, Thomas' imagination soared. He recognised the other two on Mary's amulet. Thurisaz was said to be the rune of Thor, the god of thunder and lightning, and Laguz, the rune that holds the power of the tides and waterfalls. Eihwaz was the symbol of the yew tree and of Ull the god of archery who owned a magic finger ring. And Ehwaz, a horse messenger of the gods, symbolised an unbreakable bond between horse and rider, a bond that would survive from the beginning of a journey until its conclusion.

The class were now speaking with animation about the worship of more than one god. 'It is hard to believe that they worshipped so many gods, Sir.'

Phynius hooked the thumb of his left hand into his belt whilst the middle finger of his right slid the eyeglasses up the bridge of his nose. He was enjoying the attention, and with a posture of authority, he dramatically bent forward to peruse the class. 'The Vikings brought their beliefs with them Newman and it was perhaps two centuries before they began to see the truth of Christianity. Rune symbols are scattered all over Cumberland and during the next history lesson I shall inform you of their location. We will also discuss the circles of stones which surround our district. The Vikings are said to have used them for Council meetings, sacrificial offerings and weddings. The Castlerigg site near Keswick is an excellent example, and I am determined, that one fine day I will examine them during the solstice.' He paused, raised his head, and perused the class in anticipation of their forthcoming question.

'Why, Sir?' the class chorused, and with a supercilious smile, Phynius continued to impart his knowledge.

'With the rising of the sun, during the time of the solstice, there have been sightings of strange light phenomena, white light-balls moving slowly over the stones, an interplay between the stones sacred space and the surrounding landscape.' He turned his attention to Thomas. 'And there has never been a sighting of a ghost, Johnson.' The class tittered and the headmaster was pleased with the outcome of his lesson. *He's a mischievous bugger for sure with his ghost stories, but I have to admit he's both entertaining and intelligent.* He waved his arms around in a gesture of conclusion. 'Now be off with you all.' Then as the class stood to leave, he gave out an attention-grabbing intermittent cough. 'That is, with the exception of Johnson.'

The class trundled from the schoolroom animated, discussing Norse gods, ancient beliefs, runic symbols and mysterious balls of light bouncing around a circle of stones. Church was compulsory for all grammar students and had the local vicar been in earshot he would have vigorously disapproved of their pagan chatter. Thomas was told to stay behind and help the usher clean the classrooms. The headmaster explained it was his punishment for being insolent and payment for the privilege of attending the senior class.

Thomas was alone sweeping the floor when he heard the first squeak of hinges. Phynius had left in a hurry and the usher was downstairs grumbling about the class running late. In his haste he'd been careless about locking the book cupboard and the door swung open with the weight of the key. Thomas was thinking about the ring markings and trying to remember the meanings so he could tell Mary. *She'll not believe me anyhow.* The keyring struck the wall, dislodged and fell to the floor. Thomas' eyes were riveted on the book-lined shelves. *It's the will of God.* Thomas stole a furtive look around him before edging closer. Light shone into the opening and his hand compulsively reached inside. The temptation to explore forbidden territory was irresistible and the history of the abbey was soon in his grasp. He dropped the book into his lunch sack and was careful to lock the cupboard door before he tiptoed out. *I must show Mary and John the meaning of the symbols.*

'Is that you, Johnson?' The usher was ready to lock up the schoolhouse.

Thomas' heart skipped and his lunch sack was suddenly heavy. 'I've just finished, Sir.'

'Is everything shipshape up there?'

'I think so.'

'I left the bookcase key in the lock, Johnson. Run upstairs, check that the cupboard is locked then bring the key down.'

'Yes, Mr Trimble.'

When Thomas came back down the stairs, the usher was standing at the bottom holding the lunch sack in front of him. 'Is this yours, Johnson?'

Thomas could hear his heart thumping, threatening to burst through the wall of his chest, but he could only tell the truth. 'It's my lunch sack, Sir.'

'It feels like there is half a sheep inside Johnson. A growing boy shouldn't waste food.'

'I don't feel too good, Mr Trimble. It was hot up there this afternoon.' *He knows.*

The usher gave Thomas a lingering stern look. *The lad's nervous.* He held out his left hand and Thomas was confused. 'Wake up, Johnson, and give me the key, lad. Give me the key.'

Thomas' eyes never wavered from the usher's face as in one coordinated movement he handed over the key with his right hand and took his lunch sack with his left. He walked from the room feeling the usher's distrustful gaze on the back of his neck and heard a nominal grunt from the withered old man. He never looked back and shivered with relief as he gulped in the warm evening air. His walk turned to a trot then burst into a wild run. He squeezed the lunch sack firmly under his arm and his body pumped air as he ran wildly down the slope towards home.

A visit from Phynius

Robert would never admit to his son's temptations, not even when Phynius Clayton knocked on his door threatening the law. He eventually found the book and presented it to the teacher whilst holding Thomas by the ear. Robert made his son apologise, then said he couldn't find the *Book of Psalms* and suggested the teacher must have been mistaken. He had already told Thomas that if he was so desperate to keep the book then he should leave it with his Aunt Hannah and explain that it was a leaving gift from the school. The teacher was so relieved that his treasured book had been recovered and in such good condition that he chose not to pursue the *Book of Psalms*.

'You read reasonably well, and if the *Book of Psalms* should suddenly reappear it will serve to improve your ability, especially as your place in the school has been terminated.'

'Won't I be attending class anymore, Mr Clayton?'

'No, you will not. I am responsible for the teachings of eighty-four students. Pestering school governors for my wages is time consuming enough without having to chase after stolen tomes.'

'I was only borrowing it to show Cousin Mary and John, Mr. Clayton.'

'I'm sure you were, Thomas, and without my permission I might add. You're lucky not to be having a visit from the constable. I still can't account for my lost spectacles.'

'I don't what you mean, Mr Clayton. What would I be doing with your spectacles?

'What *would* you be doing? What indeed.'

'I was only showing Mary and John that the ancient letters in the book were the same as on the silver ring.'

'But you told me the ring was lost, Johnson.'

'Er ... we remembered what the signs were like, Sir.'

'I would still like to see and touch this silver ring, Thomas. I love having a sense of the past. The writings in this tome refer to a similar ring and they were recorded hundreds of years ago. I would like to ask how it came into her possession.'

'It was her granny's and I told you the ring fell into the lake.'

'That's unfortunate, but nevertheless I would like to examine the ring if you should somehow retrieve it.' Phynius wasn't convinced that the ring lay at the bottom of the lake. After his initial disappointment he'd thought more on the subject and realised that he must have seen the ring. *Johnson said she wore it as an amulet.* Phynius had often seen Mary in church with her mother. Like the rest of the congregation he recognised the girl had a beauty like no other woman in the parish. *If only I had paid more attention to her amulet.* 'Your boy is clever, Robert, almost too clever for his own good. I'm sure that now he's left school, his help on the farm will be greatly appreciated, but if you're able to fund him, he's enough knowledge to obtain an apprenticeship. For this he must read and memorise the Ten Commandments. They're at the front of the book he calls the *Bible.* You might be able to explain the one that applies to him.'

'I don't know what you mean, Phynius.'

'Then I'm wasting my time here. It seems that your association with the Quakers has taught you nothing about telling the truth. Good day, Mr Johnson, and good luck to you both.' Phynius walked away caressing the book's cover, obsessed by the possession of the ancient relic. *I'll find that runic ring or die in the process, so help me God.*

Robert shrugged his shoulders but noted the teacher's encouraging words. Being the tenant of a Quaker landlord, he'd learned years ago that the Friends funded apprenticeships for the poor. Robert had pestered his landlord Timothy Atkinson to allow Thomas to attend Quaker meetings, just as he had the vicar for his son's entry to the grammar school. He then had to juggle attendances over two religions without breaking the law and endangering Thomas' school rights. Robert was now in another quandary. Thomas had attended the grammar school four years but was not yet old enough to take up an apprenticeship.

Robert surprised most people when he told them he'd taken Thomas away from the school. He told them his lad was now old enough and smart enough to help out on the farm. But then, after saying Thomas was to work on the farm, Robert had found casual work for his son, stockpiling the iron ore when it arrived at the Coniston Forge. Thomas had learned at school how they forged iron and Robert told him it was time he put his knowledge to good use. Aunt Hannah kept the true story of Thomas' dismissal to herself. She thought the forge work to be a blessing in disguise, and her nephew was less likely to carry iron ore home in his lunch sack than he would his schoolbooks. Hannah's son Damian worked as a gravedigger for the church, and he often visited his sister Mary at the manor house with his cousin Thomas. Mary was a domestic and husband John the head stableman who taught them all to ride. Except for the odd Quaker raid by the chief magistrate Colonel Kirkby, life carried on in the parish at its usual casual pace; until the death late that summer of Algernon Fleming, the owner of the manor house.

Residents of the market town of Hawkshead were speculating on their future wellbeing. Furness Abbey had been relieved of its tenancy as far back as the oldest parishioner could remember, leaving the district free of a resident lordship. Now almost four months had lapsed since the passing of Algernon Fleming, the holder of the estate and the king's appointed magistrate. During that time the parish thrived without the manor's authority as the locals adapted to the absence of the Crown's discipline.

After the dissolution of the monasteries, and due to a past agreement with the reigning abbot, the landholders of Furness had gained the equivalent of a perpetual freehold over their estates; for a nominal yearly rental and services to the Crown. Referred to as statesmen, they were stubbornly independent and casual regarding the king's authority. The community's Quakers were also enjoying a period of relief from persecution. There were rumours that the husband of the new owner had been a major in Cromwell's cavalry and that Vicar Braithwaite worried that his sympathies might lean towards the Quakers, who shared ideals with the Puritans. The bailiff had closed down the big house and dispersed the domestic staff, retaining only John Rigge and his young wife Mary. They were to remain in the lodge in full employment until the will had been executed. John was in charge of the stables and his duties were now extended temporarily to maintaining the servants' house, the wheat and oat barns and the dairy and piggery.

One month after the death of Algernon the parish bailiff asked John to attend a meeting in town at the manor court. On arrival he was told by the bailiff to take his place at a long table. Opposite him sat an attractive, well dressed dark-haired woman. He supposed she would be in her late forties, close to his mother's age. She appeared intelligent as her bright grey eyes focussed intensely on the gentleman at the head of the table. Her gaze shifted momentarily towards the stableman and she nodded politely as he took his place at the table.

Usually John had a word for everyone, but he felt uncomfortable in the presence of these three people. He turned his palms up to confirm they were clean and rubbed them needlessly down the front of his working breeches. He nervously spun a silver ring around his right middle finger, and then picked at soil in the grooves of the ancient symbols. The ring was Mary's wedding gift to him, crafted for a giant, too ungainly for his comfort. He wore the ring over a thick disjointed finger until he could afford to have it altered. John had the feeling he should have attended in his Sunday best, but there had been work, clearing the grounds and organising casual labour.

The woman's eyes flicked furtively towards him. She was admiring the profusion of manly chest hair curling through the neck of his over-shirt, imagining the power coiled in his muscled shoulders. John returned her gaze, saw the slight blush in her cheeks and her attention quickly revert to the lawyer. He looked across to the bailiff who was standing in the doorway, his hands behind his back, looking more than ever like a guard. The bailiff averted his gaze, looking up at the oak beamed ceiling and showing no sign of expression. *They're going to dismiss us.*

John waited apprehensively as the gentleman at the head of the table stroked the parchments in front of him, clearing his throat to commence. The lawyer's lips moved in a circular motion like a cow chewing cud, as if tasting the words before using them. The stableman, repulsed yet curious, leant forward fascinated by the peculiarities of the man. Distant bleats of sheep and the whinny of a horse entered the silence of the room.

John held his breath, waiting in anticipation for the announcement about to emanate from the parting between lawyer's thin lips. 'I must make you aware that I, Richard Swinbourne, have called you both here in my capacity as a lawyer, and as a steward by the king's orders, to execute Algernon Fleming's will.' He elevated his head as if to solicit a question, before looking down the table to read.

> I hereby give and devise to Penelope Rathbone, my niece, the daughter of my deceased brother Rufus Fleming, my lease of the aforesaid manor in the district of Furness, granted to me from the Crown.

He smacked his lips and rolled his jaw around in an apparent search for words, then seemingly satisfied, leaned forward on his elbows to spout his selection. 'The manor and the Lordship of Furness in the county palatine of Lancaster remained with King Charles II until 1662, after which they were granted away to his grace George Monck, Duke of Albemarle, for his service in the Civil War. Despite the lordship remaining the duke's, under the present agreement, the statesman owner of the manor house has the authority to will or dispose of the lease at his own discretion.' The steward squeaked out his words and with every movement of his jaw an enormous Adam's apple wobbled up and down his long scrawny neck.

John was hypnotised, unable to tear his eyes away. He was finding it hard to concentrate on the words and smiled at his thought. *The man has the looks of a turkey.*

'I must add that the said deceased acted as a local magistrate for the manor court and assisted Colonel Richard Kirkby, the impropriator of the district's tithes. This duty was instated at the request of the lord of the manor, whom I inform you once again to be the Duke of Albemarle. Any future owner of the manor would be expected to honour that position.'

The king's steward paused quite dramatically, chewing pensively as he perused the papers in front of him. Then, satisfied with the theatrical stretch of silence, he slowly raised his head and addressed Penelope. 'There are two recipients named in Algernon Fleming's will...'

> Penelope Rathbone, nee Fleming, a dear niece, our family's sole survivor; and John Rigge, who has been in my employ for many years, as a stable manager and horse trainer. For his loyalty and excellence in breeding and training horses I have bequeathed any single foal or horse of his choosing that may be in his care at time of my death.

The gentleman placed the paper on the table and stood up as he addressed John. He was very thin and pale faced, much taller than John had anticipated. 'You may leave the room now, Mr Rigge. The bailiff will contact you later to honour the contents of the will. For the present he must stay and witness the reading to Mrs Rathbone, which is rightly her private business.'

John sank a tankard of ale in the Red Lion before walking elatedly back to the manor house. He found his good fortune almost unbelievable and his future seemed assured. And the new owner was younger than he'd imagined. *She's an attractive woman. It will be a pleasure to work for her. The turkey said it would be my own choice. I'm certain that's what he said. I can be rightful owner of Prince and race him in my own name. I can't wait to tell Mary.*

Penelope Rathbone listened intently to five sheets of legalities. *How could anyone ramble on so much? Why can't he just say the manor house and its contents and the surrounding farms and be done with it?*

The king's steward droned to a finish then leaned forward to address Penelope. 'Are you in total agreement with the will, Mrs Rathbone?'

His voice filtered through cushions of drifting woollen clouds, increased in volume, and finally penetrated Penelope's thoughts. She shook her head, blinking. 'You asked if I'm in agreement. I most certainly am. The terms of the will are not unexpected, but I was under the impression that my Uncle Algernon was a titled lord.'

'No matter how much he may have tried to impress you dear woman, that's never been so. There has never been a lord in residence since the lordship of Furness Abbey. When King Henry sacked the monasteries, the reigning king held the lordship until 1662 when it was granted away to the duke, who also chooses to be absent. Algernon was an honourable man and well respected amongst the statesmen of the district, which is no mean feat. Apart from the disruptions of the Quakers, the law in the district has been upheld to our satisfaction, despite the late Judge Fell having favoured the Puritans. Since his death we've been able to deal with them more severely. You may have heard the judge's wife was dispossessed of her estate and serves sentence in Lancaster?'

'I had no idea there were those kinds of problems this far north, but I'm sure my husband, Rowan, will be able to handle the situation.' *Pray to God I hope so!* 'I know he'll be disappointed about the lack of a title.'

'Titles are earned and being a magistrate is an honour he should not take lightly. The position will only remain so as long as he commands authority. You tell me he is a retired major so I doubt that will be a problem. It's his allegiance I'm worried about.'

'My husband's a strong man in both mind and body, and he swears allegiance to the king.'

'Then he will swear it again, on oath. With his background, he should know that there is always a higher authority and that the king has many messengers.' He handed Penelope the papers and stood to leave. 'The bailiff will introduce you to the necessary people, Mrs Rathbone. I wish you and your husband well in your newfound authority.'

Algernon had told Penelope many years ago that she would inherit the freehold of the manor, as well as three surrounding farms and all his possessions. He implored her to make *sure* of her husband before informing him of her good fortune. Penelope had never been even *close* to being sure of Rowan, but she would do her utmost to retain the freehold for her family. She remembered looking across at John Rigge, admiring his physique, and him turning his head towards her. She'd imagined he was reading her thoughts and blushed, turning her face away, embarrassed. *Control yourself woman! Uncle obviously thought highly of the man. I'll make sure he remains in our employ, and he can help find me suitable staff ... if only I was twenty years younger.*

When Penelope told her husband of their new circumstances and the power he would wield, she was certain there would be little to worry over. She smiled to herself, watching him strut around their Cambridge home, puffing out his chest and ranting about lording it over all those northern peasants. The major pictured his old colonel slavering with jealousy. *A shame the old bastard's not alive to witness my elevation.*

'I've always wanted to live in the countryside, but I'm not sure you will be happy so far from your associates. I can always sell it, Rowan.'

The threat stopped the major in his tracks. 'What on earth are you thinking of woman?' He impatiently shook his head at what he considered a useless remark, missing the wry teasing lilt in her voice.

He continued pacing the small room. 'That's completely unnecessary, my dear, completely unnecessary. The district needs a strong man such as me, someone who's used to commanding and skilled in organising men. The people need someone willing to give of his time, and for little remuneration. You say my old commander George Monck holds the Lordship of Furness. What better position for me then at my age? I'll contact Hollis and offer him good employment. I hear he's married now and it's only justice that we look after our loyal army comrades.'

Penelope smiled inwardly. *Now that Rowan appears settled there is only Rufus to worry about.*

The manor house: January 1664

Penelope wiped a snowflake from her nose and looked up to the roof. Scattered laced patterns of snow clung to the tiles and patches of white flakes skated down into the gutters. Grey clouds hung low in the sky and threatened a heavier fall. The lady of the manor grew pensive. It was not the kind of day one would wish for the beginning of a new way of life. The manor house had two levels and the outside ivy-clad walls were built of pale-brown sandstone, a colour that Penelope thought of as soft, warm and secure. Four tall chimney stacks pierced the sloping tiled roof close to the guttering of each outside wall. One of the stacks was almost twice the width of the other three. The bailiff had explained it was for the dining room and lounge, and that the single brick stack rising from the peak of the sloped thatched roof belonged to the lodge and servants' quarters. Broken windows on the ground and second floors of the manor house showed signs of vandalism. *That will keep Rowan busy for a while. He'll be searching for the culprit with the local constable, probably a hopeless task and time consuming.* She smiled at the thought of an angry husband. *He's bound to take it personally.*

Penelope's first inspection of the manor with the bailiff was both officious and informative. On this second occasion, three months later, she was accompanied by John Rigge and Lizzie, a fussy and bouncy young widow, the stableman's first recommendation for domestic staff. *Mid-thirties and not too attractive dressed in that cap, over-garment, and apron. Rowan's preferences are hard to comprehend lately, but I can't imagine him knocking on her door.*

They stopped on the porch and tapped away the slush of the previous day's snowfall from their shoes. John Rigge swung open the oak double doors and they were greeted by a rush of cold air being dragged through the broken windows. Penelope remembered her first viewing as she crossed the threshold and was again impressed by the hall's high ceiling and the way it flowed towards the curved stairway that led to the second-floor bedrooms. John guided Penelope to the left of the stairs down a wide corridor and through double doors into the manor kitchen. There was a huge pantry on the right and on the adjoining rear wall a Dutch dresser had been pulled away to expose a dark timber door. John explained that the door gave access to the external icehouse and was only used in summer. They returned to the entrance, and on the right of the staircase was another double door of polished quality timber. The doors opened inwards, and Penelope proudly pushed them apart to reveal an impressive oak-panelled ballroom. The lady of the manor was feeling comfortable and she led her servants across the timbered floor into a select dining room with an adjoining library. There was a smell of mustiness about the library emanating from the walls of old books.

Penelope retraced her steps to the front window of the ballroom and pressed her forehead against the frosty pane. She swept her gloved hand over the misty glass, circled a view, and stared glassy eyed into the silence of falling snow. A white blanket covered the fells and speckled trees were dripping liquid from overladen branches. A plump red-breasted thrush emerged from a nearby tree and sprayed snowflakes as he hovered over a lower branch. Penelope watched mesmerised as he settled on the chosen perch, long, thin legs fidgeting for a secure hold, his call sounding distant through the misted windowpane. Penelope heard the wistful warble and understood. *The robin is lonely and needs a partner.* She smiled with empathy. *He's lonely like me.* She blinked and shivered, uncomfortable, realising that the chill of the manor rooms was not far removed from the weather outside. *The fireplace needs to be roaring with flames and those heavy drapes need changing.*

Penelope could see there was a lot of work to be done and doubted that her uncle's annuity and her husband's pension would be sufficient. Then she remembered Rowan was now the local magistrate and there would be remuneration from his collections for the duke and tithes for the church. There was rent from the three farm cottages and also their Cambridge property. 'We'll have to make a work list, John, in order of urgency.' Her voice resounded from the walls. Despite the covered furniture, the manor sounded empty, as an abandoned house does, but there was also a solitude that made Penelope feel uncomfortable. *Perhaps I will feel more at home when I have family around me and my own furniture in place. I hope I've made the right decision. I hope Rowan and Rufus will be happy.* Penelope was having doubts, but she cast them aside and took a deep refreshing breath. 'Put a spark to the fires, John, and have the cobwebs cleared away. The house is crying out for life. Our home needs to breathe.'

The dismissal

The major thrived with his rejuvenated career. Siding with the Puritans and Cromwell was in the past. His hair was now long in the fashion of the day and he was on a mission for his adopted King Charles. 'So, Vicar, you fear the growth of Quakerism? I finished with Puritan sympathies when King Charles II regained the throne. I'm told he supports the new laws passed by Parliament; laws implemented solely to enforce the Quaker's obedience; I might add.'

Vicar Braithwaite was a short stout man, with a balding pate and a round, jovial moon-like face. But there hadn't been too much to smile about these past few years, especially with the problem of the Quakers and the church's diminishing tithes. Nevertheless, now in his fiftieth year, he promised his wife and children that despite the problems, he would continue in life as before. He would always have a welcoming smile for his congregation, whether they slept through his sermons or not. 'The people are very stubborn in these parts major and the trait sit's well with the Quakers. Our district has become a stronghold for George Fox and his Friends.'

'That's nonsense, Vicar. I'm told you've been in the parish ever since the restoration and you have the gall to make excuses for losing your flock. I'm here to help you and mark my words, with the support of the law we will turn the tide and fill your church to overflowing. It seems to me that my predecessor was far too lenient with the Puritans.'

'I think not, Major. Only two years past, with the help of the chief magistrate, Algernon Fleming made an example of Samuel Sandys of Roger Ground. In their haste to set an example, the constables marched the poor man across the dangerous sands of Morecambe Bay to intern him in Lancaster Gaol. He still stubbornly refused to pay his tithes and consequently never returned. He died a nasty death through torture and malnutrition.'

'I'm sure I can extract the tithes in a less contusive manner, Gabriel.'

'Then how would you have handled the good lady, Margaret Fell? With full knowledge of the fate of Sandys she refused to take the oath and was dispossessed of her holdings and cast into Lancaster Gaol. She remains there to this day.'

'I have heard of the Quaker Margaret Fell. A judge's wife no less and allowed to publish her thoughts whilst serving her sentence. You seem to be in sympathy with those disrespectful of our church. Good lady you say and poor Samuel?'

'They were not poor in the monetary sense, Major, not by any means, so more the pity they refused to pay their tithes. I bear no malice major, and I only regret that these otherwise intelligent people have been led down the wrong path. They don't believe and don't practice our church's sacraments. They register their children's names but deny them a holy christening. They neglect the grace of the gift of the Holy Spirit, to be anointed with holy oil.'

'They approach a dead end. The Quakers are no good to me in shackles, Gabriel, and mark my words I'll find other means to extract your tithes.'

'The poor in the district will love you for it. I'll see you and Penelope in church this Sunday?'

'Not so soon, Vicar, I've work to do. I have to organise my own household before any other. Meanwhile you could introduce me to the churchwarden, and any jurors of importance. Oh, and you can introduce me to the constable and his watchers. We must establish our duties towards each other, collecting taxes and so forth.'

The vicar was disappointed with his reception. The major's pomposity was deflating. As he prepared to leave, the major hesitated with his next question, deciding whether it should be an order, or merely a polite request.

'Do you have a first name, Vicar?'

'It's Gabriel, Major, and yours?'

'Major will be fine, Gabriel.'

'Then I must warn you that Christian names are preferred in the surrounding districts. You could be left wanting.'

'We'll see about that. I demand respect for my position.'

The vicar smiled knowingly. *I look forward to your comeuppance.* He had failed to complain about the annoying behaviour of Pynius Clayton. The occasion hadn't seemed appropriate. He couldn't believe that a schoolteacher would want a silver ring, legally owned by one of his parishioners, to be declared a possession of the church. *The intensity of the man was unnerving.* When he told Phynius that Mary no longer wore the ring the teacher was so distressed that he thought to mention her husband, John Rigge, was wearing the finger-ring at their betrothal. No sooner was it said than Phynius became animated and shouted out. 'I knew it! I knew that boy was lying! The ring should be in the possession of the church.' *He is such an intense man. Why does he believe that a silver ring, legally owned by one of my parishioners, should be declare a possession of the church?*

Since the arrival of the major, Mary had been helping Lizzie with housework, spinning and weaving as well as helping the cook to stock the pantry and prepare the meals. For almost a month, John Rigge had been showing the major's right-hand man, Hollis, the ins and outs of maintaining the manor grounds. He'd been instructed to familiarise Hollis with the stables, piggery, dairy shed, outhouse and icehouse. But John found it hard to keep the man's interest outside of the stables, where they worked amicably as kindred spirits in their love of horses. 'You seem more comfortable around the horse sheds, Hollis. You've obviously had a great deal of experience?'

'I was attached to Cromwell's cavalry stables, John. You need know no more than that.' And John knew from his manner of authority that there would be no more questions answered on the subject. The major and Hollis had in fact been in charge of Cromwell's stables. The stables had been full of racehorses, requisitioned by the state when Cromwell banned the sport in 1654. Army friends of Hollis and the major had since found employment in the king's stables at Newmarket, and although the major was want to keep it secret, the association had favoured him admirably in the past few years. And to cap it all, their old commander George Monck was now Lord of the Manor of Furness. The major marvelled at the coincidence and was wont to voice the old adage: some things never change.

From the first day, there'd never been one word of dis-agreement between them. Edgar Hollis was middle-aged and tall with a heavily built frame that brooked no argument. He wore a long sombre face that conveyed both seriousness and a lack of humour. He had been an aide and fixer of all the major's irritating problems both in and out of the army for the past decade and was now gradually taking over John's responsibilities. It became obvious to the stableman that he was being made redundant. 'Are you merely familiarising yourself, Edgar, or are you replacing me?'

'I can't understand your thinking, John. I'm only carrying out the major's instructions. Perhaps you should have a talk with him?'

John disliked the feeling of insecurity. His frustration swelled and he found it hard to contain his anger as he knocked on the imposing oak door of the manor house. He'd told Lizzie of his need to speak with the major urgently. *I'll not be made a fool of by any man.* The stableman was taken aback by the major's effusive welcome.

'Come in, Rigge. Come in! It's just as well you came to see me. You saved me a job. Hollis will be moving into your quarters tomorrow. Mary can move in with Lizzie for now. That's if she intends to stay of course.'

The words echoed in John's skull like rolls of thunder. *How can he stand there and smile through that smug, pitted face?* 'You realise we're married, Major?'

The major hesitated for a moment, and then ignored the question. 'I'm sorry I can't offer you any other employment, but I'm convinced a man of your capabilities will soon be accommodated elsewhere. Before you leave, I require inform me of your intentions. I want this business cleared up before my wife returns with our son.'

'You never intended to keep me on then?'

'Did I promise you?'

'I was of the opinion your wife intended to use me.'

'She has no say in the matter.' *Use him indeed.* Jealousy was a new experience for the major and he felt intimidated. *Penny's got a soft spot for the man. The sooner he's out of my sight the better.*

John had an urge to strangle the major and battled his anger. *I could lift the bigot off his feet by his throat, and slowly squeeze the life out of him. It would be a pleasure to see his eyes pop and his ugly face turn purple.* John controlled the urge, knowing he would end up in Lancaster with the promise of a noose and his young wife left alone and vulnerable.

Mary was shattered with the unexpected turn of events. 'What will we do, John?'

'You must hold on to your position here, Mary, but only until such time as I've secured employment elsewhere. Timothy Atkinson was a close friend of Algernon Fleming and despite their conflicting beliefs I was often loaned for my labour. I'll try and speak with him this afternoon, but please be patient. I don't want to leave you in the major's employ. He can go and rot in Hell for all I'll care.'

'I'll be safe with Lizzie, but I shall miss you, John.'

'It will be no more than a week before we're settled, and I'll visit you every day, I promise.'

John saddled Prince, the young horse he'd chosen as his inheritance, and strapped on his role of belongings. The horse had come to the manor as a yearling. Algernon had told him it was from the king's stables, from a bloodline in Tangier, and he was to train it for racing. There were rumours that the local magistrate had won it in a wager. John had no idea where Tangier was, but he knew horses, and he knew that this one was something special. Algernon told him to enter Prince in race at the local fair, for a trial. He said that when the time was right they would all travel south to Newmarket. John realised he could never be that ambitious. The trip south would never happen and there was little chance of holding a wager race in the parish. Prince's speed was already local knowledge. They had raced twice at the High Street Summer Fair, on Racecourse Hill east of Ambleside.

They won a wager on the first occasion, but the second year there were no takers and Prince raced against older horses merely for the sport. The races at Cartmel Fair had been no different, but for John they held one of his fondest memories. Not only did he win a wager on Robert Johnson's wrestling bout, he also met Robert's beautiful niece and future wife, Mary Inman. John now realised that Prince was a horse that only the gentry could wager on, racing against one of equal breeding.

Mary held Prince's reins with one hand and stroked the horse's neck with the other. John leaned down from the saddle, cupped her cheeks in his strong hands and kissed her. 'No more than a week please, John.'

Her husband straightened in the saddle, his face stern as his heels pressed into the colt's flanks. 'I promise you, Mary. Not a day more than one week.'

'Good luck to us both, John.' Mary held back the tears, as she grasped the amber stone amulet resting on her bosom. The stone was womanly and had been passed down to John's mother by her mother. Mary's finger ring amulet was manly and had always been passed down to the first-born. It seemed only natural that the gifts be exchanged on their wedding day. During the past few months she'd come to accept the security of work and a home. With John being in charge, both Damian and Thomas had been able to visit whenever they liked, and her mother and Uncle Robert had called in on Sundays. Now, in the space of one day that happiness had been taken away from them. John had been very conscientious of his extra responsibilities, and when the Rathbones finally took residence the house the grounds were in excellent condition. John had even been preparing her brother Damian for a position in the stables, teaching him to ride and groom the horses. Now their world had fallen apart. *Why did Algernon have to die Jesus? We were all so happy. Does this* mean my young brother will remain a gravedigger for the rest of his life? I feel sorry for poor Damian. At least he'll be pleased John still has the horse. He loves Prince as if it were his own.

Spring beckoned but John and Mary's future promised to be as bleak as the snowbound winter. John turned Prince in the direction of Atkinson's Ground, and as horse and rider left the stables behind, John looked back and saw Hollis in the distance. The major's man was waving his arms frantically in the air and stamping his feet as if in frustration. *Missing me already are you, Hollis?*

Penelope arrived back at the manor house full of enthusiasm. She had already stopped in town to arrange for the tailor to call the next day. She led him to believe he may be measuring for suits and a dress, but there was no way Penelope was going to trust him with the latest fashion. She had already seen to those needs in Cambridge. *He can measure and shape the drapes, and I'll have John hang them in place.*

Penelope headed for the stables and was greeted with a smile by Hollis. 'Welcome back, Mrs Rathbone.'

'Thank you, Edgar. I'm looking for John.'

'He's been dismissed from the stables and employed elsewhere. You will have to ask the major.'

Penelope's face drained of colour and grew taut as her eyes flashed with anger. Hollis watched with interest as she raced back to the big house. *I would love to be a fly on the wall.*

Penelope found her husband in the library. 'Rowan, I've been outside looking for the stableman. Hollis said you'd know where he's working.'

The major turned slowly towards her with a knowing supercilious smile. 'I've heard he's working for the enemy, a Quaker no less. A statesman landholder named Timothy Atkinson and a defiler of the truth. The sooner his woman follows him there the better it will be for us all.' Penelope could not believe what she was hearing. She stood gaping, claustrophobic, the walls of the library closing in on her. 'I'm telling you; I've removed him from my employ, woman. He was an added expense. Hollis covers his work admirably.'

'What do you mean, you've removed him? I was going to build my domestic staff around that man, and from what I've heard there's no better horse trainer for your stables.'

'Hollis has the stables well under control. You mustn't forget the positions we held with Cromwell. The only problem we have is that rough man you admire so much has stolen one of our best horses. We have the constable and his watchers out there investigating.'

'Then more the fool you are. He's quite entitled to the horse. It was willed to him, and I agreed to his choice.'

The major's eyelid's drooped, as if veiling his thoughts. *She's involved more than I guessed. It was providence that I removed him.* 'Forget your agreement with him. I suggest to you that he will be harassed continually by the law. That horse was won in a wager and brought here as a foal. It is of the finest bloodlines. I've every reason to believe, as the branding suggests, that it was foaled in the king's own racing stables. That peasant has no right to own such prime horseflesh. I intend to race the thoroughbred and put him to stud.'

'Then we've both lost something of value, Rowan. Perhaps you should lock yourself in here and take solace in a stiff brandy, for what is done is done.'

'I could ride the horse for you, Father. I'm very good at racing.'

The major whirled at the sound of his son's voice. 'So, you've finally arrived, and have the audacity to enter unannounced and eavesdrop on our private conversation.'

'You were shouting.'

'You know he always shouts like that, Rufus. Nevertheless, your father's right. You shouldn't skulk around the corridors. I haven't even had time to introduce you to the staff.'

Rufus had given them nothing but trouble the past two years. He was let loose on society at the ripe old age of nineteen, and there was no way the spoilt brat was going to quietly exchange Cambridge or London for a quiet town in the north of the country. The temptation of money, or the withdrawal of it, had been Penelope's only leverage. Word from a dear friend of hers had suggested that they should keep a close watch on him. At the age of nineteen her son was still grappling with his puberty.

Mary and John

Mary was deep in thought. She hummed with the sound of the spinning wheel as she rolled the fleece over her thigh between thumb and forefinger and watched trance-like as the wool spun endlessly towards the bobbin. She loved the scent of the raw fleece, but it often irritated her nose and made her sneeze.

She was thinking of the markings on the silver ring she had gifted John. Thomas had fired her imagination when he'd shown her the book he'd borrowed from school. Mary thought that everything Thomas had explained about the markings on her ring could be true. She couldn't remember everything he'd told her. *Were there really gods of thunder and the sea, and a god archer that wore a magic finger ring?* John thought her silly, but she began to believe there was magic in the ring. *He said something about a yew tree. And wouldn't it be good if Prince really was a messenger of the gods?* She fingered the amber stone on her necklace and wondered about its age. Could it be as ancient as the ring she'd gifted John? The room brightened and Mary looked out of the window to see the grey clouds clearing away. The sun's rays beamed down, and the dales flaunted a patchwork of green speckled snow. She heard the gallop of a horse growing louder.

John had been calling every day as promised. *He's earlier than usual.* She paused in her spinning and smiled contentedly. She felt safe just thinking of him. She was pleased that John would be taking her away before the major returned. *I've found you a place, Mary. It's not to my liking, but at least we will be together until I can build something better for you.*

She never heard the door opening but she felt a chill and the hairs on the back of her neck bristled. A shiver ran down her spine and her shoulders instinctively hunched. Her thoughts were interrupted by the whinny of a horse, and her ears pricked at the sound of heavy breathing. Mary's neck tingled and her hands clenched with fear. There was someone in the room and she sensed evil behind her back. Her body coiled to spring from the seat, but her action only served to help her assailant. She was half-lifted from the stool and pulled backwards as two hands cupped her breasts and squeezed incessantly. She screamed as his chin nestled in her shoulder, his lips panting hot breath pressing into her cheek. Mary tore the hands away, kicked backwards and fell to the floor. She wrestled with the intruder clawing at his face. Her nails drew blood and she broke free. She grabbed hold of the edge of the bed and searched frantically under the pillow for Lizzie's kitchen knife. *Please help me, Lord.* She heard the whinny of the horse again and felt weightless. She was floating over her own body. Something was using her eyes and there was a vision enclosed in a blinding-white aura. She was suddenly consumed with rage, breathing in short heavy gasps, and holding the knife handle with two clenched fists. She saw her hands raising the blade above her head.

Rufus levered his body from the floor and looked up into the eyes of a devil. For a moment he'd been hypnotised by the woman's soft passionate eyes; at first dark brown, then suddenly bright green, piercing and angry. *It's the sunlight.* He rolled onto his knees and tried to stand, but his shaking hands only managed to reach out and rattle the doorknob. *It's a nightmare. I'll wake up soon.* He looked up again and saw the knife poised to strike down on him. 'I was only after a little grope.' His voice trembled and then choked on a scream as his hands went up to shield his face. His legs wobbled like jelly as he lifted himself by the door handle, squeezed his body through the narrow gap and slammed the door shut. Rufus collapsed onto the corridor floor and screamed out, 'Who are you?'

The slamming door jolted Mary awake, and the vision receded into the depth of her mind, to nurse some undefined ancestral anger. Composed again, she looked up with horror at the knife in her hands, opened her palms and watched it spiral to the floor. She leaned back against the door and prayed forgiveness. 'God help me. What was I doing?' She grimaced and kicked the knife across the floor, repulsed, her hands trembling, nauseated by the evil that dwelled within. Her chin dropped to her chest and she sobbed with the fear of her vulnerability. Then she laughed hysterically at her image of the cringing pathetic Rufus.

She had seen the vision once before, after losing her temper with Damian. John Rigge had been outside the cottage at the time with the young colt, Prince. The stableman had been talking to her mother when Damian started teasing her. 'Yer luver's outside, Mary.' She remembered the sudden surge of rage, the whinny of the colt and the short heavy breathing. She rushed at her brother and knocked him to the floor, surprised at her own strength. That was when she first saw her Man of Death, as she came to call him. There'd been that same feeling of floating, looking down from above, and someone else using her eyes. The face kept surfacing in a flickering spectre, an evil one-eyed face screaming pain and anger. But the screaming was coming from her mouth. She'd pulled her hands away from Damian's throat as if they were holding hot coals, then walked away in a daze, thinking she'd had a fit of madness. 'Are you scared of me, Mary? What did you scream for?'

She gave her brother a withering stare, enough to make him cower down. 'Think yourself lucky I let go, you cheeky little sod.' Mary convinced herself the vision was a figment of her imagination surfacing because of her anger. She'd never spoken to anyone lest they thought her mad. Now a few years older and wiser she worried about the lapse of her mind. The reappearance of the vision disturbed her even more than before. *Was it really because I lost my temper? I've never felt that angry before.* She had reached for the knife for protection to fend off Rufus. But her anger had turned to rage. Blinding light surrounded the flickering image of the man's head and shoulders. His hands were clamped around his slashed throat trying to stem the flow of blood. There was horror etched on his face and blood congealed in his barren eye-socket. *Could this be the evil-one that mother speaks of? The one she calls the Dobbie man.* Whatever the explanation, she had to control her temper or risk losing her mind.

Penelope heard the screaming and raced to the servants' quarters, arriving at the same time as Lizzie. Dumbstruck, they stared at Rufus. Blood was running down his clawed cheeks and his eyes registered shock. He was in trouble again: deep trouble was Penelope's estimation. He stood up, distraught. He was his father's height, a head taller than both the women and he looked at his mother with nothing to say, waiting for the lecture that followed. 'Rufus Rathbone. Why are you in the servants' quarters?'

'Er ... I was ... umm.'

'Shut your face boy, you tell nothing but lies.' Penelope eased the door against Mary's weight. 'What has happened, Mary?'

Mary breathed deeply, calming herself. She picked up the knife, placed it back under the pillow and sat on the edge of the bed. 'Nothing serious, Mrs Rathbone, but he gave me a terrible shock. I'll be happy to leave tomorrow.'

Out of the corner of her eye Penelope spied Rufus skulking away. 'Stay where you are, Rufus ... no ... forget what I just said ... leave now. I'll see you later in the library. God only knows what your father will say.' Penelope sat beside Mary. 'Perhaps you should leave today, Mary and I will pay your wages for tomorrow. This unfortunate incident may never have occurred if John had still been working here. I want you to know that I had nothing to do with John's dismissal. It came as quite a shock and as far as I'm concerned, he should still be working for me. Do you think he might change his mind? About working at the manor, I mean. I can find him work away from Hollis and my husband.'

'It's too late, and I doubt if he would ever be able to work anywhere near Hollis again. John's settled in with Timothy Atkinson now and he's found us a temporary home.'

'Then I wish you both every happiness and if I can ever help you in any way, and I mean in any way, then you must approach me in confidence.'

'I don't wish John to know about this afternoon, Mrs Rathbone. Please send him away and tell him I'm busy.'

I think he might lose his temper.' *John would kill Rufus and I would lose a husband.*

Penelope placed her consoling hand on top of Mary's. 'You may rest assured, Mary, John will hear nothing of today's trauma and as far as Rufus is concerned, it will be some time before you see him again.' She flashed a glance at Lizzie, who left immediately for the stables. She had also heard the arrival of

John Rigge and understood there needed to be an explanation for Mary's absence.

John was able to keep his promise to Mary. He called to see her every day and arranged for her day of leaving. Mary told him she'd asked Mrs Rathbone if she could leave a day earlier, and he had a feeling that his wife was unusually nervous. 'Is everything alright, Mary? I called early yesterday but Lizzie told me you were still working.'

'I know, John, Lizzie told me. It's just that I'm unsettled and think I should leave before the major returns. I don't wish to see the man again. I've never liked him, and I've recently met his son who isn't any better. Penelope is a lovely woman to work for, and if it wasn't for her this place would be unbearable.'

'Then I'm sorry you've had to stay so long without me. I didn't realise you were so unhappy. I was being selfish.'

'No, John, we did what we thought was for the best. I just want to leave before the major returns, and that reminds me of your horse, John. You must hide Prince. I hear the major is going to claim ownership.'

'That's impossible, especially as it was the major's wife that accepted my choice and it was gifted to me from her uncle's will. Timothy said he'll stable it for me until we're settled. I'm sure the major has no claim on Prince.'

'You surely can't trust the man, after all he's done to us?'

'Of course not, the man's far too devious. It's just that I can't see him going beyond the law.'

'I think he is the law, John, and that makes me worry.'

'Then I'll speak to Timothy Atkinson and ask his advice.'

Penelope waited for the major's return before she spoke to her son again. 'You are returning to Cambridge, Rufus. We've lost a perfectly good domestic, and to make matters worse she's married to the owner of the horse that your father covets. I'm telling you this before you go in to see him. Forewarned is forearmed.'

Penelope was wasting her breath and Rufus breezed into his father's study intent on having a stout man-to-man talk. 'I had no idea there was Spanish stock in the district father, she's beautiful.'

The major glared at his son and then paced the room in silence before fronting him nose to nose. 'You speak to me in all ignorance. Women are a subject you know absolutely nothing about.' Rufus couldn't have interfered at a worst time. 'You may think she's beneath you, but the young woman is married, and her breasts are not to be fondled at your slightest whim.'

'I hardly touched her, Father.'

'Rubbish! I don't expect lies from my only son. The domestic's duties are not to be interfered with. They are your mother's responsibility alone. I may add that she's ashamed of you and we both agree that you will live in Cambridge. You are not to return until we are respected here. Hopefully by that time, your misdemeanour will have faded and the status of our family will be restored.'

'But I've only just agreed to stay.'

'You're not old enough to agree to anything. I don't want to see you for at least a year. Your allowance is halved. That should help to keep you away from London and further mischief. Your mother will make arrangements for you to stay with my cousin.'

As the major had foreseen, John Rigge had no trouble in finding employment. Timothy Atkinson had sought permission from the bailiff to fell a number of choice timbers for rebuilding the farmhouses in his tenancy and the bailiff had recently called in on Timothy to supervise their markings and ensure he had a professional woodcutter. 'I've been informed that the trees will have to be felled before the end of winter, John, whilst the sap still lays dormant. I will leave it to you to employ a team of labourers. You may stable Prince with me until you and Mary are settled. After the trees are felled and the bullock teams have hauled them to the sawyer, we will look elsewhere for you. I've presently no domestic work for your wife and no accommodation other than an old woodcutter's cottage in a clearing at the edge of the forest.'

Felling trees wasn't quite the work John had hoped for. It was notoriously dangerous but at least he was to be in charge of a team of his choosing, the position he'd become accustomed to these past few years. He needed labour that could be trained by a professional woodcutter, and he went to the Hawkshead market house where men usually gathered when they were looking for work. He employed a young man named James Pritt who said he'd recently been working with the charcoal burners in Rusland. James was the only one that John could find with tree felling experience. He employed three other labourers from Kendal and encouraged them by explaining there would be ongoing work. Most of the statesmen in the district were rebuilding their old farmhouses, and the bailiff had permission to honour any further reasonable request for timber.

After her comforts at the manor house, the austerity of the woodcutter's hut came as a shock. Mary was not prepared, but she set to and had John clean out everything except an old oak table and two benches. The first priority was the brick fireplace, tripod, and cooking pot. They hadn't left the manor without thinking of their future and Penelope had donated some kitchen utensils. Her mother, Hannah, and brother, Damian, came to help with the priorities of food and warmth, and in less than two weeks, Mary had made her makeshift residence homely. In his precious spare time, John had built a lean-to for the woodcutting tools, axes and building implements that lined the cottage timber walls. He was now in the process of building a small stable for the return of his prized horse Prince. Every Sunday, Damian and quite often, Hannah, with Cousin Thomas, would call in to see them after church.

After a month of organising their temporary home, Mary came to venture outside more often. She mentioned to John that she was bored and suggested that she was quite capable of trimming the foliage of the felled trees. 'You shouldn't be employing an extra man for work that I'm capable of doing.' Mary found it hard to reason her feelings, but after watching the woodcutters, she'd experienced a compulsive urge to swing an axe.

John was at the Atkinson's estate, busily organising the bullock team when he looked across the yard and spotted Major Rathbone huddled in conversation with James Pritt. The mere sight of the major was offensive. It was the first time John had set eyes on the major since being dismissed and he had no desire to even discuss the time of day with him. He walked across to his employer Timothy, who was waving a piece of worded paper at the churchwarden William Webster. 'The bailiff signed this permission paper, weeks before we started felling trees. He even recommended a professional woodcutter to guide my labour force, and I have been under the bailiff's instruction ever since.'

'It's the major, Timothy. He has a set against you. He's against your religious beliefs and has become even more aggravated since you employed John Rigge.'

'Then he needs to have more work to occupy his mind, instead of wasting my time. Art thou organised, John?'

'We're ready to go, Timothy.'

'Then I'll see thee again in two days' time.'

John went across to join James as the major came striding towards him. The major's eyes were focussed in the beyond, and their paths crossed without acknowledgement. William was annoyed and becoming impatient with the major at this apparent waste of a churchwarden's time. 'Everything seems to be in order, Major.'

The parish's acting magistrate mounted and wheeled his horse. 'Then we had best be on our way, Webster. Will you be attending church on Sunday, Atkinson?'

Timothy's wife, Margaret, came to join her husband, wrapped her arm around his waist, and smiled her support. 'Thou know my family's religious beliefs, Major. Thy question is unnecessary.'

'Then unless you change your mind you can expect me to be signing another warrant.'

As the riders galloped past John, he turned to face James Pritt and asked him for an explanation. 'What were you discussing with the major?'

'Er ... he was asking how many trees we'd cleared.'

'That's all you spoke of?'

'He also asked where we were working.' James was annoying, clicking two coins together between his fingers and John sensed his new hand was nervous. *He's hiding something.* 'Did he hand you some coin?'

The young Rusland charcoal burner looked down into the palm of his hand and quickly thrust the two coins into his pocket. 'Now why would he be giving money away for nothing?'

'I was thinking the same thing myself.' John was suspicious and more wary of James since discovering how easily he lied and had only felled one tree before his employment. He had little experience other than clearing coppice, the growth from felled trees. *I won't ever trust him again with anything of importance.*

Mary had a beauty about her that was admired by many, but most in the village thought it a pity that she carried the sign of the plague. The purple blemish became even more prominent when she was angry and most eligible men turned away when they saw the scar on her smooth olive skin. She came to wear her long hair brushed across one side of her face to disguise the marking. Damian carried a similar purple blemish on his forehead, which was more noticeable on his pale skin. Because of their shared visible handicap, he felt a close kinship with his older sister. Damian was too young at the time, but Mary remembered the swelling of her body, the fever and the screaming pain. It was only when she looked on her brother Damian and questioned his slow mind that she realised how fortunate she'd been.

The opportunity presented to them by Timothy had more than compensated for John's dismissal. Her husband was already planning to help rebuild an old house he could rent on the Atkinson's property. Mary was looking forward to having the slate floor and surrounding sealed stonewalls that John had promised her. They would help each other in their workloads, spinning and weaving wool together. Mary would help John in the less strenuous part of his work, and then there would be children. They were only dreaming of course, but Mary knew that in time their plans would come to pass. She was surprised at how easily she'd adapted to the rigours of trimming the foliage from the felled timbers. Any stranger watching may have thought her an expert with the axe. She felt healthy, strong around her shoulders, and bounced around with her mother's agility.

John had been thinking more of the day's end than the felling of another oak. He was feeling hungry, looking forward to a steaming meat broth and a night huddled up close to Mary. He looked up into the highest branches of the tall oak and saw its spine shiver as the hammer struck a final blow and the wedge bit into the centre grain. John backed Prince away as the tree groaned and its top branches lurched forward. His team stepped back from their work and they all listened in silent anticipation, willing the familiar crack that would signal the old tree's surrender.

John heard a swish like an arrow in flight and a smack like stone against leather. Prince whinnied, thrashed the air with his fore hooves throwing John from the saddle. One foot caught in the stirrup. His head pounded the ground as he was towed towards the falling tree. John grabbed his knee with both hands and lifted his body, fighting to release his foot from the stirrup. His ankle ligaments tore as he freed himself and he clawed desperately at the earth attempting to scoop his body away from the path of the falling tree. The felled oak gained impetus, its trunk swishing in flight as it sliced the air. John looked up at the darkening blue sky and the tree branches spread wide, their fingers splayed open as if to cushion the fall. The great oak thudded into the moistened earth, pinned his body to the soil, and then buried him under a shroud of cascading leaves.

Mary was happily trimming foliage on the perimeter of the woods when she first heard the whinny of Prince and then the crack of snapping branches, a sound she'd grown familiar with since living in the cottage. She heard the usual echoing thud of timber crashing to the ground, and the after thunder of the earth tremor reverberating under her feet. But this time there was something else she heard in the whinny of the horse. An intuition persuaded her to stop work and look towards the felling area. Mary looked up in time to see the rider-less Prince galloping wildly across the clearing. Her heart was racing, booming in her ears, the colour draining from her face, and her hands shaking. She dropped the axe and ran panic stricken towards the section where John was working.

When Mary arrived at the scene the woodcutting team were struggling to roll the crushing weight of the huge trunk away from John's lifeless body. Her screams echoed in the silence of the forest. She threw her weight behind the felling team, pushing until her legs trembled with weakness and until her body drained of all energy, when she finally collapsed over the top of the log. They all knew it was hopeless, but they had to try. Even if the bullock teams had been available, they could have done little more. Mary turned her back against the huge trunk and slid like a sack to the forest floor. Completely exhausted, she lay beside the still body of her husband and wept unashamedly. *How can it be possible that John has left me? He was strong in mind and body. How is it possible I have lost my husband?* John's right arm was twisted upwards and his lifeless hand seemed to be pointing up towards his wife. Mary noticed the silver ring hanging loose, almost torn from John's broken finger. She reached out for it, and tears rolled down her face as she threaded the ancient ring onto her necklace, beside his precious amber stone. *Perhaps it's God's will that the ring should stay with me.*

Inconsolable, Mary was taken to her mother's house, where her family cared for her until the day of John's burial. Mary found it hard to recollect her husband's funeral, only remembering that the pain of the plague was nothing compared to the pain of losing her husband. They said that Prince had reared and dislodged John with the first crack of timber, and that he was probably dead before the tree fell on him. They said the back of John's head hit a rock as he fell to the ground and they saw him dragged in the stirrups towards the falling tree. Mary later had her doubts as to why the four-year-old experienced horse had reared in the first place. She'd watched John train him from a colt with such love and patience and she found it hard to believe the animal would panic at such a routine occurrence.

Mary was surprised to see the major and his wife Penelope at the funeral and even more surprised when a tearful Penelope left her husband's side to comfort her. 'I somehow feel responsible for John's death, Mary. You should both have been working at the manor and none of this would have happened.'

Her sympathy did nothing to console Mary. She'd wondered at the appearance of the schoolteacher and why he asked the vicar if he could view the body. *He must have known John.* Afterwards he'd kept staring at her, smiling and nodding. *He's creepy.* She was grateful for the attendance and condolences of Timothy and Margaret Atkinson. 'We shall make room for thee with the domestics, until thou art over thy shock.'

But Mary had already set her mind on staying in the cottage. 'Don't make me leave our cottage, Timothy. I need to stay a while, until I've made peace with the world. My memories of John and his plans for our future will keep me strong.'

'It's only an old hut, Mary, and thou art best living away from bad memories.'

'I only have good memories of our cottage. I need to work with the woodcutters until the work is finished. Please, Timothy, just for a short time.'

Timothy looked at his wife, Margaret, and the concern showed on her face. 'I'm not sure we would be doing the right thing. We are responsible for her safety and it's not appropriate that a young woman should be left on her own in the forest.'

'The hut is in the clearing, Margaret, and she will be with the men during the day.' Timothy made a quick decision, and the friendly statesman demanded only one condition. 'When the crew have felled the quota, thy employment trimming foliage will cease. That work was never meant for a woman and certainly not one possessing thine beauty. As for living alone in the woods, I would prefer thee stayed with your mother, or failing that my wife will try and accommodate you in the servants' quarters. I can do no more, and when the time comes, thou must decide if thou should stay in my employ.'

'I agree, Timothy, and I most certainly wish to stay in your employ. Thank you for your kindness.' Mary tried to reason her misfortune. She thought the loss of her husband so early in their marriage was affecting her mind. She'd wanted to tell John of the vision at the manor, but now she realised that keeping it a secret had been for the best. John could have attacked Rufus or at the worst believed her to be crazy. Mary reasoned that the Devil's face was deep in her mind and only appeared when she was angry. *I'm not normally bad tempered or angry. Am I losing control of my mind?* Mary was beginning to realise the meaning of being possessed. She finally brought herself to confess her feelings to Vicar Braithwaite and broke down crying, begging him to cast the Devil from her. 'A Man of Death haunts me in my anger. I've never hated anyone before, Vicar, never ever! What's happening to me?'

'If you perceive evil inside of you, Mary, it's because of your great loss and your wish to cast blame for John's death. In time the anger will calm, and you will find that your vision of the Devil will disappear. You should be with your mother until your soul finds peace.' Mary listened respectfully to the vicar but knew she would have to remain in the forest. Uppermost in her troubled mind, was the question posed by the festering wound she'd discovered on the colt's rump. It was only days after John's death and with the wound being close to the colt's branding, she'd almost missed it.

Hannah and Damian visited Mary as often as possible, never without food. 'You must come home, Mary. It's time we all lived as a family again.'

'This is my home, Mother.'

'You can't call this hovel a home. It's too small. It's a logger's hut.'

'It's my home, Mother. John and I were going to build a new home together. This is the forest where he died, and I will stay here until I'm ready.'

'I can't see how you are going to survive without a husband.'

'I have a promise of work from Margaret Atkinson when the felling is over. How do you survive, Mother?'

'The church provided when you were children, and I always had your Uncle Robert's help with the farm and Cousin Thomas.'

'Not for long from what I hear, and you no longer have Damian.'

'God will provide, Mary. It seems to me common sense that you should come home to live and work.'

'I know you mean well, Mother, but I have to stay here until the quota is finished. I may leave earlier if I feel it is time. It's lonely here and I must confess I'm fearful of the night.'

Hannah was at a loss and her eyes moist. 'I shall ask Thomas and Damian to keep you company at the weekends.'

'That would be nice, Mother, but I'll continue trimming the foliage for as long as I'm needed.'

'You are not needed. You are here under sufferance my girl. The Atkinsons feel sorry for you, and responsible, but for how long?'

'We shall see when the time comes, Mother.'

Mary concentrated on her work and welcomed her brother and cousin's visits. Every time Hannah called with food she would try and persuade her daughter to leave. But Mary was adamant. She imagined John was still with her. Without her memories, his absence would have been unbearable. The first week she hardly left her bed, imagining him beside her, remembering the last time they had made love, and afterwards, watching him as he slept, admiring the rippling muscles and stroking her palm over the rise and fall of his powerful chest. Mary could still feel her husband's presence and longed for him to hold her. She reached for her necklace and gripped the amulets in her fist. She raised them to her full lips and lovingly kissed the amber stone and silver ring. *No-one else will take your place, John. You will always be with me.*

Mary's nagging suspicion that John's death was no accident compelled her to stay within the woods. She immersed herself in the work but felt wasted, merely travelling through the motions of life. *Mother said that time will heal the wound. I wonder about that wisdom.* Mary worked alone most of the time, trimming branches while the loggers felled more timber. When she was with them, she felt uncomfortable and the feeling was reciprocal. Timothy told them Mary would only be working for a short time. They were to be patient and see her through her grieving.

The only sympathy coming to Mary was from James Pritt. Mary remembered that not long before the accident John told her that James wasn't to be trusted, and that she must be wary of him. He'd been a charcoal burner in Rusland, a closely-knit community that looked after their own, devious in their dealings with local farmers. Sacks of charcoal usually contained rubbish to make up the weight and having no alternative supplier, the locals were at their mercy. John should have pressed James further for the reason he had left steady and well-paid employment. He told Mary that James had been spreading dissatisfaction amongst the woodcutting team, and that he was ogling her too often for his own liking.

A month passed and as Mary's anger subsided, her thoughts became less cluttered. James had been given authority and Mary was under his supervision. She found herself studying the manner of the woodcutters more closely but became bored with the monotony of their work and endless chatter; until one day as they sat in a circle taking a lunch break while the bullock team cleared felled timber. She was distributing a jug of ale as the men unfolded bread, dried mutton, cheese and eggs from their rolls of cloth. She heard the clunk of a stone against the trunk of a nearby tree, and heard James laughing. She saw him loading another stone into his catapult and take aim at two ravens high in the branches. A picture flooded Mary's mind of Prince rearing as a stone hit his rump. There was no mistaking the suggestion of her thoughts and the confirmation of lingering doubts reignited her anger. She restrained herself, sensing the vision hovering, waiting for the door to open. *I have to control my anger.* She'd been resigned to the fact that her stay in the forest was over, that it was time to end her mourning and take up Timothy's offer. But after witnessing James' sadistic sense of humour, Mary had an instinct to stay and be patient. She was now convinced that John had been murdered.

James had taken an instant dislike to John, but he'd been desperate for employment. *Who does he think he is, prancing around on that fancy horse and giving his orders?* But although he was sullen and not used to taking orders, he was no killer. The mischief he'd caused wasn't intended to lead to John's death. The major had paid him aggravation money. *It was intended to be a joke; to laugh with the men at the boss's expense. I really did try to save him.* The tragedy was compounded by the hurt he saw in Mary's eyes. *I would like to console her, make love to her, but it's too soon.*

Mary decided that it couldn't be soon enough. She was taller than the average woman, lean and curvaceous, with an attractive high cheeked face and full lips. Her silky raven hair flowed over her shoulders, grown strong with the constant wielding of the axe. Her manly frame did little to mar her beauty. Much to her mother's annoyance, Mary had trained her hair long to curtain one side of her face. Her first thoughts were to hide the mark of the plague and to stop insulting comments, but as she grew tall her difference became an asset. There was an aura of mystery about Mary, a strangeness that made her desirable. She attracted many a furtive glance of lust from the woodcutters, yet they were hesitant to approach her. Shortly after James had taken over John's position, he began to boast of the widow being attracted to him. 'There's no mistaking her need. She lusts after me. She speaks to me with her eyes.'

But it was James' *own* need that Mary was working on. She leant close when pouring his drinks and once swept her hair aside to expose her scar. She brushed her cheek against his, and then looked down into his eyes for the reaction. James noticed the blotch left by the plague and turned his eyes away ever so slightly. *He's like all the others, but his needs will overcome his fear of the plague.*

James was drinking at the Black Bull in Coniston. It was late in the evening. He suddenly slapped down his tankard and stomped out claiming that he would be the first to bed the sullen widow. He was seen heading off in the direction of Monk Coniston, and that was the last his fellow workers ever saw of him. James never returned to work the next day or thereafter. Some say, the widow shamed him, and he left the district rather than face mockery from his fellow workers. Others speculated that Mary knew of James' mischief. They accused her of practising witchcraft and joked of her spiriting the unwelcome night visitor away. Hoping to quell the rumours she purposely stayed on at the hut until the quota was finished. But the rumours gained credence the longer she remained.

Damian's temptation

'Canna av a iuk a't body, Mathew? Canna touch it?'

'Not this time, Damian, and stop pestering me. It's not every day we lower a priest's body into the ground. You have to realise the importance of a priest's burial ritual.' *The lad's daft, not right in the head.*

Damian's jaw dropped and his lips pursed, shaping his long inquisitive face into a sulk. His grey protruding eyes focussed trancelike on his hands as they caressed the grain of the coffin's polished oak. His mind imagined the contents and he struggled to restrain the urge to slide back the lid. He'd never had this temptation before, but then, all the lids of the other caskets had been nailed down. He had overheard Vicar Braithwaite recounting old Francis' last words. 'Sixty-six is not a favourable age for a priest to die, Gabriel. If you order the lid of my coffin nailed down, as sure as the Devil exists, he'll haunt you for the rest of your life.'

Damian wondered if the priest really was in touch with the Devil. They were told to dig his grave much deeper than usual and his palms were still feeling the blistering pain from the pick and shovel. He'd been helping to dig holes and lower coffins into the ground for almost a whole year now, and he grieved that he still hadn't been allowed to help Mathew with the stiffs. Mathew was a streeker, the man responsible of preparing the dead for burial and he'd strict orders from the vicar to keep Damian at bay. He felt responsible for Hannah's son and told Mathew that Damian's mind was too fragile to be viewing freshly laid out bodies. The old streeker obeyed the vicar's orders as best he could, but there were times when he had no control. He was of the opinion that what the vicar didn't know couldn't grieve him.

Damian often peeked at Mathew through a crack in the church door, listening to him talking to the bodies as if they were still alive. He watched him paint colour into their faces, and sometimes Damian wondered if the bodies really were dead or that perhaps the old streeker was a little silly in the head. He'd once seen him stuffing something into a stiff's mouth and puffing out the cheeks. 'I think he was feeding him, Tommy.'

Damian chuckled as he remembered the time he'd looked in and been scared out of his wits. He hunched over with excitement and grabbed hold of his codpiece, a habit of which his mother despaired. It was after work on a moonlit winter night when he peeked through a crack of the door into the candle-lit room. He strained to hear Mathew as the light flickered on and off with the draft. 'Your family's gaan to be proud of you, Jane, rosy puffed cheeks and the like, just as you were in your youth.'

Damian felt hot breath, and a head resting on his shoulders and the hairs on the nape of his neck bristled cold with fear. He screamed out and banged on the door for help. Then his shoulder was gripped tight and Thomas' voice was pounding his eardrums. 'What do you think you're doing, Damian?'

'I was only having a look, Tommy.'

'We'll have to run for it.'

Mathew opened the door in time to catch a glimpse of the two boys, shook his head and chuckled. *I would recognise that gait anywhere.* The inseparable cousins flew through the mist of the graveyard and faded into the night. As usual, Damian's stride took well to the front and he slowed for Thomas' companionship. 'You were supposed to keep watch, Tommy. You near scared the shit out of me, creeping up so quiet.'

'That's nothing to what I felt standing on my own in the graveyard. I was scared stiff. I couldn't stand it any longer. I'm sure I saw a ghost.' Thomas refused to keep watch again and despite insistent begging, that was the last time they ever peeked in on Mathew.

Damian could faintly hear Mathew raving on, but his mind was elsewhere. He'd only asked if he could help him with a dead body. 'You are too young to be taught the skills of a streeker, Damian. You show too much curiosity about the dead and with your imagination you would be a nervous wreck in no time. You will have to be a few years older before I can teach you how to prepare the bodies. Be patient. Your time will come.'

Damian had almost blurted out that it wouldn't be the first time he'd handled a dead body, but he had to keep it a secret, and he liked secrets. He had made a pact with Thomas that fateful night on the Rusland track. He continued to plead with Mathew. 'It's me seventeenth birthday today, Mathew.'

'Well now isn't that a coincidence, it would have been the priest's birthday today. A pity he didn't live a few days longer and you could have shared a cake,' and as an afterthought he concocted a warning. 'They say it's sacrilege if you as much as look on the face of a priest when he's resting in his burial coffin. There'd be retribution, lad, so you'd best leave things as they are. The fact that it's your birthday is no excuse for me to stop shielding you from the face of death.'

Damian was agitated, his fingers tapping a frantic rhythm on the top of the coffin. 'Canna be a't bottom of grave when it's lowered, Mathew?'

The streeker shook his head, and then relented. 'Seeing as it's your birthday, lad, you can guide the box to its resting place.'

Damian's thin lips spread into a smile revealing a large gap in his upper teeth. His face lit up and he found it hard to contain his excitement. *They'll not be taking much notice, and I'll have a quick peek.*

Pouring rain drenched the mourners lining each side of the grave. The bearers carefully adjusted two ropes under the priest's coffin and eased it slowly over the grave. Damian was already at the bottom of the grave, squelching his clogs in a pool of muddy water, waiting impatiently for the service to end. He heard the vicar's final words 'commit him to the deep' and the sky above him darkened. When he saw the coffin lowering towards him, he breathed heavily in anticipation. His shaking hands stretched out to guide the coffin away from the sidewall but one of the ropes jammed on a tree root and the box tilted.

'Look out, Damian!'

The coffin slipped through the ropes, and as it crashed down in front of Damian the lid slid open. The young gravedigger stared at the open coffin in horror, then let go a terrible scream as the priest sat up. There was a deep terrifying moan as the corpse expelled a breath of putrid air before sinking back down into its box. That brief moment would remain etched on Damian's mind for the rest of his life. Seeing the priest's body move towards him and belch was frightening enough, but it didn't compare with the horror of being stared at with the rolled-up white of an eye in that eerie grave. His hands clawed for a grip on the muddy walls and he cried out as his feet desperately kicked away from the coffin. He grabbed hold of a proffered hand and hardly touched the sides as he shot to the surface. The congregation turned as one to witness the gravedigger's terrified flight, marvelling at his huge strides. Damian's legs flailed the air, feet splayed, and knees lifted to the horizontal as he fled downhill with a blood-curdling scream. 'It's the Dobbie man. Help me! The Dobbie man's cum fer me!' Damian was heading for home, hoping to find comfort in the arms of his mother.

Thomas often called in to see Aunt Hannah after school. On the day of Damian's birthday, he'd found the house empty and knew that his aunt would be out shepherding on the lower slopes. Thomas heard the pounding of feet down the path and went to investigate, but the door burst open before he could reach it. Damian stood on the threshold, wildly looking around. He was covered in mud from head to toe and frothing at the mouth. He slammed the door shut, pressed his back and open palms against the wood and exhaled short, heaving gasps of air. Then he lunged towards the table and dragged and pushed it hard against the door. Thomas stood bewildered in the middle of the room, trying to comprehend his cousin's actions. Then it occurred to him that it might be some kind of initiation ceremony for a seventeenth birthday. He wouldn't be surprised because the villagers had all kinds of superstitious beliefs. But when he took a second look at Damian's face, he realised that his cousin could be telling the truth. He was pushing hard against the tabletop, wild-eyed, and screaming. 'Where's Mam. I want me Mam.'

With Hannah out shepherding the flock, Thomas was the only person his cousin could turn to. Damian poured out his fears of the Dobbie man. He swore that he'd seen him in the depths of the earth. 'He stared at me with the whites of his eyes and then gave out with a terrible moan and breathed foul air all over me.'

'Was he like the ghost in the abbey ruins?'

'No! Tommy. This was different. He was more real.' Damian's voice quietened as he repeated himself. 'He was real. I think the Devil put the Dobbie man inside the priest's body.' His voice weakened, tapering off into a disturbing thought. *He was the Dobbie man for sure.* Damian gripped Thomas' shirt, his eyes boring into him like a madman.

Thomas was unnerved. He sensed evil in the room, and he wanted to leave. 'You weren't afraid of James Pritt.'

'That was different. He was really dead, and I hated him because he killed Mary's John.'

'Maybe the Dobbie man is James' ghost come back to haunt us.'

Thomas moved towards the door. 'Don't go, Tommy. Don't leave me alone.'

'I'll stay til yer mam's cum home, but only if yer promise to think of something else.' But Damian couldn't stop thinking of being trapped down the dark hole with the Dobbie man. He sat curled up in the corner, his arms wrapped around his legs, mumbling and staring at the ground. Thomas thought it strange his cousin had seen the Dobbie man in the daytime, but he was very convincing. He shivered, crossed his arms and hunched his shoulders.

There was no enthusiastic welcome for Hannah when she arrived, only a room draped in heavy silence and the air thick with tension, crowding the space between them. Her eyes went to Damian curled up in the corner and across to Thomas standing behind the table. 'Have you boys been fighting? Must I plough my way through this heavy silence?'

Thomas didn't know what to say. He looked at Damian curled up in the corner, shrugged his shoulders, and answered for them both. 'We haven't been fighting, Aunt Hannah, but Damian has something interesting to tell you. I'll be gaan home now.'

Hannah waited for his footsteps to fade away before she approached her son. 'Stand up, Damian, and stop blathering like a fool.'

'Jesus Christ, Mam, he's after me.'

'That's blasphemy. You must never use the Lord's name in vain. Now apologise before he strikes you down.'

'I'm sorry, Jesus.'

'That's better. Now tell me your troubles.'

'The Dobbie man was down in the dark of the grave and he marked me with his eyes.'

'I think you were imagining things, son. Come to Mam!'

She held her arms open and they hugged each other tight. 'I'm scared, Mam. He really was there.' Hannah patted her son's back affectionately. 'Take some deep breaths and calm down. We will talk to Vicar Braithwaite after Sunday service. I'm sure he will help us.'

That was Hannah's way. She always spoke to the church about family matters. When Mary was born with olive skin, Hannah's husband William had looked elsewhere for the father and for many years, life had become difficult for her. Only the common sense and wisdom of the parish priest had calmed William's doubts. Francis had taken William aside and explained that one of his wife's ancestors had been tainted with similar features so not to look unkindly on his neighbour, Joss Taylor. 'It's merely a hand me down from some past ancestor, William. How do you think Joss's father felt when his son popped out different from the rest of the dalesmen. The path to heaven may seem strange at times, William, but we must have faith and follow the ways of our Lord.' Thereafter, Hannah considered Reverend Francis a family friend and often spoke secretly to him of her worries. *It was providence that my only son, Damian, should help to bury old Francis.*

Damian never again mentioned his fear of the Dobbie man to Thomas. He locked it away in his mind in the same place he secreted that tragic night in the forest. Thomas was convinced that Damian would never tell anyone of that night, especially his sister, Cousin Mary. *Surely, she must have guessed they had been in the woods.* There was a wall of secrecy separating the three cousins and they avoided speaking about the disappearance of James Rigge.

The day had begun as an innocent adventure and transformed into a waking nightmare. Mary said she had a plan to catch a pig and that weekend Damian helped dig a hole for her. He enthusiastically planted wooden stakes in the bottom to spear the pig and stop it from escaping. They disguised the hole with branches and leaves and Damian said he would set the trap with a live chicken during the week.

The following weekend Mary told Hannah not to send the boys over. But the cousins had other ideas. There was no way they were going to miss out on a pig hunt. They told Hannah and Robert they were going to fish on the banks of Esthwaite Water. Thomas loved fishing and had his father's blessing when it came to winning a trout from the gentry. That evening he cast his net amongst the shallows in the shade of overhanging tree branches then went to sit on the bank with Damian. He knew there'd be little chance of a catch as it was too early in the day. There was a cool evening breeze. They chatted, threw skimmers and watched the ripples skating across the surface of the water. Later in the evening the breeze would die down and insects would start hovering over the lake's surface. The sun would begin to dip, and the fish would stir as the full moon stamped its impression on the skyline. But for the time being it was pleasant to sit, chat, and dream. 'There'll be a full moon out tonight Damian and lots of bright stars if the clouds stay away.'

'How do you know it'll be a full moon?'

'I can already see its shape in the sky. Look over there!'

Damian scanned the sky with his mouth open, spotted the pale outline and nodded his agreement. 'Mam told me the stars are God's heavenly light shining through holes in the sky.'

'That's what they told us when we were little. You can tell they're real when you stare at them. If I stare for a long time, I feel like I'm next to them. Mr Clayton said they go on forever and ever, deep into the heavens.'

'How far do they go, Tommy?'

'I told you, forever and ever.'

'How far is ever?'

'No-one knows. Not even Mr Clayton. He said our minds aren't big enough to understand the size of God's kingdom.'

'Yours too, Tommy?

Damian slapped his thigh and laughed out loud at his own joke. Thomas smirked and pointed to a lone bright star just above the horizon. 'Me fadder said that star is Mam.'

'Uh! Do you believe him?'

'No! But I like to think it is, and that she's looking down and smiling with a twinkle in her eyes, protecting us. I can remember her best that way.'

'I remember Aunty Aggie. She was beautiful. She kissed me once on me forehead.' Damian's smile widened. Thomas stared at the exposed gap in his cousin's top teeth, and he suddenly knew God's purpose. *It's a sign that something is missing.* Then he remembered the other thing that was missing and the clout across the head that he copped from Aunt Hannah. She'd caught him and Mary fondling Damian's ballbag. They were only helping him search for his missing ball. 'But I've only got one ball, Mam, and Tommy's got two.'

'Come to mother,' she'd said, and as he rested his head on her breast, she patted him on the shoulders in her usual consoling way.

'Not to bother, son. The other one will drop shortly. The good Lord is hanging onto it for a while, no doubt for reasons of his own.' But Thomas thought otherwise. *The other ball still hasn't dropped but he keeps groping his codpiece, hoping.*

'We'll surprise Mary later tonight, Damian. I wonder why she still wants to live in the logger's hut. It must be lonely and spooky.'

'That's why we need to keep her company. Mam says she's in shock, like in a trance, and she'd better not stay on her own much longer, or the loneliness might drive her mad.'

'I think she's mad already, Damian.'

'No, she's not!' Damian might be slow in thinking, but he was quick when it came to defend his sister. 'You shouldn't say bad things about her, Tommy. God will punish you.'

'Well! I wouldn't like to stay in the hut on my own with her. She boils up things like a witch.'

'That's because...'

'Shush!'

Thomas had sensed they were not alone, and his neck went cold. He smelt a horse and as it snorted, both boys shot around simultaneously. Damian's eyes popped with fright and he took off, first one way, and then the other. His slow brain might be contentious, but it needed little urging to decide on the safety of the woods. Damian had inherited the powerful legs of his grandfather, a champion fell-runner of whom it was said, over a pint of strong ale at the Red Lion, had once beaten the hounds to the fox. Thomas ran for his life, falling behind, his jelly-legs buckling with the effort, losing connection with his brain. He looked down at them paddling air, pulling his body towards the trees.

Silas Crouch sat back in his saddle and wheezed with laughter. He could hardly contain himself as he wheeled his horse and watched the boys disappear into the woods. He cupped his hands to his mouth and bellowed. 'I know who you are. You can expect the constable at your door tomorrow.' The gamekeeper convulsed with sadistic laughter. He wheeled his mount away, torso bouncing back and forth in the saddle, one hand gripping the reins and the other supporting his stomach's aching blubber. Frightening the life out of the boys had livened up his tedious evening patrol. Silas didn't have a clue about the identity of the two boys, but he'd done his best to give them a sleepless night.

When they felt it safe to leave the sanctuary of the woods it was late evening and the moon was higher and casting long shadows. They decided it was a shorter distance to Mary's and continued on with their original plan. They were not supposed to be there, especially so late in the evening, so they approached the hut cautiously. There was a dim light showing from around the door. So as not to frighten Mary, they called out quietly.

'Mary! It's me. Damian.' He rapped his knuckles against the wood, but there was no answer.

'Mary! It's me. Tommy.'

There was still no answer. They thumped with clenched fists, and as the door creaked open the draft blew out the candles. Thomas felt nervous. There was a glow from the hearth, and he could hear the cauldron simmering, but there was an unusual frosty chill in the air. Damian was stumbling around in the dark. He made a taper and lit the candles from the hot coals. 'There's something wrong, Tommy. Where is she?'

Maybe she's out collecting plants Damian. I've heard that witches pick them under a full moon.'

'Mary's not a witch. Mary's not a witch! How many times have I got to tell you?'

'Then, where is she? Perhaps she has a lover.'

Damian's hand reached up the wall and unhooked an axe. He feigned a downward blow. 'If she has, I'll kill him.'

He let out a loud guffaw. His eyes brightened and showed his excitement. 'I'll bet she's caught a pig in the trap.'

'Put the axe down, Damian, you scare me when you get too excited.' Something registered with Thomas. Prince wasn't in the stable. 'That could mean she's gone to Aunt Hannah's, and that would be just our luck. Your mam will wonder where *we* are.'

'I don't think she's gone home, Tommy.'

'Me neither. And I'm sure she's a witch. That doesn't smell like food in the pot.'

'So, what if it isn't? Anyway, witches are old and ugly and Mary's too beautiful to be a witch.'

Thomas shrugged. 'I know a story about an ugly old witch.'

'Is it scary, Tommy?'

'It could be I suppose, in this dark hut. Do you want me to tell you?'

Damian hesitated before sitting down, eyes popping in antici-pation. Thomas stood in his story-telling pose, hands clasped and rubbing together as his eyes scoured the shadows of the candlelit room. Then he dramatically cleared his throat before beginning. 'It was in the days of the monastery, when a monk was stationed at Bank Ground in Monk Coniston. The old witch lived in a hut just like this one close to Yewdale Beck on Coniston. She came from a strange family in the village and sold her soul to the Devil. That's why she could change herself into a hare or some other animal anytime she wanted.'

'How do you sell your soul to the Devil?'

'He calls on you. Stop interrupting me, Damian. There was a time when the hounds were closing on the fox, and a hare suddenly appeared in front of them, standing on its hind legs, tempting them. The hounds took off after the hare and lost the scent of the fox. Then the hare disappeared, and the hounds just ran around in circles howling. The next time there was a hunt, a black bitch hound joined in and when the hare appeared, she was the first to follow. The pack chased the hare straight into the village where the witch's family lived. The black bitch caught up and snatched at the leg of the hare just as it lunged through an open window. The witch's strange family were inside the cottage and they chanted out, "Switch Granny switch. Here comes t' black bitch. Switch granny run for your life."'

'Why were they strange, Tommy?'

Thomas had to think about that one. *He's spoiling my story again.* 'They were. They were ... white ... er ... albino. Their skin was as white as snow, and their hair was just as white. They were skinny as skeletons and their eyes were red like the Devil's.'

'That's really scary, Tommy.'

'When the hunters arrived, the black bitch was outside howling with the rest of the pack. The hunters had lost the fox and there was no hare to be seen. They went inside the hut and asked the strange family of its whereabouts. It was then that they saw the old witch sitting in the middle of them gripping a wounded leg.'

Damian's hands were clasped between his folded knees, rocking his body, his face alight with wonder. 'The witch was really the hare, Tommy.' He looked nervously over his shoulder. 'Her family scares me.'

'I said you might be scared, and I'm not finished. When the witch grew old, she didn't want to pay her dues to the Devil, so she visited the monk of the Abbey of Saint Mary. She asked forgiveness of her sins and he told her that when the Devil called for his payment, she must pray to Saint Herbert the Patron Saint of the fell country. When the Devil discovered the treachery, he called to claim the witch's soul.'

'What does he look like, Tommy?'

Thomas raised his hands like claws and snarled with crunched up eyes. 'He has horns and his lower body had a tail and hooves like a goat.'

'Is it true?'

'Yes! It's true! The old witch leapt out of the window and fled screaming the Lord's Prayer. The Devil chased her towards Bannockstone Bridge, but Saint Herbert heard her prayers. Just as the Devil was about to lay his claws on the witch, his red-hot hoof melted into a large river stone on the bottom of the beck. The cloven hoof stuck fast, and before the Devil could remove it, the witch had fled.'

Damian sat spellbound, mouth open. 'Did he catch her again, Tommy?'

'Yes! I'm sure he did. All witches have to pay with their soul. And just remember, the next time you see a hare it could be Mary.'

'Huh! She's not the Devil's witch, Tommy.' He sniffed the simmering pot and nervously looked around the cobwebbed timber walls. 'I don't like Mary staying here. It's too spooky.'

'No wonder your sister is mad. I don't think she's coming back tonight. We will have to sleep here on our own.'

'Not me, Tommy. I'm not staying. I'm scared. Let's go and find the pig trap.'

Thomas was halfway down the path when a cold shaft of air swirled past him, tearing leaves from the trees. The dark shadows grew colder and the chill in the air caused him to shiver. The door of the hut slammed shut and when he turned to Damian he was no longer there. He heard banging on the inside of the door and the latch rattling, and Damian shouting in a muffled voice. 'I'm locked in, Tommy, and I'm scared.'

Thomas walked back, lifted the latch easily, and opened the door. 'No, you're *not* locked in.' His cousin was standing in the doorway shivering and holding the axe. 'What are you doing, Damian?'

'The door slammed on me, and the room went freezing cold, and then I saw evil things.'

'Well it's not cold now is it?'

Damian looked around him and shrugged. 'Don't lock me in again, Tommy. I don't like it here anymore.'

'I didn't lock you in. Anyway, it's your sister's house. If you're scared and see evil things, then she must be a witch.'

Thomas expected his cousin to splutter a denial again, but when he saw the look on Damian's face, he felt sorry for him. His shoulders were hunched up and his head drooping. *He really is scared.* 'I don't like it here either, Damian. You had better show the way to the pig trap, that's if you're not too scared.'

'I'm not scared anymore. Let's go and see if we've caught a pig.'

Thomas couldn't agree more. He was feeling cold and after all, the pig trap was the reason for them coming in the first place. He followed behind his cousin with a feeling of guilt. *I shouldn't scare him so much.*

Damian was deep in thought and never spoke until they entered the woods. 'What colour are the Devil's eyes, Tommy?'

'They are red, like blazing hot coals.'

'How do you know they are red?'

'Because everyone says they are red.'

Damian went quiet, his mind troubled, searching for an answer. A full moon flashed shadows between the trees and the forest veiled an eerie silence. The only audible sounds were of their own heavy breathing, the echo of clogs on the hardened path and the occasional hoot of an owl. Damian suddenly stopped and turned to face his cousin, wild eyed and pleading. 'I saw two bright green eyes in the hut, Tommy. They were evil. I don't want to go there again.'

'Calm down, Damian. It must have been Mary's cat.'

'Mary hasn't got a cat.'

Thomas thought about it and couldn't remember seeing one.

'It must have been a devil cat then. Witches have them.'

'Mary's not a witch and you told me that devils have red eyes.'

'Maybe it's a she-devil.'

Thomas tried to humour his cousin, attempting to settle his own growing fears. But Damian was insistent. 'The eyes were shining in a corner and they were evil, Tommy. They were glowing like candles in the dark. The eyes were evil. I was scared, and the room was freezing cold.'

Thomas shrugged. 'Mary could have turned into a black cat and that's why she's not there. I didn't see any eyes, Damian, but if you did, then Mary could really be doing witchcraft.'

And for once Damian never argued for his sister. His enthusiasm had waned, and he led the way to please his cousin. 'It's not far now, Tommy.'

Twigs snapped ahead of them and Thomas held Damian back. 'That didn't sound like a pig. I don't think we should go any further.' Damian brushed his cousin's hand from his shoulder, eyes glowing with excitement.

They heard the whinny of a horse and the pounding of hooves. Damian was breathing heavy, jogging at an agitated pace. Thomas wanted to turn back but followed close behind. *I can't leave him alone. When Damian is this excited, he's capable of anything.*

The plague

Hannah Inman, her daughter, Mary, and her young son, Damian, survived the plague, but Hannah lost her husband, William. It was only because of her strong will during those bad times that she'd been able to keep the Johnsons and the Inmans together. Both families lived on adjoining farms. Robert looked after the cattle and helped Hannah with her quota of Herdwick sheep. He oversaw their grazing on the fells and sheared them when the time came. The sheep were easily distinguishable by their ear markings but sorting the family brands amongst others roaming the slopes was time consuming. The families continued to live apart, but Hannah took responsibility for Robert's young son Thomas as if he was her own. Thomas had since regarded her as a mother and her family as his own. He never quite understood why his mother had died of the plague whilst many others had been left untouched. Both his mother and Uncle William had died of the plague and yet those closest to them; his father and his father's sister Aunt Hannah had survived. *Could the reason be they were of the same blood?* Both his cousins had caught the plague and recovered. Damian carried a dark scar on his forehead and Mary a similar patch on one cheek. Their shared handicap created a close bond.

Mary understood her brother's slow mind more than anyone and thanked God for the survival of her own. Hannah had told the children that there were people who carried the plague and showed no signs of illness. Most people knew the story of the notorious Dalton plague. The parish clerk had made a meticulous entry in the church register. It was the most damaging of all plagues and had raged throughout the parish before the rule of Cromwell and during the reign of King Charles the first. How could anyone be so evil, as to knowingly carry the plague from London, and spread the curse as they travelled north? The story was hard to believe, but all who lived in the parish knew the story to be true. The carrier of the plague, a man named Lancaster, was a pedlar of medicine, preying on the victims of his carriage of death. Lancaster and his associate, Noble, had travelled through many towns from London to Dalton, carrying garments and precious jewels infected by plague. After the plague was unleashed on Dalton, its bridges and roads were sealed day and night. They were attended by sentinels armed with clubs, to keep the people quarantined. Many families left their homes. The vicar fled the holy thresholds of the church in fear, and the parish clerk departed stealthily in the calm of night.

Lancaster and Noble, who held no fear of death or God, committed the dead to the grave. There were as many as nine deaths in one night and the evil pair carried the bodies on a ladder and tipped them into the sepulchre, as the body of a deceased sailor would be tipped into the sea. Lancaster appealed to the people not to fear the plague. To some he sold a dark medicine that destroyed their reasoning. The poison made them so delirious that they beat their heads against doorposts or walls and perished. Others he advised to drink his vile poisons from bloody cups, so they lost their senses and all use of their faculties.

For many weeks, the doors of the church were closed and the funeral bells silent. The all-consuming plague raged for seven months and over half the population, some three hundred and sixty citizens were placed beneath the earth. People purified their houses with frankincense, bitumen, myrrh, and sulphur, and burnt their garments and infected bedding. Solemn assurances were given to the purifiers that all the infected goods had been surrendered. But at the height of the plague, the two peddlers of death had been busy, privately collecting infected rugs and many sheets, garments, gowns and shirts, concealing them in a granary amongst heaps of corn.

The Justice of the Peace cast the evil duo into a dark, populated prison that had only light from the chink in the door. On Lancaster's release the women of the township vigilantly watched all the exit roads and gates and apprehended the bearer of the plague. They took their revenge, assaulting Lancaster with stones and opening a wound in his head. They continued their assault with crooked staffs until his blood flowed freely. The cunning murderer lay feigning death and evaded the vengeance of the women. Immoral and lucky he fled the district, no doubt to spread his evil elsewhere.

Thomas had heard the story many times, and every other year there seemed to be a plague such as the one that had reduced his own family. He learned that God holds no preference and the wealthiest of families in the parish suffer the same fate as the poor.

Mary confers with Damian

Gabriel Braithwaite was feeling guilty. He had done his best for Hannah in the past and he now believed he should show some responsibility for Damian. He called Hannah and her son aside after the Sunday service. 'Your boy shows little initiative, but he's obedient, and he will take on any task as long as it's explained carefully. We must help him overcome his fear of the Dobbie man. His obsession with the Devil is hard to understand. I will try to explain to him the ways of the dead.'

'He is what he is, Vicar. I wish you luck. Nothing we can say will change him.'

The vicar placed a kindly arm around Damian's shoulders and walked him towards the graveyard. 'I want you to report for work tomorrow. Your mother is a tireless worker on the farm, but she needs the extra income that you take home.'

Gabriel was leading Damian towards Francis' grave, but the young gravedigger became aware of the path they were taking and drew back. 'I can't go near the graves, Vicar. You know I saw the Dobbie man, and he marked me with his evil-eye.'

Vicar Braithwaite smiled condescendingly. 'That was my good friend, Francis Watterson. He is no more the Devil than I. Now please walk between your mother and me. If you can persuade yourself to place flowers on my good friend's mound, it will bring ever lasting peace to your soul.'

But the closer the trio approached the grave, the more Damian struggled. The vicar tightened his grip on the young lad's elbow until they stood in front of Francis' headstone. The terrified gravedigger was wedged between his elders, choking the life out of an armful of flowers, with urine trickling down his leg. 'Now before we say a prayer, I must explain to you what you saw down there.'

'I saw the Dobbie man!' he trembled.

'No lad, you saw the body of our dear departed priest. I spoke with Mathew. He's been laying bodies out since he was a young man and he told me that sometimes when a person dies, they lay at rest with a pocket of air trapped within their body. When Francis' coffin crashed to the bottom of the grave, the air must have dislodged and escaped, causing a belch and an awful stink. It's a simple truth, so help me God. I'm prepared to swear on the *Holy Bible* if it would give you relief. Now, let us pray.'

Damian vaguely heard the vicar's distant rambling voice, his eyes transfixed on Francis' resting place. A swirling wind lifted dust from the mound, and he imagined the earth trembling over the grave. Sensing vibrations under the soles of his clogs, his fear overcame him, and his mind shouted out to him *run ... run*. He threw the flowers high into the air, and with hands over ears and legs swinging in an ungainly gait, he distanced himself before the scattered flowers landed on the grave. Damian ran until his long legs would take him no further. He was heading towards Mary's hut in the woods in the hope of finding peace of mind and kindly understanding.

Damian saw more of his sister than Hannah realised, and he knew more of Mary's habits than he was inclined to tell her. Before John's death, Damian was a frequent visitor to the manor stables and John encouraged him in the grooming of horses. He'd developed an affinity with Prince that led to John teaching both Mary and Thomas to ride. He often called at the hut, and more often than not, he was in trouble. He never spoke to his sister about John's death, and he'd sworn to Thomas he would never tell about James. *It is best I don't visit with Tommy. He can't keep a secret like me.* His fear of the hut had diminished with each visit until he came to believe that he'd imagined the evil green eyes. But he was still afraid in the dark and would never stay on his own. The first visit had been the worst. Mary had to coax him inside. She was in a nervous state and desperate for someone to talk to. Damian arrived from the churchyard gasping for air and he hammered on Mary's door with his fists, screaming, 'The Dobbie man's come back.' He startled the tethered Prince and the horse's frightened whinny and stomping hooves coincided with him crashing through the door. Damian skidded into the room wild-eyed and frothing at the mouth. Mary was standing behind the table, terrified and holding an axe for her defence. Concerned for his sanity, she hooked the axe back onto the wall and held up her palm, face out to him. 'Calm down, Damian.'

She saw that her brother was bleeding from his run through the woods and in great need of consoling. She always listened patiently to her brother's ranting, but this time he was in a crazed state and gabbling a load of nonsense. She placed her forefinger against her lips, suggesting he be silent whilst she gathered her thoughts. 'Sit yourself down brother and rest.' Mary poured Damian a drink of her freshly brewed ale and as she watched him gulp it down, he stared up at her in loving admiration. Damian worshipped his sister and looked on her as a shining light. When anyone teased him about her, he'd try to shut out the jibes. He would stamp his feet, cup his ears, and squeeze tight his codfish grey eyes. He was slightly taller than his sister, as lithe as she was but more powerful around the shoulders. His blond hair was shaped with a basin cut which sat over a short brow that was out of proportion to his long, inquisitive face. The parish church had never employed a more energetic, strong and willing gravedigger. 'Tell me why you're so excited, Damian.'

'They tried to make me pray and place flowers over the Dobbie man's hiding place, so I ran away.'

'Who are you talking about, Damian?'

'Vicar Braithwaite pushed and shoved me there and mother helped him.'

'They should be ashamed of themselves. Where is your Dobbie man and why did they take you to his hiding place?' Damian related his terrifying experience and Mary listened compassionately, concerned that her brother's mind may be slipping. 'What a terrible thing to happen, Damian. I know all about the Dobbie man. You should have come to me when you first laid your eyes on him.'

'He laid his eyes on *me,* Mary.'

'That's true. So now we must think of a way to prevent him from haunting you. Why, even mother has her Dobbie stone for protection and branches from the Rowan tree at her door.'

'And the vicar has a Rowan tree in his graveyard.'

'That's true. Even the people of the cloth understand that the powers of the Rowan tree slow down the witches and guard against black magic and ill-luck. We must think on this carefully because you've been especially marked. Few have set eyes on the Dobbie man and lived to tell the tale. Many have seen his ghost in the middle of the night, but always without witness. To have seen his body in the daytime is rare indeed. You saw him on your seventeenth birthday and Mathew said the priest was sixty-six years old on that same day. I wonder can that be a good omen or a bad one. The old priest's body was obviously possessed poor soul, and the vicar is right. He needs to pray over his resting place.' Mary's voice was calming. Damian enjoyed being cared for and being told exactly what to do. His sister was always good at that. 'We will deal with the Dobbie man as we would deal with the Devil himself.'

'I think the old priest knew the Devil.'

'No doubt he did, and that would explain why his body is possessed.'

'People say you have become a witch. Is it true?'

'No! I have learnt to extract goodness from herbs of the forest. Some may think that strange, but there is no evil in it.'

Damian looked across at the pot simmering away on the tripod in the hearth. 'Can you brew a poison, Mary?'

His sister looked angry and hissed. 'You've just drank one.'

Damian stared at Mary in disbelief and let his tankard slip to the floor. He knew by now that his sister was capable of anything when she was angered. *She must have doped James as well.* He grabbed at his throat with both hands. His jaw dropped and his tongue flopped out. One hand slid down to grip his stomach and a horrible gurgling noise came from his throat. He crashed to the earth in a foetal position, rolling around moaning and groaning with agony etched all over his twisted face.

Mary shook her head, amused at her brother's antics. 'Your tongue's flopping out, Damian. You look more like a hound dog than old Jasper. Get up off the floor. I was only fooling!'

The screwed-up tension in his face slowly unwound as he absorbed the reality. His lip curled into a grin and bared the gap between his upper teeth. He sucked a long wheezing breath of air through his teeth and expelled a deep staccato laugh. 'It was a joke, Mary?' She smiled, sat down at the table and waited for him to calm down. *That will teach him to keep his nose out.*

She should have known better. 'The villagers say you made James Pritt disappear.'

'I've heard it mentioned. What do *you* think, Damian?'

He looked at Mary with a smile of contentment. 'I think you are too beautiful to be a witch.'

'Thank you, Damian. You are not as silly as you look.'

'Do I look silly?'

'No, you don't. You know it's one of mother's favourite sayings, and it's not really truthful.'

'Then why does she say it?'

'It's just a tease. Personally, I think you are very crafty and a step ahead of most people.'

Damian's face glowed with pride. 'Did you catch a wild pig in the trap I dug?'

It wasn't only the surprise of the question that bothered her. It was also the look of anticipation on his face, the familiar dumb, jaw-dropping inquisitive look. *He's teasing me back.* Mary had to think carefully before answering. 'I want to forget about that pig trap. I was bored and it was a stupid idea, really stupid. So stupid I went to check it out and when I finally found the place the hole had already been filled. It must have been the woodcutters but I'm not asking any questions.'

Her thoughts drifted towards her visit to Ada, the Tarn How witch.

She'd called to purchase the Dobbie stone for Damian, but foremost in her mind was poison. She enquired about a cure for an irritable cough and had to listen carefully. The dialect was the same as her own, but Ada's speech was rambling and rapid. 'Yeh mun set a teaspoon wi' a gaily sizeable mouth an intul't pour in't brandy while t' mouth o't spoon's gaily weel covered ower wi't, then yeh mun put in two girt spoons o' honey, an' drink it fast as yeh can and git te bed. Yer cahld will be gaan when yer wacken up!' Ada recognised a symbol of the yew tree on her amulet and asked to examine it. The conversation conveniently led to her knowledge of the yew tree and the poisonous effects of its leaves and fruit. With a little flattery she was persuaded to divulge other ingredients: quince juice, spices, and nightshade.

'Do you use the deadly nightshade from the old abbey?'

'I wouldn't give that weed to a wild dog, lass. Not on its own that is. I would add something a little more potent, more persuasive in taste.' Mary thought she was being casual with her enquiries, but the old witch sensed her deviousness and gave out a warning. 'Don't meddle with potions that you know nothing about, lass, for if it's other than a wild dog that tortures your soul, you will surely be heading for the gallows.'

Mary grew angry whenever she thought of James Pritt, but to even think of killing anyone was against her very nature. *Why did I enquire about poisons?* Something was driving her against her will, and she sensed there would be no peace until she obeyed. The poison had been prepared carefully but it had failed. *Did I mishear the old witch? Did I miss an ingredient?* James had been neither awake nor dead. Nothing had gone as she'd planned. The grave was freshly dug and waiting, but James wouldn't die. He'd been like a zombie, dead but still alive, and that was when she first thought of leading him into the forest to wander aimlessly and hopefully die.

The next morning, when Timothy Atkinson stood in the doorway, she was almost fainting, gripping the door to steady herself, the world falling in on her. *He knows something! They've found James.* She heard Timothy talking through the fog that was clouding her mind. 'Excuse me, Timothy?'

'I said: dost thou know anything about the whereabouts of James? The woodcutters told me he left the inn with the intention of calling on thee.' Mary's mind started to clear and for the first time she noticed the statesman was holding a sorry-looking

Prince by the reins. He saw the mystified look on Mary's face. 'The horse was found on the Rusland trail and handed over to me. It was heading this way. Now, where is James and why art thou at home instead of working with the woodcutters?'

Her mind was in a whirl, but as she looked again at the dishevelled Prince an explanation of the past night formulated. 'I saw James last night. A most frightening and unwelcome sight he was, banging on my door in the middle of the night. He was demanding that I let him in. I shouted for him to go away and sober up, but he became angry and started kicking at the door. I took down my axe from the wall and stood in the middle of the room, waiting for him to break open the door. I can honestly tell you I was terrified. Then he went quiet for a while, and I was relieved to hear him galloping off with Prince.'

'That's a side of him I hadn't seen before, Mary. He seemed such a well-balanced young man. A little mischievous perhaps but there seemed no hint of aggression.'

'It's the strong ale. Some of them can't handle too much.'

'Then I must apologise for placing thee in his path, but I warned thee that the work wasn't suitable for a young woman. I can understand thine absence from work today, but if thou had informed me that Prince had been stolen it would have put paid to all of the rumours.'

'I was too upset. I could only think of my late husband, wishing he'd been there to protect me.'

'I understand. Thou hast had a lot of weight on thy young shoulders lately. The horse looks to be in distress. He needs to be cared for, and so dost thee, Mary. I don't think it is advisable for thee to stay here without a husband.'

Mary was barely listening, considering her alibi. *Is it believable?* It was difficult to wipe the previous night from her thoughts. James' advances, and her denial of him. *That must have been devastating to his ego.* She smiled inwardly, and grimaced. *It's a pity the poison didn't kill him.*

Damian's voice diverted her thoughts. 'You're dreaming again, Mary.' She smiled wistfully.

Damian's eyes rolled to the sky. 'Could you find the pig trap again?' A simple smile lit up his face, and his shoulders quivered with his wheezing staccato laugh.

She knew the signs. *He's got a secret.* 'I told you, the hole was filled in by someone and I'm not sure I could find it again. Are you hiding something from me?'

Damian's face curled into his silly smile. 'No!'

They understood each other perfectly. 'I told you, I've lost interest. Why are you so curious?'

'I thought you wanted to catch a pig.'

'Well I did, but now I don't, so just forget about it. A hole like that could cause an accident.'

Damian snorted and put a hand over his mouth, trying to choke back his amusement. 'What kind of accident?'

She had a feeling her brother was teasing her. She was becoming angry and had vowed never to let her anger get the better of her again. *I have to be in control.* 'Somebody could have fallen into those stupid spikes you placed in the bottom.'

'The spikes were to trap and kill the pig.'

There was a short silence as they stared at each other. Damian was sad when his sister upset. 'If we caught a pig, would we be fined for poaching?'

'We'd be fined or thrown into jail for killing a deer or a pig or fishing the lake, but only if we're caught.'

Damian wore his wide-open smile as he remembered their escape from the gamekeeper. That was another secret he would keep. He clasped his hands together between his knees and rocked his body gently up and down with silent pleasure. 'Can I dig another hole for you?'

Mary was desperate to change the subject. 'Perhaps another time, but I'm going to ask another favour of you later. I have been thinking of a way to stop the Dobbie man from haunting you, and it's a solution that even our superstitious mother might not be aware of.'

Damian grew closer to devour the great secret. 'You must sever the feet of ravens and bury them in the mound of earth above the Dobbie man's hiding place on the night of a full moon.'

Damian listened eagerly, his eyes wide open, then gradually narrowing into slits as the enormity of the task seeped into his brain. 'You want me to visit the Dobbie man's grave on a moonlit night? I can't do it. Not even in the daytime.'

'Yes, you can, Damian. You must be brave. You will have me at your side if you wish, and you can think I'm a witch, if it makes you feel any better, but you mustn't mention that, or the use of the ravens' feet, to anyone else. We must keep the Dobbie man in his place. If he continues to haunt you, we will scatter more ravens' feet, but it will have to be on the night of a full moon and it would be even more potent if it were on the anniversary of your birthday and that of the priest's.'

'Do you have any ravens' feet Mary?'

She raised her menacing clawed hands towards him and growled, and then laughed at her sadistic sense of humour. 'I have no ravens' feet, Damian. You must collect them yourself and I suggest you hunt with Cousin Thomas. He adds to his father's income by hunting ravens for their heads. Never reveal the purpose of the feet though and never speak of our fight against the Dobbie man.'

'What if I use something else?'

'Yes, brother?

'Er ... nothing.' *Like a human hand.* He was tempted to say but bit his lower lip instead.

'Only ravens' feet will work. Now promise me you will tell no-one.'

Damian nodded acceptance of their pact and was overcome with a feeling of peace. They had suffered many hardships together and this was a secret that could only strengthen their bond. Mary withdrew a pale-green stone necklace from a box at the side of her bed. She kissed the stone and placed it over Damian's head. His eyes lit up as he fondled it against his chest. 'Is it mine, Mary?'

'It's your birthday gift. Do you know what it is?'

'It's a Dobbie stone.'

'It's a gift that I hope you will treasure, for it will protect you from evil. You must wear it always.'

'It's beautiful. Now we both have an amulet. I will wear it like you do.'

'I have stopped wearing mine outside of the house. Thomas said that his teacher Phynius is obsessed with the past and that if he sets his eyes on the ring, he will want to claim it. The vicar told Phynius that John had the ring and he turned up at the funeral. Talk about possessive. He must be as bad as Thomas. Do you remember when Thomas ran off with my silver ring? No sooner had I placed it down on that rock than it was gone.'

'He was only teasing you, Mary.'

'Maybe so, but he often takes things he finds lying around, and I call that stealing.'

'He was only borrowing it.'

'He always says he's only borrowing. The trouble is he never gives things back.'

'He doesn't steal anything from me, Mary.'

'That's because you've got nothing to steal. Do you remember the teacher from the grammar school calling at Uncle Robert's house for the old learning book? The one Thomas showed to John and me.'

'That was a silly book, Mary. There was only one drawing.'

'None the less, that drawing still gives me nightmares. The teacher said he had enough worries about not being paid for half a year without having to worry about reclaiming valuable schoolbooks. He said he'd been waiting for a governor to arrive from Oxford to pay his wages. The man was having difficulty collecting rents from the school properties in Yorkshire. It wasn't long after Phynius called to claim the book that Uncle Robert took Thomas away from the school. He said he needed Thomas on the farm, but mother said it was more likely that the teacher made him leave, because of the stealing. She said it was just as well because he was beginning to talk like the gentry and Uncle Robert blamed it on the book reading.'

'Thomas has got a nice *Bible,* Mary. He keeps it in his father's trunk, and he swore on the *Bible* that it was a special leaving gift from the school and Uncle Robert said it was true.'

'Like father, like son, if you ask me. Thomas may tell you it's a *Bible,* but it's a *Book of Psalms* and it has the Ten Commandments written at the front. He even showed me one of the psalms we sing in church.'

'Mam said Thomas might be going to live away soon, and I think I'll miss him because he tells me lots of interesting things.'

'I can see you lonely when Thomas leaves, but I'm sure we will see him from time to time.'

'He won't come and see you anymore, Mary. He's scared of you.'

'That's silly. How can he be scared of me? We grew up together and we're cousins.'

'He says you're not the same anymore, that there's something different about you.'

'Are you scared of me?'

Damian hesitated. 'You do scare me sometimes, like the time you nearly strangled me.' Damian's hands circled his neck as he spoke.

'I'm sorry, Damian. I was upset at the time and Thomas is just as much to blame. He shouldn't have told me those stories about the ring. When he showed me and John the old book, he showed us the same markings that are on my amulet. The teacher told him they were ancient symbols and held magical and mysterious meanings. Thomas told us the true meaning of the symbols. John was wearing the ring at the time and he said he didn't believe a word of it.'

'Do you believe him, Mary?'

'Yes, I do. Thomas doesn't tell lies. But John told me not to be taken in by some silly story, and I must admit that Thomas has a vivid imagination. When he showed me that drawing of the Viking with the patch over his eye, he said the warrior had probably had his eye dug out with a knife. He gets carried away with his own enthusiasm and really makes you believe. He scared me and now I have nightmares about an ancient one-eyed warrior. And you tell me that Thomas is scared of me?'

'I believe your silver ring has magical powers. I think that's why the teacher wants it.'

'Someone else told me that the silver ring has a great presence.

'Who is someone else?'

'You're too curious, brother. Let us say that you have your secrets, and I have mine. And by the way, I need to ask you a favour. Can I entrust you with something that I treasure almost as much as you?'

'You can trust me with your life, Mary. I'll do anything for you. Nobody will hurt you anymore. If anyone else ever hurts you, I'd ... I'd ...'

'I know, I know, but this is *really* special. I feel at peace now that James is no longer in the district. Now that John's death has somehow been avenged, I feel it's time for me to leave the forest.' Damian gave Mary a strange look that made her curious 'Is it something I said, Damian?'

'No, Mary, no!'

She rapidly changed tack. 'Prince has been fretting of late and I want you to look after him. You must love him as John loved him. He was bred to race and needs room to gallop and plenty of lush grass to graze on. Take Prince to Uncle Robert and ask him to help you look after him. You will need to groom him daily. The brush stimulates his circulation and keeps his coat shiny. Don't overgraze him in summer but make sure you feed him oats and hay each evening. And keep him warm. I have a woollen duvet to strap around him every night.'

'You're not leaving me are you, Mary? Are you going very far?'

'I'm going to work for Timothy. It's not the end of the world, and you must promise to visit me there. He called on me the day after James failed to turn up for work. He was holding Prince by the reins and had the gall to suggest I had entertained the man. I put him right that I was a mourning widow and he'd no right to even consider that I would behave in such a manner. He said that nevertheless the men were unsettled, and it would be best for everyone if I started work in the big house. He said he would speak to his wife. He's such a nice man I couldn't refuse, but I asked him if I could stay until my mind was settled.'

'Did you really see James that night, Mary?' Damian's head slipped sideways to his shoulder as he asked the question, staring deliberately and causing his sister to colour.

Mary hesitated whilst she gathered the story she had told Timothy; a story that would satisfy her brother. 'Well, I didn't exactly see him. Like I told Timothy, he was hammering his fists on my door and I ignored him of course; you know I didn't like him. Then I heard him gallop away with Prince. Somebody found Prince running wild in the forest the next day, but they couldn't find the rider. They gave him to Timothy, and he thought that Prince may have thrown James off and he could be lying injured somewhere. But nobody has found him and he hasn't returned to his old work in Rusland.'

Damian stared open mouthed throughout and Mary felt uncomfortable. 'You are staring like you don't believe me.'

Damian shrugged and grinned. 'Timothy is an important man, Mary. He's a Quaker like Uncle Robert.'

Mary shook her head. 'Uncle Robert's no more a Quaker than you, or I. Just because he attends a few meetings doesn't make him a Quaker. Mother told me that all he's after is an apprenticeship for Thomas. He pestered the school in the same way and had Timothy Atkinson speak for Thomas' entry. But it's because of Timothy's religious beliefs that I must leave Prince in your care. He'd agreed to stable Prince until I stupidly told him of my intention to enter him in a wagering race at Newmarket. I was only thinking of honouring John's ambition, but the Quakers will not allow any association with gambling.'

'Where is Newmarket?'

'A long way south of here; close to Cambridge. Prince was born in Newmarket and the king races his horses there. We will race Prince when he is older and stronger. For the present, your reward will be to groom, ride, and exercise him. I promise you if he is looked after, you will never be troubled by the Dobbie man again. Believe me when I say that an Arabian black horse is almost as good as ravens' feet for protection against the Dobbie man.'

'I heard some of the woodcutters calling him the Prince of Darkness.'

'Why would they call him that?'

'They say he helped to kill John. Perhaps there's some truth in the symbols.'

Mary's face paled with shock, her voice trembling as she rebuked her brother. 'That's an evil name to call our beautiful horse. It's the name for Satan and you must never use it again. Prince is more likely to be a messenger of our good Lord.' There was a moment of silence between them and her voice was trembling when she spoke again. 'What do *you* know of John's death? It was an accident.'

'I don't think so, and neither does Tommy.'

'You will land in trouble telling lies.'

Damian shrugged his shoulders. 'Uncle Robert will help me with Prince. I'm never going to work in the graveyard again, so I'll have lots of time.'

'You will have to work sometime to help mother with the rent and you'd best hurry back or she'll worry about you.'

'I usually tell her I'm staying with you when I plan to go missing.'

'What do you mean, when you plan to go missing?'

'I don't mean anything. I mean, it's only when I'm with you that I go missing.'

She remembered their mother's questioning the day after Timothy called. 'I hope those two boys were no trouble for you the other night Mary. I told them to stay away like you asked but you know what they are like.'

The night had been complicated enough without making excuses for two wayward boys, so she shrugged and lied. 'No more than usual, Mother. It was nice to have company.'

She questioned Damian suspiciously. Where were you really, the night James disappeared?'

'You won't tell Mam, will you?'

'No! I won't. So long as you weren't misbehaving. Mam said you and Thomas came home looking as if you'd never slept. What must she think of me?'

'We were poaching fish and I can prove it, because we nearly got caught by Silas Crouch the gamekeeper.'

'Where were you for the rest of the night?'

'We were nowhere special. I feel better now. Do you think Mam and the vicar will be looking for me?'

'I doubt it. She is probably preparing a meal for you right now, and the vicar will be at home eating with his family. Will you do me one more favour?'

Mary slowly unhooked a key from her belt and offered it to Damian. 'I had the smithy shape a spare one for the cottage. I figured we could use it in the future.' Damian nodded and took the offered key, giving Mary his secretive smile. 'Can you hide it for me? I hear you and Thomas have a special place.'

'How do you know?'

'Mam told me. She knows everything that's going on. You should guard your secrets more carefully.'

'I will have to tell Tommy about the key.'

'Yes! You will and don't tell him whose lock it fits.'

Damian's eyes shifted nervously to the corner of the room.

'Have you ever had a cat?'

The question came out of nowhere, and Mary found it hard to understand her brother's reasoning. 'You know I've never had cat. Why do you ask?'

'Tommy says all witches have black cats. I know you're not a witch, but I thought I would ask so I can tell him you're not a witch.'

Mary blinked and shook her head to rid her mind of this new nonsense, not realising there was more to come. 'Are you scared at night, Mary?'

'Sometimes I am. I once thought of having a dog like Jasper, but Prince will warn me of any danger. But I leave tomorrow, so you won't have to worry about me anymore.'

'Have you ever seen green eyes in the hut?'

Mary laughed nervously. 'You're being really silly now, and I think it's time you left for home. You can call tomorrow and we will ride Prince to my new employment with Timothy. Then you can take Prince back to Uncle Robert's. Remember what I said: a black Arabian horse is almost as good as ravens' feet for warding off the Dobbie man.'

A change of stables

John's dream for Prince was ambitious and it would never have come to fruition if fate hadn't intervened in the guise of Hollis. The major's trusted servant realised he needed another assistant in the stables. The old stableman he'd taken on to replace John Rigge was limited in his skills and the other two young lads were irresponsible. His private opinion was that the major had made a grave error in dismissing John Rigge. He had overheard Penelope raving at the major, that the man would still be alive if he hadn't dismissed him. He discussed his problem with Vicar Braithwaite. 'The major grows more demanding as he ages. Just an extra hand for the stables and grounds would help me. Somebody that's familiar with horses, obedient and not too bright would be a Godsend.'

The vicar recommended Damian, and convinced Hollis there was no better person in the district for obedience and discretion. The major baulked at employing Damian but when he discovered the young man was in charge of the black thoroughbred his enthusiasm became overwhelming. The major stomped around with excitement when Hollis informed him. To the vicar's surprise and with Hannah's permission Damian was employed immediately. Hannah was pleased with her son's new employment and gave him strict instructions on being polite. 'You must always address him as Major, as he seems to prefer, and no matter the situation, you must never be tempted to call him a shit-bag, like someone else we both know in the family.'

Damian stared cod-faced in amazement. 'You swore, Mam.'

Hannah shook her head and growled with frustration. 'That man would make a saint swear, and I'm warning you not to think you can do the same.'

Damian was being shown around the stables by Hollis when the major arrived and waved him over with a forefinger. 'Come over here boy.' He paused and looked disdainfully at his new stable hand. 'I expect you to bring Prince to the stables where he can be cared for. We have expertise here my boy and you will be doing the beast a favour. You will be taught to groom and ride him in the proper manner.'

'He's not me own horse to bring, Major, and I can already groom and ride him in the proper manner.'

'You may call me sir.'

'No, I can't, Major. My mother taught me that we don't call anyone sir that doesn't deserve it. Can I call you Rowan?' Damian backed away as the major spluttered and his face reddened. 'Mam's got a rowan tree to scare the witches away. She said that's why you're called Rowan, but she was only kidding.' He thought, *shit-head,* and smiled expectantly.

'You've got a button missing boy, otherwise I would whip you. Why didn't Hollis tell me you are as stubborn as you are daft? I've already spoken to your mother. She agreed that your Uncle Robert shows no interest in the horse and not using your sister would be killing two birds with the one stone.'

Damian chuckled. He had never understood the expression of his mother's, but it now struck as being funny. 'Maybe she can help me and Tommy to kill the ravens.'

Damian's wheezing stuttering laugh grew uncontrollable, and the major left him to the sombre- faced Hollis. 'We will visit your uncle and collect the horse. You can sleep next door to Prince in the stables.'

'I'm sleeping at home like I always do, and just wait till Mary hears about you stealing Prince.'

When Hollis arrived at Robert's home to take charge of Prince, the ex-champion wrestler grew angry and lost all reason. Rushing at the major's man, he grabbed him in a wrestling hold, spun him around until he was dizzy and threw him to the ground. Robert towered over Hollis roaring victoriously, arms held high and fists punching the air. Thomas and Damian stood behind him quivering with excitement. They cheered as the major's stable-master picked himself up and strode towards his horse wobbly legged, head held high. Hollis didn't consider any loss of pride at being brushed off by such a giant. 'There are other means than brute force. I'll be back.'

Sure enough, Hollis returned the next day with the constable and three sidesmen to take charge of Prince. When Mary heard about the incident, she asked Timothy for advice. He threatened to call in the district judge so the major agreed to a meeting. Hannah and Vicar Braithwaite attended as witnesses. It was a tense gathering of residents with opposed views on vocations. Timothy rued his participation and the consequent moral ambiguities. Convening with gamblers contravened the beliefs of the Friends so he felt compelled to lie. *I feel it is my duty to protect the rights of this helpless young woman, yet it is best the Friends never hear of my attendance.*

Vicar Braithwaite felt equally uncomfortable about associating with a Quaker. *I must request that the major refrains from mentioning this meeting to the bishop.*

The major however relished the opportunity. 'Prime horseflesh is wasting away in the care of your uncle, young woman, and you must realise that it's as good as, if not better, than any other thoroughbred in the country. The horse was nurtured from a colt, in my own stables, and for that reason alone it should be legally mine. You've refused my bid to buy the horse and you are not offering any alternative that might satisfy us both. If you knew the depth of our experience in handling thoroughbreds, you wouldn't even hesitate.'

Reverend Braithwaite couldn't help goading the major. 'I had no idea you'd been associated with training horses?'

The major was abrupt. 'It is no concern of yours, Gabriel, and the less you know the better.'

Mary looked around her. She felt out of her depth and fighting a losing battle. Timothy had told her the horse was still legally hers, but she knew in her heart, that in her care, the horse would become old before John's dream could eventuate. *If I sell him I'll have no say in the matter.*

'Will you promise me that Prince will be trained to enter the king's race at Newmarket?'

'Yes, yes, of course I will, woman. Isn't that the reason I have him here?'

'And that Damian will remain in your employ to care for Prince?'

'He is in my employ for that sole reason.' *Not for much longer though if I have my way with the stupid idiot.*

'And you will allow him to ride Prince in all his races?'

The major hesitated. 'That will depend on the progress of his training.' *Not on my life will he put my wagers at risk.*

'Then I agree for you to continue stabling Prince until he competes in the king's race. I feel it will be in all of our interests, but I still wish to retain ownership.'

Her manner irritated the major and he spoke quickly and impatiently. 'Am I really standing here negotiating with a domestic? Let's get this dispensed with. We agree that I will collect the purse of any win to cover my expenses and that I have the permission to set him to stud. Hollis will keep you informed of race engagements, and any wager on the colt will be of your own doing.' He jutted his chin forward, cutting off the conversation abruptly. Hannah swore he clicked his heels and stood more erect than was usual.

Timothy Atkinson could hardly believe that he was sitting in the company of these sinners, witnessing references to their gambling traits. Vicar Braithwaite had no idea there was going to be a Quaker at the meeting and thought that his own presence verged on the hypocritical. Here he was, sitting around the same table with a past major in Cromwell's army, a statesman Quaker and two women domestics discussing the legality of a horse's wellbeing. Looking around him he found it hard to believe that he'd been coerced into the presence of such a motley gathering. *Not even a church congregation is comparable.*

Hannah accosted him on the way out. 'I hope you have some influence over the major, Vicar, for there are not many people in the parish who would trust him with their mongrel dog.'

'That is not very compassionate of you.'

'I have no time for that kind of talk. The truth is the truth and we all know of his shady dealings and his influence with the tradespeople. Locals prefer Quaker tradesmen when it comes to buying goods. At least we know they are honest with their pricing and not out to steal the last crumb from our mouths.'

'I did not come here for a lecture my good woman. I came at your request that I might witness a right of law to one of my honest parishioners.'

'Honesty is the word, Vicar, and I thank you gratefully for your presence, but you must beware of the influence of the major. When the village people see the church clerk balancing his books at the wrestling, they think you may be in collusion with the Devil himself.'

'God strike me dead if that were true. I hope you have no such evil thoughts, and that my parishioners realise that the major, as a magistrate is aligned with the law of the land and is a hard man to oppose, particularly by a lowly vicar who relies on him for a wage.'

'Forgive me, Vicar, for I'm a selfish woman, with only the interests of my daughter in mind.'

Mary's dream: summer 1664

Mary settled quickly and happily into her new employment. She was more amicable of late and pleased that Damian was employed away from the graveyard. Mary always thought deeply when she was spinning wool. It was a form of relaxation with the work she most enjoyed. Lately she'd been contemplating her vision. She felt her Man of Death was lurking deep within her, waiting to be disturbed by anger. The more she tried to forget the face, the stronger the vision became. She recalled her fight with Damian, when she noted the hands and the clothing of the upper body for the first time. The hand grasping at his open throat had a silver ring on the middle finger. His shoulder-clothing was similar to the drawing in the schoolteacher's book. She recalled he was holding a round shield and spear and in the sea behind him bobbed a strange ship with curled bows. *My vision is of the past.* Mary's hand went to her amulet. She grasped John's amber stone and her grandmother's silver finger-ring. *The ring in the vision is identical, but it was probably a style of the times.*

Mary's grandmother had bequeathed her the silver ring. Her grandmother before her had worn it as an amulet and told her how she thought it could be the cause of her visions. 'Your ancestor endured visions, Mary.'

'What visions, Granny?

'Only she knows and perhaps it was just as well. The poor woman was said to have led a troubled and tragic life. They say she turned crazy after her husband disappeared.'

'Where did he go, Granny?'

'No-one ever found out. It was said that he was working in the woods and never returned. Granny often visited the woods looking for him, and the more she looked the crazier she became. The story handed down with the ring was that her skin colour and hair were darker than that of the dales people, similar to your own. It's a trait in the family that we've never understood. Before I gift you the silver ring, you must vow as I once did, that you will never part with it. The ring has been with our family for longer than anyone can remember and must be passed on to your eldest grandchild.'

As she was spinning, Mary also thought of the runes on the silver ring remembering the words of the old witch when she showed her the symbols. The witch knew the symbol of the yew tree and gave Mary a warning. 'A yew tree regenerates life, but it also carries a poison. I've no knowledge of the other symbols my child, but the ring warms to the touch and it carries an ominous presence. The black horse you ride prowls its borders. Beware of brewing the potions you ask about, lest they begin calling *you* a witch.'

She reacted angrily to the witch's words. 'The silver ring is a gift of love from my late grandmother and I'll be brewing no evil poisons, old woman.' She stomped out the doorway with horrible cackling laughter ringing in her ears. A shiver ran down her spine with the memory of the visit.

She dragged her mind to the conversation with her grandmother. 'What if I don't have a child, Granny?'

She recalled her grandmother looking down at her sternly, with all knowing eyes, speaking with the wisdom of a lifetime as only a grandmother can. 'I can already see you with child and as sure as the good Lord looks over us, that same child will produce you a grandchild.'

'Will I be a good mother?'

'Cradle the child in your left arm and your heartbeat will give it comfort. As the child grows it will teach you of its needs.' Mary's hand slipped down to circle her stomach. She had every faith in her grandmother and smiled with the memory of her prudence.

Later that evening, after the Atkinson family had retired to their beds, Mary went to the main room and sat warming herself in the glow of the hearth's embers, deliriously happy at being pregnant and feeling safe and at home. Her body relaxed in the warmth, and she thought of her and John's baby, curled secure in her womb. *I pray to God that our child be strong.*

Two bright green dots appeared amongst the embers; ethereal eyes, flirting with the flames, invading, enticing, reflecting their image. She followed their hypnotic path as they hovered and bounced from coal to coal, like bees gathering pollen. Her eyelids flickered and closed on a gentle smile. She was being drawn into darkness, her imagination soaring. She was drowning in the depths of a most wonderful dream, her long raven-like hair streaming in the wind, her body straight in the saddle. She was galloping a beautiful black stallion that could only be Prince. They were as one, travelling through a misty sky over a mysterious white land. The outline of a long timber house materialised below them, and suddenly she was inside observing the inhabitants. A lithe and extremely tall handsome young man was walking towards a roaring log fire. Ale splashed from his tankard and dripped from a silver ring on his middle finger. His beard was trimmed short and blond hair hung to his shoulders. His clothing was strangely familiar. The huge fire flared in the middle of the room throwing flames and smoke towards an outlet in the centre of the timber roof. He lingered in front of the fire and gazed intensely through the roaring flames. A longbow and sheath of arrows were propped against the back wall, but his eyes were focussed higher, towards a mounted sword and scabbard that sparkled with each flicker of light. He scanned the length of the sword continually, his eyes illuminating pride, his mouth curled with pleasure. He squatted in front of the fire with a smile of contentment and a twinkle in his eyes. He called to a young woman tidying the table and waved her over to join him. She crossed the floor eagerly and as the dancing firelight banished shadows from her face, Mary caught her breath, overwhelmed with a feeling of love, companionship and belonging. She was gazing at a beautiful young woman with long lustrous raven-coloured hair and an olive complexion similar to her own. The woman was tall, and as slim and as lithe as her husband. She crouched down beside him and playfully pushed him away. He folded an arm around her waist and drew her close, and they began to laugh together.

The laughter down the corridor grew louder as the domestics entered the room. 'You're up early this morning, Mary.'

She snapped from her dream with tears of happiness rolling down her cheeks, the feeling of John's arms around her, and a sensation of burning inside her clenched fist. She released her grip and stared in wonder at the imprint of the runes on the pads of her palm. She hunched, tucked her hands beneath her armpits and shivered with the cold. The domestics were staring, and she felt self-conscious. She made a show of raking the ashes from the hearth and placing them aside for cleaning the pots then kneeled down to breathe more life into the embers. She vigorously fanned the coals with her apron and sighed with relief as the fresh timbers crackled and burst into flame. 'I suppose its best I make an impression, me being new and all.'

The emotion had left her, and the voice sounded hollow as it resounded in the large room. The domestics smiled knowingly and went about their tasks. Mary tried again and again to relive the dream, to sink into the past just once more, hoping that the feeling of belonging would somehow return, and that she might relive the happiness. But the magical presence was gone. She remembered the silver ring on the tall man's finger. It was like the one on the Man of Death and the one she wore as an amulet. She remembered the bow against the wall. *Was he an archer, like in the story of the rune that Thomas told me? I'm becoming obsessed. Perhaps grandmother's ancestor wasn't so crazy after all.*

Mary gave birth to her son in the autumn. He was christened John, and Hannah shared the care for the baby when her daughter returned to work at the Atkinson manor. The parish adapted to the aggravations of Major Rathbone and settled into a conciliatory rhythm that carried them safely into the yuletide. Thomas divided his workload between two industries; helping his father on the farm, and stockpiling iron ore at the Coniston forge. Behind his easy-going smile was a mind troubled by the night in Grizedale forest. He couldn't rid himself of the image of his cousin Damian, viciously kicking James' body, driving it further onto the stakes. Then putting his ear to the chest of the corpse and shouting out, 'He's still dead Tommy.' The words often echoed in his head. He's still dead Tommy, he's still dead.' And why was his cousin collecting all those ravens' feet? He often saw baby John at Aunt Hannah's, but he tried to avoid Mary whenever possible. She hadn't been the same since John's death. Damian had said he would do anything to protect his sister. *Why did I have to help him?* Damian was working for Major Rathbone under sufferance due to Mary's agreement. The major was busy establishing his twenty-four sidesmen, plotting against the Quakers, and forming an alliance with the formidable magistrate, Colonel Kirkby. In between times of office the major was more interested in breeding horses than the impossible task of training them for Mary's hypothetical race.

PART III

Ravenglass, on the Cumberland coast: January 1665

'Take in the sai...ls. Prepare the ancho...r.' Arthur Grasty's bellowing, rasping voice floated through the still night air and carried to the small group of men waiting patiently on the shoreline. They straightened on their haunches, alerted by the urgency of the penetrating voice. Seamen swarmed the *Charlotte*'s masts. Halyards screamed through their blocks as the ship's sails were rolled and secured to the yards. Grasty cast a cautious eye towards the captain's cabin. He had left Julius Laing snoring in a drunken stupor with a full bottle of brandy at his side. He was reassured that his preparations were adequate.

Shadowed by a pale winter moon, the *Charlotte*'s ghostly skeleton whispered through the cold grey sea; rippling the surface of the water as it glided with the flood tide into a harbour speckled with small fishing boats. The crewless vessels bounced in the brigantine's wake as the first mate dispensed orders to drop anchor. A thud of iron echoed against the ship's hull, and then a splash of water as the heavy metal guillotined the sea. The anchor spiralled down into the throat of the ocean; a hook spliced to a line trawling the seabed for tenure and shuddering as it bit into the shelf. The securing line tensioned, spraying seawater high into the air, and the ship's timbers groaned under the strain as the loss of momentum veered the brigantine slowly leeward. The ship rolled gently in the wake of the tide, wavelets slapping against her hull, until she finally settled with her bow facing the open sea.

'Ship secured sir...rr!' The voice emanated from a short stocky man, standing with the anchor party at the windlass. Edward Bone had followed Grasty's line of promotion. He was now the *Charlotte*'s boatswain, in charge of its crew and equipment.

The wooden hull echoed the sequence to the shoreline. Against the backdrop of a full moon and a sky flooded with stars, four nightriders stood silhouetted against the mainland. They were wrapped in leathers and heavy woollen clothing, insulating them against the biting cold of the North Sea wind. They waited patiently, stamping their riding boots into the ground, rubbing their gloved hands together to circulate the warmth in their bodies. Their leader, a tall, heavily built man, stood facing the sea with his arms folded over his chest, his legs stretched wide apart. Thick dark hair bunched out from under his three-cornered navy hat framing a scar running the full length of his cheekbone. His steely eyes never wavered as they focussed intently on the *Charlotte* rocking gently at her anchorage. He clasped his hands above his head, stretched his body to its full height and inhaled the cold night air. A smile of satisfaction creased his face. He'd never so much as boarded a ship but he loved the salty taste and smell of the sea. He lingered in his stance and held his breath, savouring the moment before lowering his arms. Edwin Sutton was readying for action. He smiled knowingly as two boats were lowered over the side, and quickly filled with sealed contraband. He watched them push clear of the ship, and when he heard oars squealing in their rowlocks he nodded and grunted with a deep sense of satisfaction. The seaport had been a hive of commercial activity before the silting of the harbour. Upon losing its trade, the port of Ravenglass had become a mere stepping-stone on the way to and from the policed port of Whitehaven. Avoiding customs and their levied duties, was a cultivated habit of many a northbound commissioned cargo ship. Edwin waved in the watch then signalled his nightriders to harness the bullocks to the wagons and prepare the packhorses. Bales of wool and boxes of clay smoking pipes lay on the ground, to be exchanged for casks of brandy, wine, boxes of tobacco and rolls of silk. They would have to move quickly to conceal their cargo before dawn. Distribution to the inns and manors of the surrounding districts would be a slow and cautious operation.

Major Rathbone holds court: January 1665

The major stood in front of the roaring fire savouring his third glass of after-dinner brandy. He was receiving Rufus, who had returned from his year-long exile in Cambridge. Rufus and his father were of the same average height and both had flapping ears that protruded at right angle to their faces, but there the resemblances ended. Rufus was a handsome man on first appearance with broad, slightly rounded shoulders, dark eyes under black heavy brows and fashionable shoulder-length hair. His full lips needed to shape a smile more often to set a character line around the smooth-skinned cheeks. But such markers would have given a lie to his true nature. The major had a craggy, potted face, partly hidden by a moustache that flowed, unbroken, into his sideburns and led to a head of straight, thinning, blond hair. His wife, Penelope, was always telling him that nowadays, periwigs were the fashion in London. But he was of the opinion that wigs should be for women. Father and son had never been close and on his many tours of duty, the major had left their son's upbringing entirely to his wife Penelope. Rufus was outlining yet another unfortunate predicament he'd brought home with him. 'If I'm to be honest with you father. I feel I can't marry the woman.'

'Now listen here, Rufus!' The major paused, grimacing, his eyes closed, thinking it was enough to turn the brandy sour. The name still jarred on him when he uttered it, even after all these years. He had a suspicion that Penelope had named him after her kin merely to defy him. He wasn't able to attend his son's christening but heard that the priest had to choke back hysterics when he pronounced the boy's middle name. Algernon! For God's sake, the poor boy never had a chance. He'd confronted Penny of course. 'Why didn't you name him after me?'

'I wanted a strong first name, so I chose my father's and the middle name to honour my father's brother. Uncle Algernon is an ageing, kind and wealthy bachelor with a considerable estate.'

The major had never complimented his wife on her cunning. On the contrary he often complained. 'I think, Penelope, that it was God's will that I should take control of the manor and suffer isolation and insolence, just so I can protect and further this ailing population.' He remembered his long-suffering wife attempting to demean him. 'The manor is in my name, Rowan, and I can always have it leased or sold.' *I soon put that notion out of her head.* 'I feel it is my duty to stay and provide for these honest people Penny. We will speak no more of it.'

The major's attention returned to Rufus. His son was standing in front of him with a hopeful, pleading look in his eyes and the major answered his son whilst standing upright with the air of one familiar with administering authority. His drunkenness caused him to splash brandy as he waved his glass to emphasise every phrase. 'I think, Rufus, that you have little alternative. The girl is pregnant, is she not?'

'That is most certain father. Her mother informed me, but the fact remains that she is ugly.'

'I can't see that having anything to do with the situation. If she is good enough to sleep with, she is good enough to marry.

Do you look at the mantle-piece when you're poking the fire?'

Rufus couldn't see what his situation had to do with the hearth. He didn't want the topic changed and was desperate for a quick solution. He stared into the embers, hunched and uncomfortable. 'I don't know what you mean, Father. I'm not interested in poking fires. Can't we send her away somewhere?'

The major hadn't realised his twenty-year old son could be so naive. He knew the young woman in question and agreed she was no beauty. Her eagle nose reminded him more of a dalesman but her figure was as desirable as any he'd seen. Eleanor was also two years older, but her family was sociably attractive. Her father, Squire Cornelius Holmes, had earned his title from being the largest landholder in his district. But the major had heard whispers of a scandal in the family, of financial failure and loss of estate. *I shall have to investigate further.* For the time being he would make his wayward son's life even more difficult. 'You will have to marry the woman! There's no other way out for you. I would have you commissioned into the king's Coldstream Guards if I had the money to waste. Go find your mother and arrange for the poor girl's family to visit. Tell her there's an engagement in the wind.'

'But, Father, I was coerced into staying while her parents were away. I'm sure they were in collusion with their own daughter. I'll not marry her!'

'Then your allowance is stopped until you see reason. On your way out tell Vicar Braithwaite I'm ready to see him. He's started fretting again over the increasing number of tradespeople in the district that are embracing Quakerism. He's worried that the disease could spread to the statesmen. We can't accept the Quakers' refusal to pay tithes. They fail to recognise the legitimacy of our government. Those infernal people even have a nerve to call themselves the Society of Friends and display attitudes similar to that of Cromwell's Puritanism. We can't afford to lose too many benefactors of our church. It's in our favour that there is only one, landholder statesmen, practising their religion. There are far too many parishioners giving in to the beliefs of the Quakers and it is worrying that they are so defiant of authority. They show no respect to rank and set a bad example to the community. It is time they were dissuaded from their beliefs and made to suffer.'

Rufus was half in and half out of the doorway, lingering, loving his father's vitriolic outburst. 'Those dammed statesmen are just as stubborn as the Quakers and it is only because of their freehold tenure. It's time the law of landholdings was changed in these parts to equal that of our southern counties. In the past, the statesmen even had the arrogance to name their holdings after their own families; such as Dixon ground, Sawrey ground, and Rogers ground. Is that decent I ask you? I also learned they were brought to heel by the monasteries for expanding their boundaries illegally. It strikes me that they believe they are a law unto themselves.' The major looked at his son in the doorway. 'Didn't I just ask you to leave and call in the vicar?'

Major Rathbone had been in possession of the manor for no more than a year and had made his presence felt from the first day. The rumour that he'd been associated with Oliver Cromwell's cavalry during his rule as Lord Protector of the Commonwealth was now considered fact. That he was a member of the Parliamentary Army and had been granted a free pardon under the Restoration, was never mentioned by the major. In fact, his manner of speaking implied he was certainly not, and never had been a Puritan. He went to great pains to show his allegiance to King Charles II and the Anglican Church by speaking openly of his hatred of Puritans. The major further distanced himself from Puritan morality openly encouraging cockfighting, wrestling, and his favourite sport, horseracing. He even indulged himself in collecting wagers from the poor in the community, a practice that didn't sit too well with Vicar Braithwaite, who was the usual recipient of his outbursts.

Lizzie entered the room and refilled the major's drink. 'Willer be owt else major?' Lizzie was looking back over her shoulder and holding up a tray of glasses. The major stared at her for a moment with glazed eyes, struggling with the speed and rolling together of the dialect. Then his eyes focussed on Lizzie's wriggling buttocks and his sexual desire took over. He impulsively leaned forward and grabbed hold of one of her bouncing cheeks. Lizzie half-heartedly tried to wriggle out of his firm grip. 'Careful sir or I'll drop the glasses.'

'If you do, there'll be a forfeit to pay my girl.' His moustache wriggled around his nose as he attempted a stuttered wink.

The maid smiled and choked back a surging laugh, then paused before squeezing past Vicar Braithwaite on her way out. The vicar couldn't help but notice the lecherous look on the major's face. 'Still wrestling with the Devil are we, Major?' The vicar might never have spoken. The major was staring as if spellbound past the vicar and down the corridor at the wriggling bottom of the fast disappearing Lizzie. He uttered a low groan of sexual yearning and then his hand shot down to grasp the sudden pain in his beloved.

'Are you in pain, or is it the Devil's payment?'

'It is merely a stitch vicar. It comes and goes. Perhaps Penelope's right and I should visit the London doctor.' He remembered the last time he'd used the bedpan in front of her. *It was like pissing needles and the bloodied water was frightening.*

Her comments hadn't helped the situation. 'I hope you haven't been a naughty boy and caught the pox. You're not coming near me again until you've seen a doctor.'

The thought of the operation turned him cold. He shook his head with irritation at the memory and turned his attention to the vicar's problem: the dwindling of his flock. 'Perhaps if you pepped up your sermons with more reality you would have a better attendance and less of the congregation would fall asleep on the pews.'

'You obviously think you could do better, Major.' The vicar might never have spoken as the major carried on with his thoughts. 'I still have difficulty understanding the kitchen help Gabriel.'

The vicar perked at this familiarity and braved a reply. 'I'm sure the domestics realise your problem. I've observed them speaking much more clearly and slowly when they address you, Rowan.'

The major was glaring at the vicar and withdrew the glass of brandy he was about to begrudgingly hand over. 'It's *Major* to you Gabriel.'

The vicar failed to hide his disappointment. He had always felt at ease addressing his congregation by their Christian names. It was the manner of the district and between statesman, tradesman or shepherd, there was never a doffed hat or a spoken sir unless it was respectfully earned. Some locals even hedged at a Mr or Mrs. A full year of residence had failed to have any effect on the major.

He's as stubborn as the statesmen he's always complaining about. The vicar shrugged his shoulders and thought to try another tack. 'Then if its titles that we're purporting *Major,* I prefer *Vicar,* or perhaps even *Reverend*?'

Before the major could reply, the vicar attempted to further retrieve his pride. He took a deep breath, and bravely added some strength to his request. 'And I don't like you using the church-warden's clerk to balance your books at the cock-fights; or the horse races or the wrestling bouts. It's little wonder to me that the Quakers grow daily in numbers when the associates of the church set such poor standards.' The vicar was wasting his breath.

'Now, now, Gabriel, calm down. Anyone else would think you had Quaker leanings, but we all have our problems, don't we? It's like I said before: you should pep up your sermons a little. My most pressing problem is trying to understand the twang of these locals. I can understand the French language much better. Perhaps we should import English-speaking persons from further south.'

'I would strongly advise you against taking that path, Major. We are a small community here and the people rely on each other for support. There would be many disruptions to your supplies and...'

'They show no respect to me as it is, Vicar. No respect at all. And I hear as many as twenty have already departed your house of the Lord for the house of the Friends. Do you realise they call our church the steeple-house. Who do they think they are? If the problem becomes any worse, the tithes I'm collecting for you will hardly be enough to cover yours and the bishop's expenses, let alone church repairs.'

'That's the main reason I requested a talk with you, Major, and before I forget my manners, that was an excellent dinner. Gladys and I thoroughly enjoyed the pheasant.' The thirsty vicar made a show of clearing his throat before continuing, and appearing absent-minded, held out his hand to relieve the major of the proffered brandy glass. 'George Fox is said to be back in the district and still persists in touring with his preacher friends. He boasts of his valiant sixty preachers roaming the country who, like himself, have no fear of serving a prison sentence. He's been released less than a week and they say he still has the aroma of the Scarborough Castle dungeons about him.'

'Well then, more is the pity, Gabriel, that he won't be staying with his Margaret Fell, unless of course, he wants to join her in prison. That woman is more of a menace than Fox himself and her from a line of the gentry. I ask you: how can the authorities allow her to publish whilst she's still serving her sentence? And she's advocating equality for women and the right to speak in church. I'll lay odds her departed husband, the old Judge Fell, is turning in his grave. She lost her immunity from persecution when he died so she can now justly serve her sentence for failing to take the Oath of Allegiance.'

'She has all the strength of Fox and more major; true soul mates by anyone's reckoning. The danger lies in her persuasive powers and influential friends. You must remember that shortly after her husband's death she visited London and had the audacity to challenge the king to put into practice his promise of religious toleration.'

'Fortunately for us it didn't work, Gabriel.'

'Evidently not, Major, but she *did* make King Charles II embarrassed enough for him to release four thousand of her kind from prison. Four-thousand Quakers released into the world! Whatever was our good king thinking? He must have known that the Fell family were Puritans and supported the parliamentarians during the Civil War. I find it hard to believe that you were on the same side major, and that now you appear to be sworn enemies. The Lord has strange ways.'

'There is nothing strange about it at all. Like my old commander George Monck, I was only carrying out orders when I fought for Cromwell. After Cromwell's death Monck was knighted for restoring the king to the throne. He was made Master of the Horse in the king's household, given large tracts of land in New England and bestowed the title Duke of Albemarle; not a reward you might think for a man who fought for the king's enemy. It was my duty as a soldier that I sided with the parliament, and I ask you not to speak of my past so openly. I am no longer in service. My allegiance is sworn to king and church. For that much you should be thankful.'

'The at least we know where we stand with *you* Major. There are people such as Margaret Fell who change their religion with the wind. Originally, she was Puritan, then a Seeker, and now they're calling her the mother of Quakerism. Better the Devil we know I suppose.'

'I would rather not be compared with the Devil, *especially* by a man of the cloth!'

'My sincere apologies, Major, but whilst George Fox remains in our vicinity, he will only become a greater nuisance to my parishioners. I fail to understand why the authorities don't keep him locked away for longer periods, but it seems the more they torture him the stronger is his resolve. A prison warden, knowing his beliefs forbid him to listen to music, sent a fiddler into his cell to play all day and torture his mind. Fox recited prayers continuously and his powerful bellowing voice, overpowered the sound of the fiddle. He drove the poor man from the cell, and the fiddler failed miserably in his task. It's a relief for us all when Fox leaves the country to spread his gospel. Would that he might stay away for good and leave us all in peace. They do seem to handle the Quakers much better down south, Major. Are we doing something wrong up here?'

'Down south they police the Conventicle Act of 1664 to the letter. If we are to be successful, we must do the same.'

'That act is pure persecution major. I feel ill at ease with the transportation of young men for their misguided beliefs.'

'You are too soft-hearted. It's no surprise that your congregation is thinning. I have a meeting with Colonel Kirkby tomorrow and will have a word with him on the subject.'

'Judge Kirkby is frightening, a fanatic. He hunts Quakers with the enthusiasm of a hungry raven gnawing at carrion.'

'You exaggerate. I find him pleasant. He's a little abrupt at times, but interesting. You should be careful voicing all your thoughts.'

'I'm sorry, but I can't altogether hide my feelings for my fellow human beings. The way they huddle in their silent meetings knowing the wolf could be at the door is commendable.'

'I think the brandy has clouded your head Gabriel. Leave the fate of the Quakers to me. I will pay a visit to our churchwarden tomorrow. You speak of Fox's valiant sixty? Well, you will find they're no match for twenty-four of our most loyal statesmen in the district, each and every one of them sworn to king and church. You may rest assured, there is going to be many a heavy fine contributing to the upkeep of our church. What we lose in tithes will be more than made up for in fines, unless of course they prefer being sent to Lancaster Gaol.' At that point the major's head turned towards the doorway and fixed on Hollis. His stature demanded attention, and as the major crossed the room, he completely ignored the presence of the vicar. The major bent his head forward and whispered. 'What is it Hollis?'

'It's the nightriders, Major. They've arrived a day earlier than expected and are waiting in the courtyard.'

'Then pay them their dues and relieve them of the goods. See that they're stabled for the night and that they leave before the crack of dawn. There are the bales of wool and a crate of clay pipes to be taken to Whitehaven this time. All the contraband can't come through Ravenglass and we must appear to have some legitimate trade. You should prepare for a journey there next week. I have arrangements to make with Arthur Grasty, the ship's first mate. It's a pity captain Julius Laing can't stay sober long enough for us to organise a more suitable trade. I'm sure we could avoid all this inconvenience.'

Vicar Braithwaite's ears were stretched to their limit but all he could hear were incoherent snatches of conversation, except for something sounding like Whitehaven. Wanting to join the conversation he asked a question as Hollis was turning to leave. 'Did you say you were leaving for Whitehaven, Major?'

'It's none of your business and no! I'm not leaving for anywhere at the moment, except perhaps bed?'

His bushy eyebrows and moustache bristled as he stared then turned to shout after his aide. 'Oh! And Hollis make sure you and your good wife attend church this Sunday. We have to keep up appearances you know.' And then, thinking to further please Vicar Braithwaite. 'You should make a list of all those attending the service and hand it to the churchwarden. If there's non-attendance we will assume they are at a Quaker meeting and fine them accordingly. You can also keep your ears to the ground for news of the Quakers' next quarterly meeting. Most of the important ones will be in attendance and we will cop them all at once. As soon as I know the location, I will sign a warrant for suppression of the gathering. There will be a letter to the church-warden and his sidesmen to lay lawful fines on all the attendants. Timothy Atkinson is a ringleader and if he's in attendance we will take him to the nearest judge.'

'What will you charge him with, Major?'

'Plotting will do for now.'

'Plotting what?'

'Plotting against the king, or anything else you can think of. There'll be enough of them there to accuse of plotting something or other. It doesn't really matter what. As long as we can get Atkinson to a judge, we can put it to him to swear allegiance and being a Quaker, he will be obliged to refuse. We will have one of their leaders in prison and his property confiscated, just as the chief magistrate Colonel Kirkby did to Margaret Fell.'

Beneath the great yew tree:
spring 1665

William Webster was a loyal statesman who the district held in esteem. He had been accepted into the twenty-four sidesmen shortly after his marriage and was only recently chosen by them to carry out the duty of churchwarden. Like the rest of his colleagues, he was well informed on the church's Quaker problem. Collecting tithes from the outlaw landowners and tradesmen had caused him nightmares, until the major thundered into the district and created a storm of unease amongst the non-conformists. As a newly appointed tithe commissioner he had thrown himself into the fray like a man possessed and fines almost equalled the unpaid tithes, a fact the major appreciated. 'Just hand me the names Webster, and I'll have the warrants made out. You can find out the location of the meeting house for me. Atkinson will be paying a long visit to Lancaster gaol after this raid. I have lost my patience. It is time our leading Quaker was made an example of.'

The Town End house appeared deserted when the major rode up with the churchwarden and his sidesmen. All they could see was one horse hitched to the stump of a tree. The scene belied gossip in the villages that most of the important Quakers would be attending a marriage during the quarterly meeting. There should have been at least a dozen horses. The major suspected misinformation. An old caretaker answered the door, visibly shaken. 'There's none such people yet arrived sir, and I've little knowledge of them ever to be arriving so late on this fine day of the year sir, although they do say there was a large gathering of travellers at the Red Lion this past night sir.'

Major Rathbone glared down from his mount. *He's too polite to be telling the truth.* 'When do you expect the next meeting my good man. Surely one in your trusted position would know.'

'In four weeks' time sir, but I wouldn't know the whereabouts. I know they were given warning of a raid and no doubt they're holding the present quarterly meeting as far away as possible. But of the whereabouts I would be the last person to know, sir.'

'There's been a notice of a coming wedding posted on this cottage door for more than a week, with the ceremony marked down for today. Are you a Quaker?'

'No, I am not, sir.'

'If I find you lying, you will be joining the wedding party in Lancaster, inside the gaol, and in the darkest cell. Now pass me that notice from the door and be careful not to tear it.'

The major read the notice then turned to face the constable and sidesmen. 'The venue of the quarterly meeting isn't specified, but the notice states that the wedding is between John Benson and Frances Dodson and is to be held today in this parish. You all inform me that Quakers don't tell lies, so put your heads together and come up with a solution.'

William Webster didn't hesitate. 'I wouldn't be surprised if the meeting was at the Benson's out at Yewdale. It's one of their regular meeting places.'

'Benson is the name of the groom on the proclamation isn't it?'

The churchwarden hung his head, feeling the insinuation. 'Yes, Major, a cousin I believe, and before you say anymore, I agree that we should have thought more on the subject before committing our full force to a day of embarrassment. We assumed too much.'

The major pocketed his warrant and glared at the churchwarden. 'If you ask me, Webster, I would say that the Quakers have plotted against us, and that puts those rebels on short notice. Set your mind as to who informed these Quakers of our business, and next time be more careful.'

He then addressed the constable and sidesmen. 'The day isn't yet wasted. Half of our party can investigate the Benson property. Make sure they take the back roads. The travellers staying at the Red Lion are also a possibility. The inn is close and if the day is wasted Webster you can placate me with a tankard of ale.'

As the major's raiding party was circling the Town End farmhouse a party of Quakers was congregating under the spread of an enormous yew tree, one of the district's most popular landmarks. The invited guests were much closer to the major's neighbouring Monk Coniston than Timothy's caretaker would have dared to suggest. Joshua Wilson was in attendance with his wife, Rachel, and their daughter, Sarah. A circle formed around the young couple as they took each other by the hand. John Benson looked into the eyes of his beautiful bride and his clear voice drifted with a lilt through the clear still morning air. 'Friends, in the fear of the Lord, and in the presence of this assembly, I take this my friend Frances Dodson to be my wife, promising, with God's help, to be unto her a loving and faithful husband, so long as we both on earth shall live.'

And the bride responded to her groom. 'Friends, in the fear of the Lord...'

A small group of outsiders had come across the gathering by accident. They assembled on the outer, curious of the ways of the Friends and they found the ceremony not altogether alien. Most of the villagers were aware that a Quaker raid was imminent and there was a degree of sympathy for them. Realising that the major and his party had been given a red herring provided amusement to the lingering crowd. Timothy Atkinson had insisted that a proclamation should be displayed at their most likely meeting place. He ordered that to conform to their beliefs, a copy should be nailed to the great yew, placed in the highest bough and out of sight.

There'd been a spate of highway robberies in the district recently, and they had a pattern about them that disturbed the major. The highwaymen were concentrating on travellers that were departing the local inns, and their knowledge of the coaches' passengers and contents was astounding. The major suspected that inside information was being leaked to the felons by the inns' employees, and possibly even the chamberlains. The major handed the reins to the ostler and sought out the chamberlain. 'Have you had any robberies on the Kendal road during the past week, Chamberlain?'

'Nothing I know of major.'

'I've heard that most of the robberies occur after a coach leaves an inn.'

'Most likely the highwaymen watch the travellers unload and note their wealth. I'll certainly keep my eyes open.'

'You will have some guests of mine arriving shortly on their way to the manor. Be sure to have them looked after or there will be plenty to answer for.'

The major scanned the room for a quiet corner. A group of chapmen with a string of packhorses had arrived at the inn shortly before the major's party and given the Red Lion a burst of energy. 'It's a pity your clientele doesn't attend church more often, landlord, and leave us travellers to a peaceful ale.'

'It's nothing compared to the crowd we had last night, Major. We had difficulty squeezing all the horses into the stables.'

'Not regulars then?'

'I did recognise a couple that stayed overnight last year and if I remember rightly, it is for the same reason.'

'Not just passing through then?'

'Not at all, they are attending another wedding, and have ridden all the way from Lancaster.'

The major's tankard thumped the table and splashed ale. He stretched to his full height. 'Just as I thought, where is the wedding being held? Which way did they ride?'

'They didn't mention the venue, but they headed down the back roads, in the direction of the Tarn.'

Tankards of ale were left untouched as the churchwarden and constable followed in the major's wake. The major heckled Webster, 'It's for sure they were heading for the Bensons'. How could we have missed them?'

'Like the landlord said, Major, they took to the back roads, and as luck would have it, they were the instructions you gave our own raiding party. Our men could have them in custody at this very moment.'

'As long as you don't include me with planning this raid, I may yet forgive you. It was fortunate that I never discussed our plans with Colonel Kirkby. That would be embarrassing.'

'If we move fast, Major, we can join the others at the Bensons'.'

'If I can serve this warrant on just one person, Webster, it will make the day worthwhile.' The major's heart sank as they approached the Bensons' property. His advance party were nowhere to be seen. They had obviously discovered the lack of a meeting and left. Apart from the dogs, the house was completely deserted. His only hope was that the meeting was close by, and that perhaps the others had found it. 'What is your second useless guess, Webster?'

'I have nothing to say, Major, except let's all go home.'

The churchwarden and constable headed for Monk Coniston. On the way they saw a party of wedding guests, most of them local Quakers, heading in the direction of High Yewdale. William Webster concluded that the wedding was over and there could be a meeting at the Bensons' property or elsewhere. The last person he would consider informing was Major Rathbone. He had come to dislike the man intensely. One day under his command would be enough to suppress the enthusiasm of a large army. His fellow sidesmen were becoming tired of carting victims to judges and often chose to make themselves scarce if they heard a friendly neighbour was to be arrested. Not only did they consider it a time-wasting occupation, but the hire of carts was at their own expense.

Timothy Atkinson was the only Quaker statesman in the district and well aware that the major intended to make an example of him. He had been a close friend of Samuel Sandy and been present when the statesman was taken from his property three years previously. Timothy was distraught at the treatment handed out to his friend in Lancaster Gaol and vowed he would never die in the same circumstances. He was a slim and energetic man of medium height with straight, shoulder-length blond hair. His energetic blue eyes showed the alertness required of an organiser and leader of men. George Fox had stayed over at their home on more than one occasion and the association had lost him the affection of many good neighbours, including Vicar Braithwaite whom, however, he still greatly respected. That he was no longer a benefactor of the church had no reflection on the deeds of the vicar; it had more to do with the failings of the establishment. He was law-abiding in the payment of tithes but rejected thoughts of further donations to the church. His immediate problems, to foil the major's plans to raid their quarterly meeting and not to postpone the Benson wedding, had been resolved. Timothy and his family had been first to leave the wedding. They were entrenched in the cottage at Town End preparing to welcome distant Friends from Lancaster into the quarterly meeting.

Timothy had observed the missing notice as he dismounted from his horse. He smiled at the caretaker as he walked through the threshold. 'Thou obviously had no trouble convincing the raiding party, Alan.'

'No trouble at all, Timothy. It was almost a pleasure being nice to the major.'

'It's just as well that thou are not of the Quaker faith.'

'We can't all be the same, Sir.'

'That is so true Alan. Life would be dull if that ever came about.'

Margaret Atkinson's empathy was elsewhere. 'It was really good of William Webster to whisper in your ear, Timmy. I don't know how our family would survive if thou were taken away.'

'Our neighbours realise that, Margaret. We were all shocked when our good friend Sandys was left to die in Lancaster. Our wounds were only starting to heal when the discrimination began all over again.'

'That they could take old Judge Fell's wife to Lancaster and confiscate her property is what frightens me, Timmy.'

'That is Colonel Kirkby's intention, Margaret. He strives to strike fear into us all, and Major Rathbone leans the same way. Our statesmen want no more of it and give the local judge time to be elsewhere before they call with a prisoner. King Charles II has sworn leniency towards the Friends, yet he fails to protect us for they say his sympathies lie more with Catholicism and the French. The Parliament starves him of funds to prevent him from being independent and that furthers his interest in having tithes collected to support the church. The country has no army to speak of and little means of supporting one, despite the hearth tax, yet our navy still meddles with the Dutch. There's no doubt that the Crown and Parliament are at loggerheads. We can only hope that the economy will improve and the persistence of George Fox and the writings of Margaret Fell will inspire the king to uphold his promise of protection.'

Monk Coniston, gathering the hounds

Robert Johnson was impatient to deal with the day ahead. There was a hint of a limp in the shepherd's step as he strode purposely through the dale. A descendant of Scandinavian immigrants, he was a tall, heavily built man with a raw-boned face, weather-beaten from a life of walking the open fells. A high forehead and bald pate served as stark contrast to his wavy dark red hair that bounced around his shoulders with the urgency of his gait. Grass compacted under his bodyweight as his oversized footprints dispersed a trail of scars in the early-morning dew. He slowed to zigzag down a grassy verge, steadying his body with a long staff, countering the tendency of his clogs to slip on the frosty dew. Back on level ground he picked up pace again, his hasty lope accenting the urgency of his task. He had arranged to meet Joss Taylor no more than two hours after daybreak at the Windermere Ferry crossing. It would be good to catch up with his old sparring partner, Rupert. *A shame he was blinded in that fall, but the Ferry contract was a blessing for him and his family. At this rate, Joss will be at the ferry long afore me.*

Punctuality was a matter of pride with Robert and he was the one chosen to hold the deposit. He pushed thoughts of his son's future away. He had agreed with his landlord Timothy Atkinson that the invitation to visit the smithy would have to wait. Favouring his left leg, he crunched the long wooden pole into the earth with each alternate step. Attached to the end of the pole were two entwined metal spirals that enshrined a family story. In his early youth, Robert was turning over soil on the perimeter of the lake when he discovered a flaking, rusty old auger-like tool. The auger had been resting inside the rib cage of a long skeleton of human bones, along with the rusty remains of a sword and axe. The find caused much speculation in the village and reached the ears of the Vicar of Dalton, a respected man of great intellect. The vicar had only recently viewed an ancient document outlining a local land dispute. More than half of the names on the scroll were Norse, none of which were in use to that day. He concluded that the remains by the lake were those of a Norse farmer, who'd been buried with the tools of his trade and his weapons of war. Few believed his analysis.

When a second skeleton was unearthed, a warrior of tall stature who had obviously been speared by an arrow, they unanimously scoffed at his idea. They all agreed with the vicar's assumption of race, as it was common knowledge that many of their ancestors were tall and of Scandinavian descent. After a few ales at the local inn, the prevailing opinion was that if there had been a battle, there would have been more than two skeletons in the vicinity. As there were only two, then there had obviously been a duel and they could have been merely passers-by. The villagers *did* agree that the function of the metal spiral was a mystery and concluded that it must have been lying in the earth at the time of the duel.

The village woodworker used a similar but smaller tool to drill holes in timber. The auger was handed over to the Coniston blacksmith for his opinion. He took one look at its rusty, knurled shape, and in the face of protestations, tossed it into the flames, suggesting that if anyone was really interested, he would forge them a new one. Disappointed at the loss of the contentious object, the villagers mischievously challenged the blacksmith's skills. 'We'll pay you to forge a new auger, but it will have to be an auger with a double spiral and nothing less.' The villagers rambled back to the Black Bull Inn, pleased they had set him an impossible task and extracted at least some amusement in exchange for the loss of their prized rusted artefact.

George Ferris, Black George to the villagers, was a man who took great pride in his work. He had been three years out of his apprenticeship when his master died and left with the task of running the Coniston smithy. With only a young second year apprentice, Black George had quickly established himself in the business and was soon married. When it became known that he had taken up with Quakers, his business suffered for a while, but it wasn't long before the locals realised his honesty in pricing. He was now taking orders from nearby Torver and Hawkshead and could afford to keep and train up another apprentice. George was of the opinion, that given time to work, no task on earth was impossible. So, he had secretly taken up the challenge of the double auger, and was unwilling to think for one moment that he could fail. At his third attempt, with the help of his apprentice, he parted the glowing end metal into two and shaped two long rounded spirals around a bar. He then trimmed the coils to length, tapered both ends to a point and brought them together. His apprentice then pushed the coils back into the glow of the forge, until they were cherry red and then plunged them into an oil bath.

The following week George paid a visit to the Black Bull Inn to collect his wager money. He proudly displayed the result of his impossible challenge, and what he considered to be a useless two-pronged implement. The auger was passed from hand to hand round the table. To his surprise, the villagers were excited by the prospects of the new design and it became the subject of some animated discussion. During the following weeks the forge man was asked to craft more of the special augers and fit them to the end of long hardwood poles. Surprisingly, it was not the woodworkers, but the shepherds who had found a use for the modified tool.

The rod bit into the ground and eased the pressure off Robert's leg. The auger had become a handy tool and only last winter he had used it to break open the icy surface of the tarn when he was stacking Algernon Fleming's icehouse. Robert pondered over their loss of the young lambs and could hardly contain his anger. *The vermin are out of control. We have to cull them now, before their litter grows.*

The shepherds of the dale had banded together against the threat, as they always had in past bad seasons. They had lost good hounds and the church its deposit, in a failed early season chase. They had to apply for extra funding from the churchwarden for a fresh hunt. Robert had volunteered to pick up the dogs with Joss Taylor, but that was before his fall in the wrestling bout. Despite waking early that morning with a swollen ankle he knew he was committed. He'd been irritated by the sound of vixen's screaming mating calls throughout the long dark winter nights. The dog fox and vixen had been mating and hunting together these past two months and now only the dog fox had been sighted. That could only mean there was a litter to deal with, and the chase would only be a success if the fox led the pack to the lair.

The journey to fetch the dogs would take him to the eastern side of Esthwaite Water, only a short distance past Hawkshead and in sight of the ferry, a distance he would normally have had little difficulty with. He patted the money in his pouch and grinned. If the vicar found out it was a parishioner with leanings towards the Quakers handling vestry money, there would be an aggravated sermon come Sunday. His long step gradually shortened as he slowed, approaching the lower ground. Hot breath steamed from his mouth and nostrils as he panted to a stop and paused in his thoughts to affirm the direction of his path. As he looked around, his preoccupation with the loss of lambs was almost forgotten as he absorbed the peace and beauty of the countryside.

The mountains behind and to the west formed a line of irregular ranges. The harsh landscape was softly coloured by purple heath and green bracken. Morning light stretched gently over the eastern hills, patterning shadows as sunbeams cast flames across the tranquil lake. The early-morning sun was going about its tasks, silently drawing up the lingering mists of the night and sweeping away the shadows of the dale, warming the land. The curtain of dawn lifted and nature's harmonic contrasts of colour stirred from their sleep, released from their nightly shelters. A trail of lonely clouds skirted the winter sky, stragglers, drifting slowly away with the swirling up draught of morning air, revealing a bloom of snow on the distant peaks.

Flocks of Herdwick sheep littered the slopes behind the lake, distinguished by grey faces and contrasting grey, dark brown or black fleece. The giant shepherd listened to their distant bleating, floating towards him on a cool breath of morning air. The sheep were grazing contentedly, peacefully manicuring the lower hillside. *If only it was as calm during the night. The vixen screams like a peacock.* Only a few miles away on Coniston Fell, a fox was nosing through the innards of a writhing lamb, searching for the liver that would nourish his vixen's litter, nestled at a safe distance in a secluded borran.

Robert squinted against the breaking sun, scanning the distant perimeter of the lake. A necklace of hazel coppice, studded with oaks, hollies and birch reflected on the surface of the deep still water. Robert focussed on an isolated farmhouse, perched on an island that almost divided the lake. Its colour and texture merged into the landscape, mellowed by coatings of lime. The surrounding dry stonewalls were covered in centuries old lichen, draped in parts with ivy that glistened with early morning dew. Inviting smoke spiralled from the chimney. Robert imagined the warmth of the constantly burning peat fire in the hearth and anticipated a friendly welcome from old Myles.

A hawk gracefully glided in a circle, silently cutting the air wings tilted, readying to swoop on its rodent prey. Robert halted his stride to admire the skills of the hunter and inhaled deeply with his eyes closed. A contented smile lit up his face as the crisp morning air nourished his huge frame. He slowly shook his head in wonder in appreciation of being alive. Memories of his long-departed wife Aggie flooded his mind. *If only she were alive and by my side to share this moment.*

He picked up his stride and headed down an emerging path that would guide him around Esthwaite Water. The path was winding and edged by a crystal-clear stream, rippling over its slate bed and slapping protruding rocks with a soothing alternating pitch. The stream passed through a wooded gorge before wending its own way, cascading down towards the lake. The path widened into a clearing and Robert's spirits lifted as he sighted Joss Taylor ahead of him. Forgetting his injury, he lengthened his stride, urged himself forward, and raised an arm to hail a greeting to his friend.

Before the words left his mouth, he skidded on the gravelly edge of the water, stumbling as both feet swept from under him and the pole flew from his hand. A chattering, brightly-plumed jay was silenced. Two frolicking squirrels froze, sensing danger in the forest's broken rhythm, and then dashed high into the fork of a nearby tree. Robert lifted himself and searched ahead for Josh, but he was no longer in sight. He cursed his limp and reached down to massage the twisted ankle. Since his loss in the wrestling bout, the once proud winner of the championship belt had been nursing doubts of his prowess. *Am I losing my fire and the will to win? Perhaps I'm growing too old. Or I'm being influenced too much by the ways of The Friends?*

Robert settled down on the bank overlooking the lake, his ankle throbbing with pain. *I'll catch up with Joss later at the farmhouse.* Spring was beckoning and Robert inhaled the pleasant scent of gorse in the air. The middle-aged shepherd listened with drooping eyelids to the continuous buzz of a large queen bumblebee. The bee was hovering over yellow daffodils, carrying pollen, searching for nectar to produce honey for the mouths of her newly hatching brood. Robert had studied the bees as a boy, followed them to their nest, and watched fascinated as they built a wax canopy over the hollow. A soft cool breeze rustled the reeds at the edge of the lake and his mind drifted back to Aggie, sweeping her broom, spreading bracken across the cottage floor. Robert thought of his wife often, especially of the times they sat on the edge of the lake amongst the daffodils. She would watch their heads bouncing in the breeze. 'Like ladies with yellow bonnets,' she would tell young Thomas. 'More like gossiping women,' he would add. His head lifted abruptly when he heard a dull thumping noise in the distance. It was the metallic crash of forge hammers clanging the start of another industrious day. Each echo lingered with the next creating a cacophony of sound: *Cunsey Forge.* To the west of the forge he could see smoke rising from Rusland. The forest had long been cleared and the resulting coppice burned for charcoal to feed the bloomeries. He remembered his father reminiscing about his youth, when the dales were peaceful during the day. Robert wrenched himself from his daydream, casting nostalgic memories from his mind. *There's work to be done and I'm responsible for more than one.* He lifted himself by the pole to a standing position and continued to wind his way along the edge of the lake. He knew that Joss Taylor would by now have crossed by ferry to the island farm. Before the day's end, the two friendly shepherds would be returning with the hounds.

Ravens and puberty

Thomas and Damian sat crouched behind a boulder on the lower slopes. The cousins observed a raven circling high above them and found it hard to stifle their excitement as it swooped down to earth. Robert had told them the site of the kill, knowing the fox had already left with his spoils. There were several scavengers fighting over the remains. The two boys cautiously worked their way towards the lamb's carcass. Jasper was at their side, eyes and nose pointed intently forward, panting, his head and tongue lolling from side to side. Thomas leaned down and affectionately patted the hound's flank 'Shhh! We're nearly at the spot, Jasper.'

The trio settled within striking distance. Several ravens were totally engrossed in gorging on the carrion. Thomas held his forefinger to his mouth to signal silence and together with Damian, his recent hunter companion, tensioned his bow and took aim. 'Yan, taen, tedderte.' On the count of three, both hunters dispatched their arrows. The missiles whistled as they cut through the air and the ravens' heads lifted, alert. They spread their wings to take to the air opening a window for the arrows to pierce their breasts. Two of the scavengers fell into their unfinished meal. One was killed and the other dragged an arrow as it hopped around in circles. Damian wasn't very good with the bow. The rest of the flock flew high, circling in the sky before descending. They settled into the highest branches of the nearest tree, wary of the intruders, patiently observing proceedings around the carcass.

Thomas cringed as he watched Damian chase after the wounded prey. He caught it by a flapping wing and swung it in a circle. 'Stop messing around. Kill it!' Thomas' voice echoed in Damian's mind. He half-heartedly clubbed the raven with the blunt end of his axe. Thomas grew impatient. He nudged Damian aside, severed the raven's head, and dropped it at his cousin's feet. 'You don't torture them. The quicker they die the better.'

Damian placed the head in his sack and then started poking the body with a stick, as if trying to shake it to life. 'What is death, Tommy?'

'It's when your spirit goes to heaven.'

Damian stroked the body with the stick, withdrew a small axe from his belt and inexplicably chopped off the feet. Thomas was reminded of the long woodcutter's axe sweeping down, cutting into James' knees. The image from that dark night wouldn't go away. Damian's eyes stared vacantly, shoulders hunched as he licked his lips and rolled his head in a circle before carelessly stuffing the feet into his lunch sack. It occurred to Thomas that Damian deliberately maimed and played with his prey. *Was his cruelty showing when he booted down onto James' shoulders?* He remembered Damian poking his finger into James' eye with the same curiosity he had just accorded the raven. *Perhaps he thought the tree-feller would come alive again? The voice still rang in his head.* 'He's still dead, Tommy'. *Of course, he was dead! What else could he be and why is Damian so curious about death? Perhaps he's worked in the graveyard too long.*

He tried to shake away the image. *I have to forget. We both have to forget.*

Thomas remembered the first time Damian asked if he could join him hunting for ravens' heads. It wasn't long after the death of James Pritt and about the same time as his cousin had stopped digging graves. *He seems to value the ravens' feet more than the heads.* Thomas was used to his cousin's curious habits and knew that to mention it would result in the usual silent blank stare. 'Nobody's perfect,' his father would say. Thomas withdrew his arrow and wiped it clean on a woollen cloth. He severed the raven's head with his hunting knife, dropped it alongside four others, rolled them into a ball and tied the makeshift bag onto his belt.

'Will you take this one as well, Tommy?' Damian held out his raven's head and was relieved when Thomas accepted. He relied on his cousin's good nature and pretended he hated bartering or dealing with the churchwarden's clerk. Thomas knew otherwise. *It's the graveyard he's afraid of.* He added the raven's head to the others then they both walked down the slopes towards the great yew tree, a part of the dales often used as a location point. The ancient tree's trunk was broader than the tallest man in the district. Damian had hitched Prince close to the great tree and Thomas watched enviously as his cousin leapt effortlessly into the saddle. Damian was a different person when he rode the black horse, full of confidence, and referring to Prince as his own. He turned towards the eastern path that would lead him to the Hawkshead village. Damian said he would ride on to his mother's farm near Monk Coniston, and then back to the manor 'See you later then Damian.'

'Are you gaan to be in the hunt, Tommy?'

'Father says I have to.'

'Are you afraid?' Thomas didn't answer.

He waited until his cousin was out of sight before starting on the long walk to the church vestry. *John taught us all to be good riders. I wish he was still alive.* He tapped the ravens' heads at his side. *Father will be pleased with the money for the heads. There'll be enough for him to trade a new pair of clogs and have them capped.* He stretched out, taking long strides like his father. He remembered when he was small, looking up to his father as they walked the fells, watching his red hair bouncing against the clear blue sky. He had trouble keeping pace, but never complained. Now he was almost as tall, and often teased his father to keep up. He had the same steel-blue eyes and raw-boned face; the wavy blond shoulder-length hair was inherited from his mother. Thomas was taller than many of the congregation and hated being looked on as a child. He'd unfortunately fallen asleep attending his first quarterly meeting. He knew his father was trying to organise an apprenticeship with the Quakers and had told Hannah to make sure he was always at his best. The ground rules for the Friends' meetings were monotonously laid down before he left home, and Thomas thought his father often went to silly extremes. 'Never wipe your nose on your sleeve Tommy, it creates a bad impression. Use the rag that Aunt Hannah gave you. And if you feel the need to break wind, never let go during the silence, squeeze it out quietly lad, and if it's a smelly, don't wrinkle your nose and look at the person next to you.'

Thomas broke out laughing. 'That's what you do father.'

'Never mind what I do. If it happens, leave quietly, and make sure you slip out with your clogs in your hand. We have to create a good impression.'

'I know how to behave father, Aunt Hannah tells me often enough, and she tells me not to pick up your bad habits. You should both spend more time with Damian. He's the one that doesn't pay attention.'

Thomas often wondered if Sarah Wilson got the same counselling before a meeting. He knew she was bored when she started sitting on her hands and kicking her legs up and down. He would wait for her to be scolded by her parents and he was never disappointed. She seemed more grown-up this year, but as far as he was concerned, she was still a nuisance, like most girls of her age. He sometimes smiled across at her though, in mutual amusement when someone happened to break the silence to speak softly of their misdemeanours. In summer when the windows and doors were wide open, he would listen to the birds chirping, or watch a bottle-fly buzzing about the room, and wish he was outside. Vicar Braithwaite's sermons were a little different. Thomas could almost wager on the first church parishioner to fall asleep. When the first snore rattled over the sermon he would look towards the major's special pew and choke back a laugh as his deathly stare targeted the culprit.

Thomas was told by his Aunt Hannah that his mother and father had been true believers and never missed a Sunday service. Then, after his mother's death, she said that his father had strayed from the fold. 'He'd been visiting your mother's grave with her favourite daffodils and stopped to listen to that preacher in leather breeches and doublet. He witnessed the poor man being stoned out of Ulverston churchyard. I've never laid eyes on George Fox but your father tells me he's a tall bulky man with a deep chest and powerful booming voice, something like your own, and his eyes are hypnotic and penetrating. Your father was certainly taken in with his preaching. Seeing such a strong man stoned, clubbed, kicked and punched without retaliation likened him in your father's words, "to Jesus bearing the cross". They say your father rescued him and the great man spoke to him kindly. The Quakers spoke of him as "the man who risked his life to rescue George Fox", and invited him to attend their meetings. The vicar wasn't impressed and warned him of the Devil's temptations. "Your late wife, rest her soul, would expect you to attend church service as regularly as she did so herself and with your sister's family." His words were wasted. The experience appeared to put new life into your father and since that day he has never been quite the same person. He welcomed the new religion with a vigour that astounded me.'

Thomas was well aware of his father's obsession with George Fox and was often reminded of the Ulverston speech. So much so, that it was now impressed on his mind. His father said that George Fox had heard the church bells ringing and been drawn towards the calling. His father was amongst other people gathered in the yard and heard him refuse the priest's invitation to preach in the house of God. He called the church a steeple-house and declared to the people that he was sent by the Lord God of Heaven and Earth to preach freely and he said that one piece of ground was no more holy that another. 'Didn't the apostles meet together and preach freely in dwelling-houses, as all who preach Christ, the word of life ought. God or Christ dwells not in the steeple-houses you worship in, but in the sanctuary of your bodies.'

Thomas' father said that he felt uplifted by the speech of this preacher but noticed the crowd around him was becoming restless. When the preacher went on to condemn idol temples and the priests and their wages, tithes, augmentations, heathenish ceremonies and traditions, the crowd became ugly and unruly. He told Thomas that his conscience insisted he protect the man. 'When I stood over them, they put down their clubs and rested their stones.'

Thomas' father related this story to the point of boredom and when he told of his belief in George Fox's preaching, he would look at his son in expectancy. But Thomas was never convinced. He knew that God was everywhere and looking down on him, especially in church. The first time he was allowed to place a coin in the silver collection plate he had made a show of thumping it down with a clatter whilst scooping two up into his palm. *'Though shalt not steal'* troubled his mind and he guiltily looked above and around him. *God sees all.* Leaving the church, he dropped the two coins into the plate held by Vicar Braithwaite and received a beaming smile. 'Thomas is such an honest and generous boy! I shall speak to our Grammar School teacher Phynius Clayton about his merits.' As he was leaving, he collected a cuff behind the ear from his father and a demand for an explanation.

From Aunt Hannah he only ever received admiration. 'He's a better example than his father, that's for sure.' She was always on about his father's terrible vices, without revealing too many details. 'I find it hard to believe the Friends suffer him at their meetings.'

When he asked her about the vices, she would quickly change the subject. He knew that gambling and drinking were a vice, and smoking. But he'd never seen his father smoking a clay pipe like most others he knew, even though it was common knowledge in the south that smoking warded off the plague. Thomas and his fellow pupils had been told there were pipes and tobacco in the schoolhouse and that if there was ever a hint of the evil death invading the district, they must be used at once. His father would have none of it, and claimed it was a dirty smelly habit. Aunt Hannah's main gripe was the women his father brought home from the Red Lion, supposedly she said, to spring-clean the house.

'It's spring-cleaning time, Thomas. Off you go to Aunt Hannah's.' When he arrived, it was obvious his aunt didn't approve of the situation. Thomas didn't mind because his father was always in a happy frame of mind when he returned home.

One day he thought he had found out why. It was the day he called back for the catapult. He was reaching for the latch when a naked woman opened the door. She waited for him to speak, but he could only stand there, dumbstruck. She smiled, reached up to cup his face between her palms, and then stood on her tiptoes to kiss him gently on the lips. 'You're growing tall Tommy. I can see you visiting the inn in a few years' time.'

Thomas still didn't know what to say. He felt the hardness inside his britches and the warm juice trickling down his leg. It wasn't the first time that he'd had the experience, but this time it was involuntary. His father always warned him to keep his hands out of his pockets and to stop playing with it or it would drop off. His father often ran around naked at home in summer, but this was the first time Thomas had seen a woman with no clothes on, and she wasn't much older than Cousin Mary.

'Are you coming back to bed Judith, or do I have to come and get you?'

'Your father's impatient, Tommy. You'd best be on your way.' She watched the red-faced Thomas walk away in a dream then called out to him, and as he turned, he could see her waving something in the air. He walked back sheepishly, and she teased him as he reached out to take the catapult. 'That's *all* you came for, wasn't it?' She noticed the wetness seeping through his wool britches. *The lad's winkle's running. His cache's sprung a leak.* 'Don't do anything I wouldn't do Tommy.'

Somewhere in Thomas' mind a small pod had burst and blossomed with illuminating relief. He rubbed himself all the way down the hill, hoping for another release, but it wasn't working and there was his father's voice, telling him to open his palms. He would hold them up, and sure enough his father could tell. He would say there was a black spot showing, but he was blowed if he could ever see one.

The vestry

Thomas tried to look cheerful as he walked through the vestry archway. He generally had an easygoing smile for everyone around him, but the room he had just entered had always depressed him. He much preferred the openness of the church and its peaceful resonance. He only missed the regular Sunday service once a month and unknown to his father he would stay late to sit alone in the peace of the church. The Friends had a silence at their meetings, but it didn't have the same effect. He paid little attention during the Friends' meetings or the church sermons and in total boredom he would amuse himself by casually observing the habits of those around him.

The vestry air was stale as usual, reeking of old books and candle wax, and smelly Ruben, hunched up in his chair with his dishevelled thin grey hair; the ever-present quill feather protruding from his red and black ink-stained hand, like a spare finger.

I wonder if he sleeps with the quill. Thomas approached the counter and Ruben's eyes and nose wrinkled as he focussed on the young boy. The churchwarden's clerk unhappily eased himself up, slid his seat back with a groan and approached Thomas with short rolling sidesteps. Ruben leaned both his hands on the front desk and looked up at Thomas with boredom. His strong body odour wafted around and drowning the mustiness of the room.

He stinks of ravens' heads. Thomas decided the clerk looked even shorter standing than sitting. His thin face displayed a large pointed nose that curved upwards, eagle-like, into a balding head. Rubbing his wispy grey beard, he looked up, black beady eyes squinting, lips parted just enough to show his few remaining teeth, yellowed with age. An ill-fitting jacket matched his well-known reputation for being miserably tight-fisted with the vestry coffers, handling the money as if it were his own. 'Don't tell me you've been killing my beautiful birds again lad?'

The shepherds knew of the clerk's fondness for ravens. Down at the inn over excess ales and much merriment it was suggested he resembled them in more ways than one. Thomas unrolled his cloth onto the countertop. 'That's six raven heads, Ruben. That will be twenty-four pennies.'

Ruben Goldsworthy's face screwed up and his head shrunk into his narrow shoulders. 'Is that so? You can't be serious lad. That's enough to pay for six days' work and it's far too many of those beautiful birds to be killed in any one day.'

'Three days' work Ruben, and me fadder say's there should be more killed.'

'I do like to see the whole raven and not just the head you know.' He looked accusingly at Thomas. 'Are you sure you haven't just cut the heads from those ravens hanging up outside?'

'Go see for yourself!'

'I only mention it because of the strange happenings around here lately. What kind of person would take pleasure from cutting the feet from my poor raven?'

Thomas' lips pursed. *Our rune pot's full of them.* He feigned innocence. 'Dunno.'

The clerk sighed and reluctantly inked his goose quill. He wrote slowly and meticulously in the disbursement book:

1665. Five raven heads: one shilling, eight pence.

He spread his hands each side of the book and leaned back to admire his flowing scribe.

Thomas knew this figure to be wrong and heeded his father's advice. 'Me fadder's Robert Johnson and he's a wrassler.'

'Aye! And a fine one at that lad, for a Quaker.'

'He's not really a Quaker.'

'Well that's what they say lad.' Rufus had handled wager money for the major at the last fair and collected with a hunger reminiscent of his beloved raven ravaging fresh meat. Ruben shuddered at the memory of Robert wrestling, reconsidered the tally, and made an additional entry in the ledger:

1665. One raven's head, four pence.

Ruben reached under the desk and unhooked a large key. He waddled across the room, unlocked the vestry box and begrudgingly counted out twenty pennies into Thomas' palm. Thomas passed them over into his left palm and stood with the right still open, looking down into the clerk's eyes expectantly. Ruben hesitated before turning back to the box. 'Of course, yes of course, silly of me. Twenty-four, it was twenty-four.'

Thomas victoriously rolled the extra four pennies around in his palm to taunt the old clerk. He knew that Ruben loved the feel of money and almost came to tears when it left his care. The clerk was of the opinion that paying for the killing of a fox or raven was a waste of church finances. *Who cares if a few lambs had to be sacrificed each year? A fox needs food, as does the raven.* But nobody would listen to him. The vermin bred as quickly as they were killed; they certainly weren't diminishing in numbers. The ledger told the story. It was similar every year. He called after Thomas, cackling sadistically, attempting to amuse himself and alleviate his sadness at monetary loss. 'Be careful of the bad man on your lonely walk home, young man.'

Thomas returned a cheeky smile. 'There's only one bad man in this district.'

The clerk's eyes squinted. 'And who might that be?'

'I can only say it's not yourself and if you don't know, I'm not gaan to tell you.' Thomas breezed out, teasing, shifting the coinage from hand to hand, and displaying a broad grin over his strong open face.

Ruben paid little attention. He was under the counter searching frantically for his missing goose quill. He preferred them to the less reliable raven quills. But the trouble was, he kept misplacing them. He had only just trimmed the tip of the missing one and had the angle shaped almost to perfection. *I know it was just here. How else could I have made the ledger entry?*

Thomas paused on his way through the churchyard to look across the dale to Esthwaite Water. The sun was breaking through banking clouds, and as he watched its rays reflecting on the pale blue waters, his thoughts turned to his father. *He will have left by now. He'll be on his way home with the dogs.*

Robert was beginning to think his day was wasted. 'You promised me at least five from your kennels Will, and now you say we will be reet lucky to have yan of them?' Robert had never seen the kennels empty. There wasn't a hound to be seen and the sheep dogs were running around in their glory.

'It's a busy season Robbie, but I have more coming back from Ambleside later this morning. They are young, and not me best, but beggars are never choosers.'

'As long as you've trained them for the fox, we're not ones to make a complaint. They will be better than nothing.'

Robert and Joss were relieved to accept three hounds that were returned late that morning. The two shepherds agreed to pay the usual price and deposit, especially when they learnt that the hounds were blooded and fresh from a kill. The old trainer promised to send extra hounds should they be returned early, but they declined the offer. With a little luck, and a successful hunt, they would have a few extra ales to sup down at the local inn.

One law for Quakers

Despite the Guild's law against Quaker apprenticeships, there was now a hint of a trade for Thomas at the Coniston Forge. Robert was cautious of being caught attending the Friends' meetings. Like all others in the parish, he was expected to make regular appearances at the Sunday church service. Non-attendance at three consecutive services was considered a serious matter by the churchwarden, and it was presumed that non-conformity was the cause of such neglect.

The Conventicle Act of 1664 was designed to persecute anyone over the age of sixteen caught attending a non-conformist meeting that totalled more than five people. The sentence was imprisonment for three months or a fine of five pounds for the first offence, double for the second offence and for the third, a fine of one- hundred pounds or seven years transportation to the New England plantations, from which escape meant death.

Thomas was nearing the age of sixteen and Robert was well aware of the dangers to his son, but he felt sure that if he was cautious, they would be safe. *We could never afford such a fine.* It seemed obvious to everyone that it was only statesmen such as Timothy Atkinson and some tradespeople that the law was making an example of. After all, they were the ones that paid most of the tithes and the fines were merely another way of collecting them.

If there were people in attendance unable to pay the fines, then they were equally loaded onto the fines of the people in attendance who were capable. The fines were often taken from goods and chattels such as a horse, a cart, or hay. Household goods as small as a kettle or pewter dish would also be sold by the bailiff and the excess distributed to the poor of the parish. The Quakers were well aware of this ploy by the law and some were stubborn enough to refuse the fine, and instead serve time in Lancaster Gaol.

Robert found it hard to give in to some of the beliefs of the Friends and even though he and Thomas were always made welcome at the meetings, he felt he was suffered more than accepted. He could never give up his sup of ale, or his loose women, or his favourite sport wrestling, and he often consoled himself. *I only take to my vices in moderation which I'm sure is agreeable with most, and I believe a man should never be denied his natural instincts. Why should I deny myself the pleasures of my soul? Moderation, that's the simple answer, moderation.* He was in agreement with the Quaker tradesmen that they shouldn't pay tithes. Why should they sustain a vicar and a church they no longer believed in? He was also comfortable with the way the Quaker's respected the habits of the dales people; believing that no-one should doff their hats or speak a Sir to anyone who considered themselves above their fellow men. Hadn't George Fox stood in the dock and refused to remove his hat in the presence of the magistrate? The habit was one of local inheritance and sat well with Robert and his kind.

The rune pot

Damian raised his hands to protect his head from another blow. 'What did you do that for Mam?'

'Take those filthy ravens' feet from this house now. Right now! How many times have I told you that they bring bad luck?'

Thomas heard his aunt's raving long before he reached the doorway. He looked warily at the crossed twigs of a rowan tree fixed to the entrance beam. They were placed there to keep away the witches and to weaken their spells. Thomas felt that somehow the charms hadn't been very successful with either of their families, despite his aunt also wearing a necklace strung with the tree's red berries. Hannah was as superstitious as any in the district and the tall rowan tree planted close to the house was ample evidence. She defended her beliefs to anyone who might question her. 'If the church feels the need of rowan tree in their graveyard to keep away the ghosts, then I'm certain I need the same to keep the ghosts and the dark witches from our door.'

There was talk in the village of his Cousin Mary being a witch, but he would never mention that to Aunt Hannah. She was a strong woman in more than one sense; tall, wiry and energetic with a will of iron. Thomas grinned devilishly as he imagined her strong arm flailing his cousin around the head again. Damian was never out of trouble with Hannah, but Thomas sympathised. *It's a shame he's a bit daft.* His father told him that Hannah blamed the plague that came up from London; the same plague that had cost his mother and her newborn baby their lives. His father told him Damian was silly even before the plague had struck. 'Don't you ever mention that to your aunt Hannah or else I'm done for.'

But he had, in a roundabout way. He had been walking home after Sunday church with Damian and Mary when they stopped to rest at a nearby stream and skim pebbles through the water. Mary decided to take off her amulet. The leather string had been irritating her neck and she was going to adjust the tie. She placed it by her side and reached out for a twig. No sooner had the ring parted her grasp than Thomas' impulses took over. He snatched up the ring and ran with Damian and Mary in pursuit. Damian was a lot faster, but Thomas was almost to his aunt's door before Damian caught him. They both rolled up in fits of laughter. Not Mary though. She was the eldest and her attitude was stern. She snatched her amulet from Thomas and then demanded a forfeit. He dutifully stood to attention with puckered lips whilst she placed her arms around him and planted a kiss. 'I'll have to marry you now, Mary.'

'Cousins can't marry, Thomas. It's a sin if they do.'

Aunt Hannah was standing in the doorway. 'And as for you Mary Inman, you're getting too old for those sorts of games.'

'If you must know mother, I've set my eyes on a man and I'm practising.'

'Then I hope for both our sakes that he's a regular churchgoer.'

'Why can't cousins marry, Aunt Hannah?'

'Because, Thomas, they might have children that are silly.'

'Did you marry your cousin, aunty?'

There! He had said exactly what his father had told him not to say. Damian bowed his head and walked away quietly. Aunt Hannah looked daggers at her nephew, and it seemed a long time before he called again. His insinuations were now conveniently forgotten. Hannah had put the blame on her brother Robert for influencing an impressionable boy. She was always happy to see Thomas' smiling face and pushed Damian aside to welcome her nephew. 'Hello, Aunty Hannah. I've brought the four pence for the raven's head.'

Damian rushed past his mother. 'It's mine Tommy.'

Hannah held her son back by the scruff of his neck and held out her hand. 'Thank you, Thomas.' Her eyes locked on Damian's. 'This time it's mine and you don't have to ask me the reason why. Now go and bury your ravens' feet with the rest of them.'

Damian looked quizzically at his mother. *How does she know I bury them?*

The vicar nearly caught him the last time. It was daytime. He'd discovered the ravens' feet worked just as well in the day, so why bother with the night? He never dreamed of the Dobbie man as long as there were fresh claws buried. He had just pushed the ravens' feet into the soil between the flowers and was stomping them into the grave mound when he saw Vicar Braithwaite riding up the hill. Gabriel was returning after doing his rounds on the outskirts of the parish. *There's a heathen dancing on Francis' grave.* When he drew closer, he was relieved to see it was Damian. 'I see you've conquered the fear of your Dobbie man my boy and you're brave enough to dance on my good friend Francis' resting place.' Damian smiled his frozen grin and stared at the vicar. Without speaking he stepped off the mound and walked away, looking back now and then, as if to make sure he had seen what he had seen.

The vicar stared at the mound, puzzled, then dismounted to scratch at the surface of the soil. He delicately drew out a raven's foot and dangled it pincer-like in front of his eyes. 'Those dammed Devil worshippers have been at it again. What have you done dear Francis, to be worthy of such sacrilege? If I could catch any of them, I'll have them in front of a judge for hanging in Lancaster.' He crossed himself and asked forgiveness of the Lord for his thought. *The next full moon I'll have Mathew call a secret midnight watch.*

Mathew saw nothing other than an owl and a few bats, but his presence at midnight was enough to set the tongues wagging in the villages about a circle of naked witches. 'They were scattering ravens' feet and dancing around Francis' grave under a full moon.' People got to thinking perhaps Hannah's young son really had seen the Dobbie man down the grave and he was not so silly after all.

Hannah knew Damian had a secret hoard of ravens' feet somewhere despite his denials. *One of these days I will take the trouble to find out where he buries them. I only hope he is not selling them to those evil people who dance over Francis' grave.* She had heard of the moonlit rituals from Robert and decided to keep her silence on the subject. *If anyone knows what he's doing it would be Mary. I must have a word with the girl and tell her the consequences if anyone is caught.* Hannah stood in the doorway with her arms folded, staring after the two boys in silence. *They will be off in the opposite direction as usual. Old Smythe said he had seen them meddling on his eastern wall. There will be time enough, one day, when I have less work to do.* She looked meaningfully at Mary's baby, John, sleeping peacefully in the cot, oblivious of the commotion around him. Thomas turned to walk alongside Damian. He felt his aunt's eyes boring into his back all the way to the first wall. He knew the direction to take as well as his cousin. West, in the opposite direction to the hoard, hop over the stone dividing wall, then north across two more farms and then back on themselves, east to the nearest stonewall. Thomas felt compelled to go with Damian, as he always did, but he only wished he hadn't been compelled to take that moonlit walk in the forest. That had been a stupid mistake. His cousin found a need to keep looking at their shared hoard, but he was only allowed to look at Damian's, and told never to touch them. They paced out ten steps from the old oak and Damian took a good look around the field before removing the first stone. As he lifted the slate off the cast iron pot, Thomas noticed the number of ravens' feet had diminished despite all their hunting. Thomas threw in another of Ruben's goose quills. Damian picked it up with a look of disdain and threw it back out. 'Hey! Damian! That's mine.'

'It's only a useless feather.'

'It's for writing with ink in books, and if that's no good, what good are your ravens' feet?'

Damian's mouth opened in a half smile, a demonic sparkle of delight in his eyes. 'Wouldn't you like to know?'

'Which lock does the key fit?'

'Wouldn't you like to know?' Damian put the pair of spectacles on his nose and stood up to walk around like a blind man with his hands in front of him.

Thomas had laughed the first time, but the joke was wearing thin. 'Pass me the silver pocket-watch.'

Damian dug into the hoard, sat the watch in the palm of his hand and brought it to his ear before passing it to Thomas. 'It's not ticking.'

'I don't care. I found out I need a key to wind it up.'

Thomas remembered the dark rain-sodden afternoon outside the Black Bull. A lad about Damian's age had leapt astride a horse and chased after a stranger to the district. As the thief shot past, something shiny dropped from his pocket and buried in the mud at his feet. Thomas watched them disappear before he bent down and scooped the object into his pocket. There were people searching for the watch all the next day, so he knew it had to be valuable.

There was an inscription on the case: a large *L* intermingled with a *J*. He also had a pocket knife in his hoard and a pair of scissors that had come into his possession at the annual fair. He still found it hard to control an impulse to pick up loose objects that were lying around ownerless, objects that he didn't really want. The knife had dropped from the stall onto the floor and when he returned it was still there. His father would make him take it back if he knew. He considered ill-gotten gains a curse on the holder. He couldn't keep the goods around the house so with his cousin's help they had found something to hide them in.

Thomas' eyes had focussed on the cast iron pot the moment they entered the smithy. Black George was shaping a large handle for it in the forge and explaining how the Atkinsons had dropped it in for repair. His father and the smith were engrossed in conversation when he casually picked it up in his arms as if to test the weight, then walked outside and placed it under a bush near the river. When he walked back into the forge Black George and his father were still talking. He would never forget the mystified expression on George's face as he turned with the new handle towards the empty space. Damian helped him carry it to the field the next day, and then they worked out the markers and buried it. Then when Damian started saving ravens' feet, he gradually took charge, calling it the treasure pot.

Thomas sat on his haunches and made an effort to humour his cousin. He tried to look interested but couldn't hide the bored look on his face. He was losing interest in their treasure.

Damian, as usual, dipped his hands to the bottom and with a greedy, possessive look in his eyes turned his hoard over and over. The feet were wrapped up in cloth and he fingered them like they were jewels. Thomas winced at the putrid smell when his cousin unrolled the ravens' feet. When he saw the skeleton of a human hand pulled out of the pile he blinked and shook his head to make sure. He leaned forward for a closer look, and realised it had to be the skeletal hand of James Pritt. Thomas' hand instinctively reached out to grab it, but Damian pushed him away, screaming, 'Keep your hand off. It's mine, they're all mine.'

'Just let me hold it'. Damian clutched the hand to his chest and his eyes glazed over. It was only then that Thomas realised how mad Damian could really be. *That night in the forest was more than a warning.* 'I thought you were going to burn the hand. Someone could find out. We agreed.'

'I did burn the hand, but I liked it better, so I decided to keep it. Nobody else knows of our secret treasure, except the person *you* told.' Thomas felt guilty. He turned his eyes away and stared silently at the ground. 'I know you told Mary because she asked me to hide the key in our secret place.'

'People will ask questions if the hand is found, Damian.' Thomas wished he had never left the house that night. Aunt Hannah told them Mary wanted to be alone, so they had told her they were going fishing instead. He had only agreed for the excitement of a night-time adventure, and to stop his cousin pestering him. Damian was excited about the chance of seeing a wild pig in the pit he'd dug. *If only it* had *been a wild pig that ended up in there.* The fact that no-one cared about James missing didn't help to ease his conscience. He even spoke with his father. 'The woodcutters told Damian that John was killed by James Pritt. Is that true?'

'Perhaps it is, Tommy, but we will never know for sure, and we are not to mention it to Mary. The poor girl has had enough misfortune in her life already, without village tittle-tattle making it worse.'

'Village tittle-tattle says Mary's a witch.'

'You shouldn't repeat gossip that you know is untrue. Mary's at peace now and says that God must have had his reasons. Reverend Braithwaite told your Aunt Hannah that Mary attends church more than she ever did before and he always finds her praying at the pew long after the congregation has left. I think that James Pritt felt uncomfortable with the accusations and decided it would be best if he just disappeared.'

Thomas wanted to tell the truth but couldn't find a way. The truth would destroy his family. He could still see James' body slumped in the hole with stakes protruding through his buttocks and thighs, and Damian kicking on his shoulders, driving the body further into the stakes. 'It's justice, Tommy. He killed John. He deserves it.'

By the time Thomas felt it safe to look Damian in the eyes again, their hoard was covered. 'We can't tell anyone Damian. No-one must ever know. Our family wouldn't be the same again.'

'I don't think it really matters if Mary finds out Tommy, but I won't be telling her. A secret's a secret, and I don't think you should come here with me anymore, because you steal things. I'm going to move my treasure to a new place, and you can take yours somewhere else. Mam told me that nothing's a secret if somebody else knows about it.'

'Please yourself, I don't care. You can have all my treasure if you like. Our secrets are becoming more trouble than they are worth.'

'If you become a Quaker Tommy, you'll never be able to have any secrets like I do.'

'Yes, I will. They're no different to you or me, except that they don't worship in church.'

'You'll have to tell the truth.'

'So, what's the problem with that?'

'You told the teacher that Mary lost her amulet in the lake, and that was a lie.'

'That was a useful lie, to protect Mary.'

'It's still a lie and what if the Quakers ask you if you have any secrets.' Damian stared at his cousin, his open grin frozen in expectancy, but Thomas never answered, and Damian smugly relaxed. *I can lie. I've got lots of secrets.* 'You'd better not tell anyone, Tommy.'

Thomas never spoke again until they reached his aunt's house. 'I have to be going home, Aunty Hannah. Fadder will be back soon.'

'Is anything wrong, Thomas?'

'No, I'm just feeling tired.'

Hannah suspected otherwise. She knew he'd had a good walk to the church in Hawkshead and back, but Thomas was stronger than most, and it could only be in his mind that he was troubled. Damian was staring after his cousin with a strange expression she'd never seen before, and she spoke sternly to him. 'You had best be riding that horse back to the major's stables or Hollis will be after you again.'

Perhaps it was only a case of Thomas growing into manhood and her son being away most of the time at the manor, but she felt things were not the same between them. Damian had always been her main worry, but he'd seemed more content of late. Mary was now her foremost concern, isolating herself after the death of John, and people thinking the worst. *As if her olive skin and raven hair wasn't enough to set her apart, she had to go and live like a witch. God bless Timothy for taking her away from that miserable hut.*

The fox hunt: spring 1665

Thomas lay on his back choking, one hand clutching at his throat, his head snapping from side to side. The slavering jaws of the fox were deep into his flesh and his legs thrashed the air as bloodied hands struggled to prise him free. Robert heard his son screaming and leapt to his aid. 'Wake up Thomas, wake up! We have to be gaan afore daybreak.' Robert Johnson's huge hands shook his son's shoulders, trying to stir him from his nightmare. His fingers brushed sweat from his son's brow and ruffled the blond wavy hair. 'Aast er gaan lad?'

'I'm alreet now, Fadder.' Thomas had tossed and turned all night; his sleep persistently interrupted by a mind restless with the excitement of his first hunt.

They'd packed their lunch of bread, cheese and dried mutton the night before; enough food Robert thought, to last for three days, let alone one. *The boy must have hollow legs, all he seems to do is eat, shit, and eat again.*

Thomas' body was entering a rapid stage of growth. He was descended from a line of true dalesmen; large-boned with a tall, lean figure, fair hair and blue-grey eyes. The strength would come later as his body matured. At sixteen, he was only a head shorter than the great height of his father. Robert lifted his rod from the wall, slung the food sack over his shoulder, and ducked under the doorway. 'We'll be away then son, we're meeting at the head of the lake.'

'You're taking the rod, Fadder?'

'There's no reason not to lad, it will steady me gammy leg and if things turn out for the worst, I'll be able to use it for its real purpose.'

'I hope not, Fadder. I hate the rod. There should be another way.'

'This was always the way in my fadder's time, Tommy. The rod's an improvement. If you can come up with anything better, then we will all listen to reason.'

Thomas said nothing but felt better having protested and left to collect the hound. Joss Taylor had taken charge of two of the hounds the day before and Robert the remaining one. Thomas held the hound on the leash and called out to Jasper. His faithful dog would have been denied the adventure had he not pestered his father. 'Surely you don't want to lumber me with that old dog of yours, Tommy. He's too slow and too old.'

'The hunt's short on hounds, Father, and Jasper's experienced. He could lead us to the kill.'

The argument drifted in Thomas' favour. Robert realised it would be his son's first full-blooded hunt and possibly his last. *Perhaps the old dog will be a comfort for the boy.* Jasper leapt up, excited, licking Thomas' hands and face. He ruffled the dog's long floppy ears and then pointed the way ahead. 'Off you go Jasper. At least I don't have two hounds to control on the leash.'

They stopped to pick up Hannah and were surprised to see Damian jumping up and down with excitement. There was no way he was going to miss a hunt. Why should he? It was *his* day of rest. The four hunters descended into the vale, catching the occasional glimpse of Thurston Lake, its misty image flickering through the shadows of scattered birch and oak trees. They entered a clearing to see the familiar long range of cliffs, standing like sentinels behind the calm water. Yewdale would soon echo with the drumming of clogs and the pounding of paws. If previous hunts were anything to go by, the melee would continue until late afternoon. They headed north towards Lake's Head, the four pair of clogs marking a curved trail through the blanket of early morning dew. As they approached the head of the lake, Robert spotted Josh Taylor and yelled out a greeting in the broad dialect of the dalespeople. 'Aast er gaan Josh.'

'A la'al kaylied from't skemmy, marra, but ahreet; drunk from strong ale in plain English.'

There was a larger gathering than any of them had expected. Besides the followers there were seven shepherds, each with a hunting dog. Hannah caught up with Robert and they watched the two boys handling the dogs.

A mutilated lamb twitched, its insides hanging out. Damian stared, fascinated by its fading life. Thomas' cheerful disposition darkened.

Any sympathy he had previously shown for the fox dissolved. The hounds sniffed at the ground around the carcass and when they picked up the scent, the whole pack started to yelp with an infectious delirium. The hounds strained against the leash and Thomas felt himself being pulled forward against his will. He broke into a trot and Jasper was at his heels when they drew close to Damian. They chased the trail through to High Waterhead where Jasper took off towards Yewdale Beck on his own. Thomas looked back at his father and saw him shaking his head. *He looks angry. I suppose Jasper should have been on the leash.*

Robert, Hannah and Joss Taylor were at least a hundred yards behind Thomas, and Damian was somewhere ahead of him. When Thomas arrived at the Beck, he found Jasper running around in circles with the rest of the hounds, sniffing the ground, searching for the lost scent. They waited for the rest of the hunt to assemble then led the hounds across the water by way of a small stone bridge. The pack regained the strong scent of fox and the handlers struggled to restrain their hounds. The dogs were being held on the leash, yelping in frustration. Then the huntsmen's cow-horns sounded. It was the signal for their release.

As one, the pack raced through the valley in full cry, long ears bouncing and red tongues flopping amongst clouds of steamy breath. Strong hind legs levered from the ground and paws scattered gravel as they distanced themselves from the followers. A bitter-cold wind raced across the fells and vigorously swirled the morning mist to reveal an occasional glimpse of the snow-capped peaks.

Thomas rubbed his hands together and drew his sheepskin jacket snugly around his chest. He could hear muffled yelping in the distant mist, and then hunters from across the way started shouting. He followed their pointing arms with squinted eyes, and saw the leading pack entering the high ground. Thomas didn't feel comfortable being alone and waited for his breathless father and aunt to catch up. He wasn't quite sure what he would do if he came face to face with a fox.

'They've spotted the fox.' Robert gasped for air.

'How can you tell?'

'I can't. It's only experience, a gut-feeling. Where's Damian?'

'He's somewhere ahead.'

'He's a strange lad that one and a fast runner. It's more than likely he'll catch the fox before the hounds,' Robert chuckled. The villagers spoke of Damian's grandfather doing that exact thing. *It was more than likely the beer talking, but he did win the fell race twice.*

The fox stopped high above the hounds on a rise. He placed the innards of the lamb on the ground between his forelegs and looked down at the pack, assessing their number. The hunters trailed a long way behind the hounds. They were spread out across the valley, ensuring at least one of the groups would be close to the kill. Removing the bushy tail earned five shillings from the vestry box, and ale would flow freely down at the Crown Inn. With no visible fear, the fox's jaws took a fresh grip on his cubs' food. He nonchalantly turned away and accelerated towards the peaks and the steep rocky ground of Holm Fell. His paws pounded the earth and his body swerved to leap over scattered boulders as he gracefully traversed the harsh landscape.

The pack followed the dry watercourse, and more than half of them fell away as they zigzagged up the steep incline. Three hounds broke from the rest of the pack and closed in on the fox as he reached the peak of the crag. With their hot breath warming his tail the fox veered towards a precipice, and the hounds yelped with excitement as they prepared to pounce. But the wily old fox was the survivor of many a chase. Two strides before the fall he swerved sharply along the ridge, and the three lead hounds sensed the danger too late. The hounds faltered in their stride as they hurtled towards the precipice, paws scrabbling desperately to grip the hard-stone surface. They skidded into a chaotic pile and the front hound was pushed over the edge, whimpering and yelping in fear. He hurtled to his fate in a long deathly silence, broken only by a short dull thud that resounded from the floor of the valley.

The rest of the pack arrived on the scene and swerved as one towards the escaping fox. He was running along the edge of the cliff with a distressed gait. The cub's food had fallen from his mouth and he was failing rapidly as the remaining hounds closed in on him. The pack bayed uncontrollably, thirsting for the kill and the hunters further down the slope thought the chase concluded. The pack skidded to a halt on the edge of the cliff, howling with frustration. Their prey had eluded them. The fox was rolling down the slope like a ball, bouncing against boulders and skidding on the slate terrain. He landed at the bottom with a sickening thud and lay deathly still only a few yards from the safety of his borran: a heap of fallen rocks creating a natural lair.

Jasper had been hunting craftily, trailing the main pack at a lower level. When the fox careered towards him, he yelped with the anticipation of a kill and Thomas became caught up in the excitement. Robert was further back, struggling with the climb. When he saw his son race after Jasper, he sensed danger and shouted out, 'Be careful, Thomas.'

Thomas' nightmare flashed through his mind, and one hand instinctively went to protect his throat whilst the other reached for the knife in his belt. He slowed down. This was his first hunt and he knew that few had been lucky enough to witness a kill. The hound's powerful jaws would snap the fox's spinal cord at the neck and cause immediate death. Thomas paled at the thought. He wasn't quite sure if the sickness in the pit of his stomach was from excitement or his reaction to cruelty.

The fox began to stir and his thick brown hair bristled as life rippled through his body. His yellow eyes and almond-shaped pupils focussed on the hazy outline of the bounding menacing Jasper. Legs flailed and kicked desperately into the earth as the fox scrambled to his borran. Jasper lunged frantically with open jaws but snapped at thin air as the bushy tail squeezed through the boulder opening, out of reach, with only an instant to spare. When Thomas caught up Jasper was on his hind legs, scraping his paws against the boulder, howling in frustration, trying to nose his way between the rocks. Thomas realised for the first time that the hound was three times the size of the fox. The hound's large frame had become a handicap and there was little hope of completing a kill. The vermin fox had eluded its hunters and was hiding in the comfort of the lair.

Robert and Hannah arrived at the borran panting steaming breath into the cold mountain air. Robert limped badly, grateful for the pole he was leaning on. 'Did we catch the old fox Thomas?'

'He's inside the lair, Fadder. Jasper nearly caught him!'

Robert bent forward, rested his forehead against the cold stone and peered down between the boulders into the gloom. His thumb and forefingers combed his coarse thick red beard and his nostrils twitched as he picked up the sharp musky smell of fox urine in the borran. The rest of the lair was empty, and he was disappointed when he realised the vixen was mothering her cubs elsewhere. The wily dog fox had led them astray. A few more of the hunters arrived and clamoured around the borran. 'Stay clear lads and give me some room.'

Robert picked up his pole and thrust it between the rocks like a lance. He could see the fox, standing up in defiance of the intrusion, spitting loud clicking staccato sounds through a vicious, open jaw. The dalesman guided the pole between the rocks and waved it around the lair. He teased his cornered foe, circling the end of the pole around its nose. The fox's clicking sounds grew louder. Agitated, he opened his mouth and snapped at the metal tip of the pole. Robert snarled and thrust the pole deep into the fox's throat, viciously screwing the metal auger down into its body. Thomas closed his eyes and cupped his ears until the unearthly screeching ceased. *It's worse than with the rabbits.* Robert struggled with the balance of the pole as he guided the dead weight closer to the exit hole. Damian drew close and started to breathe heavily with the excitement. Robert tugged, twisted and squeezed until the carcass squelched through the narrow gap with a rush. The fox-screw had served its purpose.

With one powerful arm Robert lifted the lamb-killer high above his head and roared triumphantly. His booming voice carried towards the far cliff to his fellow hunters. Blood ran freely down the pole onto his forearm before splashing to the rocky ground. Thomas looked at his father, awestruck, wondering at the warrior-like stance. Was this the same father he knew who sat so peacefully at a Friends' meeting, and who regularly fell asleep during the vicar's sermons? Damian stood alongside his uncle in a trance, holding the palm of his hand out to catch the blood. Thomas looked at the excitement on his cousin's face and was reminded of that night in the forest. He felt sympathy for the suspended animal. *I don't ever want to do this again. This is my first fox hunt, and my last.*

Apprenticeship

Thomas was twelve when he first met Black George. That was the first time he had any inkling his father had plans for his future. The smithy was the same imposing height and build as his father, with huge black hairy forearms, built from a lifetime wielding his tools of trade. Thick, black hair was cut short below his ears, and he was never without a stubbly beard. He worked at the forge bare-backed in summer, his curly chest hair hanging straight with sweat. *No wonder the villagers call him Black George.*

'Do you think I might be a blacksmith, Fadder?'

'I'll certainly do my best for you son, but I'll never be able to afford the upkeep. Just you keep on with your learning at the grammar school and when you master your letters, the Quakers may favour you. Master tradesmen are literate, and most run their own business.'

'What if I wanted to be something else?'

'What else could there be better than a blacksmith? Black George is one of the most respected tradesmen from Coniston to Hawkshead.'

'Of course, you'll be working long hours, not in the open air like you've been brought up to. There'll be the odd market day when the smithy needs to trade, and Sunday off for church. You'll have a strange bed for seven years but living close you can be home Saturday evening and all day Sunday.'

'I'm not sure that I want to be cooped up around an anvil and hot forge all day.'

'You'll think differently in a few years Thomas, you mark my words.'

The day after the hunt, Timothy Atkinson accompanied Robert and his son to Coniston forge. Thomas was four years older now and measuring his thoughts against those of his father. *I'm still not sure I want to be a blacksmith.*

Black George was keen to move on with the business. 'Thou art aware of the Guild's ruling on Quaker apprentices Timothy. An agreement wouldn't be worth the paper it's printed on in the city.'

'I know. It's a travesty that the Guild should discriminate against the Friends when we've such a variety of fine tradesmen serving society. But as you say George, the guilds show their strength more in the cities. We are less susceptible out here. It is discrimination that the law should prevent a Friend from taking an apprentice. We are hopeful that Parliament's ruling will be absolved in the near future. We also wish to make it clear that Thomas is being sponsored from our pool of contributions for the poor. Poor in this case, meaning a man who cannot afford to give his hard-working literate son the chance he so deserves in this world.'

Thomas listened with mixed feelings. He was going to miss the company of his family, and Sunday would be a day to look forward to. *My life is changing too quickly. First the fox hunt and now the smithy.* Timothy smoothed out the Guild papers on the tabletop. 'We'll need thy mark here Robert, and Thomas will sign his name below George's and my own.'

George addressed Thomas before he signed. 'Well now, except for William, our children are all married and no longer at home. Thou hast met my wife Rebecca and William, our son. William will be living at home for another year until he becomes a journeyman, and then he will travel to gather experience. Thou will take over Oliver's daily duties and I can only hope thou are more compatible with Oliver than he is with William. He is now a third-year apprentice and thou will be vying with him in more ways than one. Sharing the same room for a year until William leaves could be the worst. Before we sign, dost thou think thou will be happy living under our roof and dost thou promise not to marry until the apprenticeship is completed and to also follow the rules of our Quaker household?'

Thomas could see no alternative. He had looked at the tanners and leather workers and couldn't stand the stench. Candle making, woodworking, cobbling and tailoring were also unappealing. The more he considered the forge the more he realised how he was built for the work. He was growing fast. In another two years he would be as tall as his father, and with the work in the forge he would be as strong as George Ferris. He could travel with a trade, even to the colonies where the guilds were weak. He could become rich. His excitement increased and he realised the importance of being in the same room as his elders, determining his career, and his future. He felt guilty for his previous doubts. Feeling grown up, he strode across to the table and inked the quill. 'I'm sure I'll be happy living here Mr Ferris and I would like to thank you and Mrs Ferris and Mr Atkinson for your generosity. I'll work hard for you and I hope to learn the blacksmith trade well enough to earn my own living.'

Robert looked on proudly at his son's composure and speech. *You must be proud too Aggie, looking down on our son this fine day. God bless us all.*

'I will expect you in one week's time, Thomas, and not a day sooner. We're prompt in this business and pace our day by the clock as opposed to the sun, something you haven't been accustomed to.'

The following week flew by for Thomas, but one experience remained strong in his memory: travelling with his father through freezing weather to inform the major that the tarn surface was thick with ice. 'That's excellent my good man. The icehouse is in need of a good cleaning out. We need it to be stocked for the spring, as we plan to have an engagement party and there will be important people. You can suggest a price to fill the building, but I don't want rubbish. Only large, thick slabs are acceptable. Hollis has keys for the outside doors and make sure he's there to supervise you. I presume you know how to stack, and care for the ice?'

'I've done it many times in the past, Major. We will bring the ice down the slopes by sled. We usually borrow some horses from your stables.'

'Then you can tell Hollis you have my permission, but I want the first load tomorrow. You can borrow Damian. It's about time the fool did something useful. But make sure the thoroughbred stays in the stable.'

'I'll be using three helpers, Major. Mr Fleming always paid us fifty pence to fill the icehouse.'

'I've loaned you Damian and the horses. Forty pence is ample my good man, I only pay my bailiff two pounds for a full year's service and you're talking of a meagre two days' work.'

'That is for four workers plus the ice, Major.'

'The ice is there by the grace of God, my good man, and you want to charge me for it?'

Robert shrugged his shoulders in acceptance of the price. As they walked home, Thomas was thoughtful, and he asked a worried question. 'You told me Mr Fleming always paid you forty pence.'

'Did I really, Tommy? Now why do you think I made the honest mistake of telling the major it was fifty?'

'I don't know, but it sounded like you were lying. I didn't know that you told lies.'

'Have you heard of a black witch and a white witch, Tommy?'

'Yes, Fadder.'

'What's the difference between them?'

'A black witch is wicked. A white witch is pure and good.'

'What would you think if I said I told a white lie?'

'Was it pure and good?'

'It was almost pure and good. It brought good to us and no harm to the major.' Thomas found his father's knowledge of people inspiring. He was taught to read and write at the school and even taught a little Latin and science, but he was aware there was knowledge in the dales that couldn't be found in learning books.

Robert tapped on the thin perimeter ice, testing it with the fox-screw, working towards the thickness. When he considered it was strong enough to support his weight, he ordered Thomas and Damian to slide the timber raft across the surface and secure the hauling rope. Robert stood on the raft, chipping the ice and floating small sections across to Hannah and the two boys. They drew the slabs across the water with weighted nets and stacked them into the three oblong box sleds. Straw lined the bottom of the sleds, separating each layer of ice in the same manner as they would stack the icehouse.

The locks on the icehouse doors were rusted out. Hollis levered them open. He struggled to break the seal around the solid oak doors and as the doors swung open the hinges creaked and groaned under the weight. The brick and straw-lined room stepped up to the level of the manor house with a drainage pit dug under. A door opened onto a passageway leading to the main house. At the end of the passageway another door gave access to the kitchen. They cleaned the drain and spread hay across the base of the icehouse. There was enough ice for one layer and they covered that with another thick layer of straw before heading off for the next load. In two days, they managed to fill the icehouse almost up to its thatched roofline.

'That's an awful lot of ice Robert.'

'They'll never use half of it Hannah, but the top layer keeps the lower and there's enough to last over summer. Algernon always had large dinners for his wealthy friends and there was always a lot of waste. That's the way these rich folks live.'

The day of apprenticeship drew close, and Thomas needed to be alone. He wandered the fields aimlessly, with a feeling of sadness. He was drawn to the top of the dale and he stood still, his thoughts silenced by the surrounding scenery. The mountain caps still held a soft white bloom of snow and the air blossomed with the scent of spring. Snowdrops, primroses and daffodils were in bloom and young lambs frolicked in the pastures. He inhaled the scenery, hungrily absorbing the tranquillity of the lakes and mountain he'd for so long taken for granted. An image of his mother surfaced; sitting at the edge of the lake, surrounded by daffodils. He was running towards her with a flower in his hand. She took it from him and dangled the yellow bell against her cheek. 'Has my skin turned yellow?' She shook the stalk and watched the bell bounce up and down in her hand. 'It looks like a woman's bonnet Thomas.'

He remembered her long golden hair and the frail voice, her thin white face and the staring, sad blue eyes in their dark sockets. Looking back, he realised the day had been a special one for his mother. He knew that she was sick, and he remembered how beautiful she had been before. He could never quench his desire for those precious days.

He'd mentioned that special day to his father when he was older and smiled as he remembered his amazement. 'But you were no more than three years old Thomas. I had no idea you remembered your mother. It was her favourite place and she'd wanted to see it for the last time. I carried her down to the lake and set her down amongst the daffodils.' Thomas remembered the tears rolling down his cheeks as he told the story.

He also remembered the dark gloomy rainy day soon after her death. Horses pulled sleds to Ulverston holding bodies wrapped in linen and sheepskin. The image was impressed on his memory, but he had never spoken of it to anyone. On their journey to the abbey ruins with Damian they had stopped in Ulverston to visit his mother's grave to leave flowers. He promised himself that these memories would remain with him for always.

He wasn't sure why he'd been drawn to the top of the dale, but he felt at peace and didn't believe he was entirely alone. *I'm in the presence of God.* Tomorrow held a different way of life. His father had wished it of him and in his heart, he knew it was for the best. He scanned the surrounding hillsides on the last day of the freedom of his youth. He purposely stored the picture in his mind and created a picture he would savour forever. The lakes, hills and dales would never change. His mother's special place would always be there for him. His chest expanded as he inhaled the fresh mountain air deeply into his lungs. He took a last wistful look then turned towards home. This time tomorrow his bed would be empty and cold, and he knew that like his father, he would be lonely.

'It's about time you and I had a good talk Robert. I've mentioned this before and you've always rubbished the idea, but the time has come for us both to be practical. We're both on our own now. Damian comes and goes as he pleases, and Mary seems settled with the Atkinsons. Now you are losing, Thomas.'

'Alright, Hannah, I know what you're going to suggest.'

'It's not a suggestion. Timothy asked me to break the news to you, to soften the blow, but perhaps I'm going the wrong way about it. He said it would be a good opportunity for your cottage to be demolished and rebuilt. Yours will be the first of many. The timber's ready and waiting and the stone-walls are to be sealed. When he's rebuilt your cottage, he plans to move us in, and demolish mine; that is if it doesn't fall down in the meantime.'

'I'll have to weigh up my freedom.'

'There'll be no freedom where your women are concerned, I can tell you that now. Poor Aggie must be turning in her grave, God rest her soul. If you want your fancy women, you can take them elsewhere.'

Robert changed the way of the conversation. 'What about our loss of the sheep then? We will lose half the number we're allowed to graze on the fells. That's a fair loss of income.'

'We're going to lose them regardless, so we had best get used to it. The Herdwicks grazing the slopes can be sold. We will have to decide on the one ear marking and sell the rest. Then there are the annual rents we can save and the two one-shilling instalments of hearth tax; one on Lady Day and the other at Michaelmas.'

Robert brightened with a thought. 'I could find a good use for the two shillings.'

'I've no doubt where your mind lies, brother, but you can't spend what you haven't got. All we need to worry about is the small crops, the milking cows and the annual pig. My farm is the better for that. I say you move in now. What you save on rent we can spend on hiring labour.'

'I have to admit I'm feeling out of sorts since Thomas signed the papers, but I'll need my sup of ale and the company of good friends. I'll not forego that. Your home brew is no match for the Brown Cow or Coniston's Black Bull.'

'If you stayed away from the Red Lion, you'd make a fair saving, but forgetting your weakness brother, we will have plenty to trade with if we both pull our weight.'

'Then I'll tell Timothy as soon as possible, Hannah, before he tells me. I should be due some rent back.'

'Will you be attending church more often, now that you've had your way with the Quakers?'

'I don't know what you mean. I believe the lessons that the Friends taught me, that God is within me. I feel more comfortable praying that way than I do in the parish church. Besides which, I don't have to place my hard-earned ale money into the plate so often.'

'It's a pity that's all you think about. The church helped our family after my poor William departed this earth, and there were many like us, scraping for food in the bad years.'

'Going to church and praying to God didn't do Aggie much good Hannah and anyway, I think Timothy expects it of me to attend the Friends' meetings now and then.'

'Now and then is about the size of it. You don't fool me any, Robert Johnson.'

Late that afternoon Robert watched his son packing. Sadness lay heavy in the silence of the small room. 'Don't forget your

Bible son.' He could think of nothing else to say. They never spoke again until they were halfway to the smithy. 'It's a pity you couldn't stay at home with us, Tommy. We're certainly close enough to the smithy for you to travel each day.'

'You know that won't work, Fadder, so don't make it any harder for me. I have to be up before the birds each morning to clear the floor, bring in the charcoal and have the fires burning.'

'Make sure you keep a full belly then.'

They crossed over Yewdale Beck, clogs drumming on the wooden bridge, echoing across the water. A wisp of smoke spiralled from the heart of the deserted smithy and a candle glowed in the doorway of the cottage alongside it. Black George and Rebecca were standing there to greet them. 'Come in Robert and we will have a sup of ale.'

Robert pushed Thomas forward and they settled around the table in front of the glowing fire. *Was it only a week ago that I sat here making my mark on the apprentice papers, signing my son's life away?*

Rebecca sensed Robert's melancholy. 'Thou will be seeing more of thy son than most.'

'That will make it easier. I will just have to get used to it.' Rebecca nodded, lost for any more words of consolation. Robert wasn't in the mood for idle chat. He wanted to leave before his emotions got the better of him. He supped his ale hastily, stood up to leave then looked across at Thomas. 'You'll be alright then son?'

Thomas nodded, fighting back tears. *Go Father. Go now.*

George rested an elbow on the table and cupped his square jaw in his huge palm. He sensed the wrench between father and son and almost felt guilty of stealing the man's only child. 'Thou will see Thomas at the Hawkshead Markets from time to time. I'll be sending him over with Oliver and Rebecca.'

Rebecca looked sharply across at her husband. 'That's the first I've heard of it.'

'That's just to ease him into the trade of course. It'll give him an insight into the value of the domestic utensils we make for the chandlery and the stall.'

'Thank you, George. I'll try not to bother you too much. Just make sure you feed him well. He's a growing lad.'

'Aren't they all, Robert?'

'I'm moving in with my sister; it's for the best.' He raised his hand in a wave. 'See you soon, Thomas.'

Robert strode out towards Yewdale Beck, filling his lungs with the cold night air, inhaling and exhaling deeply with each alternate step, trying to console himself. His heart was heavy and he couldn't fight off the sadness. He was already lonely and as he headed in the direction of Hannah's farm, he thought of the future and how fortunate he was to have such a wise and compassionate sister.

Whitehaven Harbour: spring 1665

Major Rathbone organised a special journey to Whitehaven. The reasons for the trip were twofold. Extra supplies were needed for the engagement party, and the time was right for Rufus to become acquainted with the activities of the Charlotte's first mate. He planned to be away for three days, and left Penny in command. He took Hollis for support and Damian worked the packhorses with two farmhands. The major was expending untold energy on his son's engagement party with an eye to firmly establishing him in Hawkshead Parish. If Rufus and his fiancée Eleanor were to settle in the district, they would need to keep up appearances; silks, tobacco and brandy were some of the necessary and expensive items of the gentry. The major was ecstatic that Squire Holmes had direct connections to the king's court and pleased that his future in-law would take care of the wedding expenses.

Rufus emerged from his lethargy the moment he saw the amount of activity in the growing town of Whitehaven. The new harbour bustled with the arrival of three foreign ships, all anchored and awaiting a berth on the busy wharf. The major organised accommodation close to the markets in Chapel Street then led his companions down to the harbour in search of the *Charlotte*. They found the sailing ship berthed alongside two coal ships, awaiting customs officers to document its cargo. On asking the whereabouts of the first mate, Arthur Grasty, they were directed to the Blue Anchor Inn.

Arthur Grasty sat at a table in a dark corner of the inn. He was colluding with his boatswain, Edward Bone, cheeks pumping like the bellows of a forge, mouth sucking in and out like a fish on dry land. The sweet taste of tobacco was watering his lips and pooling dribble at the sides of his mouth. One hand supported a clay pipe whilst the other cupped over the tobacco bowl; sheltering the ignited coals of dried leaf and bringing them to a fiery red. He concentrated on the glow with fascination, seemingly oblivious to the world around him, yet his eyes covertly scanned the occupants of the room through nervous habit. The air was congested with chatter, the sound of guzzled beer and the clang of empty tankards on the oak tables. Grey smoke billowed from the corner of Grasty's mouth and drifted lazily through shades of patterned light towards the beamed ceiling. He rested his pipe on the scarred oak table and leaned back in ecstasy. He was inhaling what he considered to be the finest tobacco ever to fill the lungs of his slight frame. He began to speak with his boatswain then halted mid-sentence. His ever-alert eyes had spotted the major and his party walking in. He coughed up smoke, sank his head into his palms, and groaned. *Oh no! Did he have to appear in person?*

Colonel Newby had introduced him to the major two years ago. The colonel was visiting the ship's master, Julius Laing, while they were docked in London and had made it obvious that he considered the major to be a pest. He recalled the short introduction and the offloading very well. 'Could you possibly entertain the major while I conclude my business with your captain?' He had often wished his captain had conversed with both the major and the colonel, but then, the outcome would have been quite different. The major had since contributed to his lucrative side trade, so he was fated to suffer the man a little longer than he would have hoped for.

Previous to the London meeting, he had sailed as boatswain on the company's slave trading ships, running from the African coast across to Jamaica and Barbados. He would probably never know the truth, but the story he had heard was that the ship's Scottish owner, Richard Laing, had found religion. Judging by the number of Quakers that were being transported to New England, he could well believe it. Unlike the slave trade, where profits came later, the Quakers paid up front and took their chances. It wasn't always the smooth ride they were expecting. From the tales coming back from those that landed in Boston instead of Rhode Island, it seemed that many of the absconding Friends had leapt from the skillet into a roaring fire. He had heard tales of ears being cut off on arrival and fines of five shillings for not attending church. Women were whipped for the first two offences and a third saw them with a red-hot iron bored through their tongue. It occurred to Grasty that England was the lesser of the two evils.

Richard Laing's close friend, John Lowther, was the Member of Parliament for Cumberland. He was carrying on the work of his father; escalating the mining of coal and extending the wharf's capacity to harbour a larger fleet. Laing's southern registered ships had abstained from the slave trade and registered in Lowther's growing northern port of Whitehaven. Fortunately for Grasty the *Charlotte* was considered unsuitable for coal and the company continued to trade other goods with Dublin and the Indies. It was on the journey back to London, before his acquaintance with the major, that his fortunes had changed for the better.

He was in charge of the midnight watch and taken with surprise when the first mate, William Sturdy, staggered from the captain's cabin brandishing a wine bottle. The first mate was normally a man of sobriety, but the captain was a persuasive man. To see his superior drunkenly bouncing off the ship's rails, laughing hysterically as he headed for the poop deck was, for Grasty, nothing less than astonishing. He watched the first mate's body merge with the darkness. He was at first amused by his singing and laughing, then worried at the immediate silence. He decided to investigate and cautiously followed Sturdy's path. He saw the first mate wildly urinating over the aft rail with a silly grin on his face, his body swaying back and forth with the rhythm of the ship. There was a sudden lurch as the ship ploughed into a huge wave, slamming Sturdy's body against the aft rail. Sturdy almost overbalanced and was left rocking with his paunch on top of the rail, laughing hysterically at his unusual predicament. Only the weight of his feet was keeping him safely inside the ship. Grasty grabbed the opportunity with both hands and cast the first mate headfirst into the sea. It was an urge he had never been able to explain, and he would never forget the first mate's whoop of joy as he flew through the air, and the laughter mingling with the splash of water as his body plunged into the frothy abyss. Grasty turned away, rubbed his hands together, and then wiped them down his jacket to cleanse himself of the deed. He shrugged his shoulders, straightened his three-cornered hat and casually made his way back to join the helmsman. He would start the search for William at the change of the morning watch. *Such a glorious way to end one's life; laughing all the way to the grave!*

Grasty's instinct was tuned to personal gain and since that propitious day his ambition had grown. Whenever possible he sailed the *Charlotte* to his own advantage, and he had every confidence in the ship's crew. After all, less than three years ago he had been one of them, a boatswain with a thirst for knowledge and a hunger for advancing his career. The tragic loss of the brigantine's first mate, just weeks into the voyage, had given him an opportunity to gain his captain's confidence. Richard Laing, the owner of their fleet of ships, was the captain's younger brother, and well aware of his sibling's weakness. The family had long ago decided Julius would be less of an embarrassment constantly sailing the high seas. When the *Charlotte* had returned safely from that tragic voyage, the ship's owner expressed his gratitude for the boatswain's competence. Grasty gratefully accepted his promotion. *A few more years and I could be sailing the* Charlotte *as captain and who knows, with the increase in foreign trading, I could one day own my own vessel.*

He stood up and waved the major's party over. Three tankards of ale were already heading in their direction. A serving wench carried ale tankards clutched high in the air, perilously close to the tavern's oak-beamed ceiling. She swerved her buttocks away from grasping hands, weaving her curvaceous body between tall, crushing shoulders and smelly armpits. The tankards landed at their destination with a dull thud and ale splashed over the table's surface. 'Thank you, Myra, and make that two more, would you?'

'Share what you've got, handsome, or you can wait until your ship sails. I'm busy!'

Grasty offered his hand up and clicked some coins together with a shilling. The pennies are for your own pocket, Myra.'

'I'll be right back, Arthur. Don't go anywhere.'

Major Rathbone's eyes glued on Myra's disappearing buttocks as he slid his own along the bench and settled opposite Grasty. The first mate reached for his tankard and swivelled to face his unwelcome visitor. 'Now, what's the purpose of this surprise visit major?' Without waiting for a reply, he rested his forefinger on the bridge of his nose and leaned across the table to whisper. 'Didn't you receive your usual consignment?'

'You don't have to whisper Grasty. This is my son, Rufus, and you're already familiar with my man Hollis.'

'Yes, I've met Hollis once before. The nightriders speak highly of him.' *More than they do of you. I might say.*

'You'll find my son the equal of him.'

'I'm sure I will.' *But not the equal of you, I hope.*

'I need further supplies of wine and brandy, and perhaps a roll of silk, and some spices.'

'You prefer to pay taxes on your goods, Major?'

'Not really. It's unfortunate that we should both miss out our little profit, unless of course there are other means?'

'I'm sorry, Major. The customs are at this very moment taking their lawful gain.'

Hollis leaned forward. 'Do they charge taxes for runaway Quakers, Grasty?'

The major and Rufus looked at each other surprised and the boatswain sniggered. 'I don't know what you mean.'

'I've heard rumours that the ship's owner favours them.'

'Well, if that's the case, then I can't see any danger in it, can you, Major?'

'Not as long as they have paid their tithes before leaving. They are not under my jurisdiction.'

'I'm sure the master has that well in hand. He works very closely with the customs officers here.'

'Not too closely I hope.' The major attempted a half-nodded wink that amused Grasty more than the remark.

'I'll take you to the ship's master, Captain Julius Laing. Its best you deal with him in these matters. When you were introduced to me in London, you mentioned your wife's uncle was acquainted with the captain's family, Major. Well this time, you shall have the opportunity of meeting the master himself, and you'll find him sober. But if I were you, I wouldn't mention your interest in collecting tithes from the Quakers. They pay for their passage up front, well in advance, and the master reckons it's becoming more lucrative than the slave trade ever was.'

The major made a mental note of this interesting information and thought to mention it to Colonel Kirkby at their next meeting. He grunted and shook his head violently to cast the thought from his mind. *Don't do that, you fool. He would interfere with our trading.*

'Father, are you angry at something?'

He turned his attention to Hollis. 'How long have you known about the Quakers?'

'I found out this afternoon, Major.'

'You should have informed me at once, instead of trying to be clever. Now let's finalise this business of ours. The sooner those packhorses are loaded the sooner we can be on our way. I don't like Penny being in charge for too long. The last time I left her alone she gave away a prized thoroughbred and accused me of sending its owner to his death.'

The engagement party: May 1665

Lizzie stopped at the foot of the stairs, put an ear to the tall clock and drew the chain down for its daily setting. The manor house buzzed with excitement. Few could remember the last time there'd been so many important guests. The domestic staff had been tripled and Lizzie was run off her feet organising. Under the supervision of Penelope and Hollis, Lizzie had seen the icehouse stocked with meats, desserts and drinks, enough to last a houseful for three days. On ice were deer, pig, chicken, mutton, trout and game bird; crates of vegetables were stacked in the icehouse passageway.

Rufus was warming to the occasion. 'We must have musicians and dancing, Father.' The promised lease of quality land from his father and a generous dowry from Squire Holmes had heartened him. Marrying Eleanor was proving to be more rewarding than he'd imagined, but he was experiencing the first stirring of conscience. 'What about the old woman living in the cottage father?'

'The woman's name is Agnes Walker and she refuses point blank to move, says that she's lived there all her life and will stay until the end. What a stroke of luck I discovered her dabbling with the Quaker religion, otherwise her removal would prove problematic. She has a nephew in Ravenglass, name of Andrew Mossop. He might be persuaded to look after her, but it's really none of your concern. The cottage will stand vacant by the time of the wedding.'

'I'll have to keep it from Eleanor. She would never agree to the eviction of an old woman.'

'The wheels are in motion. You'll thank me for it later.'

The chandelier was lowered, and fresh candles inserted. Penelope ordered the tables be brought together and placed under the chandelier. The most important guests were to sit in the centre, befitting their position. A special effort had persuaded Colonel Richard Kirkby and his family to attend, as well as Judge Falcon and his wife. Penelope checked the guest list with the major. 'Squire Holmes will arrive with a party of four, there's the vicar and his wife plus we three. The rest of the party can number no more than twenty-five, including the most influential statesmen and their families. Who do you consider, Rowan?'

The major showed as little interest as possible in what he deemed the 'trivialities of the engagement party'. 'I'll ask Webster for a list of suitable statesmen. It is imperative we impress the squire. I ride with many yet know little of their characters. Organise the invitations with Hollis.'

'I want extra serving girls and kitchen staff.'

'Lizzie and the cook can handle that and trust Hollis to fix their wages. Hire whoever you must, but make sure the wenches are young and not drawn into conversation. The local dialect is confusing in the soberest of times.'

On the day of the engagement Penelope ensured the serving girls were suitably dressed and reminded them, through their giggles, of the correct manner of table presentation. The kitchen was in chaos and Hollis was called from his duties to regiment the staff. His suggestion that there be a dress rehearsal involving a small number was vindicated. The major had hedged at the expense and the plan was dismissed without a second thought. Penelope was spared the trauma of the bedlam behind the scenes. Out front she was composed in her new dress, relishing playing hostess to the gentry. In a quiet moment she mused on how she'd drifted from the spontaneity of her youth. *We should do this more often.*

Dinner was a total success and the toasts magnanimous. The party flowed into the garden, and by the time the last glass had scraped the bottom of the punch bowl, the inside tables were magically clear. Melodious music filled the ballroom, spilled into the hall and cascaded down the corridors. Four violinists rocked on their chairs, coaxing rhythms from their instruments, enticing dancers to the floor with each stroke of the bow. Inebriated guests danced wildly; bodies swaying, legs kicking, arms flailing like puppets on a string. Squire Holmes accepted all credit, assuring the major that the fiddlers and the flageolet player had indeed played at King Charles II's coronation.

Penelope had never been prouder. The huge effort had made every moment worthwhile. Yet there was one nagging thought she couldn't dispel. She linked arms with her husband, cornered their future in-laws before they reached the dancefloor, and coerced them into conversation. The major ranted, clueless of Penelope's intentions until she lost her patience and dug her elbow into his ribs. The major struck back, annoyed. 'What is it?'

'Say something, Rowan.'

'What on earth are you whispering about woman?'

'You know—about Eleanor.'

He lifted his head to continue the conversation. 'Ahem! Holmes. By the way, we were thinking that your daughter is delightfully slim about the waist.'

'That's very kind of you. She's the spit of her mother Catherine at the same age.'

'I didn't mean that my good fellow. There's no doubting she has a desirable figure, but I was hinting at the pregnancy.'

Squire Holmes feigned deafness, cupping his hand over his ear and leaning forwards. 'Damned fiddles and thumping feet. I can't hear a damn thing. You were saying?'

Penelope abandoned her patience and screamed at the top of her voice. 'We're talking about your daughter's pregnancy Squire. Eleanor's not large about the waist. We don't think she's *pregna.....ant.*' Her voice faded with the cadence of the music, and the last word echoed in a deathly silence. Feet shuffled nervously on the timber floor as the dancers parted. They faced each other, like rows of empty houses, still and expressionless, victims of the timeless calm before a storm. A nervous giggle broke the suspense, and suddenly the air was alive with animated chatter. The major snapped to attention then marched across the floor to berate the quintet. 'Let's hear some music. Play a courante. What do you think I'm paying you for?'

Rufus and Colonel Kirkby's son, Robert, entered from the garden, their ladies close behind. Eleanor went to her mother's side and enquired of her future mother-in-law's health. Penelope was flushed with embarrassment, silently begging the ground to open up and swallow her. Catherine Holmes took her by the elbow and led her to a quiet corner of the hall. 'We didn't know how to tell you as the engagement was so far advanced.'

'You should have informed us at once. Does Rufus know?'

'No he doesn't. It could affect our daughter's wedding. Do you think it really matters when they truly love each other?'

'You really think they love each other?'

'Yes I do. Eleanor is totally infatuated with your son.'

Penelope stared at Catherine dumbstruck. *Does she really believe that? Or is it like Rufus said all along: they connived to offload her.* 'I'll have to speak with my husband first Catherine. This has all come as a huge shock. Was this a genuine mistake?'

'I've no doubt. Eleanor is not that devious.'

The major ambled over, abandoned by Squire Holmes, who was diligently peppering an attractive young lady with political boredom. Penelope was an honest woman with an open mind. She explained the situation to her husband and determined to solve it immediately. 'I think we should tell Rufus at once.'

'Why do you want to do that?'

'Because it's the truth, and his future happiness depends on it.'

'He will have a good life if he marries the squire's daughter. They say that Holmes has an ear in the king's court.'

'So that's it. You're thinking of yourself again.'

'Naturally, the sensible thing would be to tell him a little closer to the wedding. Once he sees the advantages of the marriage, he will be more likely to go ahead with it.'

'You're suggesting he resembles yourself then?'

The major smirked and levered his chest. 'I would like to think so, Penny. I would like to think so.'

'Then let it be on your own head. I'm having nothing else to do with the marriage.'

Squire Holmes, spurned in his quest, joined the gathering. 'Have you sorted out your little problem?'

'So you knew, Squire?' Penelope was vexed.

'Not exactly Penny. Just a whiff, if you know what I mean. I thought it best to leave it to Catherine. In my opinion, women's troubles are best left for women to solve.'

The major nodded his agreement and fixed his eyes on the squire's headpiece. 'Is that a new periwig you're wearing, Holmes?'

'Yes, it is. Do you like it?'

'That depends on how new it is.'

'I had it delivered from London only last week. You should have one fitted. They're very becoming and totally in vogue in our circle.'

'I had a feeling it came from London. A pity it's so new though.'

'I don't follow you, Major?'

'The plague is raging down there. We're not entirely ignorant of the news up here you know.'

'I still don't understand what the plague has got to do with my new periwig, Major.'

'As far behind as we are of the latest news, we have heard that due to unprecedented demand, the wigmakers are scalping the dead lining the streets. You could unwittingly be the next carrier of the disease to the north.'

The squire was already scratching his neck and feeling an itch in his scalp. 'You'll have to excuse me, ladies, I have an urgent demand on my body.' He was fighting an urge to lift his hand to the wig.

The major gloated, pleased with his contribution to the squire's discomfort. His eyes fixed on the agitated man's torso as it floated through the crowd of dancers, searching desperately for fresh air. He called out after him. 'I would burn that wig if I were you, Squire. It would be for the good of the community.'

Late that night the manor house lay deathly still. Most of the guests were helplessly inebriated. Many slumbered in the corridors, having never made it to the comfort of their beds. Lizzie lay on the bed with her eyes wide open staring intensely at the ceiling, trying to unwind. Like all the domestics she was exhausted, still feeling the tensions of the evening. The party had been a heavy workload for an understaffed kitchen. She heard creaking floorboards down the hallway and someone prowling around clumsily outside. *Someone's lost.*

The creaking stopped outside her door and Lizzie's eyes fixed on the doorknob slowly turning. She shot up in bed as a crack of light sliced the darkness. Her hand reached under the pillow to grab the kitchen knife and she held it with two shaking hands in front of her terrified face. A man in a nightgown and nightcap stood in the doorway, his face partly illuminated by the flame from his raised candleholder. 'Shhhh!' a whisper emanated from under the nightcap.

'Major! What are you doing roaming the house in the middle of the night? Is there something I must do for you?'

The major's face lifted into a smile as he gleefully stroked the bulge in his nightgown. He placed the candle on a side-table and lifted the hem of his nightgown. He draped it over his beloved's protruding erection and chanted an old army chestnut:

'Strike whilst the iron's hot
Or you're bound to miss your shot.'

Still beaming, he spread his arms wide and with great pleasure proclaimed to the stunned housemaid. 'It's *reward* time, my good woman.'

'Reward time?'

'Yes! It's all yours.'

'Don't you mean forfeit time?'

'Both if it pleases you.'

'It's late, Major, and it's me time of month.'

'What's time got to do with true love, my dearest? Your buxom beauty tempts me like no other.' He shuffled towards Lizzie with embrace at the ready, beloved leading the charge. 'Grab the opportunity with both hands, my little dove.' No sooner had the words left his mouth than he let out a horrible scream and cradled his balls. 'Good God. Help me, Jesus. The pain's returned tenfold. It's pure torture.'

Lizzie rubbed her eyes in disbelief, and then slid her knife back under the pillow, baffled by her empathy for the intruder. 'If it is givin yer so much pain, Major, then yer best pop it inter me cunny. There's no sense in suffering all that agony.'

She opened her legs and for a moment the major was torn between the pain and the generous invitation. He shuffled closer and her hands guided his beloved into her warmth. The pain lay dormant for a while, and he wriggled around in ecstasy, hoping that this time there would be no painful ejaculation. But good luck deserted him, and he could no longer deny the images flooding his mind. Of late, they had taken the form of a canon. With each downward thrust he felt the powder being rammed into the barrel and the iron ball loaded. He could hear the sizzle and smell the burning gunpowder as he waited with dreaded antici-pation for the agony of recoil. There was no escaping his torture and at the height of his climax the accompanying scream would have given credit to any young aspiring leader of a cavalry charge.

The whole manor shot into life. Tinder boxes were fumbled for, candles hastily lit, and doors slammed open. Lizzie trembled with shock as the major's war cry thundered around her head. He leapt out of bed, grasping the pain between his legs. He snatched the candleholder with his other hand and completely ignoring Lizzie, rushed out of the room. He fled down the corridor dodging the human debris, one hand on the pain. Lizzie slammed the door shut and shot the bolt tight. She leaned her back against the door, bent her trembling knees and slipped slowly to the ground. She stayed there listening to the commotion, trying to distinguish the conversations and wondering if she would ever be able to leave her room again.

Penelope heard the scream and shot up in bed. She leaned across to shake her husband awake but her hands fell on cold sheets. *He's sleepwalking again.* She lit a candle, donned her nightgown and moved cautiously towards the stairs. The major was at the bottom waiting for her. He had opened the front doors and left them ajar. 'What's happening down there? What was all that screaming?'

'There was an intruder Pennykins, and I almost had him. I didn't want to disturb you without good reason. The thought of a burglar would have frightened you.'

'It sounded to me that *you* frightened *him.*' Her eyes descended to his navel.

'Is that blood on your nightshirt?'

He looked down and panicked, his mind working overtime. 'No, no, of course it isn't. Unless ... Of course, that's it! I must have wounded the blighter, struck him with my candleholder as he fled past me.' He turned to the gathering rabble of servants and visitors. 'Everything's taken care of good people. The vagabond has fled, and we can all go safely back to our beds.'

Penelope wasn't so sure. The last time this happened, Rowan promised her that he'd been sleepwalking. *Something's not right.*

After rising early, the following morning, the major sent for Lizzie. 'That was a terrible mistake we made last night my girl and I want you to make it up for me. If anyone asks questions, you must explain that a burglar burst into your room, that you were terrified, that you took your knife to him, and then he ran off when you screamed.'

'You don't want me to tell the truth then?'

'Now let me see.' His forefinger stroked his lower lip, as he thought. 'No! Not exactly the whole truth, but something very near to the truth. When I heard the scream, I came charging into the room to rescue you.'

'Well, you certainly charged off, I'll agree to that, but you didn't run into my room. You crept in with your candle ablaze from the best of my memory.'

'No, no, Lizzie, I'm suggesting that the man was a stranger.'

'He was strange alright. I've never seen the likes, but I think I know what you want me to say. Perhaps if I could have a day off with pay there would be less likelihood of embarrassment.'

'Unfortunately, my wife needs you today, but a day owing I promise.'

'Well then, as long as you explain the reason for the day off to Mrs Rathbone.'

'Leave it with me. I'll tell her you were most rewarding during the celebrations.'

'Just tell her I worked thrice as hard and deserve a day off with pay, sir.'

Squire Holmes was the next of the gentry to rise. He bumped into Lizzie as she was leaving the library. 'Did they catch the burglar last night, Lizzie?'

'I don't know what you're talking about, Sir.'

'There was a commotion after midnight, and I heard a scream.'

'Oh that. I thought I saw someone standing in my doorway, so I screamed.'

'That's a pretty deep voice you have my good woman.'

'It happens when I'm frightened.'

'It sounded more like a man's voice to me, but then, I was half asleep. I just hope the intruder wasn't our future son-in-law. I've heard Rufus has a reputation for visiting young ladies unannounced. A bit of a rascal one might say. Can you tell me anything good about him?'

'Nothing I can think of, Sir, but then I've only known Master Rufus for a short time. You shouldn't worry too much about him though as I find him more amiable then some.' She begged her leave and left for her morning duties.

The major poked his head out of the library door. 'Did you sleep well, Squire?'

'Listening in, Major? I was discussing the disturbance last night with your domestic.'

'That's all been taken care of, Holmes. I thought I heard you mention my son's name.'

'I was saying that your Rufus has quite a reputation with the ladies. We need to protect our daughter from any future scandal.'

'If you've heard rumours detrimental to my son, they are unfounded. Name the scurrilous gossiper spreading these untruths and I will be most grateful. Now, I'm sure we can find more important business than a betrothal to discuss.'

'I could certainly go a pre-lunch hair of the dog.'

'Then join me in the library, Squire. I'm a bit thirsty myself. I'm glad to see you've discarded that plague-ridden periwig.'

Holmes ruffled and scratched his short hair. 'I thought I would let some fresh air into the scalp, Major.'

'I saw your aide early on. He was outside by the stables picking nits out of the damn thing and smoking it over a fire.'

'I'm sure he wouldn't have found any. It was merely a precautionary examination. One can't be too careful you know.'

'Seemed like he had found some to me, Holmes, and he was cleansing it with the smoke. They say that smoke helps wards off the plague as well.'

'You don't like periwigs, do you, Major?'

'I sometimes wonder what Cromwell would have thought.'

'For God's sake, Major, don't ever mention that man's name in my presence or any of my acquaintances' presence. Those days are behind us. When you come the wedding, you will be meeting people with an ear to the king, so be warned.'

The major perked up. 'Do you think the king might attend?'

Squire Holmes mocked the major's naivety. 'Not a chance. My only contacts are with the outer perimeter of his court. You will of course be expected to wear a periwig.' For once the major was stunned into silence. Squire Holmes leaned forward with a supercilious smile and pounced. 'Together with a silk suit of course and I might add that you'll feel quite out of it if you presume to attend otherwise.'

The wine glass overflowed, and the major turned his back whilst he sipped it to a lower level before handing it over to the squire. 'Where can I have a wig made that's guaranteed to be free of the plague?'

'Wigs of human hair are in great demand, inflating prices. With the plague still raging and the doubts being planted in people's minds they could become even more expensive. I suggest you order one made from horse or goat hair as they would be more likely to suit your pocket.'

'You assume much about the depths of my pockets. I assure you my affairs aren't as liable to insolvency as some I know. I shall order a wig made of human hair and you may rest assured, it will be made from the hair of a clean, healthy northerner.'

'There's no need to be objectionable, I was only trying to be helpful. And as for your reference to my affairs having a bit of a wobble, they are presently most certainly on firm ground and will stay as such.'

'I'm pleased to hear that. 'The silk suit you speak of. Surely that's not essential?' *I can't believe I've been coerced into wearing a periwig. The man's more devious than I imagined.*

The squire was beginning to enjoy pressing his advantage, balancing the score of the major's indiscretion with the wig. 'I'm afraid so, Major. It's crucial to your family's acceptance.' The major thought of the roll of silk he had recently purchased from

Whitehaven, and how he could explain its loss to Penelope. *A trip to Cambridge and a visit to the dressmaker will placate her.*

'Can we talk of something other than the wedding? I will be glad when the damned thing's over and done with. You spoke last night of your connections with the royal stables, and a new annual horserace of the king's making.'

'The new race is planned for October next year. As you well know, the royal stables are in Newmarket, and that is where the king likes to race his thoroughbreds. He is expected earlier this year because of the plague, but I will keep you informed of any changes. At present there will be an entry fee of three pounds and a prize of fifty guineas to the winner. The rules are still being formulated.'

The major winced. 'Three pounds you say. With all the other expenses I will need to win the race to make the travel worthwhile.'

'It will not be the winning of the race that counts, Major. Anyone that is worthy of racing against the king's stables will elevate their standing in the right circles. But it is not something you should worry yourself over. I shall be struggling to find a thoroughbred that is worthy of entry, so it's most unlikely that you will ever have the opportunity. I suggest you don't lose any sleep over it.'

'You will be surprised, Holmes. I know more about horseflesh than you could ever dream of.'

'Then you must show me the thoroughbred that you believe to be from the king's stables.' The previous night, Squire Holmes had listened with boredom to the major boasting of his acquisition and thought to humour him rather than cause a scene. Unless the horse had bolted and fled north, he knew there was little chance of the major ever owning such a prized possession. But as soon as the squire entered the stable his supercilious smile turned to envy. He immediately recognised Prince's superior breeding. He pushed Damian roughly aside in his eagerness to run his hands over the freshly groomed horse. 'There are few horses of such quality breeding anywhere in this country. How did it come into your possession?'

The major beamed. 'It was left to my wife by the previous owner of the manor, Algernon Fleming.'

'Does the king know of this?'

'I can't say, but there's evidence the colt was won in a wager.'

'Then for your sake, Major, I hope it was an honest wager, because the king would behead anyone that stole from him.'

Holmes ran his palm over the branding and there was no doubt in his mind. It read 'CS', the royal marking of Charles Stuart.

'What do you think, Squire? Shall we continue this discussion over some sustenance at the Red Lion? You can take your choice of mounts.'

'A ride on the thoroughbred would give me immense pleasure major.'

The major picked up on the squire's change of attitude. The tide had turned, and he now held the upper hand. 'Damian! Saddle up Prince for Squire Holmes. I'll take the chestnut mare.'

The two expert horsemen cantered their mounts in short bursts, restricted by the hilly terrain, unable to stretch their charges to the full. Squire Holmes voiced his frustration at the inn, lecturing the major between gulps of beer. 'Your horse will have to be put through his paces elsewhere, Major. He's carrying too much blubber and needs to have regular strenuous exercise on the flat.'

I agree Holmes. If Prince remains in the district, there is little chance of him reaching the level required to race in the king's plate. I can guarantee the horse's stamina, but he'll never acquire the speed. I shall have to find a suitable training ground close to our parish. I shall speak with Colonel Kirkby. If all goes well, I will test Prince's progress against your string this September and enter him for the inaugural Newmarket Plate the following October.'

Rogues of the road

Everything would have gone as planned, if only Penelope hadn't invited Vicar Braithwaite to the Red Lion farewell party. After only a glass of wine the vicar became an accidental doomsayer. The mention of their guest's early morning ferry crossing set him off on a wild oratorical extrapolation. 'Naturally, you would have heard of the terrible 1635 tragedy?'

He'd been politely ignored up to this point, but upon hearing the word tragedy the visitor's curiosity was aroused. All conversation stopped as they circled the vicar with expectancy. Gabriel was delighted with the attention and paused to clear his throat before beginning the sermon. 'It was Monday the nineteenth of October, in the year 1635, and on the night of a terribly violent thunderstorm. Shoppers were returning from the market, and the ferry was heavily laden with carts and horses. Rain was pouring down, and not willing to wait for the ferry's return, a large party of wedding guests squeezed aboard. Deep thunder echoed in the hills like distant canon-fire. Lightning splintered the night with every blink of the eye. The storm was suddenly above them and the thunder deafening. A searing bolt of lightning struck the lake, then an instant clap of thunder, like the crack of a whip. The horses became terrified. They reared, bucked and stampeded to one side of the boat, and as the handlers went to calm them, the flat-bottomed ferry listed, its loading ramp dropped, and the lake flooded in.' He paused in his sermon for emphasis, pleased with a wide-awake audience for once, and for the opportunity to spout his knowledge of local history. 'The ferry sank quickly into the deepest section of the lake, and the screams of the drowning passengers were heard miles away. On that fateful evening we lost forty-seven passengers and eleven horses. There were no survivors.'

Gabriel sat back on his heels, and, being a short man, he stood on the tips of his toes to scan the standing circle of listeners. He was surprised at the absence of detractors. Catherine sat down, stunned into silence. To the squire's wife, with her strong super-stitious nature, the information was nothing short of catastrophic. Here they were in Hawkshead, intending to embark on a ferry crossing that was haunted by the death of an entire wedding party. And here she was, organising of all things, a wedding. *I wonder did all our guests at the engagement party arrive back safely.* 'Thank you, Vicar Braithwaite, for entertaining us with your fascinating story. You are indeed a man of God and bless us with your presence. You have surely been sent this evening as our savior, to rescue us from a terrible fate.'

The vicar was gratified and humbled by Catherine's godly statement, but just a little baffled by her knowledge of some future terrible fate. He couldn't remember anyone else being pleased by knowledge of the tragedy. 'Thank you, Mrs Holmes.'

Catherine faced her husband and spoke sternly. 'We're not going on the ferry!'

'Pardon dear?'

'We're going the long way around, and that's final. They say the ferryman is blind as well so that's another good reason for not going.'

'The ferryman runs the business. He doesn't guide the boat dear. He employs oarsmen.' The squire believed his wife had had a little too much to drink and would be more realistic in the morning, so he decided to agree, for the time being.

The party paid scant attention to the four men playing cards in a dingy corner of the room. Had Hollis been present, he would no doubt have walked over and introduced himself. The tall, heavily set dealer was sporting a three-cornered navy hat, army jacket and French riding boots. He had a slight squint, a pencil-line moustache, and a scar running along his cheekbone that gave character to his handsome face. The blemish was barely obscured by dark stubble and gave substance to a volatile edge. He leaned over the table to deal, expertly swerving the cards around a tankard of ale. There were few men who could slip a card more dexterously, nor better understand the advantages that could be taken of an opponent. In chosen company he took on a different guise; well groomed, cap-less, silk doublet, gentlemanly pantaloons and expensive shoes. He could carry off from ten to thirty pounds in one sitting. Such was his expertise that losers would attribute his winning streaks to good fortune, and depending on his company, few were dissuaded from playing with him a second time. His eyes darted towards the new arrivals and back again to the Red Lion's chamberlain behind the bar. A nod of recognition passed between them, and the inn's landlord beckoned over the ostler. They stood at the bar whispering, casting glances towards the major and his party. The ostler walked across to the card table, whispered in the dealer's ear, and received a coin for his trouble. The dealer stood up and made for the exit, closely followed by his three companions. He inadvertently brushed the major's shoulder, and they spun around to face each other. The major gave him a look of disdain. *Bloody peasants!* Ignored the challenge and picked up on the conversation with

Squire Holmes. 'Now don't forget our invitation, Major. We would like you and Penny to visit us in July, and I implore you not to arrive without your thoroughbred. We must test his speed and stamina against my stable.'

'We may not be able to make the journey until September for the wedding, but I'm looking forward to showing your string the back end of my horse.'

'Don't expect too much of your horse, Major. He has the breeding, but his condition has been neglected for too long. The talent in our stable is quite formidable and that of the king and the lords even more so, but you're entitled to your fantasy.'

'I'll make sure you eat your words, Holmes. Don't take me for a fool. Unfortunately, I will have to travel with the stable boy. Hollis assures me he's the only one that has any affinity with the horse.'

'That will have to change and the sooner the better. You can race against my stable in any manner you choose, but to race in the King's Plate you will have to use a gentleman rider. Those are the rules. Perhaps you should look towards my future son-in-law, despite his lack of patience.'

'I must admit that Rufus is an excellent rider but using him will depend on his length of stay on your estate.'

'And that will depend on my wife and daughter. If you don't visit in July, then you won't be available for a fitting.'

'If you mean the wedding suits, then Rufus is my size. He'll be paying more than one visit, and possibly with his mother if I can't make it. Have both suits tailored for the same size and be careful of that roll of silk in your care. It's a far better quality than we could ever expect to purchase from the mercer in Kendal. And the same goes for that cask of brandy in your care.'

'Never fear, Major, I'll guard them with my life. You won't tell me where you acquire such exquisite goods?'

'That's for me to know, and for you wonder about.'

The next morning after a hearty breakfast, a string of packhorses were led away from the Red Lion. Rufus felt uneasy about his choice of life. He felt caged and was tempted to jump ship. His future parents-in-law had a poor opinion of him, and here he was, travelling with them on a long arduous journey, with no hope of escape. He had Squire Holmes' boring political monologues to look forward to and an ominous feeling that, despite the growing ease of conversation with Eleanor, she and her mother were plotting against him. The early morning sustenance was having an effect, and as the horses settled into a rhythm so did the squire's head begin to rock on his chest. Mother and daughter quickly followed suit, their mounts contentedly following the pack.

Food had the opposite effect on Rufus. He fidgeted with the bridle, energetic and irritated. When they came to a steep incline, he urged his horse to the lead. As he approached the rise, he turned in his saddle to urge the stragglers on. 'We'll never get anywhere at this rate. Use your whips.' He rode over the rise well in front and pulled up sharply. 'Whoa up my beauty!' Two riderless horses blocked the road and there was a man on his knees cradling another's head in his arms.

The packhorses followed over the rise and as they pulled up behind Rufus, the party awoke from their daydreaming. Squire Holmes stirred and straightened in his saddle. 'What's going on?'

Rufus had already dismounted and raced over to the injured man. He leaned over, placed a hand on the carer's shoulder and found himself looking down the barrel of a cocked pistol. The man wore a mask resting on the bridge of his nose, but Rufus recognised the three-cornered hat, the pencil-line moustache and the scarred cheekbone. He was the man who had bumped into his father at the inn 'That's enough staring, young man.' He pushed Rufus backwards and he lay spread-eagled across the road with the sky in his face. A shadow cast over him and the domineering highway man stabbed a boot into his ribs. 'Back to the packhorses and unload your valuables.' For a brief moment Rufus imagined himself a hero, brave enough to grab the robber by the legs and wrestle him to the ground, until the highwayman's other two accomplices came into the open, each one brandishing a pistol.

Edwin Sutton's hunger stemmed from his youth. His parents' estates were confiscated by Cromwell during the Civil War, and they had died destitute. He had watched helpless as his younger siblings were farmed out to close relatives, who were also struggling to survive. Edwin was the eldest son and well educated in the ways of being a gentleman. Without an inheritance he learned to fend for himself. He had lost all respect for law and authority long before the end of Cromwell's reign, but despite his chosen path, he remained a devout Catholic.

After the restoration of the king, he had by chance happened on the path of a notorious highwayman and honed his talents accordingly. An early lesson had become his motto. 'Treat the ladies kindly, Edwin, and you will have a fair chance of surviving the noose,' He became a rogue of the road in the guise of a gentleman, preying on the gambling habits of the wealthy, milking them whilst charming their ladies. He plied his trade amongst the southern inns of England and the docks of London. His career came to a halt when he lapsed in his motto and fell prey to a lady of the court. He collected a recognisable scar in the process and went into hiding. Edwin was all ready to ship out when a devious acquaintance from the dockside, named Arthur Grasty, informed him of a changing allegiance. The time was ripe for his move to the north-west England.

Of late, his activities had been centred on the growing harbour of Whitehaven, the inns of Kendal, Keswick and Cockermouth and the distribution of stolen goods to favoured clientele. Some innkeepers were more inclined than others to share information about their guests. They were aware of the contents of their luggage, destination and time of departure. Their information entailed a share of the profits, and the agreement was honourable.

Edwin waved his pistol at the riders and requested they dismount. 'Keep your hands away from your firearms obedient gentlemen.' He then cast his attention toward Catherine and Eleanor who were trembling, huddled together across their mounts. 'Ladies, you have nothing to fear, I merely ask you for sustenance, and a little charity. Could you please dismount, and bring the old man to my side?'

Catherine quickly gathered herself together, urging the squire to dismount. 'Off you go now, Cornelius, we don't want to upset the nice man, do we?'

The squire staggered from his horse, fuming. 'What the hell did you dismount for Rufus?'

'Quiet, you fool. The young man came to my aid because of his kindness. Now give me the key to the lady's jewel case and untie that cask of brandy.'

'How do you know there's brandy, you vagabond?'

'I can smell it old man. I can almost taste it. Now hurry! Our day is short.'

The highwaymen cheered when the brandy cask was placed in front of them, and Edwin laughed when he saw the roll of silk. Major Rathbone would be desperately in need of more supplies. He only had to make sure there were no recognisable markings before the silk was resold to a devious mercer. *I can't think of anything more satisfying than a quick turnover.*

'Remove your jewellery, ladies. Brooches and rings are always welcome. Please place them in the sack. And you, old man, your watch, and the moneybag.'

Squire Holmes played a tug-of-war before he begrudgingly let go. 'Sixty pounds is all the money I have and I need to pay the coachman when we reach the London road.'

'You should ride your horses all the way. It will cost less and be far more enjoyable than bumping along the road in a rattling coach.'

Edwin closed in on the squire until he was almost nose-to-nose, and then poked the barrel of his pistol hard into his throat. 'It's people of your station that brought my family to grief and sent my parents to an early grave. I would be happy to never hear the sound of your voice again, so try not to tempt me, lest I choose to hang from the gallows as reward for your misfortune.' He stepped back, looking Holmes up and down with slow deliberation before assaulting him with orders. 'Take off your jacket, shirt, and riding boots, and hand them over. And before you open your mouth, be thankful that I'm leaving you with your backside covered.' Sneering, he gestured with his head for Rufus to stand up and join the squire.

He then turned his attention to mother and daughter, cowering behind their menfolk, terrified and holding each other's shaking hands. 'Come out from behind those ugly men ladies and give my eyes the pleasure to behold your beauty.' The highwayman's manner had completely changed.

'Keep your hands off my wife and daughter, you insolent rogue, or there'll be twenty pounds on your head.'

'Be quiet you fool. I find it hard to distinguish between the two ladies, but whichever is the case, I'm sure you don't deserve such a gracious wife.'

Catherine had been gazing haughtily skyward, her nose in the air, disconcerted, wishing herself as far away as possible from this embarrassing situation. She glowed with appreciation at the highwayman's flattery, smiled at Eleanor and squeezed her hand.

Eleanor was puzzled by the change in her mother, but Edwin had charmed many a woman on the open road. He had purposefully addressed Catherine, whom he rightly guessed to be the strength of the family. 'Those eyes of yours would be the undoing of me, Madam, and I would gamble my life to a farthing that a smile from you would do much more than captivate me.' Catherine smiled, curbing an urge to curtsy. The highwayman gathered his men to leave. 'I hope I have the good fortune of meeting you lovely ladies again, preferably in more amiable circumstances. Il a été un plaisir Mesdames.' Catherine fanned her flushed face, and addressed her family, breathing heavily. 'I'm certain that we've been honoured with a visit from the notorious and handsome highwayman Claude Duval. Who else would be able to steal from a woman with such charm? I've heard it said that King Charles II looks on the rogue with admiration, and I can't wait to tell everyone of our little adventure.'

'You are mad, woman. If that was Claude Duval, then I'm a Dutchman invading merry England. And as for a *little* adventure, that vagabond has just taken my last sixty pounds. Mark my words, before the year is out, he'll be hanging from the gallows with the rest of his kind.'

Catherine parted her cloak and patted beneath her breasts with deliberation. 'He didn't search for my purse and more is the pity. He may have lacked a French accent but nevertheless he spoke like a gentleman and that's good enough for me. Now, let's be gathering ourselves together. There's no sense in crying over spilt milk. We will return to the manor and explain our situation to the major. And Cornelius, you'd best be dressing yourself respectfully. I've had enough embarrassment for today.'

The squire's wife was in her element. She'd been miserable at the thought of the long ride back home, but now she couldn't wait to get started again. The sooner she was home in Cambridge and civilization, as she was wont to say, the better. It occurred to her that if she'd approved of the ferry crossing her little adventure might never have happened, and she was secretly pleased with herself. Her memories of the encounter were pleasant, but there was one thing she was certain of: superstition would never persuade her to make another detour. Perhaps *Cornelius was right about the ferry.*

Her husband was amongst the packhorses, sorting fresh clothes from a sailcloth bag. 'Darling, we *will* be taking the ferry route tomorrow, won't we?' The squire coughed a strangled reply and Catherine assumed it to be in the affirmative.

Hawkshead Market

Rebecca Ferris enjoyed the Monday markets. Once a week she was able to escape the heat and dust to socialise. 'Mind the stall for me Oliver. You can show Thomas how to barter with the customers. I'll be at the shambles buying our meat supply if you need me.' She bustled off to the market house in the square with every confidence in Oliver's ability. *He's put out by Thomas' presence, but he needs to learn how to handle the extra responsibility. George should have waited a few more months.*

Oliver was unsociable. He treated Thomas like an outsider; made him feel uncomfortable and out of place. He was nineteen and shorter than Thomas by a head. Thomas thought him a little too plump for the image of a smithy, but he begrudgingly admired Oliver's ability and there was no doubting the strength in his shoulders. They had worked together early that morning stacking huge bars of wrought iron beside the forge, and he struggled with loads that Oliver lifted with ease. He felt uncomfortable standing behind the stall and dreaded his first customer. He was only three months into his apprenticeship and selling implements he didn't even know how to make. He thought he would be much happier pottering around the smithy and learning something worthwhile. Thomas looked down at all the goods spread across the stall. Fire tongs, pokers and guards were at one side and he knew they were popular, because there was just as many again behind him in boxes. On the other side were horseshoes and nails, nails and more nails. Hanging on a rack were shovels, picks, rakes and hammers. If someone wanted shafts, they were directed to the stall of Charles Noble, the carpenter. Special orders were marked down and discussed at the smithy before agreeing to cost or trade. The more Thomas tried to remember, the more he forgot. He watched Oliver confidently serving two customers. He knew their faces but couldn't quite place them. Perhaps he wouldn't have to serve anyone, and Mrs Ferris would be back soon.

'Hello Thomas.'

He looked up and blushed. The last time he'd blushed was on the day of his father's spring-cleaning. 'Er ... hello.'

He was almost sure but didn't have the confidence to address her by name. *She's beautiful. Could it really be Sarah, and wearing a blue blouse?*

'It's me, Thomas; it's me, Sarah Wilson.'

'Oh! Hello ... Sarah.'

'What art thou doing here?'

'I'm helping in the stall. It's part of my apprenticeship as a blacksmith. I'm indentured to Mr Ferris at Coniston Forge.'

'I know thy father's a wrestler. Is that the reason he's wealthy?'

'He's not wealthy. He's a shepherd and works hard. He lives on Timothy Atkinson's land and shares the rent with my Aunt Hannah.'

'Oh.' Sarah appeared mystified and Thomas felt a need to explain.

'The Friends are paying for my apprenticeship.'

'But thou art not a Quaker.'

'I am ... Sort of. I'm not sure really.'

'I have not seen thee at the Friends' meetings these past months.'

'No, but it's in my papers that I must behave like a Quaker. I can't sup strong ale or gamble or tell lies and I can't do any courting until I'm a journeyman.'

'That's a long time to wait and more is the pity. It's lucky I found thee here. I often wondered about thee and I would never have found thee locked up in a smithy all day.'

'It's been a long time. You look different.'

Oliver sniggered. Thomas felt hot breath on his neck, and thought it smelled like shit. 'What's up with you Oliver?'

The senior apprentice pushed past him and leaned across to Sarah as her mother joined her. 'Can I help you miss?'

Mrs Wilson interrupted. 'Thou certainly can help me young man.'

Thomas had never seen Mrs Wilson outside of the Friends' meetings and he was surprised at how tall and thin she was. Thomas had been told that Sarah's father Joshua was a tallow chandler. He remembered him from the meetings, a stocky man with a weather-beaten face and a red nose. Thomas took advantage of Rachel Wilson's distraction to converse with Sarah. *She's not the same as I remember.* 'Why are you wearing blue?'

'Why can't I wear blue Thomas?'

'Because your family are Quakers, and they always wear black.'

'So, what. I just happen to like blue and Margaret Fell believes that womenfolk shouldn't be restricted. And it doesn't matter anymore because father has been set down due to his drinking. Everything's gone wrong. We've been caught twice in Quaker raids and fined. Now we have to move to father's other chandlery in Kendal and if that doesn't work, we will have to consider settling in New England.'

'I hope you don't, Sarah. I would never see you again. You look pretty in blue.'

'I thank thee for thy kind words Thomas. Will I see thee here next Monday?'

'I don't think so. I'm only a first-year apprentice. It's Oliver's duty to attend the stall.'

'Come along, Sarah.'

As Mrs Wilson walked away with her daughter, Thomas heard her lecturing. 'Did I hear you talking about your father's predicament?'

'No mother, Thomas was just enquiring about our family's wellbeing.'

'He's a lovely boy that one, but just thou be careful. Farm boys can be dangerous.'

'He's apprenticed to a Quaker, Mother.'

'Isn't that why I give them our trade?'

Sarah turned and waved. 'Goodbye, Thomas. We're moving to Kendal soon, I'll miss thee.'

Thomas watched until she was out of sight then turned back to the stall feeling empty. He was losing everybody he liked.

'Goodbye, Thomas, I'll miss thee.'

He turned to the squeaky mimicking voice, and his face drained of all colour. He smashed Oliver in the face just as Mrs Ferris arrived back at the stall. Oliver fell, landing wedged between the boxes. He was enraged and attempting to lever himself up when a firm hand pressed against his shoulders, halting his progress. 'Calm down Oliver. We'll sort this problem out in the smithy. I can't see what's got into Thomas, but he'll suffer should he be in the wrong. He shouldn't have been here so early in his apprenticeship.' *I told George. I told him there'd be trouble between them.*

Squire Holmes returns

'That's providence my good man, providence. I was only just saying to Penelope shortly after you departed that we should have left Prince in your care. Much better all around, don't you agree?'

Squire Holmes was gathering his thoughts and couldn't imagine what the major was talking about. His brain was fogged with the change of events. 'I don't understand, Major. I merely called in for a little sympathy and a short-term loan for our safe return. The rogue stole everything of value, and now you want me to feed and train your horse for a year?'

'Fifteen months to be exact. I shall pay you twenty pounds and consider that you owe me not a penny.' *What a stroke of luck they were robbed.* The major beamed at what he considered to be a clever solution to all their problems.

Holmes wished for a hasty departure, and his wife Catherine was of the same mind. She whispered in his ear. 'Do as he say's Cornelius. Caring for the horse will work to our advantage. Its pedigree will more than pay its way at stud.' The squire was pleased with his wife's reasoning, and immediately agreed to the terms.

The major grew dubious at the quick reply, and his eyes narrowed to thoughtful slits. *He's up to something. Perhaps I offered too much.*

'We shall see you in September for the wedding of course, Major, so you can check the condition of the horse then. I'm sure you'll find him in fine fettle and raring to go. If you are satisfied with my care, perhaps we could renegotiate the terms?'

'Terms that we have already agreed upon. I think not. And whilst you're still grinning, the stable boy goes with the horse.'

'You can't be serious? I have my own staff and no appetite for excess wages.'

'I've found him necessary for the wellbeing of the horse. He works hard and you need only supply him with food and shelter.'

'We have a habit of paying wages to our staff.'

'Then the boy will be pleased. I'll be generous and throw in the cost of the ferryboat. Take it or leave it.' *You pompous, old sod.* Squire Holmes and his wife could barely disguise their satisfaction.

Mary rushed to the manor when she heard that Prince was being taken away. She was even more distraught on learning her brother was leaving. She sought out Penelope and discovered preparations underway. 'Damian should see his family before he leaves Mrs Rathbone. They will want to know of his welfare and how long he will be away.'

'I can understand your concern Mary. You've lost a husband and now your only brother is leaving. I'm sure it will only be for a short while. Perhaps you can persuade him not to go. We can't make him leave you know.'

Mary went to the stables and found Damian cowering on his back over a bale of hay. Rufus towered over him, wielding a whip and trying to ward off Jasper. The hound dog had the vice-like grip of a foxhunter on his legging. 'You'll leave whether you like it or not. I can't for the life of me see it, but father say's the horse is happier in your care.'

Mary's face flushed with anger. 'Mr Rathbone!'

Jasper let go when he heard Mary's voice, and Rufus bore down on her with a lascivious smirk. 'I'm a mister now, am I? You must really be in need of something.' He gripped her shoulder with his left hand and pushed his nose into her face. 'Perhaps bedding is your need. You must miss your husband.'

She fought back her anger as his right hand fondled her breasts and then grasped her amulet. Her scar darkened with rushing blood as Prince reared and whinnied, and she sensed the Man of Death scouring her mind. Rufus tore the ring from her neck, and she spit in his face. He was using his sleeve to wipe off the spittle when Jasper and Damian pounced and bowled him over. Squire Holmes chose that moment to enter the stable. 'Rufus, desist from this scurrilous act. If you are to remain my future son-in-law, you'd best justify your actions.'

Prince had calmed down, but Jasper was still growling as Damian backed away. Mary was relieved her vision had dispersed. 'He stole my amulet. He tore the ring from my neck.'

'Quiet woman, I asked Rufus a question, and I need to know the answer.'

'The silver ring belongs to the estate, Squire. I was merely retrieving it from the thief. I would normally call the constable, but I hear the young woman has fallen on misfortune. She's lucky I'm kindhearted.'

'What is your reply to that, young woman?'

Mary knew that it was Rufus' word against hers and she would surely be sent to Lancaster Gaol for a crime she didn't commit. She spoke bravely to Squire Holmes. 'I venture that there is more than a silver ring in his hand.'

'Display your palm Rufus.' The major's son opened his hand to reveal Mary's betrothal stone alongside the rune ring.

He feigned surprise. 'Sorry about that, I didn't realise there was a stone on the necklace. Here have it back.' He slid the amber stone from the leather string, studied it with curiosity, and then nonchalantly flicked it into the hay. 'If your brother refuses to accompany us I will lay claims to the ring and call the constable.'

'He would never believe you. Everyone knows the ring belongs to me.'

'The ring was stolen when the manor changed hands, and it is common knowledge that your husband was in charge.'

Mary was enraged, her head lowered, cupped in her palms. She prayed for the vision to stay away and her prayers were answered. *The curse has left me. He's taken the curse with the ring.* Her hands dropped to her side and she raised her head to look across at Damian brushing hay from his smock, unperturbed by the situation. What could she do? She'd seen the unjust and cruel treatment to the Quakers.

Squire Holmes had heard enough. 'The boy stays. I've little use for him in Newmarket and if his choice is to remain in Hawkshead, then so be it.'

Rufus knew his father would be unhappy with the decision and spoke up. 'Father says there is no choice. The horse pines in his absence and refuses his feed. Training is difficult on an empty stomach, squire.'

Damian suddenly felt important, imbued with power. *They're fighting over me.* He took a deep breath and asserted himself. 'I'm not going anywhere unless I can take Jasper.'

There was an open-mouthed silence at the audacity of the young stable boy. Damian crouched with a silly expectant look as he waited for a response. Mary felt proud of her brother.

'Who is Jasper may I ask?'

'Jasper's me hound dog, Cornelius. And I don't want Rufus to beat me up anymore.'

'Don't be insolent. You will address me as Mr Holmes in future, and I will see to it that you are not beaten, unless of course you warrant it.'

'Mam says I'm as good as anyone else, so I can call anyone by their first name.'

Holmes held a hand to his forehead, attempting to shake the situation from his mind. 'First, I'm landed with a horse, then a stable boy who's not the full button, and now a useless old dog and a future son-in-law who's possibly unbalanced.'

Rufus sniggered and the gesture didn't escape the attention of Squire Holmes. He focussed on Mary and spoke with authority. 'I have yet to learn the truth, but I must ask if you are satisfied with your present treatment, young lady.'

'No sir, but I have little choice.'

She pointed at the smirking Rufus. 'I must tell the major's son that the stolen ring is cursed, and if it isn't returned, he will have many a torturous, sleepless night. The ring will affect his manner and bring him nothing but bad luck.'

'If Rufus had possessed the ring during yesterday's hold-up, I could well have believed you. It is noble of him to deter pressing charges. You are very fortunate and will thank him for it someday.'

'I doubt that very much, but I must ask you to treat my brother kindly. He's a simple soul, loyal and hard working for those who respect him.'

'We shall see. We shall see. Now let us prepare for tomorrow. We leave by ferry early morning then have a long and arduous journey ahead of us. You say the ring is cursed young lady? I'm not a believer of such tittle-tattle, but not a word must be said of it to my dear wife. She's riddled with superstition.' He looked purposely at everyone in the stable before turning to leave. 'Let us all pray that the plague has avoided Newmarket. Long live the king.'

Rupert Gull's wife moved diligently amongst the Holmes party, counting passengers and collecting pennies. She'd been caught before with large parties. 'A penny a passenger you say?'

'That's correct, Sir, horse or rider, and you can all travel on the same ferry together. There's room for a carriage if need be.'

But the squire's wife wasn't listening to reason. 'I'm not travelling with horses, Cornelius. I think they should travel separately with the stable hands. Think what happened to that wedding party. All of them were lost, and their horses as well. They were obviously overloaded.'

Squire Holmes knew he would have no peace until he conceded. 'What will an extra journey cost?'

'Three pennies sir, but I must say that you will be just as safe if you all journeyed together.'

The packhorses were already being walked up the loading ramps and onto the ferry. Damian and Jasper followed with Prince and the squire's stable hands. The long oars were taken up by two muscular ferrymen and the slack taken off the hawsers. 'You'll be waiting for up to an hour before you can join them sir.' The squire hesitated, but Catherine was decisive. Rufus and Eleanor sat together, relaxed, resigned to the fact that their journey to Cambridge was going to be long and tedious.

Coniston Forge: September 1665

Thomas spread his fingers wide and plunged them into the fast-flowing beck. He squatted on the bank, hypnotised by the ripples as his hand trailed back and forth against the rush of the current. He opened his ears to the chatter of birds and the call of a cockerel, and then watched the morning light fade as miniscule flickering candles in distant cottage windows were extinguished. He stretched and then followed the rushing water towards the forge.

Hot coals glimmered inside, resisting the darkness. The previous evening, he had stoked the fire and swept the floor before retiring for dinner. Such was the lot of a first-year apprentice and try as he may, he couldn't rid himself of the bitter taste and lingering smell of iron. Water from the beck swished past, prompting him to move to the far end of the building for his first task. He pulled down on a lever protruding from a slot in the outer wall to open the sluice gate and divert the beck towards the waterwheel. He stepped back to avoid the spray as water from the running beck smashed against the vertical wheel. There was a slight shudder and screeching of timbers as the huge wheel succumbed to the sudden pressure and began its journey of monotonous rotation. Thomas waited for its cadence to steady before securing the lever and returning to stoke the forge. He wasn't allowed to engage the clutch for the hammer or the bellows. That was the responsibility of Oliver. In less than an hour gasps of air would emanate from pumping bellows and echo around the smithy, accompanied by the thud of the anvil, as it pummelled out impurities to produce workable wrought iron. Market goods would then be hammered and welded into shape on the smaller anvil and Thomas would take his turn swinging the hammer. He was nearing the end of his early shift and his stomach was rumbling. Oliver would arrive soon to crank the smithy alive, testing the machinery and raising the temperature of the coals to a glow suited to the working of iron. The peace of the countryside would be shattered from dawn to dusk, buffeting the surrounding cottages with noise until that blessed day of rest. Thomas could only think of breakfast. *They must have finished eating by now.* He felt a pang of guilt for not waking Oliver. He mischievously engaged the hammer and watched hypnotised as it settled into a rhythm, before returning to stoke the forge. *It's too bad if he doesn't like it.* There was a sudden draught, and a door slammed shut just as he lifted a shovel full of charcoal. A tremendous force hit him side on and he was sent flying through the air to land headfirst in the charcoal pile. 'You never woke me up.'

Oliver was on top of him. They rolled around on the smithy floor, grappling for a dominant wrestling hold. Thomas twisted to the top, pushed down hard to break the hold and sprung to his feet. He backed away and waited for Oliver to stand upright. They prowled, circling each other, looking for an opening. There was a violent lunge and a crash of bodies. With chins on opposing shoulders, they spun around, heaving first one way and then the other. Thomas staggered backwards towards the hammer and as Oliver forced his head closer to the anvil, he felt the draft and the vibration of each thumping stroke. They were interlocked in a momentary stalemate when a bellowing voice brought them to a halt.

'That's enough!' Black George was standing hands on hips, his huge frame filling the smithy doorway. With folded arms and a booming gravelly voice, he started the morning communication. 'It's time to break up, you two love birds.' He squinted and roared with laughter. 'Does either of you fancy giving me a big cuddle?'

Oliver broke away, pushing Thomas playfully, but hard enough for him to trip sideways and fall back into the charcoal. Black George scratched his head through his soft cap, rubbed his black beard and pointed to the door. 'Off you go to breakfast Thomas, and as you've plenty of spare energy I've some extra work for you. There'll be some iron arriving from Force Forge, so you can start the day by helping our labourers unload it.'

Thomas knew all about the Force Forge bloomery, and the Rusland charcoal burners. He was good friends with Oliver now and preferred to forget his first three months at the smithy. Shortly after the fight at the markets Mr Ferris had called them aside and explained that it would be better for him and Oliver to be apart for a few months. By that time their son William would have left to gain experience as a journeyman, and there would be more room about the place. George had organised to send him to work for Margaret Fell's daughter, Sarah. Like Margaret's other five daughters, Sarah was a Quaker, and after her mother's internment she was left with the responsibility of running the Force Forge bloomery.

When he came to collect Thomas, he was disturbed to find him on loan to the Rusland charcoal burners and angrily extracted him. 'Burning timber to make charcoal wasn't part of the deal Thomas. You should have sent word to me they were using you for slave labour. And the morals of those people don't sit well with the Friends. They sell inferior charcoal to the villagers and charge six pence a sack; that's close to a day's pay. I can't understand Sarah's reasoning. The forge is becoming too much for her. From what I can see the whole place is in a state of disrepair.'

Thomas agreed and his experience with the burners wasn't exactly pleasant. 'I'm real glad you came to find me Mr Ferris. I like working at the smithy more than the bloomery, and the charcoal burning was even worse. They had me piling all that turf around the wood stacks. Then, after they had dropped fire down the centre I had to keep them damped down for two days until the wood turned into charcoal. They drank ale most of the time they were waiting.'

'Well let's hope thee learned something on the way, about life and people as well as improving thy knowledge of iron and charcoal.'

Thomas would never tell George, but one night after he'd come upon the burners drinking heavily, they lured him to the Farmers' Arms at Lowick. They plied him with strong ale, and he ended up orating on the top of the oak table. He began re-enacting his ghostly tales of the abbey; gesticulating a he'd done at the grammar school. He was thoroughly enjoying himself entertaining the burners and exhilarated by the applause. But then he became over-confident and overstepped the mark in his conclusion. 'And now they say that as the ghosts of the monks haunt Furness abbey, so does the ghost of James Pritt haunt Grisedale Forest.'

A deathly silence ensued, and Thomas was now looking down on a threatening audience. The entertainment was over, and it was the boss of the charcoal burners who broke the silence. 'Whad'yer ken of James me lad?' Thomas' left shoulder twitched, and the side of his face winked in unison.

'Don't be insolent boy. This is not a laughing matter, and no time to be pulling faces. Now tell us. What do you know of James Pritt?'

Thomas could hardly believe that he'd been stupid enough to transgress his vow of secrecy. He'd been told often enough that James had worked in the charcoal gang. The ale had weakened his mind and loosened his tongue. He bit his bottom lip and broke into a cold sweat. The crowd began asking him pertinent questions. The madam of the house said she had a bone to pick. 'I'd like to lay my hands on that mongrel, and I'd be obliged if you can tell me where to find him. My daughters grieving and he owes me a month's rent money.'

'He just disappeared one night Mrs Green and nobody's seen him since. 'I ... I ... don't know anything really. It's just a joke about the ghost because the villagers and the woodcutters said he just vanished into thin air.'

'Ran away eh? That's true to his form then.' All agreed and were unanimous in their anger. Thomas was relieved to hear James had been unpopular, yet his guilt remained. He suffered from a spinning and pounding head the next day, 'kaylied' the locals called it. But he put his head down and worked hard, laying turf over the cone-shaped timbers, purposely avoiding any probing conversation.

When Thomas returned to Coniston, he found some dramatic changes in the family. Damian had left for Newmarket and Mary's baby John was now one year old and being cared for by his Aunt Hannah while Robert cared for the sheep, farm animals, vegetable holding and milking cow.

Mary was working fewer days in Timothy's employ and on his recommendation, helping out his son Samuel, working three days a week at the chandlery in town. Mary hadn't been sure about working for Samuel Atkinson. For a start he was unmarried, and to her way of thinking a man forty years of age should have taken a wife many years ago. He was slightly taller than Mary, stocky, clumsy and hesitant in his speech, but neat in his appearance. He was stubborn and wilfully independent, the only Atkinson sibling not beholden to the Quakers. Fortunately, Timothy was a man of wisdom; God fearing, lenient and kind of heart. There was no mistaking Samuel needed a woman about the house but from what Mary had heard his parents had long ago given up hope. Timothy had been presenting eligible women for many years and only sent Mary to absolve his own guilt at the death of her husband while in his employ. Mary settled into the work easily and felt comfortable in Samuel's employ. She soon had the cleaning in hand and was finding time to help in the store on market days. Since the birth of her baby, Mary appeared much calmer. The farm had been quiet without Thomas' cheery face and even more so when Damian had left with Prince and Jasper. The altercation in the stables and the ensuing loss of her amulet had lifted a weight from her shoulders.

Not long after Rufus stole the ring, the schoolteacher called to see her. She recognised Phynius easily now. *He still gives me the creeps.* He became agitated when told Rufus had taken the ring away. 'I need to examine the runes on that ring, Mary. I have known all along your cousin lied to protect you, but I shall be patient and wait until the major's son returns. I will not be made a fool of and mark my words; I will determine the truth of that ring or die in the process.'

The wedding: September 1665

Penelope had seen the estate in her youth, but she was completely taken by surprise, overwhelmed by its size. The Holmes' manor was situated close to Newmarket, in Fordham, Cambridge. The house, stables and grounds were more than double the size of her estate. She was tired, her body sore from the long tedious ride and she promised herself a decent side-saddle before they returned. The grounds were chaotic; impressive teams of wagons offloaded food into the kitchen storerooms and icehouse. They entered the stable-yard and heard a cacophony of sounds coming from the big house. Musicians were rehearsing for the coming ball, seemingly filtering in and out of the house at will. Catherine came out to meet the Rathbones' entourage with a male domestic. They were cupping their ears against the noise. 'Welcome major. I'm relieved to see you Penelope. You left it a little close, arriving two days before the ceremony. Don't tell me you had trouble with highwaymen on the road?'

Penelope dismounted, brushing down her doublet and long riding skirt. 'Thankfully there was nothing as exciting as your trip north. The inns were comfortable and thank you for sending the guide. He was most helpful and shortened our journey considerably. We stayed over at York for two days which was probably a mistake. Forty miles a day and a week on the road is enough for anyone with a sore backside.'

'Well the sooner we have you all settled the better, then you will have all day tomorrow to prepare. We have a travelling dance master available. He should be able to help the major.'

'Did you hear that, Rowan? Isn't that nice, thinking of you?' But the major had already disappeared into the stables.

The congregation went silent, and Rufus became apprehensive. He sensed Eleanor walking down the aisle but feared to steal a glance. *The organ's too loud. I can hardly think.* He was wearing a red velvet doublet, with white silk undershirt laced at the collar and cuffs. Below the waist he wore white pantaloons, long red stockings and brown leather shoes. The garments were nothing unusual, but he felt uncomfortable and overdressed, because of the weight of his father's sword hanging from his hip. He would have trouble lifting the sword in defence, but the major had insisted. It was military, traditional, and a manly show of strength. Eleanor was suddenly beside him and the echo of the organ's final chord faded away. She held her head high; proud of her appearance, knowing the design of her silk dress was much admired. The open-necked full-length gown was in a beautiful blue and gold silk brocade, plain blue silks and satins. The dress was adorned with silk taffeta ribbons and bellowed sleeves with laced cuffs. Her mother, Catherine, had demanded the best and was not disappointed. Rufus looked at his bride from the corner of his eye. Eleanor's face was radiant, framed by a cluster of curls that fell to her bared shoulders from each side of her temples, and eardrops that complemented a short string of pearls encircling her neck. His eyes flicked back to focus on the altar. He was astonished; his bride was stunning. They spoke their vows and the priest slid the wedding ring on and off the bride's thumb, then her index finger, then the middle finger, invoking the Father the Son and the Holy Spirit. He placed the ring on the wedding finger, the third finger of the left hand, and voiced the final words, 'I pronounce you man and wife.'

Rufus relaxed from the tension, and kissed Eleanor on the forehead. They looked each other in the eyes and focussed, searching for acknowledgement of the occasion. For the first time since their engagement Rufus had a longing for Eleanor. They beamed happiness as they walked into the churchyard, Eleanor laughing as she ducked under the traditional corns of wheat thrown over her head. Rufus cast his eyes over her, not believing his luck. *Pity about the nose, but like father said she has fine curves.*

He had come to understand his father's adage: 'Don't look at the mantelpiece when you're poking the fire', and his playing field had widened considerably. He had been dreaming incessantly of his mother's Spanish servant ever since he took her amulet, and the dreams were often wet. *Mary.* He almost spoke her name out loud. *So much fire! To think she had the audacity to wield a knife at the son of the manor.* He'd ejaculated on the spot and wondered whether it was from fear or excitement. She was now a widow, and the possibilities excited him. Even on this most prestigious day, her amulet rested secure in his pocket. He ran his palm over its bulge for assurance. He pictured one side of her face, secreted by shoulder length silky black hair, and was excited, experiencing an uncontrollable desire to draw aside the curtain and reveal her blemish. She had become an obsession, but whatever Rufus' thoughts were during the consummation of the marriage, groom and bride never left the bedroom for two days.

The banquet, the ballroom and the orchestra; everything was big. The Holmes were making a statement. After the scandal of their only son and his eventual disinheritance, a grand show was deemed necessary. Cornelius had honoured his son's gambling debts with part of his estate and dispatched him overseas. His name was never to be mentioned again in the family. The Holmes' two eldest daughters had married well and Catherine was able to concentrate all her energy into marrying off Eleanor, her youngest and least pretty daughter. Choosing Rufus had been no accident. He was from the outer-circle, devoid of his father's gambling traits and, despite a fondness for the ladies, the squire believed him young enough to be moulded. *A banking career will be suitable if he can keep his nose clean.* Catherine was also looking to the future. Her daughter and future grandchildren would be living nearby, and she was ready to foil any plans Penelope may have for luring Rufus to the north.

The major's sister and her family were in attendance, mystified by their invitation and uncomfortable in the extravagant surroundings. The nephews were jealous of Rufus marrying above his station and consoled themselves with spiteful thoughts. *From the looks of the bride, he must have been desperate.* The major observed their attitude and smirked. *They show their feelings too easily. They all know that Rufus is on a winner.*

The major had discarded his wedding trappings and for the first time in a week, he felt comfortable. 'The wedding was a splendid affair, Holmes. I must congratulate you on the turnout. The reception, the orchestra and the ball all made a lasting impression on Penelope. She was delirious with excitement.'

'That's a little over the top, Major, but Catherine and I thank you for your most pleasurable comments. I must admit that it did surpass your small engagement party.' The major grimaced then fired back. 'It was a pity there was a lack of dignitaries at the wedding.'

Squire Holmes was taken aback. 'You can't be serious. I'm travelling down to London tomorrow with the Earl of Aylesbury, his son Thomas, and my good friend Sir John Lowther, the young parliamentarian. I saw you in their presence more than once during the reception.'

'That may be so, but there could have been more like them, especially with the connections you're supposed to have. And I must tell you that I took no pleasure from being in their company. For a start, I felt uncomfortable in their presence and being dressed up like a bloody peacock didn't help. I don't take kindly to your false hair or the lace and silk fashion. The earl's son, Thomas Bruce, continually boasted he would show my horse a clean pair of hooves in the Town Plate. The race is a year hence and I haven't even entered Prince, let alone been accepted.'

'Neither has his father, the earl, or anyone else for that matter. That's youthful exuberance and one-upmanship. He talks to all possible rivals in the same way. You shouldn't take offence. Leave it to Rufus to create a good relationship with him that would be beneficial to us all.'

He might have a chance with Thomas, but he'll have no luck with the other one.'

'I don't understand, Major.'

'I'm speaking of his friend, John Lowther. They were both having a go at me. Thomas was downing Prince, and Lowther was insulting our parish.'

'I'm sure they were only teasing. Cajoling you into a livelier discussion perhaps?'

'I don't think so. When Lowther discovered I was from Hawkshead he kept harping on about losing a piddling little pocket-watch. He said it was stolen from one of our inns and was a twenty-first birthday gift from his Uncle John, the Baronet of Lowther. The watch was apparently crafted especially for him in Germany, and he had to wait another year for a replacement.'

'John is also the Baronet of Whitehaven and much closer to your district than ours. You should speak kindlier of him. His family connections are widespread and influential. This is his first year in Parliament and now is a good time to strengthen our bond. We travelled with his entourage part of the way to your engagement party. He is very entertaining.'

'He accused our parish of harbouring thieves and allowing highwaymen to roam unchallenged. Then he waved a spare watch key in my face, saying that was all he had left of his coming of age gift.'

'You are off to a bad start, Major. Sir John is in great favour. Duties from his expanding sea trade are filling up the country's coffers. He carried on where his father left off. Increased coal production and the growing harbour of Whitehaven are all down to his enthusiasm. Perhaps if you retrieved his watch you would be on better terms.'

'He can go to hell for all I care, and talking of hell, we have that long journey north in front of us tomorrow. Penny isn't looking forward to the ride and said it would be her last for a long time, unless of course a grandchild happens along the way.'

'She won't be coming for the King's Plate?'

'Not a chance in her present frame of mind, but she'll be happy to see Rufus and Eleanor before then. We are expecting them to stay with us in the spring.'

The eviction: spring 1666

Rufus was about to dismount when he caught a glimpse of his father outside the stables. He motioned to the other two riders and they wheeled their horses. Major Rathbone was in deep conversation with Hollis and spun around, surprised at the sound of his son's voice. 'Hello, Father!'

'What on earth are you doing here boy? You weren't expected until late spring.'

'We've come to claim our dowry.'

The major's face remained static. He folded an arm across his chest, propped his chin with his free hand and contemplated, his forefinger incessantly flicking his lower lip. Rufus had seen it all before and as always, his father's stance irritated him. He concentrated on the vibrating lower lip, waiting patiently for an answer. The major's expression suddenly changed, suggesting that he'd come to a decision. He sighed, dropped his arms to his side, and without another word turned to continue his conversation with Hollis.

'You didn't answer me, Father, and you didn't say hello to Eleanor.'

The major turned and squinted as he elevated his head towards his son's wife. 'Hello, Eleanor, you're as pretty as ever.'

'Thank you, Major. Do you have any particular day in mind for the transfer of the lease?'

The major ignored the question then noticed Damian for the first time, sitting upright on a packhorse behind Eleanor, grinning. He stared in disbelief. 'What on earth is he doing here?'

'The squire said he didn't need an extra stable-hand.'

'But he does need him. Prince frets without the boy's presence and I certainly can't use him.'

'He can still help in the stables.'

'I already have stable-hands and I'm not paying wages for another. He can go back digging graves for the church; if they will have him.'

Damian looked back and forth from the major to his son and back to the major again and his smile faded into a look of anxiety. *They don't like me.*

'I'll have a word with the vicar. Failing that, you'll have to pay his wages until we return for the race in October.' The major had other problems on his mind. Many of the Quakers refused to pay tithes and the statesmen showed distaste for hauling their neighbours before a judge. Even the adjudicators of the district were rebelling. The judges were inventing urgent appointments in fictitious outer districts as soon as they heard a cartful of prisoners was about to be delivered.

Rufus had expected the old rented cottage on the acreage to be cleared and the old woman Agnes Walker, departed. 'Eleanor is impatient to have a house of her own for when we stay in the district father. We were promised the leasehold.'

'So you are demanding already, Eleanor? I don't envy our son's future. I can't see the problem with you both staying over at the manor when you visit. You'll be living most of the year in Cambridge, so why do you need to establish another home?'

'We would have more freedom than being confined to the manor house.'

'Penny won't be happy to hear that. When is the baby due?'

Rufus was taken by surprise at the change of tack, stuttering an answer. 'What b...b... baby, Father? We are still trying.'

'There we are you see. One false alarm after another! Let us hope you make up for the first mistake, Eleanor.'

'I'll not remain here any longer listening to your insults. Come with me Damian. We will seek out more amiable company and let father and son stew in their own juice.'

The major watched them all the way to the manor house. *Penny will sort her out.* 'Now Rufus, we had best discuss the land being cleared of the cottage. The old woman's nephew Andrew Mossop has been contacted in Ravenglass and he's due to call for her in March. In the meantime, her Quaker friends have organised for the Bensons of Yewdale to take care of her. I'll expect rent from you the moment she leaves. We can't build until the end of summer, and of course, we will be attending the king's Newmarket Plate in October. So that leaves you with a little time before winter sets in.'

Rufus was puzzled 'It's not what you promised father. We were expecting the leasehold to be free and that we could sublet the land for farming.'

'Then you have a misconception of the promised leasehold. Your mother had grandchildren in mind when she agreed on the terms. If you had chosen to stay permanently and work the land, the leasehold would have been free. As that is now no longer the case, I will require rent. You can still alter your decision of course.'

'That's blackmail. You know I can't stay here more than a few months. I have a career to think of.'

'We'll talk more about the arrangements when the new cottage is built.'

Rufus hadn't expected any complications and was starting to panic. 'Can we let the old lady stay a little longer and build next year?'

'Too late my boy, I kept my word: the deed is done. The cottage must be demolished, and the lease renewed.'

'What am I to tell Eleanor?'

'Have you told her you are the instigator of the eviction of an old lady?'

'No, I haven't.'

'Then you will have to invent a few lies. That shouldn't be too hard for you. And while we are on the subject, you had best have a word with your future neighbour, Vicar Braithwaite. The allotment he leases from me adjoins your boundary. He has already heard of our intended eviction, and despite the old lady being a Quaker, our actions don't rest well with him.'

'I had no idea the vicar leased an allotment from you.'

'The man also uses Agnes' land for a fee. He has a large family and a horse and cow to feed and receives poor wages from the church. The tithes I collect are not enough to sustain them all. I'm afraid we've given you a sheltered life. Let us hope that you can make good of your career in Cambridge.' The major paused, losing concentration.

'What are you staring at, Father?'

'I'm staring at that thing hanging around your neck. Shouldn't it be on your finger?'

'It's a lucky charm. It will help me win the race.'

'It looks stupid. See a silversmith and have it polished and fitted to a finger. That would be far more suitable for a gentleman. What with silk suits, wigs and now necklaces I don't know what the world's coming to.'

Agnes Walker didn't understand why she had to leave. Her husband had left her secure, with ample income to pay her rent.

Vicar Braithwaite was incensed and wished the Devil on the officers as they served notice on his elderly neighbour. He didn't even consider her a Quaker in the true sense. He knew she was often visited by an overseer, but he turned a blind eye as she no longer attended meetings. He paid her in kind for the use of her leasehold and he saw to it that his parishioners and his wife contributed to her embroidery. He had gone to great lengths to acquire a pair of repaired eyeglasses from Phynius Clayton as her needlework was the only thing left in her life. 'Why can't we all live in peace in the house of the Lord?' Damn you and the Rathbones to hell.'

His wife tried to calm him down. 'Careful my dear, or our own tenancy may falter.'

'I'll have none of it. She's being evicted from her home because she follows the Friends, but she harms no-one. I'm sure Penelope knows nothing of these dealings. It's time I informed her.'

The more Penelope Rathbone listened to the vicar, the more her anger grew. By the time she found her husband and son in the stables she was livid. 'How dare you throw an old lady from my land? And how dare you serve a warrant without my permission?'

'I thought it was our land, Penny, and it was for the good of our son and his wife.'

'You've known for a long time that Rufus wouldn't be able to live here permanently. We could have worked our way around the old woman staying. The land is already sublet, and Rufus and Eleanor will own the new cottage.'

'They were being greedy, expecting to have a free lease and then charge a tenant rent for the use of the farm.'

'I've no interest in your conniving ways of saving money, especially at the expense of our son.'

'All the cottages have to be demolished and rebuilt, and the Crown has given permission to fell trees in the district. The old lady would have had to leave eventually, and besides, she is a troublesome Quaker.'

'That's no excuse, and surely there was other land that you could have leased. Does Eleanor know about this evil deed? Rufus shook his head and dropped it to his chest.'

'You're cowards! The both of you are cowards. I'll have the woman reinstated at once.'

'It's too late. The Friends have already taken her to a safe house and her nephew has arranged to take her to Ravenglass.'

'Then you must tell me where they are keeping her. I must console the poor woman and compensate her for this travesty.' Penelope rode out to the Bensons' property with Damian and one of the stable hands. She'd insisted on keeping Damian on the staff, despite her husband's resistance. 'You know he'll have to return to Newmarket for the wellbeing of the horse. The fault lies with Rufus. He's easily manipulated. You only have to look at his marriage to Eleanor to realise he carries no air of authority; unless he's bullying the stable boy that is. Damian can help in the grounds and in the kitchen until you leave for Newmarket.'

'Have you decided to journey with me, Penny?'

'You know I have to stay at the manor, Rowan, so why bother asking. You can't expect me to make that terrible journey again merely for a horse race, and especially with that old saddle. Keep in mind that I'll not be welcoming you back without the bladder-stone operation. The surgeon will be there and there's no excuse to avoid it.'

'I'll only be risking my life, that's all.' The major's hand went to guard his crotch. He cringed and groaned at the thought of the knife.

'Don't be a coward. It's for your own good as well as mine, and don't forget to call in on the saddle-maker. I can't remember his name.'

'It's Andrew Millhouse.'

'That's him. He was very friendly, lifted me up for a fitting, and told me he'd made saddles for the king. He suggested the most expensive side-saddle, one of extra-good quality, so make sure you pay without complaint. From what we know of the operation you may have to use the saddle on your return journey.'

Penelope laughed openly at the thought of her cavalry husband riding side-saddle and the major growled back at her. 'If the operation is as successful as Samuel Pepys', you could be begging me into your bed come December.' Penelope's mocking laughter carried in the breeze as he made his way to the stables.

Yewdale was on higher ground than Penelope had realised. The wind blew icy from the snow on the high fells. She shivered as the cold air penetrated her clothing and goose-pimpled her skin. The winter sky was grey with heavy snow clouds, and the Bensons' manor house looked dark and uninviting. The horses were led to the stables, and Penelope was admitted into the house with caution. 'Agnes has been badly treated by thine husband, Mrs Rathbone. She's frail and mentally distressed.'

'You may find it strange, Mrs Benson, but I've only just heard of her plight, and I mean to do all I can to rectify the situation.'

'I'm afraid the damage has already been done but try and console her if thou must.'

Penelope found Agnes huddled around a roaring log fire. Fine grey hair straddled her wool shawl and her head bobbed around as her long gnarled bony fingers worked at the embroidery. She looked up as Penelope approached, fire flickering in the glass of her thick, ungainly lenses.

Penelope sat down close to the fire and opposite the old lady. She thought of her late mother and smiled with a genuine compassion. 'Good morning, Agnes. I see you're keeping busy.'

'There's little more a woman can do at my age, but thou art cold, young woman. Thou shouldn't be outside in this kind of weather.' The voice quivered with the frailty of age.

'I had to come and see you, regardless of any weather. I can't sleep because of your predicament. You've been evicted from land that I own without my permission, and I can only offer you a weak apology for the actions of my husband. Nothing could reward you for the anguish you must have suffered, but I would like to assist you in any way possible.'

'I could scarce accept an apology and money would cure nothing. Thine visit on such a cold and miserable day is reward enough. I will say a prayer for thee before I sleep tonight, Mrs Rathbone. Thou art a brave woman to be living with such a cold-hearted monster.'

'There is a better side to him, Agnes, but I must admit that I haven't seen it for quite some time. He is no longer the man that I married. He suffers constant pain, as we all do at times, and he is often too stringent in his responsibilities. That his actions may be related to his condition is no consolation to the people who suffer around him.'

'Then I will also say a prayer for thine husband, Mrs Rathbone, to remove the Devil from his soul.'

'I came to apologise and ask your forgiveness, and you reward me by offering a prayer for my husband. That is hard for me to comprehend.'

'It is the way of the Lord Jesus.' They both looked into the flames, sharing a thoughtful silence.

Penelope wished the peaceful moment longevity but knew in all reality that she must soon leave the kind old lady. 'I'm relieved to find that you are being cared for Agnes, and sorry that I can't stay longer, for the fells are dangerous and unkind to late travellers.'

'Thank thee for caring, young woman, and may thou travel kindly.'

Penelope left feeling as miserable as the weather and on the threshold, she pressed coins into Mrs Benson's hand. 'I won't feel any better for it, but make sure they are placed in her luggage.'

Penelope turned her horse on the rise and looked down at the Bensons' manor house. Smoke was circling the chimneys, burning candles flickering behind lace curtains, and gusts of wind slamming loose shutters back and forth. Driving sleet whipped Penelope's face, and she wheeled her mount, relieved the wind would be at their backs. The sleet was already building another layer, obscuring the path to the manor house.

The following day the weather had cleared sufficiently for the Bensons to attend the Friends' meeting. Agnes Walker's frailty had made her an absentee since her husband's passing, but the Quaker overseers often called. To leave her alone with the domestics wasn't considered unkind. 'After all's said and done, the old lady's been living on her own for years.'

Agnes accepted her fate. Her nephew, Andrew, was expected to call and see her soon to arrange travel in the early spring. She'd set her mind on moving and was now looking forward to his visit. Her mind wandered more frequently these days, and she often lost track of the time and day. The night was drawing to a close when the cook called to say the family must be stranded out at Town End and she shouldn't expect them until early morning. She left Agnes with a supper before retiring and made sure the fire was well stoked, before telling the old lady not to stay up too long. When Agnes awoke the fire was down and her supper untouched. She placed a log on the fire, stretched back with a yawn, and tucked her cold hands beneath her armpits. She leaned forward to rake the glowing embers and shivered as she waved her long bony fingers across the fire. Her eyes glazed, captive to the ever-changing shapes of the hearth's black and red coals. Agnes' mind drifted, and she thought of her nephew. Her head snapped back and forth as she fought to escape her dream, then she anxiously scanned the room in agitation. *He could be on his way at this very moment.*

She made a quick decision, pushed herself up from the chair, rested with hands on hips, and arched her back to loosen the pain from her aching bones. She pulled her shawl tight around her shoulders, inexplicably pocketed her needlework glasses and placed the untouched supper in her embroidery bag. *Andrew will be hungry.* She shuffled down the hallway, leaned against the heavy entrance door, and struggled to lever the latch. The door gradually creaked open, a blast of cold air whistled down the passageway, and the fire roared into life. Agnes crossed the threshold onto the porch then wandered into the night. She looked up and saw sparks flying amongst the chimney's soot then blinked as her face was sprinkled with fresh snowflakes. She heard the whinny of a horse in the distance and peered into the dark misty night. The moon was struggling to break through the heavy clouds. *That has to be Andrew come to visit. He's looking for the farm.*

Agnes walked unsteadily down the path towards the manor gate. Oblivious of the falling snow, she squeezed through an opening and headed up a slight incline in the direction of the horse whinny. The path behind her was no longer visible. The mist swirled; cold and suffocating, thinning for a moment, only to be replaced by driving showers of sleet. Her exposed hands were paining, pierced by pins and needles, the icy wind chilling her to the marrow. She fought on and stumbled into a slush-filled hole in the snow-covered road. Her basket flew through the air and her arms spread wide to diffuse the fall. Embroidery, cheese, and bread were callously washed down the slope. She crawled onwards through the snow, fingernails snapping as they dug into the road for leverage. *I must find Andrew. He will lose his way.* She fumbled with her numb hands, dragged the embroidery glasses from her pocket and held them above her nose, hoping to clear a window through the mist. Clouds raced across the moon and cast intermittent shadows through the showers of sleet. She saw the ghostly outline of a man on horseback, wavering, dismounting. *Andrew has come to fetch me.* Agnes Walker's eyes brightened. She crawled towards the grey ghostly vision, smiling. *God bless him.* With a surge of excitement, she lifted to her feet, and stumbled forward with open arms. The young trees branches quivered and showered flakes as the old lady embraced its trunk and slid down into the deep warm blanket of snow. Behind her a final gust of wind rattled the manor house shutters, and the night quietened as it yielded to the calming sound of soft cascading snow.

The burial

A search party discovered Agnes Walker's body the following afternoon after a break in the weather, shaded by the branches of a young yew tree. A messenger was sent to her nephew and Major Rathbone was informed. The story circulated in the village and the entire district believed the major was responsible for the old lady's death. Penelope was distraught. 'First you dismiss John, a good honest worker, forcing him to take a dangerous job which took his life, then you evict Agnes, a helpless old lady and send her to her death. You are nothing short of a mercenary and may you suffer the pain of your victims tenfold.'

'I can't see how you can blame me. It's more your son's fault than mine. I can't stop a woman who's lost her mind from wandering on the fells.'

'She should never have been there in the first place, and Rufus is your son as well as mine. You'd best put your thinking caps on and do something to compensate or I'll not be able to hold my head high in the parish. The manor has been shamed and needs to save face.'

The major called on Vicar Braithwaite. He offered to organise and pay for the funeral but was surprised at the reply.

'You can feel free to bury a Quaker, Major, but it won't be with my authority.'

'That's understandable, Gabriel, and as I proposed, the funeral will be at my expense, and under my authority.'

'The Quakers don't believe in your authority. Besides, a Quaker can't be buried in the soil of our hallowed cemetery. It is against the law, and don't forget, you are a servant of the law.'

Vicar Braithwaite was enjoying his superiority, but the urge to dominate was tempered by his wife's words of wisdom. Like church bells ringing an alarm her words interrupted his games-manship. *Be cautious in your dealings with the major, Gabriel. Remember he's the landlord.*

'Good God my man, can't you see I'm trying to help?'

'I'm not your good man, Rowan, and please don't use the Lord's name in vain.' He had smugly let the major's Christian name slip and paused, waiting for a reaction. But the major's eyes were closed, screwed-up in thought, oblivious to the game, paying little attention to the vicar's words. He came to his senses with a sudden grunt of satisfaction. He unfolded a plan of action that he believed would appease the district and elevate him as a man of compassion. Vicar Braithwaite listened reluctantly with growing impatience.

'Give me permission to prepare the body for burial in the church. Mathew will spread word of my grief and my insistence that the old dear have a fine burial. Impress on them it will be at my expense. The coffin will be of the finest oak. I will let it be known that my preference is for an interment in the church grounds.'

'Where *will* you have her buried, Rowan?'

'Address me as major if you please, Vicar.'

'It was a mere slip of the tongue ... Major.'

'I hadn't actually thought of a place of burial. Where do you usually bury Quakers?'

'The church refrains from interfering. The Friends bury their own, in their own grounds.'

'Then what should I do?'

'I suggest you speak with Timothy Atkinson.'

'I'll not be seen dead with the man. He's a renegade, and his body will be rotting in Lancaster before long.'

'He was once a loyal parishioner, but he's now a Quaker who commands authority. Who else would you expect to talk to?'

'The Bensons would be more reasonable and they're holding the body. Penelope knows them well. I'll send her over with the stablehands, and they can deliver the body to the church.'

'I'm afraid it's not that easy, Major. I'll have to mediate on your behalf, or your good intentions will provoke a riot, and if we are to prepare her for burial, I shall have to enter her in the death register.'

'Good. That's an excellent idea, Gabriel.'

'Not so good, Major. It's against the law of the church to register Quakers.'

'Then make a mistake. We have to account for them somehow, even if it's for the collection of taxes.'

'Taxes are your domain. Leave the registrations to the church.'

The major pledged his stable hands, two Galloway ponies, and a sled or cart, whichever might be suitable. As an afterthought, he spoke to Penelope about sending Damian to help hollow the grave. 'After all, the boy's experienced and doing nothing useful for his pay.'

'What would you know about my use of Damian? Your head's never out of the stables.'

'The Quakers will take offence at you attending the funeral, Penny.'

'Not as much as if you decided to go. They know I'm attending out of respect.'

'I'll organise for the coffin to be taken to Town End. It's the least I can do.'

'You say it's the least you can do? You've shown no compassion and done nothing except give orders. I can't see them ever forgiving you.'

'Then it's just as well that I won't be attending. I couldn't live with myself being a hypocrite. I have a meeting with the Kirkbys at Kirkby Hall. I would hate to think what the colonel would think if I attended a Quaker funeral. You will have to see to the finer details on the day, Penny. Don't let me down.'

Penelope had planned to arrive early for the viewing then discovered that the coffin hadn't been collected the day before, and the weather had turned sour. She went immediately to the stables, but Edgar Hollis showed no interest in the major's whereabouts and only thought to complain about the loss of his stable hands. 'They left to collect the coffin from the church at the break of dawn. The major gave them instructions and set aside two Galloway ponies and sled.'

'The body should have been delivered yesterday. There is a viewing later this morning.'

'Then they'll have to delay the burial.'

Penelope rode to the church to ask Mathew of the coffin's whereabouts. 'They left early and will arrive in ample time for the viewing. The grounds are slippery with the rain, but I can't see why you should worry unduly. We're experts at this, although I must admit it was the first time that I had prepared a Quaker for burial, and hopefully my last. I might add that it was a beautiful piece of workmanship I performed on the old lady. It was a pity the Quakers refused the major's offer of an oak coffin and an engraved headstone. They prefer to remain humble and never use coffins or headstones. They consider a wooden box far too splendid for a Friend so normally roll bodies up in sheets for burial.'

'My husband was pleased to respect their wishes, and save the expense, but would like it said that his heart was in the right place. I can't think how he managed to persuade our stable boys to deliver the coffin. They are both superstitious and would fear to carry any corpse, let alone a Quaker's. And you also refused your services at first. Was it the vicar that persuaded you otherwise Mathew?'

'Not entirely. He believed that it was most inappropriate and bordered on being illegal. Then he appeared to have a change of heart, and I can only think it was compassion for the old lady. She was his neighbour after all, but on the other hand your husband is a persuasive man.' He smiled faintly, lifted his eyebrows, and thought fondly of the brandy cask.

'I'm not sure what you are hinting at.'

'It's best you concentrate on the burial, and rest assured that everything is proceeding as planned.'

'I wish I had the same confidence in my husband's activities as you obviously do.'

The old streeker looked at her studiously before deciding to speak his thoughts. 'Your husband must have the power of the Devil over Vicar Braithwaite. I fail to understand how he could allow a Quaker to be prepared for burial on hallowed ground.'

'You must refrain from speaking of the Devil in relation to my husband. Now I've no appetite for attending an hour-long service but I would very much like to show my respects at the burial. Which path did they take with the coffin?'

Mathew watched Penelope canter her horse down the well-worn path and tried to dismiss a nagging thought. *He should never have bribed those two young lads. Not with a whole bottle of brandy.*

Damian was racing Jasper through the woods, exhilarated at having the rest of the day off work. The last thing he wanted was to attend a Quaker funeral. Timothy Atkinson had sent him back to his employer on the condition he kept his eye open for the hearse.

'The carriers should have been here more than an hour ago Damian. If they're in trouble, report back to me immediately. I should never have allowed the major to interfere. His self-preservation is obvious, and it's fortunate for him that he has such a compassionate wife.'

Damian had walked just short of a mile when Jasper started barking and racing ahead. He thought the dog must have scented a rabbit, so he slowed to let him play. Then there was a short silence followed by voices breaking into song, and Jasper yelping and howling in harmony. A grin shaped Damian's face and he started laughing as he ran towards Sammy and Chas from the stables. They were sitting under a tree at the top of an incline passing a bottle back and forth, the Galloway ponies standing idle, reined to an empty sled. 'Hi Sammy, where's Agnes?'

The stable boy swayed, waving the brandy bottle against the motion of his body. He pointed his forefinger to the bottom of the incline then sat down heavily on the stump, chuckling to himself as he passed the remains of the bottle to Chas. Damian looked down the slope and gasped. The coffin had skidded down the muddy slope and brought to a halt by rocks in the middle of the fast-running beck. He was stepping forward to take a closer look when Jasper shot through his legs, unbalancing him. They both followed the path of the coffin, in an uncontrollable helter-skelter, skidding helplessly down the muddy incline. Damian's feet hit the bottom first, his progress halted by the rocks balancing the coffin. He raised his head to examine the wooden box and was horrified. The lid of the coffin had slid across and exposed an arm. He was experiencing his nightmare all over again. *It's the Dobbie man.* Damian raced up the slope, hands and clogs slapping wet clay, searching frantically for a hold. He was almost halfway and in sight of the stable boys when the muddy bank released its suction on his clogs. He slid back down towards the coffin and his eyes widened, looking for escape as the waving arm closed in on him. Jasper howled and barked, alternately frightened and aggressive, confused as to which voice he should use. Damian desperately tried to climb the slope a second time, but his legs were shaking and weak. As he slid back again, his eyes transfixed on the vibrating coffin, and the arm bouncing around, reaching out to search for him. He rolled his body over at the bottom then saw Jasper heading upstream. He shot to his feet and not daring a second glance at the coffin, he took off after his dog. Behind him the two stable boys were looking down, baffled by the commotion. The coffin seemed alive, rocking back and forth on the pinnacle of the stones. It had skewed with the power of the running beck and with the force of momentum, the exposed arm waved again, urging Damian on his way.

Penelope was a mile from Town End and had seen no sign of the stable boys. She concluded that they had made it in time for the viewing. Then she heard twigs snapping ahead of her and the pounding of feet. She recognised Jasper as he flashed past. Damian followed, chin skyward, splayed feet scooping the air. He was covered from head-to-toe in mud and obviously terrified, staring ahead into the distance. He flew past Penelope without any sign of acknowledgment. She slapped her heels back, urging her horse into a trot. There was something ahead that needed investigating. One look at the isolated coffin and the drunken stable boys was enough. *How much more must that woman suffer?*

Penelope rode in all haste to Town End and returned with help. The viewing was cancelled in respect to Agnes, and

Penelope sighed with relief when the coffin was finally lowered into the ground. The thoughts of the Quakers attending the funeral were divided. In their eyes, the major would always be an enemy and an interfering intruder. His wife on the other hand was obviously a woman of compassion and determination. She could see no harm in the Quakers and had earned their respect. Because of her position in the community and Protestant religion, she would have to remain at a distance, a predicament she would have to live with. That she was respected in the district was first and foremost in her mind.

Damian may have been terrified, but his thoughts were clearly focussed on the grave of his Dobbie man. *I should have done it before.* He made straight for the buried rune pot, furtively looking around for farmer Smyth as he secreted the wrapped hand under his tunic. He picked a bunch of primroses from the field and then ran all the way to the graveyard with one hand holding the parcel to his midriff, the other holding the flowers. When he arrived, the churchyard was deserted. He grabbed a shovel resting by an open grave and started digging frantically into Francis' mound. He muttered and cursed the Dobbie man as he dug down to the length of his arm and then carefully positioned the skeletal hand pointing towards the headstone. He had filled the hole and was shaping the mound around the primroses when the vicar came over the rise. Damian stood up to stamp the earth around the flowers and then wet himself in excitement as he saw the vicar riding towards him.

Gabriel Braithwaite was returning from visiting his outer parishioners, and had spotted Damian stamping down the earth over the old priest's grave. 'Hello Damian. Dancing on Francis' resting place again? Your mother told me you were still fearful of the Dobbie man.' Damian looked at him open-mouthed and never spoke. 'Lost your tongue, then have you?'

The vicar focussed on the grave mound, surprised at the flowers. 'Those are fresh primroses. Did you plant them?' Damian nodded vigorously. 'That's a fine gesture my boy. I'm happy to see you making amends to my good friend, Francis. There have been many evil rumours about this grave since you left the district. Perhaps we can now put them to rights.'

'I'm not afraid anymore, Vicar. I've fixed the Dobbie man good and proper this time.'

'You've come to your senses at last. Good lad. Then I'll expect to see you at my next Sunday service with your mother and sister Mary, especially as you are leaving soon for Cambridge.'

Damian nodded and held his silence until the vicar rode away. It had come to him quite suddenly that a human hand would be better than ravens' feet, but he couldn't tell Mary. *She would want to know where it came from. That was clever of me, picking the primroses from the hillside as an excuse to visit the grave.* Without warning, his protruding eyes lit up. He grabbed at his crotch, and rocked back and forth, laughing hysterically, imagining the hand grabbing the Dobbie man by the throat. Gabriel Braithwaite heard Damian's laughter. He swivelled on his mount to see the object of amusement; shook his head and continued on his way. *I'll never understand that boy of Hannah's.* Damian rocked on his haunches, staring at the priest's grave, trancelike with a devilish smile on his face.

PART IV

Newmarket: 25 September 1666

Smoke rose from the smouldering fires of London. Parliament was in recess and the king had moved north for the racing season. Newmarket was bursting at the seams, a hive of excitement as the town entertained members of parliament and the king's court. The turf resonated with thundering hooves, and the eyes of the king's entourage focussed on a distant curve in the track. A ghostly figure of horse and rider burst through the early-morning mist; followed by a string of horses no more than a length apart. Bunching behind the leading chestnut they galloped head-on over the rise, seemingly slow until they drew level then flashed past, muscles straining, hooves pounding the earth as they closed in on the finishing line. Sporadic clapping greeted the chestnut as it entered the enclosure. Its tall rider slowed him to a canter then stood high in the stirrups and waved confidently to the admiring crowd. He steered his mount through parting spectators, the chestnut's close-cropped mane glistening with sweat, its body heat steaming the air. The rider's bunched raven hair swung freely as he dismounted and flamboyantly handed the reins to a stable boy. The man was over six feet tall with an athletic body, and he dwarfed the young handler. He patted a handkerchief over his forehead, mopped around his swarthy face and then carefully wiped his pencil-thin moustache; first one way, and then the other.

An elite group of gentlemen made their way towards him, and it was the commanding heavily built figure of George Monck, the Duke of Albermarle, who first addressed the king. 'That was an admirable ride Rowley. The trial augurs well for your first Newmarket Plate.'

'Do you think I should ride her George? I mean, will it sit well with the people?'

'You worry too much about how your subjects perceive you. They still speak of your ride from the Tower of London to Whitehall. My wife said you looked resplendent donning the ostrich-plumed hat, as your father did, dressed in true cavalier fashion. You were rescuing them from the Roundheads and the restrictions of Cromwell's Puritanism. Believe me when I say the people still welcome you. They tilt their glasses to your kingship.'

'I will always remember the welcome they gave me in London. Did you know it was also my thirtieth birthday? After the death of my father and my reclusive years in France, their acceptance of me as their king was a revelation of joyful significance. I wish to reward their loyalty and maintain their respect throughout my reign.'

'The people's minds are occupied with the fires ravaging London, and nothing else.'

'That is precisely my worry. I tried to help out with my brother, James, but the fact is, I fled from the great fire to Oxford, as I did from the plague. You advised me to flee both catastrophes and I had to agree, but it doesn't sit well with me. To exacerbate matters I've recently been informed that the fire started in our own Pudding Lane bakehouse, and that the fire will be burning for months to come. I don't envy your task of maintaining order. Is London's eternal punishment hellfire and damnation?'

'Last year I was called from my sea duties, and as commander of the fleet, ordered to contain the great plague. The dead carts were piled high, the drivers, bell ringers, gravediggers and searchers for the dead were all overworked. When the graveyards were full we buried them in pits outside the city. Many poor people went unrecorded, and the Quakers and others refused to have the bell rung for them, so the number of deaths is uncertain. It is estimated there were ten-thousand victims in one week alone. Thieves were abundant, looting the shops of the dead, many of them poor women, who flaunted their stolen finery. Now I am asked to contain the great fire. I shall need more help. My duty is to king and country, but my opinion is that the fire is a beneficial cleansing. Good must emerge from the bad, and London will be rejuvenated.'

King Charles II gestured with an open palm towards his summer house on the hill, suggesting they walk with him. 'I hope you're right. I pray to God that the future of the king, the church, and the people will be safe. The buildings will be rebuilt as a soon as possible. There will be less timber to fire in future; stone, bricks, mortar and slate will be the preference. Six commissioners have already been appointed to redesign the city and Christopher Wren has been commissioned to design and oversee construction of the churches. He is studying the city of Florence at present. My architect assures me of his competence. We were fortunate that Westminster was untouched, and that both houses could reply to my speech. After the catastrophe of the fire it was thought insolent to ask for extra funding to pay the navy. But the navy is our defence against the Dutch. It shouldn't be necessary to beg for funding.' A small entourage were following, and he addressed the master of his stables. 'How many entries can we expect for the race, Henry?'

'The clerk is holding twenty-three deposits, Your Majesty.'

'That's far too many. I want them whittled down. Hold elimination races, and make sure there are no more than eight competitors on the day. Five would be admirable.' He turned his attention back to the duke. 'Do you have an entry?'

'I have two deposits.'

'I can only guarantee you one start. You may enter the other horse in the preliminaries. There will be a break of two days before the plate is run, allowing ample recovery time. Familiarise yourself with the rules as they will be rigorously applied.' Charles raised his eyebrows to the duke and smiled. 'I'm open to side-wagers of course.'

The Duke grinned, accepting the statement as a challenge. He had been a Puritan for most of his life until he was advised that gambling would be a distraction and thus good medication for his wellbeing. Wagering on the Sport of Kings appealed to him as a prestigious entertainment. 'I will take up your challenge. The strength of the field will determine the size of my wager.'

They were approaching the summer house and as the king looked to the viewing balcony a huge smile illuminated his face. He opened his arms and gestured a welcome to three beautiful women. They ran down the steps, giggling and bustling their way towards him; one lady was holding a wig, another one a cane, and the third trailing two of his favourite spaniels. He fitted the periwig over his tailed hair then spun in a circle with his arms widespread, posturing to his entourage. 'Ladeeeez, Quelle surprise plaisante vous m'avez donnee.' The king ignored his close friends to concentrate on one of his greatest pleasures. He hugged each of the women in turn, ruffled his dogs behind the ears, and then vigorously fondled his codpiece as he stepped onto the viewing platform of his temporary home. His loving and faithful Portuguese wife, Catherine of Braganza, was waiting patiently to welcome him. 'Darling, did you see me win the race?'

'Must you embarrass me, Charles, bringing your floozies with you? Send them back to Cambridge, away from our home.'

'Darling, today is sports day. The London coach journey is tedious and uncomfortable. The ladies suffered greatly to be in my attendance. You must know that they are merely playthings and could never compete with a woman of your beauty and intellect.'

'Your sexual appetite is a disease. You wouldn't survive one week in Portugal. The church would dethrone you.'

'But we are not in Portugal, my love. We are in England and I'm the king. I'm a little Italian, a little French, a little Scottish, a little smitten, but nevertheless I'm the King of England.'

'And a little Protestant when it suits you, and a little Catholic when you require a woman that I will not name, to beg money from King Louis to fund your Coldstream Guards. Parliament demands that you be Protestant, yet it will not grant funds to pay guards for your protection. Is that a true measure of their faith?'

'Parliament invited me back because the people were tired of being ruled by Cromwell's army, crushed by Puritanism. They gave me fifty-thousand pounds to return from France and quickly punished those responsible for beheading my father. The people chose to return to the rule of king and church, but to place a ruler in charge of an enlarged army goes against the grain, and it will take some time. The most important thing is the people have their freedom back. They can play music and dance in the streets if they wish. They can gamble and attend the theatre, and scientists can think clearly, without fear.'

'The Quakers are not free Charles. George Fox has limited freedom but Margaret Fell remains in prison.'

'I once honoured that woman with an audience and now she constantly writes to me from prison. Her daughters requested that I intervene in her plight, but they should know by now that

I haven't the power to overturn acts of parliament. I pledged my word that the Quakers should not be molested for their peculiar scruples, with the proviso that their conduct was peaceable. She wrote to inform me that my ruling was being abused, and that they were being hounded by the district's chief magistrate, Colonel Richard Kirkby. He apparently had property confiscated by Cromwell and has since developed a hatred for the Puritans, and now his son, Roger, is lending a hand to his crusade. Several Quaker meetings were interrupted on the surmise that they were plotting against the king and were thus not peaceable. They were then asked to swear an Oath of Allegiance to the king, which all refused. She went on to say I had her allegiance, she loves and honours me but Christ Jesus the King of Kings had commanded her not to swear. Now to my mind we have a play on words, and she is truly being persecuted. I remain virtually powerless, but I must confess she influenced me in the case of George Fox. Before the last sitting of the house I ordered his release from Scarborough Castle. The man had more than served his sentence. Four years have passed since I relinquished the Furness lordship to George Monck. I thought his background as a Puritan would allow him some empathy for the locals, but he shows no interest. The Quakers are stubborn and obviously feel a need to suffer for their cause. I learned during my brief two year lordship that many of the people are born with this attitude and the area has been a fertile ground for breeding Quakerism.'

'I had no idea you were so familiar with the district, Charles?'

'I'm not familiar. It's off the beaten track, and from the day of my coronation, which was the day of my inheritance, I showed little interest apart from the collection of taxes. The district has a strange freehold, and that was my main consideration when I relinquished the title to George; it was too problematic for my liking. The tenure was never changed on the dissolution of the monasteries, and with tenure for life the statesmen have grown stubborn with a misguided sense of power. They say that their underlings have inherited the same attitude. How can anyone have tenure for life that is neither freehold nor leasehold? Not even parliament can fathom it.'

'Can't they change the law?'

'One day, they will change the law, but only when it suits them. If I had the wealth to rule I would sack the parliament and put the country to right. My steward was the last official to visit the parish, and he informed me of growing problems with the church attendance and the collection of tithes.'

'So, the Quakers really are a problem?'

'They are not so much my problem as George's problem. I may have to concede him further powers to enforce the collection of tithes. But that's enough of politics and courtiers, Catherine. They bore me. The courtiers speak only of the war with the Dutch whilst parliament turns a blind eye to the funding of my Coldstream Guards. Today is my sports day. Will you watch the rest of the morning trials and entertain our friends on the viewing balcony?'

'Change into something more suitable and arrange for the departure of your playthings. Then, perhaps, I could be enticed into entertaining your advisors and our friends, the Dukes of Buckingham and Albermarle.'

'Will you abandon your card games and play tennis with me this afternoon?'

'When we are alone, I will do anything for you, but you must respect my pregnancy. Your desire for a legitimate heir is paramount.'

'And what of this evening, my love? Ce soir?'

'You look handsome in your periwig, my husband. I love you dearly, but you smell worse than your dogs. Tonight, we will bathe, and I shall perfume you.'

'There are whispers in court that I should divorce you, my darling.'

Catherine smiled confidently. 'You tease me. We both know that in your heart and mind you are Catholic, and that your hidden beliefs would demand the impossible, to ask the Pope's permission. What a tragedy that you must live your life as a Protestant. But then, your so-called gift of fifty-thousand pounds from parliament *was* a lot of money. If only you'd envisaged my dowry of Bombay and Tangiers before we were betrothed, perhaps you would never have accepted the obligation. But then you wouldn't have been the king and we would never have married. What a tangled web you weave.'

'The gift from parliament was a godsend. Without it I would still reside in Holland or France begging for food and clothing, and as you have inferred, my greatest misfortune would have been not to have such a loving wife.' He smiled at Catherine, and she coyly acknowledged, humouring him. 'Those miserable days on the run from Cromwell were the worst. You could never imagine the suffering I endured in exile. Did I tell you the time I...?'

'Pardon me Charles, but you're wandering again. I've heard the tales of your adventures too many times, and you always neglect to tell me you were also travelling with ladies of the court.'

The king pursed his lips in a sulk and gathered his thoughts. 'Your dowry wasn't as huge as it first appeared to be, my love. The chest of this new drink, tea, was the most appreciated surprise, but both of the trading rights have proven to be a handicap. The ports are expensive in their upkeep and it has been decided that the rights to Tangiers will be sold and those of Bombay will be leased.'

'Then my dowry has been badly managed, Charles, and you have been ill-advised to part with your valuable assets.'

'I only act on what I consider to be expert advice. I can do no more.'

'There are rumours that another gifted asset will be racing against you in the plate.'

'That is news to me. I can't remember gifting a thoroughbred horse. If that is true, I will investigate its credentials during the trials.'

The Town Plate: October 1666

'The boy on the black stallion rides well. He displays an uncanny feel for the horse. He has strength in his knees and a good balance, but a most unusual style of riding.'

'He's only the stablehand, Your Majesty, but as you say, he has an obvious rapport with his mount.'

'I'm interested. What's the stallion's name?'

'Prince, Your Majesty.'

'The horse sports Arabic lines. If that is so, his colour is rare. Investigate its breeding for me, and whatever today's results are, reserve a place for him in the plate.'

Henry took his leave and immediately headed for the stables to intercept Prince and his rider. He had been present in the royal stables when the mare gave birth to a black foal on the night of a blue moon. He was convinced that for such a rare event to occur the foal had to be something special. Being gifted to him, the colt was beyond his wildest dreams, but his ownership had brought nothing but bad luck. He knew more about the major than he intended to share with the king. He had served with Rowan in Cromwell's stables and his present position was due to his association with their old commander and Master of the Horse, George Monck. He had been pleased to welcome his old colleague, but to have him appear with a horse that he'd once owned, and tragically lost, didn't sit well with him. He wanted to know why the major was in charge of the horse, and how the registered owner had come into its possession.

Henry could still see the four tens fanned out in his hand like it was yesterday. He had noted an ace, king, and queen being discarded and had upped the ante with supreme confidence. He was aware that the two so-called gentlemen sitting opposite were there with the sole purpose of bleeding him dry, and they had coerced a naive bailiff from the north to make up the numbers. One of the gentlemen lay down the first, the second, and then the third king, his thumb pressing each card down with theatrical deliberation, while looking up at him with an irritating smile. His partner half-heartedly showed two pairs and then he spread out his four tens, grinned triumphantly, and lunged for the pot.

'Excuse me gentlemen!' He froze and turned his head up towards the squeaky voice. They were the first words the novice had spoken all night. 'Should I show my cards now?' Algernon had been unsure of the value of his cards throughout the game and had discarded aimlessly, most of the time through ignorance. This time his hand was full of pictures and he felt a surge of excitement. He lost control of his senses and followed the rest of the table in the bidding. The tense silence of the room was shattered when the novice opened his palms to expose the four curled up cards to the table.

The two gentlemen rolled about their seats laughing and he'd stared in disbelief at the four jacks. 'It's not possible.' He'd had no hesitation in risking his most prized possession and had lost it to the unbelievable luck of a first timer. He had never forgiven himself for signing the animal over to Algernon Fleming. One wild night of gambling and false bravado had urged him to throw his ownership into the centre pot. His prize colt had been lost on the turn of a card. Such unbelievable luck told him that the colt was never destined to be in his possession. The Master of the Stables had been aware that the gift from the king had created jealousies and that he'd been enticed into the game because of them. That was four years ago, and he still cringed at the memory. The horse had obviously been on-sold and there could be complications with the paperwork. Perhaps it was providence that Prince had been returned to his sphere of authority. The most important and urgent matter now was to assess the speed of the horse and take a measure of its ability to challenge the king's stable.

Damian was about to dismount when he was spotted by the Master of the Stables. 'Come over here my boy, and don't dismount. I need to speak with you.' Henry was sitting astride a magnificent chestnut horse at the entrance to the stables. The air was heavy with the smell of fresh manure and scattered hay. Damian smiled as he walked Prince over to the stable master. He loved the sound of hooves clattering out their rhythm on the cobblestones. 'What's your name, boy?'

'Damian.'

Henry thought the voice firm and honest, but he'd been told the boy was backward, and there was a hint of suspicion. *He squints as if searching my mind.* 'Your horse needs more exercise.'

Damian kept on staring, his eyes flicking from the head of the beautiful chestnut to Henry. He was in awe, but to the stable master it appeared he was deaf.

Henry shouted louder. 'Your horse needs more exercise.'

Damian smiled and his eyes widened. 'Major Rathbone and Rufus tell me how much Prince has to exercise.'

'Naturally they do, but I'm the stable master. You can call me Henry if you wish.'

Damian nodded and remained silent. *I think he might be a nice man.*

'I know your horse is called Prince and he loves racing. We must race him once around the track with my favourite horse. I'm sure they'll enjoy racing against each other. There'll be an extra bag of feed for the winner.'

Damian rolled his lower lip over his bottom teeth, bit down with his upper lip, and thoughtfully nodded. Then he looked up at the stable master and grinned. 'Prince will win for sure.'

The major lodged his deposit of twenty shilling for each of the three heats without a grudge. He had been a witness of the race between Prince and the king's highly regarded chestnut mare. *With Rufus riding he's a certainty.* He even managed a smile for the Clerk of the Race as he handed over an extra three pounds for the plate entry fee. 'You'll be handing that back to me after the last race my good man.'

'As long as you pay "your good man" his dues, he'll be happy.'

'What do you mean, pay your dues?'

'Twenty shillings from your winnings will be donated so I can keep the course plain and free from cart grooves.'

The major looked the clerk up and down with disgust. 'You must be joking.'

The clerk straightened and took on an air of authority. 'You should be more familiar with the rules my good man. The winner must also pay the Clerk of the Course the same amount. The sum of twenty shillings is to be distributed to the poor on both sides of Newmarket. If you have any further queries you can take them up with the race judge.'

The major was nonplussed. He could see his winnings already being depleted and the race was not yet run. *Holmes never mentioned any charitable expenses.* He placed a heavier than normal side-bet on the first heat.

Even Squire Holmes had to admit that Prince had improved beyond all expectations. He had placed a larger proportion of his wager on the major's horse than he had on his own. 'The king's two horses must start as favourites major, but we must have faith. Everything depends on the fitness of each horse on the day.'

Race day: 16 October 1666

The great day had finally arrived and the weather was glorious. It was the sixteenth day of October 1666, the second Thursday of the month. Eight horses had qualified to contest the king's inaugural Town Plate and the rules were to be adhered to the letter. The reward for the winner would be a prize flagon and a side purse of one-hundred guineas, drawn from a horse registration fee of three pounds and contributions from the attending noblemen and gentlemen. To many, the prestige of winning would be worth more than the monetary value of the purse.

Damian was pleased to see Henry. He'd been friendly after their secret race and had complimented him on his riding. He said that he'd once owned Prince as a colt and then lost him foolishly playing cards. Damian felt sorry for him and related the story of Prince and how he came to be owned by his widowed sister Mary. He also mentioned being bullied by Rufus, and Henry sympathised with him. He promised to visit the stables before the race to help with Prince's preparation, but not to mention it to Rufus or the major. 'I don't really like them either, Damian.'

The Master of the Stables arrived carrying a bucket full of apples and he set them down in front of Damian. 'I witnessed

Prince's birth in this very stable five years ago to the day. Do you realise what that means Damian?'

He watched the stable boy's eyes light up and his grin widen. Damian was so excited he found difficulty blurting out the words. 'It's ... it's Prince's birthday!'

'You're right, my boy, and as I was present at his birth and I consider myself to be his godfather. The apples are a present from me to him, but we must keep it a secret. Best make sure he eats them all before Rufus arrives.'

Damian could hardly contain his excitement. 'It's my perfect day. I like secrets, and Prince loves apples.'

'Prince has to run the four miles three times over Damian, and there's only a half hour between each heat. If he's to win, he must be well fed.'

The crowds were gathering, and the posts and flags being marked out on the round course. The first and last heats would be run clockwise with the flags to the right side of the rider, and the second heat anti-clockwise with the flags on the left. Midday was less than half an hour away and some of the horses had already been weighed in.

They were parading in front of the stand and trotting the course. Rufus was carrying one stone of lead in his saddle, bringing him to the twelve stone required. He was an excellent rider, more than capable of matching the skills of his opponents, and he puffed up when his wife, Eleanor, remarked that he looked smart in his riding gear. He felt important knowing that his mount was creating as much attention as the king's. The king was riding the chestnut from his own stable and he was being backed heavily, but there was an equal amount being gambled on Prince. Word travelled fast in Newmarket and the result of Henry's secret trial had become common knowledge.

As far as the betting was concerned the heats were a three-horse event. The only other contender thought to be a danger was the Earl of Aylesbury's grey, ridden by his son Thomas Bruce. Squire Holmes thought himself fortunate to have a runner. He knew that his horse and those of John Egerton, the Earl of Bridgewater, and of George Monck, the Duke of Albemarle, were there to make up the numbers. Henry had his own thoughts on the winner and had gambled accordingly. After pulling Damian aside to confirm that Prince had eaten the bucket of apples, he had bet heavily on the king's chestnut. The meeting hadn't gone unnoticed by the major and he accosted Henry as the trumpet was calling the horses to the starting line. 'I saw you speaking with my stable boy. If you require any knowledge of my training methods, you have only to ask.'

'I was asking your stable boy about the horse's condition. He seems to have an unusual affinity with the horse. I'm not usually taken with sentiment, but I've bet heavily on Prince and because I once owned him, it may have affected my judgement.'

'You have nothing to worry about, Henry, and you mark my words when I say that he'll be showing the grey and the king's chestnut his tail more than once in the Town Plate.' The stable master could hardly contain his pleasure and choked back a smile. Even when Prince held the lead at the first milepost he smiled. Four miles was a long haul for any horse carrying a bucketful of apples in his stomach.

Rufus was on top of the world. He was leading in the first prized race in England and showing his back to the best of the gentry. There was no doubt in his mind that Prince would lead all the way. He was striding out with the same effortless gait that he'd displayed in the trials. His instructions were to stay close to the pack and not to overexert his mount. If Prince fell behind a horse, he had the ability to fight back, but he loved to be at the front and setting the pace. Rufus thought his only danger was the king's mount, and he'd been trapped inside for the first two miles. Passing the three-mile post the field was bunching up behind him. The king was moving the chestnut to the outside and the grey was following close behind. Henry was beginning to feel uneasy about the result but then relaxed when he realised the king had made his move at the right time. The last mile was a gradual uphill slope and he expected that Prince would soon be coming back to the field. *His stomach must be souring.*

Rufus had seen the king make his move and urged Prince forward. Normally the horse would have responded immediately but he seemed content to stay on the same pace and the grey and the chestnut continued to make ground. The major was pumping the air with exasperation. 'Whip him forward, son! Whip him!'

Henry was gritting his teeth and his hands were gripping his tunic, threatening to tear it from his body. 'Fall back! Fall back!'

Damian was shouting hysterically. 'Come on, Prince. Come on boy!'

Rufus kept urging Prince forward, but his pace never altered and as the finishing line approached, he sensed the emerging presence of the king's chestnut on one side and Thomas Bruce's grey on the other. The thudding of hooves and spiralling turf had the crowd roaring as the three horses passed the finish together. There was a buzz amongst the crowd, and none were willing to declare a winner.

Damian ran over to greet Prince and held the reins as Rufus dismounted. 'I think you won, Prince. I think you won.'

Rufus gripped him by the shoulder and glared. 'We won't know until the judge has made his decision, and they'll give it to the king for sure. Father is going to be furious. Make sure he's rubbed down and made ready for the next heat.'

The judge called the trainers together for his decision and only the major was involved. The major was becoming suspicious of Henry. In his experience a trainer of that standing would never back an opponent of equal ability unless there was mischief afoot. He concentrated on Henry's face as the judge was about to confer his decision. But the adjudicator gestured the major towards him and the opportunity was lost in the excitement. 'The black horse was judged to be the winner and the king and the Earl of Aylesbury have conceded.' The major's world exploded, and he turned around to celebrate his success with Henry, but the head of the stables was nowhere to be seen. Damian was speaking softly to Prince as he groomed him. 'I think you won, Prince, but you look sick. Perhaps you had a bad apple.'

His head shot around when he heard the familiar loud voice from behind. 'What did you say about an apple?'

The major was standing over him. 'I thought Prince would like an apple. He looks sick.'

'Not as sick as you'll be if you ever give him an apple before a race.'

'Prince likes apples and it's his birthday.'

'He's not allowed apples in training and it's not his birthday. What was Henry talking to you about?'

'He wanted to know if Prince was going to win and I said yes.'

'You tell him to speak to me next time, and what's this you say about Prince being sick.'

The major took the bridle and proceeded to examine Prince. 'His eyes look sad that's for sure. He's been ridden too hard.'

'Did he win, Rowan?'

The major glared and left Damian without another word. He had seen enough to be worried and Rufus' instructions would be to give him an easy ride. All bets would be off until the third heat. *Let's hope we can win that one. If there's to be a decider, we've no hope.* He caressed his money pouch and changed his plans. Half the winnings would be paid up front to the king's surgeon, and the rest would be his stake for the third and hopefully the last heat. *If we win, there'll be a hundred guineas bonus.*

Henry was thinking exactly the opposite. In all his years as a trainer he had never seen such stamina in a horse. *If he can win after swallowing a bucketful of apples, nothing will beat him.* The stable master borrowed heavily and bet Prince to win against the king's horses. Rufus found it hard to understand his father's change of plans. 'If he's good enough to win, Father, shouldn't we try and win?'

'We'll see how the others have been affected first. That was a hard race and the rest of the field were a mile away at the finish. Keep the king's horses close and feel your way. If you don't think you can win, then save the horse's energy for the last heat.'

The trumpet was blaring out for the field to assemble, and the moment Rufus sprung into the saddle he knew there was a change in Prince's attitude. 'He's no good, Father. There's something wrong.'

'He's fatigued, Rufus. You took too much out of him in the first heat. Just restrain your enthusiasm and do as I told you a moment ago. We will save him for the third heat.'

Henry found a comfortable seat and was smiling contentedly as he watched the runners parading. But when Prince trotted past and he saw the condition of the horse he'd gambled heavily on, his heart sank. He tried to pull his bet but to no avail then walked away with little intention of witnessing his own downfall. *That horse is the ruin of me. He's been a jinx ever since I first laid eyes on him.*

The second heat was run at a leisurely pace and for the first three miles Rufus coasted Prince at the rear of the field. When he considered it time to urge Prince forward there was no response, and the rest of the field began to draw further away. With the weakened competition, the chestnut and the grey led throughout and the king's chestnut was cantering to a win when the grey burst on the scene late and overhauled him in the last stride. The king had been beaten, and the race was an anti-climax. When Prince and his rider laboured to the finish, the crowd jeered. Rufus was angry and embarrassed, wishing he was elsewhere. He had been convinced that this was going to be his day of triumph, his day of recognition. He dismounted amongst the crowd and when Damian approached, he became the recipient of Rufus' hate. 'You fool! You idiot! The horse isn't fit.'

Rufus stomped off in the direction of his father. The major had been watching Prince's every movement and it was obvious to him that the horse was distressed from a sickness. He greeted his son with all the sympathy he could muster. 'We shall be better prepared next year, boy.'

'I'm finished, Father. I shall never ride that horse again.'

The major watched his son being consoled by Eleanor then turned his thoughts to the next heat. He was relieved that he'd refrained from placing a bet, happy that he'd saved a tidy sum. The major patted his belted money pouch with pride. *Enough to aside for the operation, and the remainder will cover my expenses.* He searched for Squire Holmes to ask his advice, but he was nowhere to be found.

The squire was in a quandary of his own, troubled with by his losses, and the poor performance of his horse. *Rathbone can go to hell for all I care.* Then the major thought to ask for an audience with the clerk of the race with the intention of withdrawing Prince from the field and claiming back his deposit. He told Damian to unsaddle Prince and take him back to the stables. 'What are you crying for boy?'

'Prince is sick, and I think he's going to die.' *Henry's an evil man.*

'That's nonsense, it's only a little sickness and he must be cared for. Unsaddle him, towel that sweat off, and take him for a walk. There's no way we could ever allow the horse to run in that condition.' The Master of the Race had rotated his timing glass. The last grain of sand would indicate the end of the half hour allowed between races and be a signal for the trumpeter to call the runners together.

Damian was talking to Prince as he walked him around the yard. 'I shouldn't have made you eat all those apples. They must have been as bad as that evil man who gave them to you, and he made me promise not to tell anyone.'

Prince suddenly stopped his gait, turned his head to the rear, and let off a great fart. Damian let go the reins to hold his nose as Prince's tail lifted and the diarrhoea had its way. The stable boy ran for a bucket of water and then another and then another. Prince whinnied as he continued his onslaught. Justice was being done, and in more ways than one.

The Clerk of the Race had seen the major approaching and smiled a little sadistically as he held out an open palm. 'You've come to pay the race stake of the horse that came second?'

'That's ridiculous. My horse is ill and isn't even running.'

'Your horse came last in the second heat, and therefore you are obliged to pay twenty shillings for your own stake and twenty shillings for that of the second horse. The contributions go to the winner of the next heat. Must I always explain the king's rules? Can't you read my good man? You were the beneficiary of the same rule in your first heat, so pay up or be fined and disqualified.'

'But I'm withdrawing my horse.'

'That is of no consequence, but I beg to differ on the status of your horse.' And the clerk of the race slanted his eyes towards the weighing-in enclosure. The major gave a start, and his eyes popped. Damian was astride Prince and waving to him with a huge wide grin on his face.

King Charles II had been astride the bay horse and on his way to the starting line when he sent an officer to enquire about the condition of the horse that he'd so much admired. 'I feel the black horse has been interfered with. His performance in the last heat was most unusual and for his rider to dispense with him in such a manner makes me suspicious. If I'm to win this Town Plate, the race must be run in an honourable fashion. I want to be satisfied there is no foul play.'

The officer found Damian cantering Prince around the stables and reported back to the king in the affirmative. 'The horse seems sprightly, Your Majesty.'

'Then he shall challenge the grey and the chestnut. The rest of the opposition is of little consequence, devoid of stamina.'

'The stable boy is the only rider available, Your Majesty.'

'Then send him to the Clerk of the Race and have him weighed in and tell the clerk to hold the start until horse and rider are prepared.'

'The rules state the rider must be a gentleman, Your Majesty.'

'Don't put obstacles in my way. The horse will be disqualified if he wins, and the owners stripped of the prize, but I say the stable boy should be allowed to ride. He rides expertly and on the black horse he will test our speed and stamina.'

Damian saw the major talking to the Clerk of the Course. He waved to him and then turned to trot Prince towards the starting line. Two heats had to be won before the Town Plate could be claimed, and both Prince and the grey had one win each. If the king won on the chestnut, there would have to be a deciding heat between the three winners. Damian just wanted to ride, and he knew the major would be pleased if he won. He could see the major pushing his way through the crowd yelling and waving at him, and he strained to hear above the noise of the crowd. 'Come back here you bloody fool. I can't afford another last place.'

The king was on the inside running, at the far end of the line of horses. He leaned forward in his saddle and as the field settled for the off, he smiled and shook a forefinger of friendly recognition towards the stable boy. Damian's head turned quickly away. His face flushed and his eyes opened wide as he stared ahead with a silly embarrassed grin. He was dumbstruck, and Prince was left at the start. The major clamped a fist around his money pouch and groaned. 'God help me. I'm being ruined.'

After his dismal showing in the second heat, few had been game enough to gamble on the Prince. Some thought the change in the direction of running had been his undoing, others that his stamina was lacking. Henry pulled his small bet on the grey when he saw that Prince had recovered. *With that horse around I can only lose.*

Damian gradually caught the tail and stayed with them for the first two miles. He had listened to the major's instructions to Rufus and at the end of the third mile he urged Prince forward. The black Arabian horse was travelling beautifully, and Damian's right arm was loose and swinging like a pendulum, alternately brushing Prince's rump as he closed in on the leaders. Within half a mile of the finish he drew level with the Earl of Aylesbury's grey. The two horses came together, and Prince was forced outwards. Damian saw the grey veer to the left with the impact and he concentrated on the king's chestnut less than two lengths ahead. 'We can win, Prince. We can win.'

The major found it hard to believe. Prince had changed from a cart horse into a racehorse in the past half hour. Rufus had come forward to console his father and wasn't prepared for the tirade of insults. 'You bloody fool. Do you realise we had a chance of taking the plate? You're no better than that idiot who's riding out there against the king. You should have been out there instead of him. If we win with that boy riding, we lose, and it's all because of your stupidity.'

Damian was jousting with the king, stride for stride, length by length. And then the stable boy sensed a falter in Prince's stride. The slope of the ground was upwards towards the finish and the day's events had taken their toll. A normal horse would have been drained of its stamina long ago, but Prince was no ordinary horse. Damian lifted in the saddle to coax Prince into one last effort and as he drew alongside the king, he caught a glimpse of the stand and heard the crowd cheering. *You're going to win, Prince. We can beat the king's horse.*

Then as his head came up, he stole another look at the finish and his heart sank as he realised the cheering was for the Earl of Aylesbury's horse. The grey had taken the inside running and streaked ahead whilst he was jousting with the king. King Charles II looked sideways and smiled as his chestnut surged away. Prince crossed the line two lengths behind the king's bay, in third place. Damian watched the earl's son, Thomas Bruce, waving his arms around in triumph and as the grey was paraded amongst the crowd Damian felt sad for Prince. Tears were welling in his eyes as he patted his exhausted horse affectionately. 'Next time you will feel better, Prince, and we will win for sure.'

He staggered back as the reins were torn from his hands and Rufus pushed his nose into his face. 'There'll be no next time you bloody fool. I'll be handling Prince next time.'

'You'll have to see Mary first. It's her horse.'

The major had been following his son to the stables and saw him intercept Damian. 'Hold him there, Rufus!'

The major was panting, from an aggravated temper and his face reddened as he chastised Damian. 'What the devil do you think you're doing, boy? There have been large amounts of money gambled on Prince and the losers are shouting foul play. They're inferring that there has been a mischief in our stables. What do you say about that, boy?'

Damian shrugged his shoulders. 'I dunno.'

Henry was hovering in the background and Damian caught a warning look. The stable master was protecting his own interests and ruing his late decision to pull his bet on the earl's grey. *That black horse holds a curse over me.*

An audience with the king

When the major was called to the king's company he saw his old commander, George Monck, at the king's side and became excited. *This could mean a lordship. Why else would I be summonsed to attend with so many luminaries? Surely, he will recognise me.* He was introduced, but without a second glance the duke waved him towards the king's steward. Richard Swindbourne stretched his thin body to its substantial height and coughed to clear his throat. As he commenced his announcement the major's eyes were drawn hypnotically towards the man's wobbling Adam's apple. By God, *it's like a turkey's neck.*

'The king wishes to discuss the collection of taxes and tithes and the handling of Quakers in the Hawkshead parish.'

The major's chest extended, and his bottom lip almost curled into a smile. 'I knew it. They have finally recognised my authority.'

'Mr Rathbone, as an acting magistrate of your parish, you have an agreement to maintain order for the Duke of Albemarle and to collect dues owed to him and to assist a Colonel Richard Kirkby, the lay impropriator of the district tithes.'

The major looked straight into the turkey's eyes. 'That is correct, Sir.'

'Then are we to ignore these letters being sent to His Majesty by the Quaker woman, Margaret Fox?'

'The woman is in prison for holding meetings to denounce the king.'

'The letters say otherwise, and the Crown will soon be authorising officers to investigate her claims. I mention this as a warning to you that in future that any unwarranted excessive behaviour towards the Quakers will be dealt with decisively by the king. How familiar are you with Colonel Richard Kirkby?'

The major sensed trouble and went on the defence. 'I'm only slightly acquainted sir, because of his authority over tithes. However, his son Robert is a close friend of my son, Rufus.'

'Then you must warn your son to tread carefully. The Kirkby's, both father and son, carry a grudge against the Quakers and could be a bad influence. Apparently, the problem relates to Colonel Richard Kirkby's property being confiscated by Cromwell.'

Major Rathbone was nonplussed. He couldn't see where the questioning was leading. 'Am I being investigated, Sir? Am I under suspicion?'

'No, Major. This is merely a warning that we wish you to convey to all concerned, both inside and outside of Hawkshead Parish. The duke wishes your agreement with him to continue with no amendments. All responsibilities will remain the same leaving your position unchanged, assuming you wish to continue as magistrate of the parish. All future matters will be referred as usual to me, and I will be acting for the duke with the permission of the king.'

The major would have been completely shattered had it not been for a timely compliment from the duke. 'I hear you're still breeding thoroughbred horses major, and from your result in the plate I see you've lost none of your skills. A pity the horse and rider were so erratic, but perhaps you shall go one better next year.'

'Thank you for the compliment, Sir. I thought you'd forgotten our acquaintance.'

'I never forget men of authority who serve under me, Rathbone. I remember you serving me well in the past, and I expect you will continue to do so in the future.'

The king remained seated during the conversation, appearing bored, one hand resting on his cane, as was his habit. When King Charles II deemed the *tête-à-tête* concluded, he leaned slightly forward and directed his comments to the major. 'Le cheval, monsieur! It has the markings of the royal stable. Pour quelle raison?'

The major jolted at the sound of the king's strong voice. 'The horse was won in a wager when he was a colt, Your Majesty, and he was later willed to my wife.'

'We shall have to look into the original wager. I can't recollect.'

The major was hesitant to reply to the king and shuffled nervously. The turkey coughed as a way of interruption and the major turned to him in anticipation of being rescued. 'I have all the details required by Your Majesty. I remember the will and how the colt's ownership was thoroughly investigated before the reading. The colt was granted to the master of your stables at the time and it was within his power to transfer ownership.'

'Ah yes! That would be Henry. He has a losing habit. Remind me to talk with you about reclaiming the black horse. I would like him to be settled in my stables by this time next year and put to stud. Impress on the trainer that until that time, the horse and the stableboy should be looked after with more care. Prince's condition in the second heat was deplorable.'

The major's head lifted at the king's criticism of his training ability. He considered the insinuation an insult. *Why doesn't the king speak to me directly?* King Charles II seemed satisfied that the meeting had concluded. His hand fluttered, waving all matters aside before leaning back to resume his static position.

The Duke of Albemarle nodded to the king's steward before turning to the relieved major. 'That will be all, Major. The steward will be in touch. And who knows, perhaps one day soon I shall pay a visit to the district of my lordship. They say the lakes are quite magnificent. We wish you and your family a safe journey home.'

'I'll be returning home soon, but there's the obstacle of an operation to overcome first.'

The duke's eyebrows lifted. 'Is the operation serious major?'

The major turned on a sad, screwed-up face and his head dropped to his hand clasping his codpiece. 'It's a bladder stone, Sir.'

The duke grimaced. 'That's bad luck. Good stone cutters are hard to come by and I have heard of many deaths through bad surgery. Frère Jacques of Beaulieu is highly respected, and you can use my name if need be.'

'Thank you, Sir but Squire Holmes has already arranged the operation with a Doctor Joyliffe. He assisted Thomas Hillier with Samuel Pepys' operation and comes highly recommended.'

'I hear that Pepys was one of the lucky ones under Hillier's knife. The doctor is failing of late, possibly because of his age. They say he's lost his last four patients. Young Doctor Joyliffe is a most admirable choice for the operation. I wish you good luck. You're certainly going to need it.'

Damian was grooming Prince when the stable master approached. Henry had no appetite for the task he'd been allotted. Damian was to have an audience with the king by special request, and he was to attend the garden party with the very stable boy he'd deceived.

Henry was rightfully worried. If the simpleton exposed him as the one who'd interfered with the training routine, he was finished for good.

Henry called on the major before taking Damian away. 'Surely the officer has made a mistake, Henry. Rufus is the gentleman who was the registered rider of Prince.'

'There's no mistake, Major. The officer was emphatic in his description, and he left me in no doubt that he was insulted by my audacity to question him. "His Majesty wishes to communicate with the stable boy to whom he had given permission to ride in the last heat." Those were his exact words, Major.'

The major shook his head in dismay. Once Rufus found out that he'd been overlooked for Damian, there would be friction. He had been present when the king suggested that Prince and the stable boy should be looked after. *The king's taken a shine to the boy and perhaps there will be something to gain from his interest. Rufus will need to be spoken to. He'll be in charge of Damian in my absence and we need to avoid trouble.*

When he realised he was left alone, Jasper sniffed around the stalls and nonchalantly picked up his master's scent. With head bobbing and ears flopping, the hound padded innocently along the scented trail, faithfully following at a distance, attentive and excited at the activity around him. Damian looked back and was reassured. The shy stable boy would forego his meeting rather than attend without his best friend. Henry stopped at a table where the crowd was thinner and told Damian to stay put until he contacted one of the king's officers. Jasper brushed against his master whose hand dropped to ruffle his ears. 'I'm going to talk to the king, Jasper.'

The old hound dog whimpered and then left his master's side when he spotted the king and his ladies' entourage of spaniel dogs. The ladies were on the outer rim of the king's party and Jasper moved amongst the spaniels, sniffing and agitating. An officer had drawn Damian aside to explain his imminent audience with the king while Jasper nosed a spaniel away from one of the king's mistresses. Out of the corner of his eye, Damian saw the spaniel scamper off into the woods with his hunting dog in hot pursuit. The partygoers were oblivious to the goings on, paying more attention to their all-consuming party gossip. Shortly after, Jasper was standing on all fours in front of his master with tail wagging and body panting like a foundry bellows. Damian sensed the floppy eared hound had something to show and was asking him to follow, but all he could focus on was the blood around Jasper's mouth. He took a rag handkerchief from his tunic pocket and looked nervously around before quieting Jasper and wiping the blood away. He was tucking the bloodstained rag back into his pocket when he heard one of the king's ladies shouting as she moved amongst the crowd. 'Poopsy, come here, Poopsy. Has anyone seen my little pet?'

Damian looked down at Jasper and growled disapproval. 'You're a bad dog.' The old hound dog hung his head in shame and trailed behind his master as he was being led towards the seated king. The officer stopped Damian two paces from the king and tried unsuccessfully to drag Jasper away.

'Leave the dog at his side my good man. A dog is the measure of his owner.' Queen Catherine sat beside the king on a lower seat. She was slim, much shorter than the king, with large, dark eyes and slightly protruding teeth. Damian thought her almost as beautiful as Mary, but not so much as the king, with the colour of his skin and his long black hair. 'Is that a hunting dog, young man?' Damian gawked, his voice frozen on a gasp as with open mouth he nodded in the affirmative, terrified at the consequences of Jasper's kill. The king's three spaniels growled, and one mistress hugged another on her lap whilst the distraught lady continued on her search. 'Perhaps it is best that you leave your dog in the care of the officer, young man.'

Damian felt relieved, and as soon as Jasper was taken away, two of the king's spaniels came to settle at his feet. The king smiled and nodded. 'My dogs are the best judge of a good man.' He wriggled in his seat and fondled his codpiece, whilst his free hand beckoned Damian closer with a forefinger. Damian stared in disbelief at the king's bad habit. His hand covered his mouth and his cheeks ballooned as he choked back a snigger. *Mam shouts at me when I do that.*

He drew close to the king and Charles II leaned forward as if to whisper. Damian's eyes widened and his mouth opened as he went into listening mode. His eyes focussed on the king's mouth, fascinated by the eloquent accent, and hypnotised by the king's waving fingers opening and closing like the petals of a flower. It was as if he were drawing the words from his lips and casting them towards his attentive listener. As the king leaned forward Damian caught a whiff of perfume, and he was overwhelmed by a temptation. His head extended; lips pursed to kiss Charles on the mouth. He almost overbalanced and the king reached out with his palm to push him back.

'Do you not feel well boy?' Damian nodded and the king leaned back in his seat with a wrinkled expression as he enquired of the nearest officer. 'Does the boy speak?'

'His master tells me he's not the full shilling, Your Majesty.'

'Commentaire de? Not the full shilling?'

The officer leaned closer to whisper and gestured with a tapping forefinger to his temple. 'He's a few pennies missing, Your Majesty.'

And the king's face lightened with understanding. 'Ah Yes! Of course, that may explain his shyness.'

'He may speak when he overcomes his fear of the occasion, Your Majesty, but you will have great difficulty in understanding him.'

'What is the stone he wears as an amulet?'

'The villagers believe that wearing such a stone will protect them from the Devil and witches, Your Majesty.'

'Well he certainly rides like the Devil.' The king laughed at his considered wit, then turned in his seat and leaned back to his entourage for their approval. He extracted a lace handkerchief from his cuff to dab tears from his eyes, and then leaned forward, squinting a challenge to the shuffling stable boy. 'Are you a good Christian? Do you attend church?'

Damian was still staring wildly with pursed lips, like a dying codfish gasping for air. He nodded positively.

'Good! Good! And you should pray more often as our good Lord has obviously favoured you.' The king beckoned with a finger to his officer, who bent down so the king could whisper in his ear. 'He has the sign of the plague on his forehead. I have seen the mark on survivors in London.' The officer agreed and then handed the king a parchment. Charles perused it before speaking again to the stable boy. 'Your name is Damian Inman and your sister, Mary Rigge, is the owner of Prince?'

'Y ... yes.' Damian stuttered as he nodded his agreement.

Charles shook his head in exasperation and opened a raised palm to his Officer of the Law. 'Explain to the boy.'

The officer cleared his throat and proceeded. 'Less than a year from today, your sister will be required to pen her mark on this document, relinquishing the ownership of her horse, Prince; a horse which carries the markings of the king's stables. For the privilege of ownership, His Majesty King Charles II is tendering the princely sum of ten pounds. As a replacement, a suitable workhorse will be exchanged on the same day.'

The king addressed Damian again. 'Your master, Major Rathbone, will be informed of the transfer, but not the fee involved. You must convey this message to your sister and the amount of money she receives must remain a secret. I also believe your skills as a rider should be rewarded and a place found for you working at our stables under the guidance of Henry.'

Damian was visibly shocked and vigorously shook his head in opposition. Henry felt a weight lifted from his shoulders. He was already reeling from the shock of hearing that Prince, the horse responsible for his run of bad luck, was to be reallocated to his stable. To be saddled with the stable boy as well would have been a tragedy ready to unfold. King Charles II listened sympathetically, and then turned an open palm to the officer to gather in a leather pouch. 'In that case, young man, I have something to offer you that must also be kept a secret between us.'

Damian was now on familiar ground and his eyes brightened. He had understood that the king was buying Prince and that Mary was going to be rich, and it was a secret. The king handed him the leather pouch and he placed it in his pocket.

'There are five coins in that pouch. You are to keep it secret and tell no-one lest they rob you.'

Charles turned to his stable master Henry and their eyes met in an understanding before the king finally waved them both away. Damian was frightened of losing the leather pouch and his hand cupped around his pocket as he rubbed the coins together all the way back to the stables. Jasper ambled behind his master feeling a change of attitude and sensing that he'd been forgiven his instinctive misdemeanour in the woods.

The major's operation

Squire Holmes offered the major a room for his operation and, most importantly for the six weeks required to recuperate. He said it was the least he could do to relieve the pain of the father of his beloved son-in-law. The major wasn't quite sure if they were manicured words or words of genuine compassion, but he wasn't going to quibble, as he was indisputably thankful. The newlyweds agreed to stay with the racing entourage until the operation was considered a success. Holmes bade them farewell. He was travelling to London with parliamentarians, looking forward to frequenting the surviving coffee houses to exchange political banter with men of his own standing.

Two days before his operation, the major paid a visit to the Holmes' stables, pushed an astonished Damian aside and took over the grooming of Prince. He needed to reminisce, to breathe in the air most familiar to him; to enjoy the scent and the feel of equine sweat leather saddles, the aroma of horse manure and the hay that irritated his nostrils. He worked away with the brush with thoughts of his days in the cavalry foremost in his mind. He was only now beginning to realise that his life could end just as abruptly in this peacetime and that his time on earth could be short.

Damian observed the new major in silence, not quite believing his eyes. His shoulders hunched nervously as the major suddenly stopped smoothing Prince's coat, then angrily threw the brush into the water pail and stomped out.

The feelings of the major on the day he was called into the makeshift surgery were reminiscent of his first day on the battlefield. He stood to attention before he entered the door wavering as he crossed the threshold of the makeshift operating theatre. They had quarantined him for a whole day and served him only liquid. But he'd managed to procure liquid of his own and on an empty stomach the brandy had gone straight to his head.

The drapes had been removed to allow maximum light for the operation. His footsteps echoed as he approached the centre of the sparsely furnished room. Four heavily built men stood in a circle behind a bare table, listening attentively to instructions from Doctor Joyliffe. The young surgeon was leaning against a side-table supporting a swab bowl and a knife. The major took long, deep breaths to calm his nerves and attempted a brave smile as the men turned and faced him. Their eyes were threatening, and he stepped back as two of them came forward and stood each side of him. The doctor forced a smile. 'Not to worry, Major. Everything is under my control.'

He gulped nervously. 'I most certainly hope so, Doctor.' If he'd heard a trumpeted retreat, he would have unashamedly run back to his room.

'Not having second thoughts then?'

The major took a deep breath as he was lifted by the elbows and carried to the table.

'No, I am not. I was in the cavalry you know.' His boots and breeches were removed, and he felt the coolness of the room wash over his bare skin.

'Just lie back nice and easy, Major.'

The major took a last glimpse of the trees through the tall window and prayed it wouldn't be his last. Birds were flying to and fro, accentuating his loss of freedom. He wanted to be outside there with them, soaring. He had been praying more than usual these past few days and was surprised at his total confirmation of the good Lord. *I vow if I survive this operation, I will never again fall asleep during Gabriel's sermon.* Penelope had also been in his thoughts which had also surprised him. *If I'm cured, she'll have less reason to reject me.* It was as if the torturous pain had already gone away and he didn't really need the operation. Thinking about the future had made him feel much better.

'I don't need the operation anymore, Doctor.' His hands searched for and gripped the edge of the tabletop and he made a great effort to slide his feet from the table. Nothing happened and his face wrinkled into an expression of surprise. There was an attendant assigned to each of his legs and the other two were busily tucking his arms in and finishing off strapping his torso to the table. The major attempted to struggle, but only his head moved. He bent his neck and saw his thighs and knees elevate as his legs were folded back towards his chest. 'I've changed my mind, Doctor.'

Doctor Joyliffe seemed unconcerned. He was already busily soaping and shaving the major's genitals, used to witnessing the behaviour of patients in this predicament. But he cringed at the sound of the loud military voice. 'Untie me at once. I command you.'

An assistant placed a wood-piece in his mouth. 'Bite down hard, Sir.'

Doctor Joyliff's hands were fully occupied. He cupped the major's balls, shaved a passage to the anus and noted his entry point for the three-inch cut. The major closed his eyes and prayed, resigned to the fact that he must suffer and be brave. He thought of his wife's words in her anger at the fates of old Agnes and John Rigge: *You're nothing short of a mercenary and the lord will make you suffer their pain tenfold.*

Penelope's words echoed around his skull as he struggled against the straps. He saw the flicker of the surgeon's knife as it curved down between his legs and ground his teeth on the wood-piece like a dog gnawing a bone. He waited an eternity for the incision and when the pain finally racked his body, he spit the wood from his mouth and roared like a lion.

The leg holders bore down hard, and the air was suddenly full of cannon smoke. He licked his trembling lips and tasted salt. He was leading the cavalry like never before, driving his mount forward, and feeling the friction of horseflesh between his thighs. The nostalgic smell of gunpowder and the stench of blood was all around him. He was in the midst of a battle and there was groping and tearing inside his body. He writhed with pain, followed by more pain, a spinning darkness, and peace.

Damian was ready to return home. Hanging around the stables waiting for the major to recover had seemed to him a waste of time. It had been three weeks since his meeting with the king and he was impatient to relate his adventures. He found a quiet corner in the stable, sat down on a bundle of hay and took out the king's pouch. He looked around cautiously before tipping the contents onto the floor, and his face lit up as he scanned each coin separately. For Damian, one coin stood out from all the others. He picked it up and rolled it between his thumb and forefinger. On one side of the half-crown was an imprint of the king astride a horse. Damian knew he would treasure the memory for ever. He remembered the king's words. *You must tell no-one.* He kissed the coin and tucked it carefully into the pocket of his tunic. *I'll keep it safe in my rune pot.* He then turned his attention to the other four coins. They all had the same imprint of a woman's face and he smiled as an idea occurred to him. He picked the first one up and spoke out loud as he popped it into the pouch. 'That one's for Mam, and that one's for Mary, and that one's for Uncle Robert, and that one's for Tommy.' He pulled the cord tight on the pouch and held it up in front of him. Damian had never been so proud or experienced so much pleasure. He was imagining himself presenting the coins and already enjoying the surprise on the faces of the four most important people in his life. Even Jasper growling wasn't enough to pull him from his dreaming.

When the shadow fell over him, he knew there was no escape, and he was slow to react. The pouch was snatched from his grasp and he looked up into the eyes of a triumphant Rufus, holding the pouch out in front of him, admiring it at arm's length. 'And that's four for Uncle Rufus.'

'You can't take my pouch. It's a gift from the king.'

'The king has long departed for London you idiot, and you're now in my charge.'

'I'll tell your father.'

'My father has been close to death's door these past weeks and he's only now recovering from his operation. He's certainly in no mood for trivialities. We leave for Hawkshead tomorrow stable boy. Make sure the horses are saddled and ready.'

'But the coins were my gift from King Charles II.'

'The coins were meant for the official rider of Prince and it was I who should have been presented to the king. I won a heat with brilliant riding, against the best in the land. You interfered with my glory and the less you say to anyone about this matter, the better it will be for your good health.'

Damian was frustrated and close to tears. 'You steal all our good things. You took Mary's horse and her amulet and now you've taken my coins. The king said you would steal my coins.'

Rufus laughed. 'The king told you nothing. But he did tell my father that he would be taking Prince back from your sister's ownership.'

'The king's not taking it. He's going to...' Damian's voice tailed off. He'd nearly blurted out about the money. He'd just learned his lesson in time. *The king's gift must remain a secret.*

Return to Hawkshead

Rufus and Eleanor arrived home in the middle of November with Damian and the packhorses in tow. The major was still in pain and in no condition to ride. He had insisted that as soon as he was fit and able, Hollis should accompany him home. The morning air was crispy cold, and the countryside littered with the brilliant colours of falling autumn leaves. The tops of the distant fell were powdered with snow and the sun was rising in a clear blue sky. Damian scanned the surrounding dales, filled his lungs with fresh homely air and smiled with relief. He was happy to be back. Rufus and Eleanor hadn't been the politest companions on the road.

Damian had secretly fantasised about a royal welcome. Surely news of his valiant ride against the king and his subsequent audience with His Majesty had filtered back. *My friends will be lining the village streets to cheer my exploits.* When they stopped at the inn Mary ran out from the chandlery and was quickly joined by the ostlers and kitchen staff craving news of the outside world. Mary grasped Prince's halter and ran her palm down his brow before looking up to greet her brother. 'Welcome home, Damian. Did we win?'

Damian felt proud sitting up high in the saddle. He was about to relate his story when Rufus butted in. 'I won the first heat against the king and his earls and then, unfortunately, Prince took ill in the second heat.' He deliberately flicked the newly polished silver ring across his puffed-out chest, hoping to aggravate Mary and succeeding.

'You still have my amulet.'

Eleanor, puzzled, grabbed her husband by the elbow. 'What does she mean?'

'I'll explain later.' He flicked his wife's hand away and turned back to Mary. 'Let's not go into that again or you'll find yourself in trouble.'

Mary sneered. 'The ring brought you bad luck. I warned you it would.'

Rufus looked down from his mount with arrogance. 'I don't consider winning the first heat against such eminent company bad luck. You can ask your idiot brother why the horse took sick in his care, and how he came to ride him illegally, disqualifying him from contention.'

'My brother's presence was necessary for Prince's wellbeing. It was the stolen ring that cursed you.' Her anger was building, Prince was twitching, and a vision flashed across her mind. *My Man of Death still haunts me.* Mary struggled to stay calm.

'The horse is now yours to care for. Father has washed his hands of all involvement.'

'Because he lost, I suppose?'

'You can ask him when he returns.'

The major had taken the king's parting words to heart. *Prince and Damian should be looked after.* He had given orders for Prince to be returned but he was flummoxed as to how Damian could be cared for. Prince's return spurred Hannah into action. 'I've enough on my plate looking after baby John without trying to feed a useless horse.'

'But Prince was John's horse.'

'He's not built for heavy work and you're right when you say it *was* John's horse. You may think me cruel, but John's gone, bless his soul. It's time you were looking for a husband; a good strong man who would put that son of a major on his backside. Don't think I haven't seen his hungry eyes devouring you. That wife of his should take him in hand.'

'What am I to do, Mother?'

Fortunately, Margaret Atkinson had taken a shine to Mary. She noted that Samuel was happier in his work of late and it was no coincidence that he'd failed to complain about the domestic help as was usual. He had always called them 'interfering domestics', but this one was always 'Mary'. 'Mary keeps to herself, Mother. Mary works conscientiously and doesn't hang around like the others, fancying themselves up, trying to impress me.'

Margaret gave him his head and contentedly sat back in her rocker, listening. It wasn't often Samuel spoke of his work and least of all about a woman. 'She's not unattractive, Mother, which makes me think I should introduce her to the front counter.' *It's a pity she's so much younger and a widower with a child at that.*

'We loan thee Mary for three days a week. Thou should not overwork the poor lass.'

'I really do need help at the counter, Mother, especially on market days. Perhaps thou could loan her to me for a few weeks to see how things work out?'

'We pay Mary a weekly wage for three days work at the manor and three days at the shop.'

'Yes, but we share the profits from the chandlery. If I had some free time I could travel and stock the shop with items that would increase our profits.'

Margaret leaned forward in her chair to peruse the phenomenon. 'There is still some life left in thee my boy. I'll have

to discuss it with thine father. I'm sure he will be very interested.'
Flabbergasted will be more the like.

Mary pleaded with Timothy to stable Prince, claiming there would be no more racing and that she hadn't placed a wager on the king's race and had no intention of frittering away her hard-earned pennies. That her late husband's horse had raced at Newmarket was reward enough for her.

Timothy put on an appearance of being delighted; Margaret would have it no other way. 'We'll just let things take their course, Timothy, and see what happens.'

Penelope was enquiring of her husband. 'How was your father, Rufus?'

'I have to tell you that he was near death after the surgeon returned to London with the king's entourage; not that the surgeon could have helped any. Before he left he explained it was simply a matter of healing and patience. Can you imagine father having patience?'

'It's not a word he's familiar with. I have sympathy for your poor mother-in-law, Catherine. Having him confined under her roof for six weeks is more than any poor soul should have to suffer.'

'It was a terrible time for everyone in the household, but Squire Holmes was well out of it, Mother. He departed for London on business shortly before the operation.'

'That was both astute and selfish of the man, but we can't underestimate his generosity in allowing your father a room in his house.'

'Father refused to eat solids for the first week and became very frail. He was in great pain and afraid that his bowels would open up the wound. The pain subsided during the second week but then he caught a fever that raged for three or four days.

That was when we thought he was drifting so we asked the vicar to call.'

'I always told your father he should pay more, but he showed no fear of the Lord and he too often missed church service.'

'He told the vicar to go to hell.'

Penelope smiled. 'That should have been enough to tell you he was on the way to recovery.'

'Yes! That was when we knew he was going to survive and he insisted we leave immediately, before Hollis arrived lest you had trouble at the manor.'

'That was nice of him, but it's more likely he's worried about the stables.'

'Andrew Millhouse delivered your new saddle before we left. Father insisted he should keep it as a surprise for you.'

'I hope he will surprise me with more than a saddle.'

'What do you mean?'

'Oh! It's only a wishful thought, Rufus. I live in hope.' Penelope could hardly imagine her husband riding side-saddle and smiled in anticipation.

'Before we departed, father made me promise that Damian should be looked after. Can you understand that?'

'I can understand the poor boy having to be cared for, but I can't see your father having any sympathy towards him and to ask you of all people to look after him can only be a plot. Are you sure he's alright?'

'He seems more amiable as the days go by, Mother.'

'Then let us pray that his change is due to the absence of pain and not the loss of his mind.' Penelope was nervous at the thought of being confronted by a new man. *Rather the Devil you know, they say.* Her gaze fell on the silver ring from her son's neck. 'I see you're still wearing John Rigge's necklace. It should be returned to his widow. Mary is the rightful owner you know.'

'I believe he stole it from the estate.'

'I doubt that very much. John Rigge was an honourable man and a conscientious worker. I saw him wearing it the first day we were introduced.'

'I never had the pleasure of meeting him, Mother. Do you remember that you sent me away?' Rufus cupped the ring defensively.

'Eleanor objects to me wearing it socially. I only wear it as an amulet when I'm riding, and it's proven lucky for me.'

'If you consider yourself lucky, then so be it. I'm more of the opinion that the amulet reminds you of the young widow. I've seen the hunger in your eyes when you look at her. You covet the woman and I'm sure that it hasn't gone unnoticed by Eleanor. Perhaps sending you away from the manor wasn't such a good idea. I should have left you to John. He would have taught you to be more respectful of a man's wife.'

'John Rigge's no longer on this earth.'

'And you know I blame your father's interference for that.'

'He said you had too much of a liking for the peasant.'

Penelope ignored the inference and paused to gather her thoughts. 'Hmmm. Now, where were we?'

Rufus scowled. 'We were discussing the stupid stable boy.'

His sullen response encouraged Penelope to let loose with another tirade. 'Damian is not so much a boy as a man and he's not as stupid as people make him out to be. They say he can keep a secret, and that's the sign of wisdom.' Rufus burbled air through his lips in disagreement, but Penelope carried on regardless. 'That's his sister's amulet you are wearing and as I'm employing him in the stables again you will be hearing more of the truth.'

'You can't be serious about him being a stablehand again.'

'Oh yes I am. You've just made up my mind for me. And he'll stay as long as I'm the owner of the manor house. Don't you *ever* forget that the house is in my name?'

'Hollis won't like it.'

'You said it was your father's wish that we take care of Damian, so Hollis will have to comply with the situation.'

The major's jewel

Edgar Hollis couldn't care less about Damian's presence. He was only happy to be home, with his wife. Nothing could compare with the torture of his return journey. He had never realised there were so many coach inns and the hullabaloo every time he lifted the major on and off of the side-saddle had been embarrassing. When he handed over the major to Penelope and the reins to Damian, he felt a wave of relief wash over him.

'I trust you had a safe journey, Edgar?' Hollis' face was grey and withdrawn. He simply nodded, grunted then sloped away with his arms around his wife. The major seemed unconcerned and wondered what the fuss was all about. 'Lift me down then boy. For reasons unknown to me, the king requested I should be kind to you. But there'll be no shirking your duties, I assure you.'

'The king requested the favour, Rowan? That's news to me. I had no idea you were so close.' Penelope teased.

The major regretted the slip of his tongue but tried to make the most of it. 'King Charles II and I were talking about horse breeding. He mentioned that Damian was an excellent stable boy and recommended that I should take care of him. He developed an unfortunate soft spot for the boy. I can't for the life of me fathom why.'

'It surprises me that the king was even aware of Damian's existence. How did such a meeting take place?'

The major looked disdainfully at Damian. 'Oh! It was something to do with him riding Prince around the enclosure illegally.'

'I rode against the king, you saw me.'

'You did my boy, of course you did. But only in your dreams.'

'How was King Charles II?'

'I'll tell you later, Pennykins. Just help me to my bed. Careful lad or I'll have your hide. Take it slowly. Where's that boy of ours?'

'He's readying to leave. He said that he doesn't intend to be locked in the north for the winter, but I think it is more Eleanor's idea than his own. She misses her family.'

The major wasn't quite sure how it happened, but he suddenly found himself walking around without any sign of pain. The past few weeks he'd been fearful of putting weight on his feet. He stopped with the shock of discovery and gingerly took a few steps holding his backside. Then he released his hands and started to gently jump up and down on the spot. 'Penelopeeeee.'

Penelope charged through the door in nightgown and cap. 'What's wrong, Rowan? Is it still painful?'

The major was standing in front of his wife naked, with his arms out wide, displaying an oversized erection. 'I'm cured, Penny. I'm cured.'

'You've lost your short and curlies.'

The major looked down in dismay. 'Is that all you've got to complain about woman? I had a bit of a close shave, that's all. My beloved is healthy and raring to go.'

Penelope whimpered humorously. 'You'd best come back into the bedroom then, but don't bother me unless you can finish the job off properly without screaming. I've been left too long in the wilderness to be hopeful of half-hearted promises.' Penelope found it hard to admit that the past few years had encouraged a hunger that she thought had deserted her. *And to think I castigated our son for harbouring similar thoughts.*

The major wore a lecherous look as he gathered a small oak box from his bedside, tucked it under his arm and eagerly entered the bedroom. He set the box down on the dresser and made an elaborate gesture as he turned the key. Penelope imagined an extravagant gift that he'd bought her from his winnings. When the lid of the box was lifted, she pinched her nose with her thumb and forefinger and covered her mouth to banish the foul odour. 'What is it?' She was unimpressed by its contents, a pitted stone, about the size and shape of a hen's egg.

The major gleefully explained its origin. 'The surgeon cut it from my bladder and before he left for London presented it to me in this beautiful box, a memento of my years of agony.'

Penelope turned up her nose in disgust. 'If you can't rid it of that smell you can burn the ugly thing. I don't need your insides to remind me of your pain.'

The major's feelings were hurt but the following week he perfumed the box. Penelope conceded to allow his memento to rest on the bedroom dresser, as long as the lid was closed. Whenever she left the bedroom, she would lock down the lid knowing that it would be undone when her husband returned. She was often tempted to throw away the key but knew that her actions would be both temporary and futile. The major was proud of his operation and the more he insisted on the box being open, the more it become a game between them. Rowan was now as she remembered him to be, but she had an intuition the change was temporary. *Best make hay whilst the sun shines,* was the thought most foremost in her mind.

Word filtered through to the domestics that the major had brought back a jewel box of polished oak lined with velvet.

It was said to house a rare stone, and the major was so obsessed by its beauty that he gazed upon it daily. Penelope overheard the whispered words, 'jewel', and 'size of an egg', and was amused that the domestics were gossiping about the new addition to their bedroom. *News travels fast.*

Lizzie had to admit that initially she had no interest the locked box, but curiosity got the better of her and the more she thought of it the more cynical she became about its contents. She shared her views with Mabel Fowler one evening before dinner. 'If you ask me Mabel, it's the bad parts of his stomach inside that box and not a jewel. I overheard her say something of the sort to Rufus. It's forever in and out of the top drawer like a jack-in-the-box. They are playing games, like a couple of young lovers.' Mabel didn't say much, but Lizzie knew it would be all over the parish the next morning.

Christmas of 1666 held a jolly atmosphere for the parish. There hadn't been a raid since the major's return from Newmarket. The Quaker community felt an armistice had been declared yet were still wary. Nobody could change so dramatically in such a small space of time. The gossip around the village was that he had made some choice wagers and the winnings had paid for an operation to relieve him of ongoing torturous pain.

The manor house staff had never experienced a more pleasant Yuletide. Penelope was buzzing and gathering the staff around her like a queen bee. A banquet was to be held and most of the guests from the engagement party had been invited. A pig was to be slaughtered, trout taken from the lake, casks of ale brought from the inn and the icehouse replenished. Large yule logs were to be placed at the side of every hearth in readiness for the day and extra-large candles would be ordered for both church and manor. Penelope had decided to order the candles through Samuel Atkinson's chandlery. *What Rowan doesn't know, he can't grieve about.*

Mary had called into the manor house the previous week asking to visit Damian. Their conversation led to the subject of Mary's employment in the chandlery. The following day Penelope walked resolutely to the stables, asked Damian to saddle two horses, then spoke to Hollis. 'I'm taking him to see his sister at the chandlery, Edgar. There must be some way that I can make amends for the poor girl's misfortune.'

The chandlery was in a side street off Market Square, set back from the beck running through the centre of the village. Damian was helping Penelope to dismount in the loading yard when Mary came out to greet them. She'd expected Damian's companion to be Liz and when she saw the finery, she was taken aback. 'Hello, Mrs Rathbone. It's quite a surprise to see you shopping in the village.'

'I can't see why, Mary. It's not the first time.'

'I meant you visiting a shop with Quaker affiliations. Samuel is away on business for the day.'

'Then he's taking advantage of a hard-working woman. I'm not entirely in agreement with Quaker principles, but I do think that both my husband and my son have been excessive in their treatment of the non-conformists, especially how they hound them for tithes.'

'It's best I don't see Rufus again. He has brought nothing but bad luck.'

'I agree! Stealing your amulet away was a crime. I saw your husband wearing the ring before his passing, so I know the ring belongs to you. I will do my utmost to see it's returned.'

'Thank you, Mrs Rathbone. You know Samuel Atkinson isn't a Quaker.'

'I'm told that he's a mind of his own and refutes the Quaker religion. That is refreshing to hear. It must make working here easier for you.'

'It's the happiest I've been since I lost John.'

'I'm pleased that you are in good employment. I am aware of my son's mistreatment of you and Damian, and I don't understand. And taking your amulet was nothing short of a crime. I saw your husband wearing the ring when he was in my employment, and I shall do my upmost to see it returned.'

'Thank you. I wish your husband was of a similar mind.'

'Rowan's manner has softened of late, so I still live in hope of being respected by the community.'

'You *are* well respected. I've thought of you as Mrs Rathbone ever since being in your employ. All the domestics are of the same mind. You have earned our respect and I couldn't think to call you Penelope, unless you asked it of me. Your husband is different. He hasn't earned the right to be addressed as Mr or Sir; not in this parish; not by anyone who's worth their salt. If he wants to be called Major then so be it, but his actions decry respect.'

'I've heard you address Samuel's father by his first name. Doesn't he hold your respect?'

'As much as anyone I know. Out of habit I call him Mr Atkinson but he insists his name is Timothy and it pleases him to be called that. He's not as uppish as some. Perhaps it's because he's a Quaker. They doff their hats to no-one you know.'

'When we first took residence, the vicar warned Rowan of Quakers addressing people with thee and thou, and of obstinate parishioners who had their own way of addressing people. Unfortunately, respect has never bothered him. He's too thick-skinned.'

'Damian doesn't much like him, or Rufus, but he thinks highly of you, Mrs Rathbone. Isn't that so Damian?'

Damian had wandered into the back of the shop, unin-terested in the conversation but fascinated with the choice of implements scattered across the earthen floor and hanging from the beams. *Tommy would pick up lots of things here.*

Mary still couldn't fathom why the lady of the manor was so interested in her, or why she was considering buying from a Quaker's shop. 'I shall have to order the candles in for you. They're larger than we normally stock.'

'That will be fine, as long as they're ready by tomorrow. Damian can pick them up. You've no need to worry about your brother. I feel he's my responsibility and will continue to employ him as long as he works hard. And don't you worry about Rufus. He won't be visiting until summer at the earliest. Eleanor is finally pregnant.'

'That must be a relief for you and mother will be pleased to know that Damian is being looked after.'

'I hear you've borne a child, Mary.'

'John left me with a special gift. He's more than a year old now; a healthy boy John would be proud of. We christened him John.'

'I'm pleased for you.' Penelope took a shilling from her money pouch. 'That's a late christening gift for young John. I'm only sorry I wasn't in church for the ceremony. I would like you to join the domestics the day after the banquet to dine on the leftovers. Liz and Damian will be there, and you can bring Hannah.'

Penelope walked from the chandlery humming, immersed in the spirit of Yuletide. Damian helped her into the new side-saddle. 'We must bring a choice young fir tree from the forest, place it in the ballroom and decorate it with apples, nuts and paper flowers. Everyone should be happy at this time of year. We will call in to see Vicar Braithwaite and his family on the way home.'

Quarterly meeting: spring 1667

Flower buds glistened with morning dew, petals coiled, ready to unfurl and display their seasonal colours. Snowdrops and daffodils blossomed, lambs bounced about the fells, and blackbirds dashed to and from their nests. The air was fresh with the bite of spring as the last of the seasonal snow clung desperately to the peaks.

Rufus arrived at the manor unannounced taking his mother by surprise. 'I didn't expect to see you until the birth of the baby. How is Eleanor?'

'Fine, Mother, but she's always complaining I get under her feet and her mother's always fussing around. I wasn't surprised when the squire left for London. I felt the same way, bored. So I came to help father in the stables and for a bit of sport.'

'Which sport, Rufus? Are you referring to racing horses?'

'I was thinking more of helping father to disrupt the Quaker meetings. But if Roger can organise a stay with the Prestons at Holker Hall then we may be able to run the horses at Cartmel.'

'We've an extra two foals — a filly and a colt, thanks to Prince. I've no doubt your father will be asking to stable him again.'

'Prince is stabled with Timothy Atkinson, Mother, and I don't think father would ask a favour of a Quaker.'

'You might be surprised by your father's demeanour since the operation. If you think you'll be hounding Quakers for sport, you could be in for a disappointing visit.' Rufus found that hard to believe, but his mother's comments were confirmed on his first meeting with Roger Kirkby.

The district would have remained calm throughout spring had it not been for the infiltration of Colonel Kirkby's son. Years ago, his father had pursued George and Margaret Fox until their imprisonment. Now Roger had an obsession to emulate his father and have Timothy Atkinson dispatched to Lancaster Gaol. When the Rathbones had first taken residence, the Kirkbys had been impressed with the major's attitude. They had thought him a man of passion, but lately they had been forming a different opinion. 'Your father's gone soft on collecting tithes. While the Quakers run amok in front of his nose, he thinks only of the rents due to his precious Duke of Albermarle. We need assistance in your parish if we are to achieve results.'

Rufus tossed down his brandy and agreed. 'I can't understand what's happened to father. When I left the manor last November he was in full recovery. When I returned, he was changed, not as aggressive and smiling too much. It's as if the surgeon removed more than his stone.'

'It more than likely he cut your father's balls out. Has his voice gone squeaky?' They roared with laughter.

'I can't imagine father with a high-pitched voice.' Rufus' face was flushed with alcohol and glowed like a beacon, but he persisted in holding his glass out for a refill. Roger had made a lasting impression during his attendance at the engagement party and Rufus had found an ally in the young renegade. They were in total agreement that the district was in need of a rude awakening. 'When do we start, Roger?'

'We'll start as soon as you find out where and when the Friends' next meeting is being held. Then we can arrange the warrants with our fathers.'

George and Rebecca Ferris had persuaded Thomas to attend the Friends' monthly meetings. 'It's the least you can do, to show appreciation of your funding.' He could easily have said no to Black George, but Rebecca was a different proposition. The professing of his true beliefs fell on deaf ears and he reluctantly agreed to go, as long as he could attend Vicar Braithwaite's morning sermons three Sundays in the month. He wasn't interested in the vicar's sermons either, but he had Aunt Hannah to contend with. With resignation he organised his Sundays to appease both families.

When the Wilson family returned from Kendal, the Quaker meetings suddenly became more sociable for Thomas. Sarah affected him in a most agreeable way. He'd been attracted to her at the markets when he was an apprentice, but now she'd grown taller, her face was more defined and her breasts curvaceous and womanly. She walked with the confidence of knowing she was beautiful and accepted the admiring looks from men of all ages. Her hair was straight and dark and trimmed neatly to her shoulders. He imagined what she'd look like without her bonnet, and then without her blouse, and then he thought of the young naked woman with his father and he blushed. Thomas had been hesitant to approach her but Sarah had no such inhibitions. His heart pounded as she spoke, and he found it hard to think clearly. 'Hello Thomas. It's been a long time since we last said our hellos. I always knew I would meet thee again.'

'I'm glad you came back. I was sad when you left. Now you've returned more beautiful than ever and you're dressed in blue. That's the way I remembered you.'

'I thank thee, Thomas. I'm still the rebel and I don't care what the Friends think. Wouldst thou sit close to me in the meetings?'

Thomas smiled shyly and nodded. He considered himself strong but in the presence of Sarah he felt weak. The ministers, elders and overseers were sitting on a two-tiered stand so that they might be better heard. The women's benches were on the left, separate from the men's, but it was sometimes possible to sit at opposing ends and still be close. On those rare occasions Sarah would sidle closer and reach out her hand to touch his and smile. He sensed a warmth pass between them and hardened. He now viewed the silence of the Quaker meetings in a different light. He was into the third year of his apprenticeship and filling out. Mrs. Ferris tried to dress him well for the meetings, but she was struggling with his growth and endless appetite.

At first, the elders had been wary of the changed major but as time went on they grew comfortable with his apparent lack of drive and lax authority. Even the return of Rufus was considered a non-event and a quarterly meeting was organised for the Atkinson manor. The Friends had been lulled into a false sense of security and Timothy's usual source of information was found wanting.

The major's party was tucked away on the hillside and becoming restless. They had been counting the arrivals and Rufus was impatient to begin. 'They must all be in attendance by now father. We should move quickly, before they suspect anything.'

The churchwarden had four constables and a clerk for support, each one of them with a desire for a rapid closure to the raid, so they could be home. All that is, except Ruben, who couldn't care less. He sat at ease on a pony, caressing a small box that contained a ledger book, ink and quill. The major finally conceded, dismounted and scanned the landscape one more time. He had made himself familiar with the converted barn with its thatched roof, windows on only one side and a door at each end. 'Dismount gentlemen and be patient. We need to go over your positions again. I want a sentry at each door and one to cover the stables to withhold the stable hands. Rufus, Roger and the churchwarden will confine the dissenters while I organise the fines with the clerk. Remember we are here to witness a meeting of dissent, non-attendance of our church and of conspiracy against the king. When they become animated, we will enter and arrest them.'

The major was ready to wave them on when he spotted two horses approaching. William Rawlinson and his wife had been delayed on their ride from Lowick. He tethered their horses and gestured his wife to enter the meeting ahead of him. William removed his Quaker beaver hat, stooped under the low lintel and entered into the silence. They had travelled almost twelve miles of packhorse trails to attend the monthly meeting and he expected the benches would be just as uncomfortable as the saddle.

William motioned Thomas to move along the bench and Sarah frowned as he separated them. He sat with the beaver hat resting on his knees, brushed back his long, dishevelled white hair and ran his fingers irritably over his sideburns and plump jowls. He leaned back and yawned as he crossed his arms and dropped the lids over his dark, penetrating eyes. Thomas resumed the same posture, head down, eyes loosely closed, perusing a member of the assembly as she unloaded her burden. 'I have followed the peace of the inward light and grown familiar with God. I hear him. He speaks to me. He is my life. He is my fountain.'

She sat down amongst the silence and a male Friend stood, encouraged. 'I *also* listen for the spirit of God. I search for the inner light, but it avoids me. I worry that we Friends are not recognised. I feel like a criminal and seek within that I may be comforted by God.'

There was no comment from the gathering, only the silence of the believers, communing with their inner peace. The raiding party had made their way to the meeting house on foot and the major was waiting patiently outside, ear to the door. He was straining to hear a comment or a discussion that might be interpreted as conspiracy. But there was only silence, broken occasionally by some indefinable mutterings. Rufus was stretching to peer through the windows and whispered. 'They're just sitting there doing nothing. Should we go in now?'

'Shhh. Patience you fool. They're worshipping. That's how they do it, and they do it for one hour.'

'I can't wait that long.'

'Listen! Someone is speaking.'

'I am wearing a wig and fear that thou will judge me vain. I ask thee for understanding as it was the pox that stole my hair.'

Thomas was losing his concentration. The gentleman who'd pushed him along the bench was fidgeting in his slumber. He suddenly snorted, sprung to his feet and bellowed out in a deep resonating voice. 'Get behind me Satan. Get behind me.' He paused, wavered, and then continued. 'Cast the Devil from thy soul and he'll never bother thee again.' He sat down with a thump that reverberated along the bench, stretched out his legs and stomped the heels of his riding boots on the compacted earth floor, completely oblivious to the fidgeting row of Friends. Thomas wrinkled his nose and sniffed. He caught a whiff of leather, salty sweat and cow dung that had fallen from his neighbour's boots. Timothy thought it timely to interrupt and came down from the stand. As an elder he called an end to the silence by shaking hands with the closest Friend, a signal for everyone to shake hands with their neighbour and exchange pleasantries.

'They're all shaking hands and talking father. I heard one shouting to the Devil.'

'That doesn't surprise me, but the chatter will do for a conspiracy. Everyone go to their stations!' He burst through the door and stood in the middle of the room, arms crossed. He scanned the room until his eyes settled on Timothy. He was on the way down from the loft, holding the attendance book. The travelling minister had failed to appear, and Timothy's mind was on the sermon which would have to be voiced by another elder. As an elder himself, he would be arranging meetings for any future birth, marriage or funeral. The overseers looked after the wellbeing of the members and maintained personal and spiritual contact with those unable to attend because of age or illness.

For a moment the room was as still as the Quaker silence. Then reality set in and protests were proclaimed. The families were herded into the women's meeting room. Wives held their husbands' arms for comfort and terrified children cried and screamed, clinging to their mother's dress. The overseers moved amongst them, reassuring and calming. The major shouted for them to calm down whilst he declared the reason for serving the warrant. 'There is no point in protesting when we have witnessed you all attending a dissenter meeting. In doing so, you have breached the Conventicle Act of 1664. You are guilty of non-attendance of church and conspiracy against the king. Write him a letter of protest if you must.'

He looked particularly pleased overseeing the clerical work. He noted the names in the attendance book, called out the offenders and read out the conviction and fine. Nobody suffered more than Timothy. 'Timothy Atkinson. Is this your first offence?'

'Thou know it to be so.'

'Then for breaching the Conventicle Act above mentioned you are fined the sum of twenty pounds, to be paid to the churchwarden by coin, goods, or chattel.' He looked at Timothy with empathy. 'A man of your stature should seek better company.'

'There is none better than I already have.'

'Joshua Wilson, tallow chandler of Hawkshead. Is this your first offence?'

'Thou know I cannot lie. It is my second offence.'

'Then for being present at the aforesaid conventicle and for having been before committed and been duly convicted you are fined the sum of ten pounds.'

Ruben sat at his desk penning furiously, smiling gratuitously.

John Birkett of Skelwith, carpenter, second offence, ten pounds.
John Satterthwaite of Colthouse, mercer, second offence, ten pounds.
Edward Park of Skelwith, hatter, first offence, five pounds
William Rawlinson of Lowick, gentleman, first offence, five pounds.

Thomas and Sarah were each marked down for five pounds. There were twenty-four people in all including yeoman, tanners and husbandmen from the surrounding district, most accompanied by their wives. Timothy swore it would never happen again. There were few who could afford the third offence, a fine of one hundred pounds or seven years' transportation to the New English plantations.

The second raid was a poorly attended weekly gathering. The raiders rounded up nine dissenters, most too poor to pay the fines. They were destined for a three-month sentence. The expense and time consumed didn't sit well with the churchwarden and his constables. Unfortunately for Thomas, he had agreed to meet Sarah at the meeting. For Rufus it was disappointing, an anti-climax after the success of their first raid. In his boredom and not for the first time, the attractive woman in blue caught his attention. He pushed forward, gripped her by the elbow and drew her close. 'I remember you from our last raid my colourful flower amongst Quaker weeds. Sarah Wilson, I believe and foolish enough to be caught a second time.'

She snatched her elbow away and glared defiantly. 'It's a pity you have nothing else to do with your life other than to hound innocent worshippers.'

'Are you innocent enough to be caught a third time and be transported in shackles? Perhaps it was your boyfriend who persuaded you to attend?'

He looked purposely at Thomas then stepped back nervously at the white anger in the apprentice's face. Thomas was furious and about to leap towards Rufus when the constables gathered around him. The major sensed it was time to intervene, but his son only gained in confidence with his protection. He taunted his victim, moved closer and whispered obscenely in her ear. Sarah slapped him across the face in return. The constables restrained Thomas, one hooking arms around his neck and another his limbs. Roger Kirkby intervened. 'Rufus, the warrants have been served and you're becoming an embarrassment. We are ready to leave now with the constables.'

Rufus wasn't satisfied. Sarah was slightly taller than him, and her bonnet emphasised the fact and irritated him. He pulled it from her head and as he cast it to the floor Thomas snapped. He cast off the two constables either side of him, tore the other's arm away from his neck, and then crash tackled Rufus to the floor. His huge hands circled Rufus' neck with a grip usually reserved for an iron bar in the forge and his victim's face adopted a similar glow. The three constables fell on top of him but failed to force him back. It was Sarah's screaming that saved Thomas from the gallows. He let go his grip and turned to her with a sorry look as the constables walked him away. Outside the meeting house, Rufus ran a hand around his neck as he climbed into the saddle. The major shook his head in disgust and ordered the constables to release Thomas. 'Your father is respected in the parish for his skill as a wrestler, not for his connection with the Quakers. If you choose to continue down this path, then I can no longer help you.'

'If he lays another hand on Sarah. I'll kill him.'

'Save your strength for the forge young man and perhaps some genuine wrestling. Another attack on my son will see you sailing the high seas.'

Thomas nodded, showing respect rather than obedience and as the constables rode away, he placed a protective arm around Sarah and pulled her close. They watched the raiders ride out of sight before Thomas voiced his concern. 'I wonder how long this can go on.'

'It seems we've come to the crossroads Thomas and I worry for the safety of my parents. We seem to be moving all the time and now fathers told me he's sold the Kendal chandlery. I wish I could stay until you've finished your trade, but I don't know what the future holds.'

Thomas' future depended on staying clear of the Rathbones. For the fines owing, he would once again be in debt to Timothy and his employer George Ferris. Joshua Wilson was furious. 'You'll stop attending meetings until this round of disruptions is exhausted and explain that to thine apprentice friend. I can't afford one hundred pounds. We could all be marked down for transportation next time.'

'Do you really think they would transport me, Father?'

'I can't see it myself, not a woman to the plantations. But I wouldn't like thee to be the first. Thine mother's worried.

We're both worried that young Kirkby seems to be targeting us. We must tell thee now that your mother and I have discussed migrating to the New England colony rather than risk a prison sentence. And thou must avoid the attention of Rufus. His eyes are all over thee so be careful.'

The major heard of the trading ship *Charlotte*'s imminent arrival in Whitehaven and seized on the opportunity to stock his larder. Penelope persuaded her husband to take Rufus. 'The Kirkbys are a bad influence and the trip will give him an opportunity to assert his own authority.' The major, Rufus, and two stable hands rode into Whitehaven the day before the *Charlotte*'s scheduled arrival. They watched the ship dock on the early morning tide and later that morning headed for the tavern to seek out the ship's first mate. The dockside tavern was bursting at the seams. Grasty and his boatswain were at the head of their usual table. The major saw them huddled in conversation, heads clouded by tobacco smoke spiralling through shafts of light. He looked up as the major and Rufus approached. 'Good morning, Major. Is your visit to the harbour for pleasure or honest trade?'

'We would like to think a little of both. We arrived early in the hope of claiming our usual discount.'

'I'll see what I can do, but there's no promise until I see who's in charge. There are no rolls of silk this trip, but we've ample brandy casks, wine, a small cargo of tobacco and sacks of tea.'

'I'm not a lover of tea anyway; it takes up too much space.'

'You should persist with a sample. The ladies are taking to it and you could make yourself popular in the right circles, if you know what I mean.' He concluded with a wink the major ignored.

He turned his attention to Rufus with more hope of success. 'Do you do your father's bidding, or do you have a mind of your own?'

Rufus hadn't the slightest interest in his father's acquisitions, only that he be generous with his brandy. His interests lay with the exodus of Quakers. He had promised Roger Kirkby that he would endeavour to find out how many Friends had booked passages from Whitehaven to New England. 'I've a mind of my own and I never heard you mention your most rewarding cargo.'

'Then you should enlighten me, Rufus. Which cargo are you referring to?'

'I'm referring to Quakers. Many in our district disappear overnight without paying their dues.'

'Once a Quaker boards our ship we are sworn to secrecy. If you think that is illegal, then consider that your father avoids paying import taxes.'

Rufus ignored the inference and thought of another way to acquire information. 'Would it be possible to examine the quality of your passenger accommodation? Perhaps we could see one of the cabins?'

'That can be arranged after the cargo's unloaded.' He turned to his boatswain. 'Can you see to that, Edward?' His boatswain nodded with a grunt.

The major showed little interest, but Rufus was determined. After his inspection of the cabins he introduced himself to a slightly inebriated captain and discovered exactly how many Quakers would be boarding, their names and the date of departure. *Roger will be pleased.*

The summer fair: 1667

The major suggested to Rufus that, for the time being, he should abandon his obsession with the Quakers to concentrate on enjoying the summer fair. 'Two full days of excitement my boy and crowds will be pouring in from all over the parish. We must take advantage of the situation. We will be attending the Newmarket Plate again this year and there will be opportunities to cover our expenses. Can you arrange a short horse race with Roger? Perhaps the colonel would like to ride as well.'

'Will you ride, Father?'

'I will leave the riding to you. I'm busy organising other events. We will be holding wrestling matches in the field near the Red Lion Inn. That should make for easy pickings. The Ambleside champion, Titus Armstrong, is competing. There'll be many a sucker wanting to take him on after the championship.'

'Is that his real name?'

The major shrugged. 'Who cares? He's the champion and holder of the belt, so he can call himself what he wants. He's a woodcutter and shearer, six-foot-three-inches tall. He weighs sixteen stone and he's only eighteen years old. He trains between the shafts like a horse, lugging heavy loads of wood down from the slopes. The common opinion is that he's only the champion because of his immense strength, not for his wrestling skills. You could be in with a chance there, my boy. Perhaps you'd like to challenge him?'

'The horse race sounds great. I'll ride to Kirkby Hall and have a word with Roger.'

'Good for you! I'll be taking wagers on the wrestling Thursday and Friday afternoon. The cockfight is set down for Thursday evening in the inn's barn. I'll be charging one shilling a head to circle the pit. That should make the landlord happy, keep out the riffraff and ensure genuine wagers and good returns. I don't want the problem of hanging defaulters from the rafters in a basket cage. That's not a pleasant way for anyone to finish off a day at the fair.'

'How does the vicar feel about you using Ruben to keep the books?'

'I'm donating a penny to the church from every wager over five shillings and Ruben will accept the same. Gabriel calls it corruption, but I explained to him that the church had accepted large donations from the Quaker fines these past two months, and that its folly to rely solely upon generosity and tithes for their upkeep.'

The fair was scheduled to run for two days commencing on Holy Thursday, the day of the Ascension of Our Lord. The day before the event, stalls were set up in the field overlooking the wrestling arena. Dalesmen and buxom farm wenches flocked from near and far and the roads were blocked with cattle and sheep heading for the sales yards. The inns were overflowing with customers and hot meals being served. There was anticipation in the air that guaranteed the village candles would burn well into the night.

The major oversaw the shaping of the cock pit and conferred with the feeders and setters. Money and goods would change hands the following evening, so he wanted the terms of exchange understood without confusion. He had seen too many brawls over wagers, so he negotiated in the constable's presence. The pit was measured to eight yards in diameter. A shallow trench had been shaped around the ring for the feeders and setters, and the earth thrown up to form a barrier to the spectators. More than fifty cockerels had been caged for the contests and the leatherworkers handed the task of supplying ten sets of spurs fitted to leather straps. On the evening of the cockfights a large contingent gathered outside of the barn entrance; more than twice the number inside. Those inside were assured of the correct verdict whilst those unfortunates outside had to rely on the honesty of the bookmaker when he called out the winners.

'All bets have been taken!' A penetrating voice distracted the rowdy spectators and a hush of expectancy gripped the barn. The silence filtered to the outside and the crowd settled as the bookmaker moved amongst them, repeating the call. The gamblers held their collective breath as the setters took their respective birds from their feeders and set them beak to beak in the centre. When the birds became aggressive enough the setters drew them apart and stepped back into the trench. The cockerels' wings flapped angrily as they circled, threatening each other. Their neck feathers flared and as one leapt into the air to attack, the other sprung to meet the challenge. Legs clawed with razor-sharp spurs and the crowd was up and roaring in frenzy. Hooked beaks pecked their oppenent's eyes until suddenly their bodies soared into a mid-air collision, both birds probing and lacerating with their spurs. One cockerel dropped dead and the maimed victor fell over him, dragged down by the deeply embedded spur, to lay limp amongst the scattered blood and drifting feathers. There was confusion amongst the crowd until the judge declared the maimed cockerel the winner. The dead bird was discarded into a barrel and the winning owner appeared to claim his reward.

The bout had lasted for less than three minutes and the crowd were satisfied but not sated. A buzz returned to the spectators, rising and falling as they perused and speculated on the two handsome game birds proudly parading before combat. Ruben had twenty contests marked in his ledger for the evening, with the balance of wagers leaning heavily in the major's favour. He was looking forward to the morrow and the chance of another successful day at the wrestling bouts.

Mary rode Prince to the Rathbones' stables hoping to surprise Damian. She walked in on Rufus standing over him, cutting him with the whip, her amulet swinging wildly from the bully's neck. 'I told you not to speak of Newmarket and if I ever hear of you saying that you rode against the king, I'll have my mother send you away for good.'

Mary was incensed, Prince unsettled, and her Man of Death stirring. *Go away. Go away.*

Rufus felt a presence and turned on her. 'Come to rescue your brother, have you?'

'One of these days he will turn on you.'

'Like a mad dog, I suppose?'

'You should be careful. He *can* be wild and uncontrollable.'

Rupert looked down at Damian thoughtfully, and then sneered as he pushed Mary aside and stomped out of the stable. 'I don't want you here when I return.'

Mary stared after him murderously. *So that's what the one-eyed man wants.* The words of her faith defended her. *Thou shall not kill and thine eye shall not pity. But life shall go for life, an eye for an eye. That appealed to her. Does my Man of Death want an eye for an eye? Will he then leave me in peace?*

On her next visit, Mary arrived prepared, deliberately leaving Prince tethered in sight of the manor house. She sat down in a corner of the stable with Damian and waited patiently. When Rufus arrived, she stood and greeted him. 'I didn't expect you so soon, Rufus. You never fail to surprise me.'

He hesitated, taken aback by her confidence. 'I saw your horse. You must understand that you are not welcome here.' He was unconvincing and Mary walked towards him swinging her hips, allowing the key ring to dangle enticingly from her waist. 'Your key ring looks ungainly, woman.'

'It holds a key that is most important to me and if you think it ungainly, then perhaps you should look to yourself. You are not manly enough for the stolen ring to fit your finger, so instead you wear it around your neck like a woman.' Rufus' face flushed with anger, and he closed on her, threatening. 'You'd best leave our property and take your brother with you, peasant, before your life becomes unbearable.' He pushed his nose in her face and his left hand went to the key at her waist.

Mary was too quick and brushed his hand aside. 'The key is worthless if it has nothing to open.'

'Then what does it open?'

'It's a cottage and if you've the nerve, you can visit me there on the last evening of the fair.' She looked Rufus squarely in the eyes and ran her forefinger suggestively along the inside of her moistened lips.

Rufus was dumbstruck, hypnotised by her sensuality. His hand reached out to brush away the long curtain of hair from the side of her face. He ran his fingers over the mark of the plague, fascinated, excited. He was losing control, panting and hardening between the loins.

Mary placed her palm against his chest to halt his progress and moved to caress the ring's necklace. 'The ring is a part of my dream. It is a part of my being. I must have it.' She could feel his hot breath on her face, but her eyes never wavered as she ran her fingers slowly up and down the leather string. 'I promise you, on the last night of the fair. It will be more enjoyable.' Her hand dropped to her waist and her eyes never left his as she unhooked the keyring. She held it out to Rufus who snatched it without a word. 'A ring for a ring would be a fair exchange.'

Rufus sniggered as he fixed the key ring to his belt. 'The ring is my lucky charm.'

'Then you have a useless key and your luck has run out.' Mary held out her hand. 'You must miss your wife something terrible.'

Rufus tore the leather string from his neck, unhooked the key and threw them both at her feet. 'The final night of the fair it is then. I know where the hut is, and the last thing I need is a key. If you fail to be there and in good humour, then your brother will suffer accordingly.' Damian was curled up in the corner of the stable listening. He could hardly believe his ears. *No, Mary! I don't want to. Not again.*

The fair was blessed with fine weather. The stalls overflowed from the market square into the adjoining fields. Thomas was free for the whole day. He had left early in the morning with his father, Aunt Hannah and Damian. His old dog Jasper was happy to see him and the hound loped alongside the two cousins like a proud pup. Beneath the market hall in the shambles they watched five butchers trading their wares before they found Mary helping out on a stall near the chandlery. They had purposely gone early to visit her, but she seemed to have her mind on other things. Thomas still didn't feel comfortable with Mary. He found it hard to imagine how she could act so innocently. *She really is a witch.*

Thomas and Damian arranged to catch up with their parents later and drifted together into the crowd. They could never remember such a large fair or one with so many activities. Colourful jesters, troubadours and travelling minstrels moved amongst the stalls. Everything was hustle and bustle and Damian's excitement was more than he could contain. 'Mam said to watch out for the jugglers. They do tricks and cheat you.'

Thomas' nose wrinkled, sniffing in the aroma of food, his mouth watering, his stomach rumbling like distant thunder. 'That's fresh bread and cheese I smell. Let's go!'

They pushed their way through the crowd to the food stall where they supped light ale and munched away on boiled bacon and cheese while listening to a group of strolling players acting out their parts. 'They can't tell a story as good as you can Tommy. Will yer tell me the one about the giant Great Will and Lady Eva and the ghosts under Yewdale Bridge? Was the giant really nine-feet-six?'

'Well, we saw his grave, didn't we?' Damian grinned and nodded his agreement.

The cousins hadn't seen a lot of each other during the past year and they were talking like maniacs, making up for lost time. They sat down to finish their meal on a verge overlooking the fields. There were some scattered stalls amongst the activities. 'Where's Jasper, Damian?'

'I saw him run after some bitch on heat. He'll find us when he's finished. He always does. Did I tell you he chased a funny little dog into the Newmarket Woods?'

'No, you didn't.'

'Well he did, and he came back with blood on his mouth like when he catches rabbits and excited like that time when he caught the fox. I was talking to King Charles II at the time and he had lots of the same dogs and many beautiful ladies around him.'

'What were you saying to the king?'

'I said nothing! I was too nervous. But the king gave me a present and he said to keep it secret.'

'What did he give you?'

'It's a secret.'

'Well then, why did the king want to talk to *you?*'

'Because he liked me, and he liked Prince.'

'There are stories all over the place that you rode Prince when you shouldn't have, and he was disqualified. I can't see how the king would like you for that.'

'Well he did and anyway it was the king's officers that asked me to ride. Rufus said he would never ride Prince again after he came last. I thought you would believe me, Tommy.'

'I do but it's not easy to meet the king. What does he look like?'

'He's tall like you but a lot thinner and he's got a thin moustache but no beard. His hair is black and long like Mary's and a lot curlier than yours.'

'Is that because he wears a wig?'

'I dunno, Tommy, but he smelled nice and his skin was the same colour as Mary's. There was a lady with the same dark skin looking just like Mary and they were all dressed up in fine clothes.'

'I often wonder about your sister. She's different from everyone else around here. Maybe she's from another country and has a different father.'

'Old Francis said not to talk like that.'

'Well he's dead now and from what I've heard he was in touch with the Devil. They say the witches dance on his grave at full moon.'

Damian became silent, and Thomas looked at his cousin suspiciously. 'Were the ravens' feet on his grave from our rune pot?'

'No! Mam asked me that as well, and it's not true.'

'I'm only kidding. I know you wouldn't go near his grave. Not with the Dobbie man being down there.'

Damian gave one of his secret smiles. 'I've fixed it, so he'll stay down there but don't ask me how, Tommy, cause it's a secret.'

'I wouldn't dream of it. Did Rufus meet the king?' Damian's face beamed as he shook his head. 'Then that's why he hates you. He's jealous. Mary told me he whipped you. If I had known, I would have punched him even harder.'

'Has anything happened to you for punching him?'

'Not so far. Black George told me to stay away from him, because if it happens again, they'll send me to the slave fields.'

'Mam says you should stop seeing Sarah and stop gaan to the meetings. Are you a Quaker, Tommy?'

'Dunno.'

'Sarah likes you. I can tell. Are you gaan to marry her?

'No! I'm an apprentice, and I'm not a Quaker, so I doubly can't.'

Damian was pleased with himself for asking the questions that his mother had told him to. 'Mary asked Rufus for the ring and he gave it her back. She's going to meet him tonight at the hut.' Damian blurted it all with a rush, as if fearing the words might never leave his mouth in time. 'She's boiling her pot again and she asked me to dig another pig hole. She said to make it a bit longer and not to put any stakes or a chicken in it.'

Thomas closed his eyes and sighed despairingly. 'Not again. It's not going to happen again. Don't do it.'

'I have to. She's my sister.'

'Then I don't want to know about it.' He looked around him and whispered. 'Don't become involved Damian. I won't be there to help you this time. Rufus is too much of an important person to go missing.'

'Mam said Mary was good all the time we were away but not now. She's obsessed with the ring and believes those rune stories you told her. And the teacher didn't believe that lie you told him about losing the ring in the lake, Tommy. Mary said so. He keeps asking her about it.'

'Do you remember the time I ran off with Mary's necklace and she chased after me?' Damian nodded. 'I wish I'd run a bit further and really thrown it in the lake, and then we would never have had any of this trouble.'

Damian was thoughtful. 'I wish you had thrown the ring in the lake too, and then I would have the real Mary back, like when Rufus stole it from her. When she told Mr Clayton it was stolen he got mad.'

'She should tell Mr Clayton the truth and sell the ring to him, except he probably wants it for nothing.'

'I wish we could get rid of Rufus. I don't like working in the stables when he's there. Mrs Rathbone's the best one. I like her.'

Thomas stood up, wiped his palms together and turned them to brush crumbs away from his new woollen shirt. Damian stood up and copied his cousin's gestures. Hannah had fitted them both out with new shirts for the fair and they wore them proudly. 'Let's enjoy the fair, Damian, but let me know if you catch a glimpse of Rufus or Mary.'

The cousins moved on to the spinners and weavers and then the leatherworker's stalls, but they were soon bored. They left the craftspeople to follow the sound of drums, enticed down the slope by the dancers on the common. They had decided to visit an archery contest nearby when Thomas stopped walking and took Damian by the arm. He'd been thinking of their conversation on the embankment. 'Did you really think the pig trap you dug for Mary was for a pig?'

Damian acted like he never heard the question as his protruding eyes scanned around him. 'There's a falconer.' Thomas chased after his cousin, who was running to the centre of the common, shouting back to him. 'Hurry, Tommy, we'll just catch the start.'

They arrived, breathless, as the falconer was taking the hood off the hunting bird's head. Its claws were wrapped around the falconer's leather forearm strap. It had a small bell attached to one leg. Damian was fascinated by its talons, his mind working overtime. *They're bigger than my ravens' claws.* The falconer was holding a fresh cut of meat in his fingertips, waving it in front of the falcon's beak to tease it. He lifted his arm and unleashed the falcon. The bird took off immediately, its spreading wings beating a rhythm in the air as it soared gracefully into the sky. The small crowd ooh...ed and aah...ed as the falcon circled higher and higher before swooping down to perch in a tall tree. All eyes turned to the falconer's helper. He was positioned in full view of the falcon in a clearing away from the crowd. The assistant raised the cage and waved it in front of him. At falconer's whistle he lifted the cage's gate. Three captive sparrows flapped rapidly into the air. The falcon swooped, gracefully dipping and swerving, tailing its prey. The crowd ducked as the falcon closed on them and the cousins felt a downward draught from the falcon's wings. The hunter gathered his prey only inches from the ground then flew to a private space and settled to gorge. The crowd clapped their appreciation and dropped coins into the falconer's hat. They left, animated in their chatter with the anticipation of finding further entertainment. Thomas headed for the wrestling bouts and Damian left to look for Jasper. As Thomas drew close to the wrestling, he saw parts of the crowd were drifting away in the direction of the Red Lion Inn. He was about to turn back when his father spotted him and waved. 'Over here, Thomas.'

The second day of the wrestling bouts were frivolous compared to the championship of the previous day, but a wager was a wager where the major was concerned. Titus Armstrong had retained his title and the honour of possessing the belt for another year. The championship belt was on display and could be worn around the waist for the sum of one penny. With the major's promotion Titus had become the central attraction and he was taking on all challengers. The major had promised him one tenth of the winnings. Ruben sat at the wagering table with the dubious permission of Vicar Braithwaite. 'I deny all knowledge of my clerk's private life, but any contributions to the church will be most welcome.'

The vicar had long since given up hope of having any influence on the major. Despite the occasional objection from some overzealous parishioner, he discovered that his life was less complicated if he turned a blind eye to the major's activities. Ruben sat at the major's side with quill and ledger at hand, on a wooden chest that held the takings. At odd intervals he would smile and pat the chest to sound out its contents and then affectionately stroke his hand along the grain of the oak top. It was a comforting habit that ensured him of the chest's presence.

The wrestling was scheduled to finish by late afternoon, but the major was running short of contestants. He was scanning the dwindling crowd for a likely opponent when his attention was diverted by Robert's call. He looked towards the large frame of the long-striding Thomas and a mischievous smile flickered across his face. He recognised the young apprentice who was responsible for his son's comeuppance. *This is divine intervention.* His arm lifted and his forefinger pointed dramatically towards Thomas as he arrived at his father's side. His bellowing voice echoed across the common. 'The Quaker boy will be fair competition for Titus. What say you? I throw out a challenge to the young Quaker boy, whom I know to be a forge man of great strength. I will stand any bets on the best of three falls.'

Thomas shook his head and looked down at the ground. A buzz of excitement travelled around the ground, convincing gamblers heading for a taste of the Red Lion's strong ale to turn back. Thomas was embarrassed and trying to show a lack of interest, but he was being taunted. 'Aweeeez Tommy. What are yer scared of, lad?'

His head lifted, eyes scouring the sky, trying to ignore the growing cries, wishing he was elsewhere. He was being coaxed. 'Aweeeez Tommy lad. Wrassle him like yer fadder would.'

Robert felt an urge to walk into the circle and save his son the embarrassment. He had never been able to instil into Thomas his own love of wrestling, or to inspire him to participate. Yet he encouraged his son. 'You need to have fire in your belly lad. A fire that roars like the forge you're caring for.' Thomas was being pushed unwillingly into the wrestling circle. Robert's heart went out to his son. 'Good luck, Thomas! At least he's having a try. God bless him.'

Another voice came from the crowd as deep and powerful as Robert's. 'Two falls for the forge, Tommy.' Oliver was shouting encouragement. He was risking the wrath of Black George by attending and placing a wager.

Sarah and her mother Rachel were bartering at the stalls on the rise when they heard, 'Quaker', shouted out amongst the commotion of the adjoining field. The walk of the challenger seemed familiar to her.

'I hope that's not Thomas wrestling, Mother. He'll be sent down if he's seen wrestling for money.' She turned to look down the aisle of stalls, and saw Damian skipping in and out of the crowd, his head bobbing up and down as if he was searching for someone. Then she saw Rufus heading towards her, and her heart skipped a beat. Damian had followed his cousin's instructions faithfully. He watched Rufus stop and talk to Sarah. The excitement from the wrestling was carrying over and Damian decided it was time to inform his cousin.

The major couldn't believe his luck as he watched Ruben greedily taking wagers. The villagers were confident that Thomas could win at least one throw. After all, wasn't his father a winner of the belt in his youth? Both contestants were the same height, but Titus was broader and heavier. Their shirts, belts and boots were discarded, and they came together chest to chest. Both placed their chin on their opponent's right shoulder and grasped him around the waist, his right arm above his opponent's left. The referee positioned them and stood back. After what seemed to Thomas like an endless pause, he shouted out, 'Hold!'

Titus lifted Thomas and hurled him to the ground. The back of his head thudded against the earth. When the blackness cleared, he was staring into the eyes of his grinning opponent and listening to a groaning crowd. 'Bad luck Thomas,' a wit heckled. 'One more throw lad and you can go home and learn how to wrassle.'

Titus was already counting his bonus and the major rubbing his hands as he smiled at Ruben. 'That was just a bit of bad luck for the Quaker lad. The champion caught him off guard. I'm sure he'll be more alert for the next hold. I'll wager you three to one for the second fall if you couple it with a third fall, or I'll risk even money on the second.'

'Thanks for nothing, Major. You'll have nothing else from me.'

The rest of the crowd murmured agreement and the major conferred with the champion. 'Very well then, you all win. It's two-to-one for you all if the Quaker boy wins the second, but you'll have to be quick before I reach my limit.'

Robert called Thomas over whilst Ruben was recording the wagers. He put his hands on his son's shoulders and gave him a shake. 'Are you all together now, lad?'

'Yes. But do I have to continue?'

'There's no way you can quit. Neither of us would be able to hold our head up in the parish again. Now pull yourself together. He's strong, but no more than you are and he possesses little skill. You've already experienced his surprise lift. Be prepared and move him from side-to-side to keep his weight on one leg. If you sense he's unbalanced, you have a chance of a throw. Remember, that with the exception of his feet, if any part of his body touches the ground you have a fall. Now gaan concentrate. And whip up some fire in yer belly, lad.'

Thomas walked back into the circle feeling miserable. He couldn't gather his father's enthusiasm for wrestling. The crowd were deathly silent. They had seen Robert talking to his son and were expectant of a good run for their money. But as the wrestlers locked chins on shoulders, Thomas was feeling ready to submit. They were in a clinch, both tensed in an effort to anticipate the referee's call, when Thomas caught a glimpse of Sarah. She was standing by the stalls on the rise, looking anxiously at the sky, embarrassed by Thomas' failure, resolutely turned away from him. *She doesn't want to see me wrassle. She's ashamed of me!* Thomas was disgusted with himself. He gritted his teeth and growled. His face drained of all colour and his hands began to shake as his whole being surged with a power and rage that he'd never before experienced. It was as if another being had taken control of him and the champion's body felt inexplicably light. Thomas shuffled Titus from side-to-side as his father had told him and then suddenly threw all his strength to the left. Titus' body wavered as all his weight was transferred to the one foot and Thomas spun him around and pushed forward. Both wrestlers fell to the ground as one, but the referee judged Thomas to be on top and he was allowed the fall. The crowd erupted in roaring approval, but as the major stomped around and argued with the referee, Ruben sat firm. The fragile, miniature, tight-fisted clerk sat like a leprechaun perched on a rock, holding a death-like grip on both sides of his money chest.

Thomas was shaking, weakened by the effort of lifting Titus and the champion was confused by his turn in fortune. The forge apprentice had been stronger than he'd anticipated, but there was another fall left in the contest. This time he would not be taking the Quaker so nonchalantly.

Sarah turned her face away from the sky when she heard the cheering, and focussed on the wrestling circle. She felt strangely proud when Thomas' hand was raised and surprised herself by shouting out and waving. 'Thomas! Thomas!'

Rufus was now upon her and he grabbed Sarah's elbow to pull her towards him. 'Will you be cheering the apprentice when you sail away and leave him, Sarah Wilson?'

Sarah tried to pull away from him, but he maintained a firm grip. 'What do you mean? I'm not leaving Thomas, not ever.'

'I paid a visit to Whitehaven recently and looked over a ship called the *Charlotte*. Your parents are going to be arrested and prosecuted.'

'What do you mean? *I must tell father.*'

'There's no escape for your parents.' He placed his hand to Sarah's cheek. 'That is, unless you are nice to *me*.'

Thomas had now gathered support in the betting and the major had reduced his odds to evens. But the odds did little to deter and there were many takers. For the first time during the summer fair the major had an uncomfortable feeling that he could lose money. As the two wrestlers came together for the third time Thomas looked to the rise and saw Rufus talking to

Sarah. She was trying to pull away from him. Thomas lost all sense of reason. His shoulder lifted and the left side of his face winked. Titus believed he was being mocked and reacted with rage. Their bodies crashed together without formality and the referee hastily backed away. Both wrestlers were growling and whirling around when Damian arrived with Jasper. The old hound dog took exception to Thomas being attacked and headed straight for Titus' ankle. The champion roared with pain and lifted his leg in the air with Jasper attached. He lost his footing and overbalanced with Thomas still clinging to him. All three hit the ground together and the crowd roared, excited at the added entertainment. Thomas levered himself away from Titus and took off to rescue Sarah from Rufus.

Major Rathbone was unusually indecisive. The crowd were declaring Thomas the winner and demanding their winnings as he repeatedly bellowed out. 'Bets are off. All wagers are void.' He called the referee to his side and demanded a verdict. Ruben clasped his hands in his lap, not knowing whether to laugh or cry. Then the major saw the reason for Thomas' run to the rise. He saw the giant apprentice pummelling Rufus into the earth and called his constables around him.

Roger Kirkby was one of the first to respond. He had been heading for the Red Lion, on his way to meet Rufus, when he heard the major announce the Quaker challenge, and become an interested observer. A Quaker wrestling for a wager was a little hard to comprehend. The more he studied Thomas, the more he believed he'd seen him somewhere before. He had sensed it at the meeting when Thomas had first attacked Rufus. It was dark, but there was something about him even then that itched at his memory. It was during the commotion at the end of the bout that a picture of a rainy night in Coniston almost four years ago came to mind. He was outside the inn tending to the horses. His father and the Lowthers' relatives from Whitehaven were inside drinking strong ale. The singing had ended abruptly then cries of 'Stop, thief!' filled the air and a youth ran from the inn. He had mounted his horse and caught the thief less than a half mile away, surprised that the culprit had surrendered so willingly. The thief assumed wrongly that he would be released when the stolen watch was nowhere to be found. Roger's cousin, John Lowther, left for Whitehaven the following day and he had been given the task of searching for the watch. He was sure there had been an accomplice and remembered riding past a young lad standing on the roadside. The lad had disappeared by the time he returned with the thief, and the more he thought about it, the more he realised his suspicion was correct. 'I will arrest him for you before nightfall, Major. Thomas Johnson the Quaker is wanted for another crime that you are unaware of.'

Thomas didn't hesitate as he tore into Rufus. Sarah was screaming as he bunched the neck of Rufus' shirt in his huge fist and dragged him away. With the other fist he drove Rufus to the ground then lifted him to his feet and continued the onslaught until Sarah's voice brought him to a halt. 'Stop it, Thomas. You're going to kill him.' He turned to Sarah and saw the horror in her face. Rufus was unconscious. Thomas let go his grip and dropped him to the ground. He was shaking, exhausted by his vengeful rampage.

He saw Damian next to Sarah, holding out the shirt and boots he'd left behind. 'Uncle Robert told me to chase after you with your clothes, Tommy. We have to run. The constables are coming for you.'

Thomas couldn't think straight. He looked at Sarah with anguish on his face. 'What have I done, Sarah? What have I done?'

Damian was tugging at his arm. 'We have to run, Tommy. I'll show you where to hide.'

Thomas goes to ground

Rufus was humiliated by his beating. He urged his father to join Roger in the raid on the Atkinsons' property. The major felt obliged to avenge his son's beating so assembled his own constables for the search. Roger had a hunch that Thomas would look for shelter under Timothy's roof and that there was a good chance of locating the Wilsons there too. But by late evening, after searching every known meeting house in the district, the search had proved fruitless. They were all bitterly disappointed and Roger Kirkby decided that for the time being, they should leave the search for Thomas to the major. His primary interest was the whereabouts of Joshua Wilson and his family. Roger's plan remained to keep the family in close attendance and arrest them as they boarded the *Charlotte*. The family were due to sail in two days, but he'd lost track of them already. Rufus was aggravated at the thought of Thomas escaping, but reluctantly left the chase to his father and agreed to share his knowledge of the port of Whitehaven with Roger. In high spirits they set off the following morning at the break of dawn with two of Colonel Richard Kirkby's constables.

After the incident at the fair, Joshua and Rachel Wilson had called on Timothy Atkinson desperate for a change of plans.

'I've already organised the ship and paid for thy passages, Joshua. The *Charlotte* leaves in two days. The money will never be refunded.'

'The major and Rufus have the passenger list and the date our ship sails. They have no doubt informed Roger Kirkby who will certainly arrest us as we are boarding, if not before.'

'Does your daughter know about this?'

'Sarah was the one who informed us. Rufus was threatening her with it when Thomas intervened.'

'Well, Rufus has quickly recovered and is presently out hunting for Thomas. So thou may be overlooked in his obsession to find him.'

'I doubt that very much. The major's son seems to be equally obsessed with our daughter.'

'They came to our house first to search for Thomas. Can thou imagine me doing anything so obvious?'

'You know where he's hiding then?'

'I only wish I did so that I could save him. The lad's future is insecure, and I hear that thy daughter is partly responsible for his folly.'

'Sarah attended the last meeting against our wishes and placed her own life in danger. They are both fools to themselves.'

'Leave your problem with me, Joshua, and I will mediate on a solution. Everything has happened so quickly, and time is short.'

'Are you there, Tommy?' Damian entered the barn with food from the Rathbones' kitchen. He heard a thud, followed by the flapping feathers of clucking hens and a rustle in the straw behind him. Thomas had leapt from the roof beams of the barn and scattered the chickens.

'Good to see you, Damian. I'm starving. Did you manage to see me fadder?'

'Mary rode out to see him. She was pleased you'd beaten up Rufus.'

'At least it stopped her from meeting him at the woodcutter's hut. You'll have to keep an eye on Mary for both our sakes. We can still be caught for murder and don't you forget it. I don't think I'm going to be around anymore to protect you. I might have to escape to Scotland.'

'I'll miss yer, Tommy.'

'Did you miss me last year when you were in Newmarket?'

His cousin thought slowly before deciding on his answer. 'Yes!'

'I think that you'll soon get used to me being away.'

Damian smiled shyly. 'See yer later, Tommy.'

Penelope caught Damian walking away from the barn and called him over. 'There must be some hungry mice in the hay this early summer morning?'

He stopped in his tracks, jaw sagging, eyes alert. 'Er ... yes, Mrs Rathbone.'

'Come inside, my lad. I need to talk with you.'

Penelope was sick of all the Quaker searching nonsense and had already decided on a plan of action. 'I know Thomas Johnson has been in the barn all night. You had a nerve bringing him here, right under my husband's nose. It's fortunate I have the mind to help you both.'

Damian looked at her dumbstruck when she told him to ride out and take his Uncle Robert to Timothy's manor house. 'I'll be taking care of Thomas until we sort out this mess.'

Penelope spoke to Timothy with confidence. He told her that there was a ship sailing from Whitehaven in the next few days. The knowledge made her task much easier. Together with Timothy and Robert, she devised a plan that would hopefully foil Roger Kirkby and his constables. 'We are helping each other this time, Timothy, but when this is all over, I will retreat, for I can't be seen favouring your flock. But there is a favour that I ask of you. I would like you to employ Damian in your stables, if not permanently, then at least until Rufus leaves for Cambridge.' The statesman agreed and was thankful for the help from this surprising ally.

Penelope returned home from the Atkinsons', satisfied that she could save Thomas. She called Lizzie to the library. 'You and the rest of the domestics are to take the day off work. I want the house to myself this afternoon. You can visit your cousin in the village and please inform Mabel and her kitchen help that I expect them back in the house tomorrow.'

Lizzie wasn't surprised. The atmosphere in the house had changed for the better since the major returned from Newmarket. Mrs Rathbone often had a smile on her face and the major sported a hungry look that persuaded her to bolt her door. She shuddered every time she thought about the night of the engagement party. *I never want to go through that again.*

It was fortunate for Penelope that Hollis and his wife were in Kendal for a few days and that the stable hands were in the village. There was no time for an alternative plan. Penelope let the manor settle for an hour before she went to the barn. Penelope cocked her head to listen, but apart from the quiet cluck of a chicken and a rustle of straw the air was still. 'You can show yourself now, Thomas.' She felt fur creeping along her skin, gasped, and then pulled her leg away. The barn cat was marking her with the length of its body. 'Go away you stupid cat.' The silence was unnerving her, so she shouted louder, 'I know you're there Thomas. I've sent Damian away and if you don't come out now my husband will find you here. I've been helping your father to organise your escape, but you have to come to the house with me.' The floor shook behind her as Thomas dropped from the beams. Penelope spun around to face him. 'You didn't need to frighten me like that. You took my breath away.'

'I'm sorry, Mrs Rathbone. I wasn't sure what to do.'

'Then follow me to the house, and I'll show you. We've no time to waste.'

Penelope walked briskly away, and Thomas followed sheepishly behind. As they drew close to the house, he felt nervous and uncertain of his fate. As soon as they crossed the threshold, Penelope turned left and ordered him to follow her. She walked down the passageway leading to the kitchen and was about to open the door when she heard a door slam inside. She panicked, retraced her steps and pushed Thomas towards the stairs. 'Quickly, follow me!' She turned right at the top of the stairs, opened the second room on the left and sat Thomas down on the edge of the bed. 'Stay there until I call you.'

Penelope turned to leave and then hesitated as she glanced at the dresser. Her husband's jewel box lay with his stone on full display. Penelope's back was to Thomas, but he saw her close the lid of the small box, lock it and place the key in the top drawer. She turned back and gave Thomas a quick, nervous, embarrassed smile. 'I'll call for you.' She quietly closed the bedroom door behind her.

Thomas realised he was in the lady's bedroom and grew embarrassed by his thoughts. *Mrs Rathbone is an attractive woman.*

Penelope casually walked along the landing and raised her head as Mabel Fowler appeared at the bottom of the stairs. 'I thought I heard you come in Mrs Rathbone. I wasn't going to leave without your permission. I was preparing the evening meal so I couldn't take Lizzie's word for it just like that, now could I?'

'It's all right Mabel. Everything is organised. We will see you tomorrow morning.' Penelope was becoming impatient. As soon as she heard Mabel's footsteps fade away, she banged on the bedroom door. 'You can come out now.' She led Thomas down the corridor and into the kitchen. 'Help me with this.' Penelope was gripping the edge of the Dutch dresser, trying to pull it away from the wall. Thomas tipped it with one hand, levering it away with an ease that excited her. He opened the icehouse door and a draught swirled around the room. He had never seen the icehouse from the inside but remembered helping his father stock the ice from the Tarn. 'Hide in there for the time being. It's the safest place I can think of.' She went to a chest in the corner, lifted the lid and pulled out a blanket, a pair of mittens and a Monmouth cap. 'You had best wear these or you will catch your death of cold.'

Penelope's hand reached out to proffer the garments and her eyes fell on Thomas as if for the first time. The blanket slipped from her fingers and fell to the ground. Neither of them stooped to pick it up. There was an awkward silence as they stood looking at each other, entranced. Penelope gasped a lungful of air and fought to control her feelings. She attempted to breathe out slowly and quietly, but her ears were drumming, and her heart was pounding. Her breasts rose and fell hungrily. Chilled air raced from the passageway, but Penelope felt warm and she no longer cared. She reached up into Thomas' open shirt and placed her palm against the firm muscles of his chest, her delicately splayed fingers caressing his curled hair in an ever-widening circle. Thomas hardened and he nervously licked his dry lips. Penelope tore open the buttons of her silk jacket and took his hand to cup her breast. Her arms reached up to circle his neck and as her body arched against his hardness, she lifted her face, mouth slightly open and enticing, begging to be kissed. Thomas lowered his head and during that moment of passion, the peace of the manor was shattered by a commanding call.

'Penneeeeee! I'm home!' The opening and closing of doors reverberated throughout the house as riding boots pounded the stairs. 'Where are you?' The major had been searching for the runaway since early morning and had arrived home irritable and frustrated. Penelope gasped. 'It's my husband!' She pushed Thomas away from her into the passageway to the icehouse. Thomas' travel sack was on the floor in the middle of the kitchen. She rushed to pick it up and dragged it into the entrance. 'I hope you can handle this better than I, and I don't mean dragging your heavy sack around. Your father will be calling for you as soon as he's able, but in the meantime, you must try to keep warm.'

Penelope heard the hall doors slam and the footsteps fade, then her husband shouting orders outside. She struggled to slide the dresser against the wall, and finally stood with her head bowed, palms pressed down above the cutlery drawers. She was panting as much from sexual anticipation as she was from moving the furniture. *That boy's a man ripe for the plucking.*

The hall door slammed again and then footsteps echoed through the house and down the corridor. Penelope was leaning towards the Dutch dresser, putting on a show of rearranging the dinner plates, when her husband barged in. 'Hiding from me are you. I'm hungry. Where's the cook?'

'I gave everyone the afternoon off, Rowan. I thought it was time I prepared a meal for you myself.'

'The manor's deserted. Why did Hollis have to take his wife to Kendal at the busiest time of the year?'

'They are away for that very reason. You know they hate summer fairs.'

'And where is that idiot, Damian? He was seen running off with Johnson and in case you decide to ask, that's why the constables are searching our house and grounds.'

'Damian has been here all morning. I've only just sent him out on an errand. He's got talent that lad. He's very much in demand you know.'

'You're beginning to sound like the locals. Talented lad indeed! An inadequate intellect I would say.'

'They say he rode well against the king.' The major closed his eyes and turned his head away. 'Is it true, Rowan?'

'Who's been talking to you about Newmarket?'

'Does it matter? The truth will out sooner or later, and the locals will think less of you if they thought you had lied about one of their own.'

The major deliberated and Penelope waited. She had an intuition about the situation. Damian was too simple a lad to invent such a story, especially about the bag of coins. He was adamant that there were four coins and it was a low level that Rufus would stoop to. The silver ring was a perfect example of that. 'I lied to protect our son.'

Penelope smiled. 'I knew it!'

'Rufus had set his mark on being introduced to the king and rode beautifully to win the first heat. Then during the second heat the horse took sick and they straggled into last place. I'm sure there was skullduggery. I shouldn't put a name to the culprit, but I've a fair idea it was the king's stable master.'

'But that's Henry. He's a gentleman.'

'You know Henry?'

'Yer I do. He's the one who introduced me to the king's saddle-maker.' She waved a hand in front of her face, trying to recall. 'You know, the short thickset man with sandy frizzy hair. I can never remember his name.'

'Andrew Millhouse. I'm sure I've told you that before. His initials are on your saddle.'

Penelope gestured dismissively. 'It's not important. You accuse Henry of skullduggery, Rowan, but I don't believe it.'

'You don't know him like I do, Penny. He was one of my stablemen in the army and something of a Jonah. We had all kinds of problems wherever he was involved. Nothing ran smoothly. I had a feeling that Henry was up to something in Prince's stable and that that silly boy was keeping it from me. He often looks at me with shifty eyes, as if he's trying to read my mind. He's not as stupid as he looks you know.'

'Of course not, but he looks at you with those eyes because he's afraid of you. I know he's very good at certain tasks, especially with animals. You must realise by now that I don't employ him for charity. He told me that he has a lot of secrets and one of them used to be a bag of coins. He was being faithful to the king by keeping them a secret until Rufus stole them from him.'

'You can't seriously believe that nonsense.'

'I think he's romancing about sharing secrets with the king. He was obviously overcome by the occasion. I don't know where the truth lays, but if our son continues to abuse the lad I will have to find employment for him elsewhere.'

'Hollis won't miss him; I can assure you of that.'

'Rufus carries too much hate and not only for Quakers. He's the same with Damian's sister, Mary, but I think that leans more towards passion. At least he's stopped wearing that stupid amulet around his neck. It belongs to Mary you know.'

The major ignored the inference. 'He seems to think it is a lucky charm.'

'He can think what he likes but he'll have no luck with Mary. We can only hope that being a father will bring him to his senses.'

'He is in Whitehaven and out of harm's way at present, but he will be back in two days' time. We should suggest that its time he returned to comfort Eleanor.'

'Tell me more about Newmarket, but please, not your operation again.'

The major sat back in his seat, resigned to telling the truth, holding the silence before continuing. 'The problem in

Newmarket was that Rufus boasted of winning and was subsequently humiliated with last place. He flatly refused to ride in the final heat. Prince made a miraculous recovery and even though Damian was ineligible and would be disqualified if he won, the king unbelievably sent word for him to ride in the last. To top it all off, Damian was given an audience with the king. I must admit that I was quite put out myself and sorry for Rufus. I felt the need to back up his story. All that needs to be said is that your precious Damian met the king, came third behind him in the Newmarket Plate and rode well.'

'Was he rewarded by the king with coin?'

'The lad's certainly romancing. I know nothing about a reward, but we did win handsomely on the first heat.'

'Penelope leaned across the table, cupped her hands behind his head and kissed him on the forehead.'

'Thank you for being honest with me. There's hope for you yet. I'll let the news out gradually to the domestics. You will be praised of course.'

The major sat back, surprised at his relief for having told the truth. He then began to rant on about Damian. 'The stupid boy should have taken his pathetic old mongrel with him, or at least he should have fed it before he left.'

'I thought he'd taken his dog with him, but any way, you can't say the pets aren't well fed from the kitchen leftovers.'

'Well the cook must have forgotten them. You *did* give them the day off you know. The mongrel's sniffing around the icehouse like he's starving and your cat's scratching around there as well. There must rotten fish in there. I'll send for the stable hands to clean the food out immediately.'

Penelope's heart skipped a beat. *Jasper was Thomas' dog.*

'Hollis will be here tomorrow, Rowan; I'll see to it then. You should concentrate on what you have in hand.'

She drew close to the major, opened his shirt and brushed her hand through the hair on his chest. 'We should have had more children, Rowan. You neglected me during those long campaigns.'

'Not now, Penny, I'm shattered. Food! I need food.' He shifted uncomfortably in his seat. Penelope busied herself sorting through the larder, and came out with some cheese, boiled hambones, a cob of bread, and a jug of beer. 'That's peasant food, woman.'

Penelope ignored her husband's complaint and sat down beside him. 'You're running after that apprentice like a man possessed. Rufus only received a beating that was coming to him. It was something that you should have done years ago but you were never home. You were always too busy playing war games. Rufus should be in Cambridge caring for his wife instead of harassing single women.'

'I promised Colonel Kirkby I would keep the Quakers on their toes.'

'I wouldn't bother. Robert is more than adequate at hounding Quakers. What will you do with the young man when you catch him?'

'The decision will be Colonel Kirkby's, but there's no doubt the lad will be sent away and he'll lose his apprenticeship.'

'What will they charge him with?'

'Attending an illegal gathering and conspiring against the king or attacking an officer of the law. Kirkby will think of something.'

'But none of that is true, Rowan. You know he was at the fair, that there was no meeting and Rufus is no officer of the law.'

'The truth can be arranged. Kirkby has already made out warrants for the Wilsons' arrest. He's charging them all with attending a third meeting and Joshua for failing to pay his tithes before fleeing the country. He plans to arrest them boarding the *Charlotte*. No doubt he has already added Johnson to the list and acquired the witnesses.'

'I hope you're not one of the witnesses.'

'I may be many things but I'm not an outright liar. His constables' signatures and that of his son will be sufficient.'

'You *did* lie about Newmarket though.'

'That was different. I was protecting our son.'

'How do you know they are fleeing the country and how do you know the name of the ship?'

'Rufus found out.'

'Just like that was it? Rufus found out. And neither of you told me.'

'We had to keep it a secret.'

'Keep it a secret! You are no better than Damian, keeping secrets.'

'Even at this late stage the Wilsons could escape our net.'

'So, what if they do escape. Does it really matter?'

The major rested his elbow on the table, scratched his head and thought on the matter. He dropped his hand back to the table and sat back to reply, then hesitated and repeated the same gesture. Penelope sighed and continued giving her opinions. 'If Richard Kirkby serves those warrants, they are all in danger of being exiled.'

'I have no other choice, Penny. It's my duty as a magistrate to maintain the law. I must seek out the law breaker.'

'That's a shame, Rowan. He's a nice boy placed in a difficult situation.' Penelope gave out a weary sigh and sat down close to her husband. She rested an elbow on the table and cupped her face in a palm, allowing her delicate fingers to stroke her thought-wrinkled brow. She almost spoke out then hesitated and appeared to reconsider before making a show of sharing her information. 'I must tell you of the whispers I overheard in the kitchen this morning. There was a mention of Whitehaven and a freedom ship. It could be the same ship that you failed to tell me about. Isn't that where Rufus has gone with Roger Kirkby?'

The major paused to absorb the kitchen staff's trivial gossip. 'If the rumour is true then we've not much time. We've already searched the Atkinson property.'

'That was this morning.'

'The *Charlotte* leaves on the morning tide in two days. It makes sense. I had a feeling Timothy was hiding the lad. He booked the Wilsons' passage on the same ship and he could be thinking of saving another of his kind.'

'He would need a horse. Do you think he would steal one?'

'He would be desperate enough to try. But if he has Timothy's sympathy, there would be no trouble with a mount. We will check out the Atkinson stable. He only has four horses capable of that journey. If Thomas is already on his way to Whitehaven he will run into Roger and Rufus and save me a lot of trouble. On the other hand, if he's stabled nice and cosy at the Atkinsons' place he will probably leave before nightfall and we will have him.'

William Webster thumped his fist on the kitchen door. 'The house and grounds are all clear, Major.'

'I'll be with you shortly, William. I have some inside information. We'll be riding back to the Atkinsons' for another search. We may have him this time.' The major listened for William's footsteps to fade. 'I'm losing my appetite for hounding Quakers, and they are testing my patience to the limit. Why can't their traders and husbandmen be reasonable and pay the tithes? After all, it's the law of the land and a mere tenth of their produce.'

'It's their faith, Rowan, and their stubbornness will never lead to a solution. You must be more reasonable with them.'

'I've no time for reasoning. If they don't pay in future, I'll refer them to Colonel Kirkby, which could be a fate worse than death.'

The major had made his decision. He pressed his palms on the table and went to stand but Penelope slowed him. She placed an arm around his shoulder, thrust her hand through his shirt and reached down to cup his balls. 'Must you always be in such a hurry, Rowan? Can't you send them all away?'

The major faltered and then smiled as he stood to leave. 'I don't know what's got into you lately woman.'

Penelope smirked. 'I think it was you, Rowan. I think it was you.' *And almost the apprentice you are looking for.* She closed her eyes and pictured Thomas. *To think I had him in the bedroom and had to let him go.*

The major was beaming as he left the kitchen. He wasn't in the most conducive mood to hunt down a criminal, but that's how he'd been since the operation; relaxed and savouring life to the full, although not so much that he forgot his duties. One of the stablehands had returned and when he saw the major, he wished he'd stayed in the village. 'Search the stables and the barn again, and the pigsty if you have to. Johnson was seen heading this way with that idiot cousin of his. I'll be at the Atkinsons' grounds. If you find anything, let Mrs Rathbone know immediately.' *I would hate to think I was harbouring the villain myself.*

The major's raiding party were circling the outer perimeter, working into position, when they were alerted by a whinny from the stables. A horse emerged at a canter, its rider crouched low clinging desperately to the reins. It pierced the cordon of constables and headed for a path that would lead them to the north. 'There's the culprit.' The major gathered the constables around him and gave orders to Colonel Kirkby's men. 'I know that horse and you'll not hold your ground with him. He's heading north and will make for the quay in Whitehaven. Keep to the packhorse trails and when you make the arrest, bring him straight back to me.' The major knew that Thomas was the son of a shepherd and would know the fells like the back of his hand.

Timothy came running out from the stables. 'What's thy trouble major?'

'You've obviously been harbouring a criminal and given him a horse and passage to freedom.'

'I don't think so, Major, that was my stablehand leaving for Whitehaven with an urgent message.'

'Then when your messenger has been returned by the constables you should invent a more suitable excuse for Colonel Kirkby. For whatever reason, his son, Roger, has you marked down for Lancaster and no matter my respect for you I can do little to help.'

'I've heard that the colonel is organising a commission for Roger with the Coldstream Guards. The sooner he goes the better it will be for all of us. The lad can then perhaps rid himself of his boredom and disperse his boundless energy elsewhere.'

'That's news to me, Timothy, and it may be good news for all, but only when your so-called messenger is brought to me will our standing be known. Until then I can only hope for your sake that what you say is true.'

The *Charlotte* left its berth early on the morning tide as expected, but much to Rufus and Roger Kirkby's bewilderment it had set sail without taking any Quakers aboard. The two constables had policed the boarding platform until it was taken in and the seamen had let go the ropes. By midday Rufus and Roger Kirkby were drowning their disappointment in strong ale. They were drinking at the Harbour Inn and Roger was questioning his friend's diligence. 'I can't see how you could have made such an obvious mistake. Perhaps it was an old logbook you turned out of the drawer.'

'It was no old logbook. The date was current, and the passengers were marked down, "to be picked up".'

'You're sure it was marked, to be picked up?'

A bell rang somewhere between Rufus' ears and the tankard stopped halfway to his mouth. He was looking through the smoke-filled tavern towards the corner where he'd once sat with his father. *Grasty had been talking about contraband and the usual drop-off point.* His tankard thumped down and splashed ale across the oak table. 'It's Ravenglass!' he shouted out. 'They're leaving from Ravenglass.'

'Calm down. My father told me the harbour was silted up years ago. The ships can't tie up there anymore.'

'They don't have to. I'll explain later. We must leave at once. There may still be time.'

Ravenglass, on board the *Charlotte*: July 1667

The brigantine's sails billowed. The ship heaved to one side, and then corrected as the first mate set course to run with the tide. The *Charlotte* pulled slowly away from the rain-swept bay, and the timbers creaked and groaned as they yielded to the power of the sea. A shower of rain splashed Thomas' face, but his expression never altered as he looked towards the shoreline and the diminishing figure of his father.

They would have missed the ship if it hadn't been for the highwayman arriving late on the scene. At least, that's what Thomas surmised him to be. The man was jumping around, pounding the shingle in exasperation, and screaming out across the water, 'You bloody fool, Grasty. Did you think I paid my passage for fun?' He turned to the speechless Thomas. 'They probably think I've been caught. Are you on the run as well?'

Robert shook his head as he nudged his son, but Thomas nodded sheepishly, and backed away as the man took out a musket and fired it into the air. 'That should bring them to their senses.'

Grasty had been preparing to pull up anchor when he heard the shot. When he looked to the shore and saw the trench coat and hat, there was no doubt in his mind about the culprit. 'He'll roast me alive if we leave without him and he survives for the *Charlotte*'s return.'

'Lower the boat again, Mr Bone, and be quick about it. From what I've heard those two out there are lucky to be alive. Keep them below decks or in the steerage; as long as they are away from the cabin passengers.'

Rufus was the first to see the black stallion thundering towards them. He reined in his horse and pulled to the side of the track. His companions followed suit to allow free passage. As the horse loomed close, Rufus thought there was something familiar about its rider, with the arm circling the air before striking the horse's rump. He would have recognised the unconventional style of riding anywhere. It could only be Damian and he was galloping Prince as if his life depended on it. The stableboy was urging his mount forward and as he flashed past, he turned his head and gave Rufus one of his silly grins. Rufus half turned his mount, hesitating on whether to take up the chase. Roger, who'd stopped further on, called out to him, 'Do you know the rider?'

'I know him well, and I think he's stolen that horse.'

At that moment the first of Roger Kirkby's constables arrived. 'I can't stop, Roger. The major told us to arrest the lad and return him to Hawkshead.'

Robert stared until the ship was out of sight, oblivious of the drizzling rain. He was remembering the conversation with his sister the previous night. 'Do you suppose we will ever see him again?'

'I've a feeling we will. I'm not sure what he'll find over the other side of the sea, but his ties are too strong for him not to want to return.'

'The law will have to change before that happens. The injustice of it all, Hannah, is that he's not really a true Quaker.'

'If only he'd chosen to be with a woman other than Sarah, he would still be with us, Robert. I heard the Wilsons were leaving the district anyway, so it was all for nothing. He's lost everyone he loves.'

'He has his life, and that's all that matters. Timothy said you can achieve great wealth in the new land.'

'What good is that without a family?'

Robert thought of Damian and Mary and Hannah's first grandson and he could only agree with her. Thomas had disregarded the danger and agreed on stopping to see his Aunt Hannah before they left. He walked the nearby fields for the last time, remembering that special day, soaking up the beauty of the dales before he began his apprenticeship. He had thought of that day as his last day of freedom. Now he had another day to remember and a different kind of freedom. He regretted not being able to visit his mother's grave one last time, but Ulverston was too far away and time was short. He vowed that someday he would return to her resting place, and to his special place on the hill, and God willing, he would be a free man.

Sun filtered through the showers of rain. The *Charlotte*'s sails faded and merged into the fog of the bay. Robert stopped waving and turned away with a heavy heart. He grasped the tether of Thomas' horse, mounted his own, and left the abandoned horse to graze. *Someone will be thankful. From the looks of its rider the horse was probably stolen.* He saw four horsemen galloping down the hillside and, as they drew closer, he thought he recognised Rufus. The riders pulled up on the foreshore and they looked a sorry lot, shoulders sagging, heads shaking in disbelief. They were focussed on the horizon, shielding their eyes against the summer showers. As if to taunt them, a rainbow curved over the *Charlotte*, highlighting the diminishing ghost of the brigantine. The four horsemen remained silent, disconsolate with failure. Robert's long unruly red hair and beard were dripping wet. The giant of a man shivered as he pulled the sheepskin clothing tight around his broad shoulders. More than seven hundred years ago his Viking ancestors had travelled the same path, and their profile had barely changed. He nudged his horse along, preferring not to be noticed. *I had best take to the side trails lest they recognise me. I wonder how Damian is faring. The lad has risked his life to save Thomas.*

Damian was at that moment being arrested by Colonel Kirkby's constables. They were on a rise and in sight of the port of Whitehaven. He seemed pleased to see them and smiled as he handed over the rolled paper he was to deliver. The message was to inform the *Charlotte*'s captain of the cancellation of a cabin for three passengers. The constable had no way of knowing that the ship had sailed, and the worthless message was placed in his saddle bag unopened. 'Let's go home, Thomas Johnson. Major Rathbone is certainly going to be pleased to see *you.*'

Damian didn't mind being called Thomas Johnson for a while. Timothy told him that if he didn't recognise any of the constables he must keep his real name a secret and he liked secrets. He wouldn't be seeing much of the major or Rufus anymore. Thanks to Penelope he was going to work in Timothy's stables. *She's a nice lady.*

Thomas felt abandoned. He had never felt this lonely since the first day of his apprenticeship; the day his father left him with Mr and Mrs Ferris. That seemed so long ago, and now he was alone again. He was going to be separated from his family for a long time and by miles of endless sea. He had also lost Sarah, and it was because of her that he was being hunted. Aunt Hannah told him that Joshua Wilson had sold his business and his family were leaving the district. *Sarah should have told me.* Robert rode all the way to Ravenglass with him. On the way he explained how the major's wife had coordinated his escape. Why Mrs Rathbone had befriended him was a mystery. He still felt guilty about being alone with a married woman, and for having sexual feelings for her. Now he could only fantasise about what would have occurred had the major not returned. He had survived two nerve wracking hours in the icehouse and having Penelope's jewel box in his sack didn't help. First it had been Jasper and the cat nosing around, then he'd heard the constables searching close by. After the search party had left he'd expected Mrs Rathbone to call, but it was his father that eventually awoke him from his slumber. He had heard the rattle of the lock, and then one of the double-doors swung open. His father was standing there with two fresh horses. 'Hurry up, Thomas! We're riding to see your Aunt Hannah. There's no time to waste.'

Moonbeams on the lake

Damian was feeling miserable. 'Do you think we will ever see Tommy again, Mary?'

'I don't know, Damian. I'll miss him just as much as you.'

'He didn't really tell any big lies, except for a few, and that means he could be a Quaker if he wanted to.'

'What lies?'

'He told one to protect you and he told another one when he was with me, so you'll never know that one.'

'I think I know *that* lie, already. You told Mam that you both stayed with me on the night that James Pritt disappeared. What about the other?'

Damian had thought often about the other lie and had come up with a clever solution, but he was fearful of using it. Mary would never let it happen if she knew. But he was clever with secrets. Slow, but clever, and he'd already decided. 'I've been thinking a lot, Mary, that if you make a lie happen, then it's not a lie anymore, and if it's not a lie anymore, then I can tell you.'

'I've told you before not to talk like you are daft. People will laugh at you. Like they did when you said you'd raced Prince against the king's horse.'

'I did race against the king. I really did.'

'There you go again. You only rode Prince around the enclosure and got disqualified. You can't stop dreaming, can you?'

Damian ground his teeth and stomped his feet with frustration, then suddenly stopped his antics when he saw Mary laughing. 'Why are you laughing Mary? Are you teasing me again?'

'I'm proud of you Damian and Mam will be too. She knew all along that you were telling the truth, that you rode Prince against the king's horse. Mrs Rathbone told me when she called in at the shop. She asked Samuel if she could speak to me in the back storeroom. Very secretive she was but said to keep it quiet until Rufus had left for Cambridge.'

Damian couldn't stop smiling. 'I like secrets and I like Penelope.'

'I like her as well, Damian.' *But not the way she looks at Samuel, like she's hungry for something.* 'She said you nearly won the race and the king asked specially to see you.'

Damian's grin widened and his eyes almost popped out as he listened to his sister, hardly believing his ears. 'Everyone will say good things about me now.'

'Mrs Rathbone also said you told her the king gave you some coins.'

Damian had been in a quandary at the time. *Don't tell anyone, lest they steal them.* But when he thought further, he realised the coins had already been stolen. *All the coins, except my special one.* He nodded guardedly, with a lingering question mark on his face. 'Rufus stole them from me.'

'Well then, we will never know the truth now, will we?' And Damian smiled his glassy eyed secretive smile. 'You are going to be famous in the parish now, my brother. They'll have to be paying a penny to talk to you.'

'I won't charge them. I wish Tommy was here to tell them. He makes up stories better than me. Are you going to make a lie truthful with me?'

'Alright then, just for some peace, we will let the lie happen. And hopefully, now that you're about to be famous, you can tell me a truth.'

Damian's face lit up. 'Tommy will be pleased, and I hope you will be as well. We have to take a boat out on Lake Windermere, near where the ferry leaves.'

'That sounds nice, Damian. As long as you row, I'm happy to go with you.'

'We have to leave when it's dark.'

'Then I'm not going.'

'But Tommy made the lie to protect you.'

Mary muffed her ears as if about to scream. 'Alright, Damian, It's alright. I'll go with you!'

They tethered Prince away from the ferry house. Mary left Damian on guard with Jasper. He pulled off his clogs and long woollen socks and threw them into the boat. 'Where are you going, Mary?'

'I'm going to pay for the boat.'

'You must have a lot of money.'

'I took a penny from your pocket.'

She disappeared into the shadows leaving Damian searching his pockets. He waded around deep in thought with his hands folded across his chest, wincing as the lake's pebbles pinched his bare feet. His hand went to his pocket again and he puzzled as to where the penny might have come from. He quickly forgot his dilemma and breathed a sigh of relief when Mary reappeared. Damian could still see Prince's silhouette. He was tethered to a tree, nosing his reins, attempting to undo them. He thought he saw the shadow of a man behind and his heart skipped. He whispered, 'I think the ferryman's coming, he's over there near Prince.'

'That's nonsense. You're seeing shadows. I've just left his door, and anyway, he's blind. Don't be so scared.'

Jasper started to run towards Prince then suddenly stopped, ran around in circles and cowered away whimpering. The old hound then came back to squat at the lakeshore with his nose pointing towards their boat. 'Good dog, Jasper. Don't be afraid of Prince. You're a good dog. Don't bark.' He turned to his sister. 'I was worried. You took a long time.'

Mary whispered 'Shush!' and leapt into the boat with dry feet as Damian made to glide the boat into the water and tilt his body aboard. They had drifted almost to the middle of the lake before Mary spoke. Damian was rowing and she whispered, knowing that their voices would amplify across the lake. 'Can you tell me now?'

'Not just now, but soon.'

'Why do you keep looking over your shoulder?'

'I have a feeling we're not alone.'

The moon had clouded over and he could hear a distant rumble of thunder. Damian levered the oars into the boat, lifted them from the rowlocks and rested them on the benches. He stood up to move towards Mary and the boat rocked on the deep, calm lake. Water slapped the hull and a fine spray mottled his face as his hands spread to the sides of the boat to steady the roll. 'Be careful, Damian!'

'Do you feel scared, Mary?'

'No! Should I be?'

'It's that sort of a night. It's spooky and we're out here all alone in the dark.'

'I don't like thunder, Damian, and neither does Prince. Things happen when God moves the furniture. Prince always whinnies as if he's afraid, and then I see horrible things.' Her hand tightened around the ring.

'Why are yer holding the ring so tight? Yer look frightened.'

'I am frightened. I grip the ring because my senses tell me to. I only have the feeling when I'm in danger or angry. I think Prince and the thunder protect me from the evil face.'

'What evil face? Do you see the Devil?'

Mary bit her lip and hesitated. *I shouldn't have told him. I've placed him in danger.* 'It's nothing, only a nightmare I sometimes have.'

Damian thought of the night he was in the forest. 'Does it send you crazy?'

Mary could feel the anger rising inside her. *He's taking over.* 'Only when I feel the danger, and bless you brother, for I'm feeling the danger right now.'

'Can I feel the danger in the ring, Mary?'

She opened her palm and as she mouthed her next words, she saw a flashing vision of her Man of Death, clasped hands holding back the blood from his gaping throat, one eye screaming pain, the other a dark, empty socket leaking red tears. 'You can try if you like, but only a touch.'

Mary heard her voice fading away and saw herself looking down on the small boat from above. She opened her hand and when Damian saw her eyes glaze over, he snatched at the ring, tore the leather necklace from her neck and cast it into the lake. A flash of lightning illuminated the placid water, and a clap of thunder rolled over the hills. Prince's whinny floated in the air, but Damian was deaf, numb from his act of bravery. Staggering backwards, he lowered himself onto the rowing bench, folded his arms across his chest and rocked his body slowly back and forth. His body shivered with the cold of fear. His knees trembled and his shaking hands clasped as he looked to the heavens. A silent flash of lightning illuminated the sky and for the first time in his life, Damian prayed to God for help and forgiveness.

A veil of clouds drifted, and moonbeams splashed the surface of the lake. The silver ring danced along the trailing necklace, flirting with the light as it was coerced towards the deep. Damian stretched forward, hypnotised, and compelled to stare. His head pounded and his skull threatened to burst with the pressure. Something was controlling his mind. He couldn't stop his hand reaching out. He watched helplessly as his fingers splayed open, dipped down into the cold water and grasped the trailing string. A hand came over his shoulder and pulled it from his grasp. He swivelled and let out a terrifying scream. 'No, Mary!'

Blazing green eyes bore down on him, penetrating, searching his soul. His mind darkened and his heart slowed, pounding heavier. The air was stale and hard to breathe. He was mesmerised by an outstretched hand holding the loose leather string. An object bounced on the deck and rolled towards him. Mary was bellowing in a foreign tongue, her voice deeper, resonating as if under water. 'Jeg ma ha hans leder ... Og ringen, Hrolfr, det solv ringe med det runes.'

Damian couldn't understand the strange words, but he knew that his sister was raving mad. *It's not Mary.* He was exhausted, his legs shaking, urine dripping into his clogs. He clamped his hands over his ears and closed his eyes to block everything out, then gathered his remaining strength, and screamed out, 'Leave her alone. Please, God, send Mary back to me!'

The ring was at the end of its spiralling descent, and as it settled on the bed of the lake a dark shadow passed over it. Damian's senses floated in the eerie silence. He took his hands away from his ears and opened his eyes. Mary's body stiffened and the colour drained from her face. He watched the green glint of madness dissipate, her eyelids close and her body slump into the bottom of the boat. His heart pounded as he stared at the crumpled bundle in horror. *Mary's dying!* He grabbed the oars and rowed recklessly towards the lakeside, extremities trembling, and the oars paddling more air than water. He hit something wooden and an oarless boat drifted past, swirling around with the impact. There was a shadowy figure in the boat and Damian leaned forward as it spun towards him. He saw two staring, wide-open, bulbous eyes and let out another scream. 'It's the Dobbie man.'

He was still rowing frantically when the boat's bow ploughed into the shingle at the lake's edge. He leapt onto the shore and saw a man standing there with a dog on a leash. The man walked towards the boat and as he drew close, Damian could see the anger on his face. It was Rupert Gull, the blind ferryman. 'What in God's name have you been doing out there?' He appeared to be focussing over Damian's shoulder, and the nervous intruder looked behind him for another presence. 'Explain yourself!'

Damian was in shock and could only mumble. 'I think my sister is dead.'

'What do you mean you *think* your sister is dead? Where is she?'

'She's in the boat.'

Do you think I'm stupid, lad?' Damian had heard the ferryman was blind, but it was said he could see in the dark.

'You had best step back into the boat until the constable arrives. I've been dragged out of bed in the middle of the night by my terrified wife. I've heard a clap of thunder and my wife said she saw lightning with not a cloud in the sky. I've had a boat stolen and now I'm supposed to have a dead woman at hand. I pray to God I'm having a nightmare.'

The ferryman's wife was hurrying from the house. 'Go back, Elizabeth, and prepare to ride for the constable.'

'It's the middle of the night.'

'I meant in the morning then.' He squinted with concentration. Keep your eyes on the young lad for me.'

Damian was trying to lift Mary from the boat, and he let go with a yell when her eyes shot open. 'Is that you, Mary?'

'Who else would I be? Why did you throw away the ring?'

His eyelids closed, and he drew in a deep calming breath. *She's come back to me.* He sat down on the rowing bench and his Mary settled beside him. Rupert Gull was puzzled. 'Am I to believe there is a girl in the boat, and she's alive? Speak up woman. Why did you steal the boat and why does the young man think he's your brother?'

'He thinks he's my brother because he *is* my brother. I know of you, Mr Gull. Our mother Hannah speaks highly of you. She says you're a kindly man.'

'I can't place your mother and compliments won't clear you of stealing a boat.'

'I left a penny at your door for the loan of the boat. Do we owe you more?'

Elizabeth arrived at his side and answered for him. 'There's another boat missing.'

'Then thar'll be one more penny owed.'

'We only took the yan boat.'

'That remains to be seen. A penny is satisfactory for the time being young woman but waking me in the middle of the night is not. The noise from that horse and dog of yours woke up the whole household and near frightened us to death. I've never known such a commotion. What is your business?'

'I can only say it was an adventure and hope for your forgiveness. I took a nasty turn and it frightened my brother sick.'

'You certainly look sick, and your brother looks worse.'

'We need to rest, Mr Gull. Could we sleep in your barn until morning?'

'After all you've put us through you've the cheek to ask a favour?'

'I can pay another penny. I'm sure you know me mother, Hannah, and me Uncle Robert, the wrestler.'

Mary had touched on his favourite subject. 'I know Robert well. We both wrestled in our young days and earned some fair money on our bouts. When I fell and was blinded, I was given the contract for the ferry. All the old wrestlers help us out. Our chief boatman was a wrestler who fought your uncle more than once. We had a wager on Thomas at the fair. Now that was a strange bout. We had trouble claiming our winnings from the church clerk. That man would balk at giving away a bad tooth. What's this we hear about Thomas disappearing? We heard that with his Quaker ways he was lucky to escape prison.'

'He's gone to the New ... ouch!' Mary stamped hard on her brother's foot before he could finish.

The ferryman opened his mouth to comment then decided enough was enough. Rupert was feeling the cold and so decided on some action. 'Let's cut out the cackle and be off to bed. Elizabeth! Take a penny off this young lady and I'll settle them with the horse and dog in the barn. Your horse's coat feels like it needs grooming young man and a blanket wouldn't go astray. He seems a fine horse and should never be neglected in this manner. You should be ashamed of yourself.'

Damian never said a word. He was simply happy for his sister to be back and when they had settled down in the barn he rejoiced. 'I think you're my sister again, Mary. I really think you're my real sister.'

'Yes I am. Now tell me why you threw the ring into the lake.'

'I threw it because it was taking you away from me. You were dying. I was losing you and I've already lost Tommy.'

'The ring was handed down from our ancestors. It was a symbol of where we came from, and you have a lot to answer for. How can I explain the loss of my young son's inheritance?' Damian couldn't answer, but nevertheless, his mind was working overtime, although ever so slowly. Mary couldn't understand why she was feeling so calm. 'I've lost something other than the ring. I feel a great weight has lifted from my shoulders and I no longer fear the evil vision that drifts across my mind. I had the same feeling of freedom when Prince was away, and Rufus was in possession of the ring. When Prince and the ring were close, and I became angry, terrible things happened. I tried to be calm, but the vision kept aggravating me. Now the ring has gone, it's as if a spell has been broken. Does that sound stupid?'

Damian shrugged. 'I dunno.'

'My marriage stone was an even greater loss though. I often held it when I thought of John.'

Damian's face lit up. He reached down into his tunic pocket and withdrew a clenched fist. His soft grey eyes focussed on Mary as he unclasped his hand. She gasped, and Damian's grin widened when he saw her amazement. The beautiful amber stone sat in his palm like a pearl in the cushion of an oyster. Mary's heart pounded as she dipped her fingers into his open palm to retrieve her late husband's wedding gift. She held it in front of her eyes, staring in disbelief, then looked at the pleasure on her brother's face and smiled. There was no need for words. The amber stone had fallen to the bottom of the boat and rolled towards him. He watched in silence as his sister made a necklace and patted the amulet against her breast. 'I can't thank you enough, Damian. This amulet could never be replaced. When I said a part of me was missing, I meant the evil inside me, something I can't explain.'

Damian had never felt so pleased, and sat with his hands clasped between his knees, rocking back and forth, sharing the peace of silent contentment with his sister. He studied Mary's face, wondering if she really was his sister. Mary was quietly reflecting on her past, and suddenly blurted out what had been preying on her mind. 'I am sure you and Thomas saw me in the forest that night. Why didn't you say something?'

'We were both scared of you, Mary. You were different.'

'I admit I was possessed by a She-Devil. My man of death was nothing in comparison. Her powers overcame me when we were out there on the boat. I could feel her using my eyes.'

'We vowed to keep it a secret. It was Tommy's idea. He said we would be blamed because we were supposed to be staying with you. And he said that we would all hang in Lancaster if anyone found out.'

'That was why you both lied to Mam and I had to say it was true.'

Mary took her brother's hands in hers to comfort him. 'Nobody is ever going to find out. There are only two of us now that know of the Devil's deeds, and they will always remain a secret between us. Thomas is best out of it, far away in the new land.' Damian smiled contentedly. 'You must tell me your story of that evil night, Damian, and I will tell you mine.'

Damian spoils the lie

'**D**id yer catch a wild pig in't trap I dug Mary?'
She remembered her brother's curiosity, his devious look, and her reply.

'I lost interest, Damian. It was a stupid idea.' *And the hole was too bloody small.*

She had planned it so meticulously: the full moon, the prepared grave, the invitation and the ready potion with the poisons from the yew tree—roots, leaves and fruit—mixed with nightshade, quince juice and spices. She'd simmered the brew for almost week through the period of a full moon, exactly as Ada, the witch, had instructed; but the potion had failed. The witch had been absorbed with the ring's symbol of the yew tree. She explained that it was a tree of life which held the power of regeneration and that as the tree lays in death, daughter trees are already growing inside to replace them. She said there were sacred yews that bleed red resin like blood from never healing wounds. *Like the running blood from my Man of Death.* She'd stomped out of the doorway with the witch's horrible cackling ringing in her ears. *She was mocking me. The old witch kept her poison secret. She deceived me.*

The potion worked quickly, but he'd refused to die. She helped him to his feet and walked him around the table like a zombie. *Like death warmed up, Mam would say.* She pushed him and there was no reaction, so she took hold of his elbow and led him back to the table. He just sat and stared ahead with glazed eyes fixed. *Die!* She leaned across the table and shook him by the shoulders, but there was no reaction. She shouted, 'Can you hear me, James? I'm going to take you and Prince for a ride in the forest.'

His eyes never wavered, and she felt confident of leaving him on the Rusland track. If he was found and he recovered, she would deny ever being with him; it would be her word against his. Timothy would take her side. She prowled the table, frustrated, her anger surfacing. Prince was unusually restless in his stable, stomping his hooves and whinnying. Her anger increased and all she could see was her Man of Death. She was hypnotised by the hands clutching the slashed throat and the vision flashing on and off, like lightning scarring the night. Anger turned to rage, and she was looking down on herself tearing an axe from the wall and viciously slashing it through her flickering vision. James' head lurched back then slumped forward onto his hands. She lost track of time but there was a feeling of relief; peace, like the calm after a violent storm. Then her eyes snapped open as if awakening from a trance and she stared in horror at the corpse in front of her, its blood lapping around her fingers. She looked at the bloodied axe on the table and there was no doubt in her mind that she'd committed a murder. But her recollection of wielding the axe was hazy, like a dream. *Something used me. The Devil inhabited my body.* She stared vacantly at James' corpse, unable to cry. *The poison was meant for a peaceful death.* She was surprised at her own calm as she methodically mopped up the blood and rolled the body in sacking. Her mind was now her own; clear and sharp as the axe her arms had just wielded.

She tied a rope to Prince's saddle and dragged the body by the feet along the forest trail, thankful for the moonlight to guide her path. She found the pig trap and dismounted then pulled away the brushwood cover and was struck in the face with beating wings. Damian had insisted they use a hen as bait. She watched the clucking bird scuttle into the shade of the woods and gathered herself together. She grasped the reins and as Prince dragged the body across the length of the hole, the sacking came away. James' buttocks thumped down onto the stakes, piercing the thighs locking the body in position, with the knees protruding above the hole. She pushed and shoved but the body was locked firmly onto the stakes. The knees refused to slip below the level of the earth. She became desperate. The body was in a crouching position, its head resting against the back wall just below the level of the soil. The elbows were wedged against the side wall and the hands locked onto the jutting knees. She screwed her face, squeezed clenched fists against her temples, and screamed with frustration, lifted her head to the sky, stamped her feet and cursed. 'If only Damian was here to help me.'

Poor Mary, poor Mary! I have to help her. Damian made to step out of cover, but Thomas dragged him down. He was closer than Mary could ever have imagined, and if he had been alone perhaps their future would have taken a different path. They were hiding behind a bush staring goggle-eyed at Mary's strange behaviour, her pushing and shoving at the dead body, frustrated by its defiance. Suddenly she swivelled around and ran back down the track towards the cottage.

When the forest quietened, Damian came out of hiding. He approached Prince and found the horse sweating and agitated. He calmed the horse before examining the pig trap.

He was curious, trying to comprehend why a body should be in the hole instead of a pig? He put the weight of his boot behind the shoulders and tried to push the body down into the pig trap, but it was locked into the stakes and he only drove the pointed sticks into the flesh further. He lay down on his side and peered into dead man's face and then shouted out to Thomas. 'It's James Pritt and he's dead.'

'I can see that he's dead. Just leave him alone. I don't like it out here and I'm going back home. Your sister's mad. She's a black witch. What about the two bright green eyes you saw in the logger's hut? You know Mary hasn't got a cat.' Thomas felt a cold chill and wrapped his arms around his body. He was shivering and his teeth chattered. The more he thought of that dark corner in the hut, the more fearful he became. 'I think you saw the Devil, Damian.'

'Mary's not a witch. The eyes must have been a stray cat.'

'Do you think she killed James?'

'I am sure she did. He murdered John, and deserves what he got.'

'John was killed in an accident. Anyhow, what exactly *did* James get?'

'His throat's been slashed. There's blood everywhere. I heard the woodcutters talking. They said John must have been murdered, and that his horse was the Prince of Darkness.'

'It sounds like witchcraft to me. I'm scared. Let's go home.'

Damian was walking around erratically, becoming excited. Despite a year of digging graves this was the first dead body he'd ever touched. His second viewing, the dramatic bursting open of the old priest's coffin was soon to happen and enhance his superstitious fears. Out of the corner of his eye he caught a movement and he turned in time to see James' left hand slip off his knee and dangle loose. 'Ugh!'

Damian was frightened. He backed away, eyes bulging, and then bravely returned to take a closer look. He crouched down on his knees and cautiously poked a finger into James' eye. There was no reaction and he stood up, relieved. 'He's still dead, Tommy! He's still dead.'

'Of course, he's still dead and if we don't leave soon, we'll be caught and hung in Lancaster.' Thomas spun around as he heard feet pounding the path. 'Mary's coming back. Hurry up, Damian. We have to hide.'

Mary found the axe lying on the table and was puzzled. *I thought I had hooked it on the wall.* She hastily snatched the axe from the table, latched the door and raced into the forest with something nagging at her mind. *They looked like cat's eyes but an unearthly bright green.* She was tempted to go back, but there was no time, and a stray cat could wait. The path looked different and she became nervous and frustrated with the loss of time. Sweat ran from her forehead and she felt a chilling cold. *There'll soon be people about.* She had often seen the charcoal burners from Rusland with their packhorses and James had been one of them. Twice Mary turned to retrace her path before she finally found the body. She looked intensely at the knees protruding from the grave, certain that the corpse had been interfered with. *There's something different about the body.*

She heard a rustle from the trees and raised the axe to her shoulders, stalking the sound. The vision was flashing inside her head. The two boys saw Mary walking towards them, and Thomas felt a trickle run down his leg. Damian couldn't tear his eyes away. He reached out blindly with his arm to touch Thomas, to feel the comfort of his presence, but he wasn't there, and he whirled around in panic. He saw his cousin behind an adjoining bush crouched down with his pants around his ankles, arms wrapped around his stomach, trying to choke off a groan.

Damian was relieved to find he hadn't been deserted. *Tommy's just scared.*

The tension left Mary and the axe dropped to her waist. *It's just my imagination or that stupid hen.* She returned to the grave, anxious to avoid further delay, but she was unable to look at the body. Frustration turned to anger, and the vision flashed intermittently. She was moving away from her own body again and her arms were swinging the axe, cutting into the knees.

Thomas was transfixed. When Mary lifted to her full height her eyes were blazing green. *It's a trick of the moonlight.* He remembered his teacher's wisdom. *Do you believe what you see, or do you see what you believe?* He came to his conclusion: *Mary's definitely a witch.*

Damian was hypnotised by the flight of the swinging axe and the sound of it severing bone. A hand spiralled into the air to land in front of him and he took it as a sign. He was reaching out for the hand, when he felt a tug on his clothing. Thomas had recovered and was dragging him back. 'Shush! Keep out of sight!'

Mary blinked as if awakening from a dream and stared in disbelief at the carnage. Prince whinnied as he tossed his neck from side to side, then suddenly reared and broke loose from his tether. His forelegs pounded the earth as he galloped down the narrow forest track and melded with the darkness. Mary was exhausted. She dropped the axe to the floor and cursed as she turned to her unsavoury task, working frantically with the shovel until the body was covered.

When Thomas saw that Mary was totally occupied, he tapped Damian on the shoulder and gestured to leave. But there was no way Damian was leaving without the hand. He remembered Thomas scoring the silver pocket-watch and considered he was being given a similar opportunity. James' hand was worth more than ten ravens' claws. He turned back, scooped up the hand, and then ran after his cousin.

Sounds of snapping branches and brushing leaves cut through the still night air. Mary stopped shovelling. Hairs bristled on the nape of her neck and a chill ran down her spine. She sensed danger. The rustling sound had come from the same place. She whirled and caught a glimpse of a moving shadow behind a swaying bush. *It's the night creatures.* She continued to fill in the hole. The vision of her Man of Death still haunted her, floating in and out of her mind. She breathed deeply to calm herself and then returned to look down on the covered body. *The Devil's eye stares at me from beneath the soil.* She filled in the hole and levelled it with the forest floor. Satisfied that nothing could be noticed, she rolled a log over the grave and then slumped down, exhausted. Tears rolled down her cheeks as she looked down at the grave, hardly believing what she'd done. Her hands went to hide her face and she sobbed uncontrollably until she lapsed into a restless sleep.

She awoke with the cold forest air, thinking of John, pleading for him to forgive her. She cried out, her voice echoing amongst the witnessing trees. 'Please help me, God. I beg of you. Please forgive me my sin.' But she knew the burden was hers alone, one that she must learn to carry if she was to survive. She picked up the shovel and axe and ran back to the hut as if the Devil was closing in on her.

When Thomas and Damian reached the clearing, they felt a sense of relief and as they unwound from the tension, they burst out laughing. 'You smell, Tommy. You've got shit on your clogs.'

'At least I didn't shit my pants. Fadder would have killed me. I'm sorry if I scared you.'

'You didn't scare me and neither did the dead body. Mary scared me though.'

'She scared me as well. I can't understand what's happened to her. She's always been gentle. Did you see her slashing the axe with her eyes closed? And when they opened her eyes were flashing green.'

'Like I saw in the hut?'

'It was only the moonlight reflecting. You've too much imagination. It's too late to go home now. We will have to hide until morning. Where should we say we've been?'

'We'll say we stayed with Mary. If she doesn't help us then we will have to tell her what we saw. But don't worry. I know Mary. She'll help us for sure.'

'I don't want to tell her what we saw. If she's found out, then we will all hang in Lancaster.'

'Nobody will find out from me. Nobody! Not even Mary, not even Mam.'

'Best get rid of that hand then; burn it or bury it.' Damian patted his lunch sack, smiled inwardly and nodded his agreement.

Mary had listened carefully to Damian's side of the story, and worried that so much had happened whilst the Devil controlled her.

'What did you do with the hand, Damian?' When he told her, she broke out laughing and he felt pleased.

'It was your idea, Mary, and the hand's working better than the ravens' claws.'

'I was only kidding about the ravens' claws.'

When Mary saw her brother's disappointment, she tried to make amends. 'Well, I was only kidding a little bit. The witch told me that ravens are the Devil's messengers.'

Damian seemed satisfied and nodded, understanding. 'I thought you were going to kill Rufus as well when you asked me to dig another grave Mary.'

'He was cruel to you. I wasn't sure how, but I was going to make him suffer. Anyway, everything changed when Thomas attacked him at the fair. He's going back to Cambridge now so we will never know.'

'Do you like secrets, Mary?'

'No, I don't. Now, what has our being here to do with making a lie happen? Isn't that why we came?'

'Thomas told his teacher that you lost the ring in the lake. Mr Clayton wanted to see the symbols on the ring, and Tommy told a lie because he thought his teacher would take it away from you.'

'He pestered me more than once, and it's just as well that Thomas warned me.'

'Well, now Tommy's lie isn't a lie anymore and he can be a Quaker if he wants to. And if you are feeling better then...' Damian paused. He puffed out his chest and smiled at Mary. 'Throwing away the evil ring has helped my two best friends.'

'You've killed two birds with one stone.'

Damian's face screwed and he shook his head. 'I don't kill things. I just threw away the ring and it helped us all.'

'You killed the raven.'

'Tommy kept telling me to club them, but he always finished them off himself.'

'You enjoyed killing the fox though.'

'I didn't kill the fox, Uncle Robert did. I just liked the chase.'

His sister smiled and spoke with a whisper. 'If only I could tell Mam. She would be so proud of you for helping me. I feel like a new person. I can think with a clear mind again.'

Damian sat with his hands between his knees. His face beamed as he rocked back and forth. Mary grasped the amber stone amulet as she once had the ring and thoughtfully looked out of the barn towards the water. 'I'm certain that the symbols on the ring were messages from the Devil.'

'The ring was evil, Mary.'

'It wasn't completely evil. The ring belonged to honest people. I have seen them in a dream and had a feeling of belonging. Our ancestors were kind and loving people but something bad must have happened to them, perhaps the same evil that happened to me. In my dream I travelled with Prince through the sky. There was a woman who looked like she could be my sister. It was a wondrous dream. I feel that Prince and I went on a journey to a strange land where I once lived. Maybe the destination in the symbol was the lake and our journey has now ended.'

Damian was sitting with his mouth open, enthralled. 'It's a good story, Mary. Tommy used to tell me *ghost* stories too. We saw some ghosts at the abbey.'

'I know. You keep telling me, but did you *really* see ghosts?'

Damian quietened. 'No. Not really.'

'Then why did you say you had?'

'Tommy asked me if I could see them, so I said yes. I wanted to, but I couldn't.'

'I'm not sure mine is a ghost story, Damian. I wish it were all a dream. God will never forgive me for what I've done.'

'It wasn't you. It was the Devil inside you. We drowned him in the lake.'

'The Devil came to me when I was angry and only when Prince and the ring were close. Perhaps I really was mad.'

'Tommy was frightened of you, Mary. He wished he'd never shown you the meanings of the symbols on the ring. He thinks you are two people, one a madwoman from another time, long before the abbey existed.'

'Thomas can think what he likes. He's too clever for his own boots and I don't care, now that he's gone, and my devils have gone as well.' Mary suddenly stopped talking and became lost in thought. She was puzzled by something she'd just said. 'Why did I say there were two devils?' She thought again of the boat on the lake. 'You said my eyes were like green fire, as bright as burning coals. Were they truly different eyes?'

Damian nodded, open-mouthed, still in awe of the vision. 'Not yours, Mary.'

She remembered the night of her dream in the Atkinsons' manor house. Gazing spellbound into the fiery coals, head drooping, eyelids flickering, focussing on the glazed reflection. The bright green blur melded with her vision, like a glow worm hovering between the coals, flirting dangerously with the roaring flames. Her eyelids closed on the vision and she was hurled into a magical dream world. Reliving the dream brought a realisation to Mary that struck her dumb. She paused awhile to calm herself, and then vent her feelings. 'The blurred image in the fire was the Devil!' And she shouted out again, 'It was a reward!' Then she placed her head in her hands and sobbed.

'Are you sick, Mary?'

Mary couldn't bring herself to answer. Her beautiful dream had been shattered. 'My Man of Death was no Devil. He was only a vision.'

'Where did he come from?'

'He came from my mind, sent by a she-Devil. I have been possessed by a she-Devil and rewarded for killing.'

'What did she give you?'

'She gave me the dream of our ancestors. Thomas was right to fear me. I was possessed. My mind was tormented, and I was close to madness. I can still see the Man of Death in my mind, but his presence has gone. The she-Devil no longer gnaws at my soul. I'm at peace with myself and I will be able to visit the chapel and pray to God for forgiveness. You drowned the she-Devil in the lake, Damian, and it has returned to hell.' Mary looked affectionately at her attentive brother then closed her eyes and smiled. 'The danger is over.'

They heard Jasper whine and looked towards where Prince was tethered. The hound was no longer barking and backing away. Jasper fearlessly stood between Prince's forelegs and pointed his face in the air. Prince's head lowered to nuzzle the proffered nose. Mary smiled, satisfied that the evil surrounding her had departed. She turned back to look across the placid water of the moonlit lake and now thought it to be a veiled innocence and a shiver of fear ran down her spine. 'You were very brave, Damian.'

Her brother's grin widened, and he nodded in agreement. 'I saw the Dobbie man as well tonight.'

'Where did you see him?'

'I saw him on the lake when I was rowing back to shore. He was in a boat.'

'I don't think it was the Dobbie man.'

'It was. He had the same eyes.'

'I think it was the man who took the other boat. Do you think we should tell Rupert about him?'

'No!'

'Then we had best tell no-one in case they think us both mad. It will be another secret between us to strengthen our bond.'

'Mam keeps on telling us that blood is thicker than water and that you always look after your family first.'

She stroked her hand down the side of his face and looked into his bulbous, questioning eyes. 'Yes! We are of the same blood, my brother.'

He looked at his sister's beauty, her long black lustrous hair and her olive skin. He wasn't so sure about the blood, but he smiled. He wasn't scared anymore. Not now that Mary was back. He thought of his cousin, Tommy, sailing to the new land. He thought of his mother and Uncle Robert at home around a warm fire with his new baby cousin and he knew the place he liked best. He drifted off to sleep with a contented smile on his face.

Mary woke at dawn and drew the smell of hay through her nostrils. She stretched her body then lay on her back for a while, thinking of their experience on the lake. *I had no control over my body, the same as the night in Grizedale forest. Did it really happen or was it all a dream, a strange dream?* She sat up with a start. Damian had been waiting patiently for her. He looked down at his sister and begged the question, 'Can we go home now?'

Mary felt exhilarated and leapt to her feet laughing. 'I'm free, Damian. I'm free! You can run ahead with Jasper and I'll race you with Prince.'

Damian's eyes lit up, and he ruffled the hound's ears. 'Come on, Jasper, we're going home.'

Damian's long legs stretched to the full and his knees kicked high and outwards. He loved running wild with the wind in his face. His back straightened, his head leaned slightly backwards and his arms flailed the air; not exactly the style his grandfather had taught him. As he ran he remembered his mother's father, and the hounds, and the chase. 'It's only four miles!'

Mary was pleased to see Damian carefree again. She waited until they were almost out of sight before kicking her heels and urging Prince forward. She smiled at his running style. *He's a strong runner. Grandfather would be proud of him.* As Mary closed the gap, she made a promise to herself. 'You'll be running in the fell race this year, brother, and it will matter little whether you win or lose; we will all be proud of you.'

Without breaking his stride Damian's head turned and he shouted out. 'You're gaan to be rich, Mary. The king's officers are coming with papers and to give you money for Prince. And I'm gaan to share a secret with you when we're home.'

Mary gave him a knowing smile and waved him on. She had her future to think of now and lately she'd been paying serious attention to Samuel in the chandlery. She made a mental note to remind him that Penelope Rathbone already has a husband. *Samuel's older than John was, but he's a kindly man in need a good woman. He refuses to be a Quaker like his parents. I like a man with a mind of his own.*

'Come on, Mary! Stop dreaming!' Damian was impatient to visit his rune pot, to show Mary the king's coin.

The final escape

The *Charlotte* rolled from side to side as its bow plunged in and out of the heavy seas. A cargo of livestock slid across the deck, and a cage of chickens was lost overboard. Seasick passengers couldn't care less. The wheelhouse passengers had been ordered below for their own safety, and the hatches battened down. Their sleeping berths were shelves along each side of the underdeck, divided by low boards; not much advanced from the remnants of the old slave accommodation. The upper deck had six enclosed cabins for the wealthier clients, and each had four berths. Thomas was clinging to his shelf bunk in the lower section. His body swayed with the movement of the ship as he stretched out his arms to reach his travel sack. They had been in heavy seas for five days and he wondered if the brigantine had made any headway at all. A hint of salt in the stale air failed to overcome the stench from the vomit barrels secured mid-ship. Thomas was one of the fortunate few able to keep down the ship's rations. His newfound friend was leaning over a split ale barrel and heaving. The man lifted his head and wiped a sleeve across his scarred face. Yellow liquid dripped from the dark stubble of his chin. He looked worn out, as frayed as his three-cornered hat. Thomas stood upright against the bunk and looked cautiously around before delving into his travel sack. There'd been some thefts on board, and he felt a daily compulsion to count the money he was gifted by his father and Aunt Hannah. Edwin had warned him of the need for security. 'There's no law on a ship such as this one Thomas. Make sure you keep your travel sack close.' They had agreed to keep watch for each other if they were ever parted from their baggage. There was whispering amongst the passengers that Edwin Sutton was a highwayman fleeing the noose, and Thomas had to admit, that had been his first impression. But he was willing to give the benefit of the doubt and recalled his Quaker teachings, *Judge not lest you be judged.* The man had obviously fallen on hard times and his ragged garments belied the manners of a gentleman. Thomas' hand dipped into his travel sack and came out holding the pocket-watch.

He'd easily found Damian's new hiding place and was sure that his cousin wouldn't have objected. There'd scarcely been time to consider. When his father and Aunt Hannah gave him the money and they had said that every little thing helps he'd felt justified in finding the rune pot. He ran his hand over the engraving on the outside cover of the watch. It looked like an *L* intermingled with a *J.* He'd often wondered whom the watch belonged to. It was obviously someone important judging by the number of gentlemen he'd seen pouring from the inn. He'd heard later that a wealthy party had been travelling from London to Whitehaven. They were relatives of the Kirkbys and young Roger Kirkby had apprehended the thief. Thomas gave the watch an extra spit and polish. *I'll need to have a key made afore I can use it.*

He caught Edwin Sutton's side-glance as he carefully placed it back in the sack. 'You don't have to be shy about it, lad. I can see it's a pocket-watch. Now I ask myself; what would an apprentice blacksmith be doing with a gentleman's pocket-watch?'

'I never stole it, if that's what you're thinking.'

'Let me see it then. I've had dealings with such trinkets.'

'I saw your pistol, Edwin. You're a highwayman, *aren't* you?'

'I can't deny it. My choice was the noose or fresh territories. You were in a similar predicament I gather.'

Thomas reluctantly handed him the watch. 'I knuckled the son of a magistrate because he was molesting a girl I was fond of. I was on my last warning for attending Quaker meetings, under threat of transportation and seven years in shackles. The Friends organised my escape and passage to New England.'

Edwin looked up at Thomas with an ambiguous smile. 'Perhaps you should have stayed and saved them the money.'

'I don't know what you mean.'

'I mean that Boston is to be avoided at all cost. The Friends are more vilified there than they are in England. The king granted a Royal Charter four years ago declaring Rhode Island independent and authorising freedom of religion. Find your way to Providence. You will find religious tolerance at the Rhode Island colony and nowhere else.'

Edwin had confirmed Timothy's warning. He had reread the letter obsessively during his first two days at sea.

Dear Thomas,

This letter is written in haste. God willing, when it is read, thou will be safely aboard the *Charlotte* sailing toward a new life. I feel personally responsible for the situation in which thee find thyself, although thou have not helped by breaching thy contract with George Ferris. Thy fondness for a certain young lass is common knowledge. Perhaps in New England the situation will be regarded in a different light, but I doubt that very much. The ten-week voyage will provide thou time to reflect on thy past and consider thy future. Deliver the sealed letter of introduction to Joseph Farrington unopened. He is a native of our parish and will welcome you. I knew the man for many years before he was driven from his country to seek a life elsewhere. When you disembark in Boston do not linger. You must move swiftly to Rhode Island where there is safety. In thy time of uncertainty never fear to look inward for the spirit of God. Search for the inner light, God will be with thee.

Timothy Atkinson

'I have an introductory letter to a Quaker blacksmith on Rhode Island, Edwin.'

'I suppose you have little choice but to go where the path leads you. Fortunately, it is a safe one.' Edwin flicked the face open and perused the watch's innards. 'Do you have a key?'

'I intend to have one made when I'm settled.'

'Then the watch is no more than a useless trinket.' Edwin handed it back to Thomas. 'I've seen the insignia before. If you are caught with the watch in your possession you may lose your head.'

'Do you know the owner?'

'I've only set eyes on him the once, but I know him to be the man most responsible for hunting me down. The least you know of him the better.'

Edwin joined a woman and her husband around a half beer barrel. They all leaned over and heaved in unison. Edwin lifted his head and as he looked around the stinking enclosure, he craved the freedom of the open road. 'More space. We need more space. I feel like a pig at a trough.'

Thomas tipped out the remaining contents of his sack and looked puzzled as he shook the sack again and again. *The little oak box is missing.* He caught Edwin looking at him. *The man has the eyes of a hawk.* The highwayman turned his gaze away and Thomas was sickened. *He's stolen from me.*

Edwin watched Thomas frantically shaking his sack and smiled inwardly. He turned away from Thomas' gaze and focussed on the ship's bulkhead. *There's bound to be good value in the polished box and the lad's fearful of confronting me.* He decided on a positive move and joined his shipboard companion. 'Have you lost something, Thomas?'

'My valuable jewel box has been stolen.'

'You're carrying jewels? I'm beginning to think that we have much in common—and that we have more than an apprenticed blacksmith in our midst. Did you steal the box with the watch?'

Thomas didn't know what to say. He had never thought of it as stealing and he didn't even know the contents of the box. The whole incident had been unfortunate. He had been all alone in Penelope's bedroom, sick of staring at the walls. He saw her lock down the lid, drop the key in the top drawer and leave the room. He was sitting on the edge of the bed with the highly polished box staring him in the face. He was curious about the contents of the box. There was talk in the village that the major possessed a rare stone in a felt-lined box, and the fact that the lid was locked down annoyed him. He picked up the box and sat down with it resting on his thighs, admiring the workmanship. Then he rolled it between thumbs and forefingers and fantasised about its contents. He was still holding the box when he heard Mrs Rathbone outside, banging on the door, calling his name. He had simply panicked and dropped it in his sack.

'I place no value on the box, Edwin. The thief could be disappointed.'

'Then you've suffered no loss and I wouldn't cast suspicion on those around you. I hope you're not accusing me of stealing from a friend. This ship is full of thieves and you can't say I didn't warn you.'

Thomas was more disappointed at the loss of his newfound friend than he was of the wooden box. He turned his back on Edwin and once again fanned his fingers through the contents of his belongings. How ironic that he'd outgrown the rune pot and yet here he was, hiding away more of his possessions. He had noticed the key for the woodcutter's hut was missing, as well as the skeletal hand. *Damian said Mary was simmering her cauldron again. There's no doubt she's a witch and she's probably thrown in the bones of the hand for good measure.* He smacked his forehead with his palm. *I must forget and hope for all our sakes that the grave remains a secret.* He separated a coin from the contents of his sack and picked it up. The silver coin had been a complete surprise. *Why would Damian hide such a coin and where did he find it?* Thomas rolled the coin between his fingers, admiring the stamping of the king on horseback. Then with a tinge of guilt, he dropped the coin into his bag.

Damian was at that very moment emptying the contents of the rune pot, feverously scattering his treasure. The king's coin was gone, and he searched again and again for the pocket-watch. When the solution dawned on him, he looked forlornly in the direction he imagined Thomas would be. *Tommy's the only one clever enough to find the pot.* He became angry, and for Damian, that was an unusual feeling. He felt a surge of strength and tore the pot from the earth, lifting it high above his head and with another surge of anger he threw the pot far into the field. The treasure pot turned over in the air and descended onto a boulder with a clang, the contents dispersing in the surrounding grass. A pair of cracked spectacles glinted in the sun alongside a pair of scissors, a pocketknife and numerous quills. Damian had discarded some of his best kept secrets and walked away without a backward glance. His secret treasure was unearthed, exposed to the world. *That's the last time I'll be helping Tommy to escape.*

Days later, farmer Smyth picked up the scattered contents and on his wife's instructions, delivered the pot to Black George at the smithy. The blacksmith was asked to shape a handle for the pot and was left scratching his head. He was thinking that there was more to the Smyth's than met the eye. *That's the pot that disappeared years ago. There's little doubt it's the one that belonged to the Atkinsons.*

The major's missing jewel box was the talk of the village. Penelope was just as surprised as her husband at the theft and when the major's temper exploded, she prepared for the worst. He was in no doubt about his wife's loathing of the stone and she was the first to be accused. Penelope made no bones about being insulted and strengthened her position through verbal attack and inference. 'How could you think such a thing of your own wife after allowing our household to be searched by all those strangers? To think they invaded our bedroom with your consent while you entertained me in the kitchen. Did you ever doubt that I would be embarrassed? Don't you care about my privacy? Don't you care if you hurt my feelings?'

'Calm down now, Penny. It was only a passing thought. We must think further on the subject. It couldn't have been you. Could it have been the domestic? Lizzie has access to our room.'

'She was away visiting her cousin. I sent all the staff away, and I'm thinking it was just as well I did.'

'I've every confidence in the churchwarden's men. Kirkby's constables were the only strangers searching inside the house the day my stone went missing. It has to be one of them. I will let it be known that they are under suspicion of stealing the box. The truth will come out eventually.'

'The colonel won't be very pleased, will he? Not with you going around casting aspersions on his constabulary and each and every one of them God-fearing members of the church.'

'That doesn't mean they are all honest. Did you notice the small constable, the one with the shifty peephole eyes? I didn't like the look of him from the first. I'll ask Roger to keep an eye open in case he tries to sell the box.'

'Who on earth would want to buy, sell, or steal that monstrosity?'

'That's not very kind. You know very well I have a strong sentimental attachment to the stone.'

'Strong is the right word. I would like to be there when the thief opens it.'

The major was visibly hurt, and Penelope tried to console him. She almost felt a tinge of sympathy for him even though she was secretly happy. *Whoever took the stone has my blessing.* There was only one other person who could have taken the box that day and Penelope could never divulge his presence. She thought it unlikely that Thomas would steal from her, yet she felt compelled to speak with his cousin Mary at the chandlery. Her excuse for the visit was to inform her of Rufus' premature departure. 'He was reluctant to leave the parish, but I persevered until he returned to Eleanor. I tried to retrieve the silver ring for you, but he insisted it was no longer in his possession.'

'He gave it back to me on a condition that would disgust you.'

'I would rather not know. Rufus doesn't let go of possessions so easily.'

'You can tell him that the ring has been cast into the lake and it lays somewhere between Long Holm Island and the ferry.'

'Why did you cast it into the lake?'

'I believed it was evil. My husband was wearing it when he died, and it also troubled my mind greatly. I think it drew Rufus to evil as well. Perhaps he will stop pestering me now and become a better husband to Eleanor.'

'You are very wise for your age and your manner pleases me. I will inform Samuel that as long as he employs you, he can count on my trade. Rufus can swim to the bottom of the lake, if he so desires, and retrieve the ring with your blessing.'

'Thank you, and if you happen to see the schoolteacher please tell him about the fate of the ring. Hopefully he will also stop bothering me.'

'If you are referring to Phynius Clayton, there is to be an inquiry into his death.'

'He passed, away? I never heard. When did he die?'

'He died a few days ago. Where have you been lass? They found him swirling around in a boat on Lake Windermere. The poor man's heart had failed him. Mathew said he must have suffered a horrible death; there was terror in his eyes, and he had to stitch his eyelids closed. The ferryman said it was the teacher's habit to stay over on the weekend and take the early morning ferry. But it was unusual for him to take a boat out, especially in the evening.'

Mary's heart raced. 'That must have been the night we threw the ring into the lake. That explains why the churchwarden and a constable called to ask me some questions. They asked me if we had seen anything unusual that night. I told them no. They said they couldn't get any sense out of Damian, only a silly smile and something about fishing. I wonder why they never told us about the teacher.'

'Perhaps they thought they were investigating a murder.'

'Maybe that's why William Webster said those terrible things to me. Do you know what he said, Mrs Rathbone?'

'No! Go on Mary, tell me.'

He said, 'A lot of people seem to die around you Mary; first Algernon Fleming, then your husband, and then the woodcutter mysteriously disappears. He said that I was close to all of them. That's what he said, and now that I've heard about poor old Phynius, I suppose he was thinking of him as well. I just shrugged and told him that people die all the time and there is always someone close by.'

'Why did you choose the nighttime to throw the ring away?'

'It was Damian's idea. I never realised I had taught him so well. There has to be a full moon when you meddle with evil. Perhaps the ring brought the teacher bad luck as well.'

'I'm not a believer in such superstitions.'

'I feel sorry for that poor man. He didn't really pester me that much. I didn't know him very well or understand his obsession with setting his eyes on the ring. He was only interested in the ring's history. He believed it should belong to the church and that he would determine the truth or die in the process.' *The Devil took his payment.*

'Well he most certainly died and he's never going to see the ring now. He was well respected in the parish and a teacher that will be hard to replace. His funeral is tomorrow.'

'I'll be attending, Mrs Rathbone.'

Penelope smiled approvingly. 'We should all show our respect. I'll be on my way now. You must bring Samuel to church more often.'

Mary smiled and breathed a deep sigh of relief. Penelope feigned hesitation. 'Oh, there *was* one other thing. You may find it an offensive question but did your cousin Thomas, ever steal anything?'

Mary smiled and humoured the lady of the manor. 'I remember he did when he was young, but he's grown out of that bad habit now.'

Penelope walked from the chandlery chuckling at her memory of dragging Thomas' sack across the kitchen floor. *I was helping him steal Rowan's beloved stone. That's my consolation for not taking his virginity.* She smiled wistfully at what his thoughts would be when he palmed the box's contents *and* sighed at what might have been. *What a waste!*

Thomas awoke to the sound of water swishing along the sides of the ship. He was curled up inside his sleeping bag, feeling clean for the first time in five days. An oversized seagull flew over the billowing mainsail. He overheard one of the deckhands calling the bird an albatross and say that an island was in sight on the portside. The brigantine was on a southern tack and would take on fresh food and water before sailing west. He leapt from the sleeping bag, folded it alongside his travel sack and walked to the ship's rail. He'd been striding the deck during the night, revitalised by his barrel bath. He was itching to place his feet on dry land and dirty his hands. He had spoken to the boatswain, Edward Bone, about his boredom and the deckhands had welcomed his strength with the ropes. But he was impatient to secure his future and believed that the sooner he was earning an honest living, the healthier he would feel. He had watched the sun rise from behind the sea and flood the horizon with its orange glow. Its rays were reaching out, illuminating the island and splashing reflections across the waves. It was a different sun from the one he'd always seen rising above the fells. There was a haze surrounding the forge-like molten mass and it seemed larger and warmer. He closed his eyes and filled his great lungs with the fresh morning sea air.

A movement on the starboard side caught his eye and he saw Edwin Sutton trying to attract his attention. The previous day Thomas had seen him talking animatedly to Arthur Grasty, the first mate. *I could have sworn they were old friends.* Edwin was looking splendid in his Sunday outfit, clean shaven with pencil-line moustache, doublet waistcoat, and gentleman's pantaloons, and most noticeably minus his old tri-cornered hat. He had decided that his road disguise was a thing of the past and the time was ripe for him to seek better company at the card tables. *It's a pity these Quakers on board are opposed to a little speculation.* The polished box was sitting in his opened palm and there was a sneer on his face. The lid was open, and Thomas caught a glimpse of a dark stone. *It doesn't sparkle.* The highwayman growled in Thomas' direction, leaned over the ship's rails and flamboyantly tipped the contents of the box into the sea. He snapped the lid shut, stretched out his arm and pointed an accusing hand towards Thomas. 'Take me for a fool do you, lad?'

Thomas looked around, but apart from a few of the crew making busy he was alone. Edwin was now walking towards him, a threat in every ponderous step. He stopped less than a foot away, grasped Thomas' right hand and slapped the empty box into his open palm. Thomas twitched nervously, his left shoulder lifted and his eye winked. Edwin's eyes narrowed at the apparent insolence. He glared as he leaned forward, his jutting, well-defined square jaw serving to accentuate his increasing anger. Thomas caught a whiff of perfume and it clashed with his vision of the face, sweating and red with rage, then Thomas' eyes crossed as the barrel of a pistol touched the tip of his nose. 'Make a mockery of me once more young man and your handsome face will be scarred by the fire of my pistol.' The highwayman turned abruptly and made for the upper deck, leaving Thomas with his heart pounding.

Passengers from below deck were beginning to stir, stretching their legs, feeling well enough to brave the calm conditions, and to attend the ship's first morning service. Thomas breathed heavily from his scare, trying to clear his thoughts. 'Edwin is acting like a madman. I feel sorry for him. The sea sickness must have affected his mind.'

His thoughts went out to Penelope, imagining how she would feel. He could still see her carefully, almost lovingly, closing the lid and turning the key in the lock. *The contents of the box were obviously very dear to her. Why would Edwin cast a rare stone into the sea?* Thomas was at a loss, but then it suddenly came to him. *It's so obvious. The highwayman is starting a new life, sacrificing his chattels, casting away his temptations.*

He looked down with guilt at the stolen box in his palm and thought he should offer his own sacrifice. After all, he was also at the crossroads of a new life. He watched the polished oak box spiral down and splash into the sea then surface amongst the slipstream to be carried away in the wake of the ship. When the box finally disappeared, he gave a sigh of relief. *No more stealing and no more hoarding.* He would keep the coin though. That would have to be returned to Damian and the more he looked at the engraved initials on the pocket-watch the more he could see a *T* and a *J. The watch was meant for me. It is God's will.* He would keep the pocket watch; it would be a timely reminder of his wayward past. He smiled at his own humour, and then became wistful. *I've lost all my family and friends.*

'Thomas!'

He was staring out to sea, reminiscing on his past and attempting to concentrate on his uncertain future. Just a moment ago he had leapt to his feet full of life and expectancy. He thought of his father and Aunt Hannah tending the flock, and Damian and Mary and baby John. *Please God keep them safe.* The picture of his mother flashed again, holding the daffodil against her gaunt cheek. *Look, Thomas! The bell's like a lady's bonnet.* His eyes welled and his heart felt heavy. He had always remembered her last words. *Be a good lad for yer fadder, Thomas.*

'Thomas!'

He wouldn't miss Mary so much, but as he pinched the coin in his pocket he thought kindly of Damian and felt a twinge of guilt. *I should never have taken the coin. It's a shame him and Mary are a bit daft. The plague damaged them more than I realised. Did Damian know what that pig trap was for? Did he lead me there, playing games with his secrets? He was so excited. Poor Mary, I have to help her. Just as well I pulled him away.*

'Thomas!'

He thought of Sarah and what his life could have been. He imagined her voice, soft and lilting, carrying in the breeze, drifting around in his mind.

'Thomas, wake up, Thomas!' She shook him gently.

He blinked his thoughts away, disturbed by the insistent call. Sarah, forever the rebellious Quaker, was wearing a blue long-sleeved blouse with a dark linen dress flapping about her ankles. The persistent ocean breeze firmed the garments to the curves of her tall slender body and swirled a curtain of ribboned dark locks across her face. She brushed the strands of hair aside and looked up to Thomas with an earnest face. Thomas gaped, surprised by her presence and stunned by her beauty. She was more beautiful than he could ever have imagined. His gloom immediately left him, and his spirits soared. He looked down into her soft brown eyes and blushed unashamedly, his face beaming with happiness, his heart pumping faster, pounding his inner drum.

'I need you, Thomas. I need you to hold me.' Sarah drew close, and as his arms enclosed her, she reached up and clasped her hands behind his neck. Her breasts tingled as she stretched to her full height and arched into his tall muscular body. She rested a cheek against his chest, inhaled his manly scent, and felt comforted. She lifted her head, leaned back, and looked deep into his eyes, questioning. She was afraid. 'Hold me tight, Thomas. Tell me we'll be safe.'

Thomas nodded his assurance and gently pressed her head back to his chest. There was a silence between them that nothing could invade. It would be forever their own. In that intimate peace, Thomas knew that his future life in the new land would be shared with Sarah. The boyish smile deserted him for a moment, and a glimpse of steel flickered amongst the blue of his eyes.

Appendix

The United Kingdom Parliament
Lords Hansard: 17th July 2006: Column 1023
(Excerpts from the National Trust Debate 2006)

Lord Inglewood: I hope I will be allowed a few moments just to say a big thank you to the Minister, his predecessors and not least his officials, and to convey to them the appreciation of the Federation of Cumbria Commoners for having introduced in the other place a prevision that permits but does not mandate transfer that I describe as 'within the parish'. Across England, the law of common land and the common law in its manorial aspect developed differently from place to place. In Cumbria the smaller owner-occupier farmer-known as a **'statesman'** was well known for his independence and indeed his stubbornness, as some of those who may have been involved in this debate will appreciate. They separated their rights emphatically from those of the owner of the soil very early on. There are well documented 17th century examples of manorial courts fining the manorial lord. After all, it may have been the lord of the manor's court, but the law that was being applied in it was the common law of England in its manorial manifestation. Equally, very early on, rights were quantified and became severable by agreement. In the 19th century, statutory provisions were introduced from time to time making this possible. Therefore, I believe that the government were absolutely right not to introduce with this legislation a move back towards feudalism in the fells.

Lord Livsey of Talgarth: My Lords, we were concerned that the situation in Cumbria is very different from that in other parts of the United Kingdom. We were concerned that accepting what happens in Cumbria with regard to severance as a generality vis-a-vis other parts of the United Kingdom would cause considerable problems with severance.

Furness Abbey excavation

Rare treasure found by chance in a mystery grave at a ruined medieval abbey will go on display after lying undiscovered for more than half a millenium. The silver-gilt and copper crozier, the staff of office shaped like a shepherd's crook held by high-ranking members of the church, was found along with a jewelled ring during emergency repairs carried out in 2010 at Furness Abbey in Cumbria.

https://www.english-heritage.org.uk/visit/places/furness-abbey/

Other books in the series 'Circles of Time' by David Thomas Kay
Book 1: The Sword of Saint Isidores
Book 3: The Inscription

Lightning Source UK Ltd.
Milton Keynes UK
UKHW020637170820
368376UK00009B/222